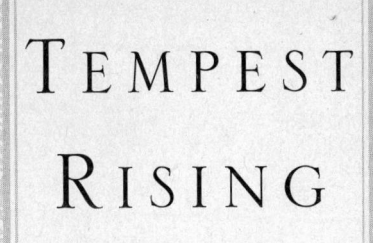

Tempest Rising

ALSO BY DIANE MCKINNEY-WHETSTONE

Tumbling

Tempest Rising

a novel

Diane McKinney-Whetstone

WILLIAM MORROW AND COMPANY, INC. / NEW YORK

Copyright © 1998 by Diane McKinney-Whetstone

All rights reserved. No part of this book may be reproduced
or utilized in any form or by any means, electronic or mechanical,
including photocopying, recording, or by any information storage or retrieval system,
without permission in writing from the Publisher.
Inquiries should be addressed to Permissions Department,
William Morrow and Company, Inc., 1350 Avenue of the Americas,
New York, N.Y. 10019.

ISBN 0-688-14994-4

Printed in the United States of America

BOOK DESIGN BY JO ANNE METSCH

www.williammorrow.com

To the memory of my sister, Gloria S. Chase,

AND

To the fulfillment of the dreams of the next generation:
Taiwo Whetstone, Kehinde Whetstone, Aaron Chase Keys,
Gerald Paul McKinney Mars, David Anthony Abrams II

Part One

I

THE grand stone Victorian tried not to show off, even though it survived that sudden March storm, stood tough while the roof caved in on the house next door, and the front palladian blew out in the one across the street; a half-dead pin oak died for real and crashed through the attic of the house on the corner. But this house blushed inside, still intact with an endless center hall and windows that stretched from the floors to heaven, waiting patiently for Clarise and the girls to get back home. Finally, after all they'd been through leading up to the mammoth March storm, they so deserved this house with its pervasive elegance. Understated, though. Because Clarise knew better than to have an ostentatious house.

Clarise had been raised by her two aunts and two uncles, brothers and sisters to one another, who earned their living making exquisite bar soaps, coconut and honey, by hand. The four had never married and shared a tidy Queen Street row house on the other side of town from where the sturdy, blushing house stood. They dunked their lives into bringing up Clarise, their dead fifth sibling's only child, and had exceptional taste: the uncles; and thick-knuckled attitudes: the aunts.

The sisters were tough, hardworking, ample-chested, husky-voiced women who didn't believe in indulging the child. They both had Georgia-clay red complexions; both were tall for the generation of women born around 1900. And even while they were raising Clarise, through the 1930s and 1940s, and packaged meats had caught on in cities like Philadelphia, the sisters were the type who always bought their pork whole and fresh-killed from the waterfront, drained it, skinned it, hacked it into ham and rump and chops while the brothers and Clarise covered their eyes.

The brothers were soft, immaculate, and artistic; they kept spotless bureaus and chifforobes, played the melody harp, cooked like the French. Both were the color of ginger: one tall and thin, back straight as a paper birch; the other, short and round, no neck, built like a mushroom. They adored Clarise, and from the time she was a baby they would conjure up desserts and make like magicians, pretend as if the tapioca, her favorite, had just gathered itself together from the mist in the air and settled on the table in front of her. They had to sneak, though, when the aunts weren't around, who insisted that too many sweets would turn Clarise into a weak, crybaby type of child.

Clarise was tough in her own right, at least when it came to crying. She could will herself not to cry and shut down her tear ducts so that no fluid fell. She wasn't so tough when it came to men, though. She would go weak for men from the time she blossomed into adolescence. Had to squeeze her thighs together so she wouldn't let herself go wide open every time she got a whiff of Aqua DiSilva, or Old Spice original, or Noxzema aftershave. She'd been well trained though, by the aunts, who, tough and celibate as they were, understood a woman's nature, had watched Clarise's strong-natured mother die a hard death from female problems: a growth, a ruptured vessel, a massive bleed, according to the doctors; too many lying men with their tainted naked things getting too close to their trusting baby sister, according to the aunts. They told Clarise what to look for when her own nature came down. Told her to run like hell from any man who said, "Baby, I'm for real." Told her she'd do well to marry young.

So when Clarise was sixteen going on seventeen, and graduated early from high school because she was smart and had been skipped a grade, and Finch was walking through the streets of Philadelphia, taking leave and his final pay from the merchant marine ship where he'd duly served as assistant cook, he saw Clarise in the cream-colored graduation dress that had been hand-sewn by the uncles with beads at the top and layers and layers of voile. Clarise took note of Finch's eyes, how they went liquid for her like brown gravy seeping down the curve of a rump roast; she knew then he was the one she would marry even before he tried to woo her with his financial worth. He'd flash a wad of bills, lick his index finger before he peeled off the dollars to pay for their drinks at the Showboat.

But Clarise knew it was all for effect. The sailors whose ships always docked at the navy yard made similar spectacles of their earnings. Even when she was a child walking through the streets of downtown, she'd watched them, pausing before they went into the penny arcade, or Horn & Hardart, or McCrory's dime store. They'd heist their pants up higher on their waists before digging deep in their pockets to bring up a mound of paper money. And if Clarise appeared even minutely impressed, she'd feel her aunt Til tug her arm. "Man with real money doesn't flash it in public for all to see," her aunt would say.

So even though Finch tried to show off his money, which Clarise knew meant that he was broke as a grasshopper in the snow, she sensed that he was the type to turn a dollar into twenty time and again. It wasn't just the way he puffed his cigars and mashed his feet flat into the earth when he walked or the way he'd slap the backs of the men in the clubs, with a gregarious authority; it was the way the air smelled around him. Clarise had a heightened olfactory sense that revealed more about a person or thing to her than her eyes could see. And whenever she stood within two feet of Finch, no matter how much his Old Spice tried to get in the way, she detected the unmistakably crisp scent of heavily inked, fresh-cut, new paper money.

Plus Finch was dark, meant the children they'd have together would have some color. She herself didn't have much color. Her father was rumored to have been an Italian from the other block of Queen Street, so Clarise had an odd look: skin color like the shell of an egg when it wasn't quite a brown egg, but not a white egg either; eyes the tint of a dusty gray dawn; long silky hair that went bushy when it was humid out; well-defined nose; nicely padded lips. She was often teased about her look. Would run home after school and stand straight as a board in front of the aunts, hold her tears like she was trying to keep from wetting herself. "They called me a half-white African," she'd say.

"You tell them you as white and as African as their mommas," her aunt Til would say.

"They called me shit-colored," she'd say.

"You tell them shit comes in all colors, even black like their mommas," her other aunt, Ness, would say.

The aunts helped Clarise to be tough and unflinchable in the face of hurtful childhood insults. They knew firsthand the starchy taste of persistent teasing. Spinsters, they'd been called; old maids, hags, he-women, funny honeys. Had to teach their baby sister, Clarise's mother, how to hurl the insults right back when she'd come home crying, telling the aunts the names they'd been called. So they were expert when it came time to help Clarise become a master at quick comebacks to the assaults on her strange looks. Soon the other children were so terrified of Clarise's ability to string words together like beads on a necklace, wrap them around some child's neck, and send that child home crying and choking, they promptly stopped calling her half-breed, mulatto, massa's child, witch's nose. And even though her odd look as a child metamorphosed itself into an exotic form of beauty when she became a teen, she didn't want her own children to tote the barge of her childhood looks. She knew Finch would dilute her looks in their children and give them thick, pressable hair and earthy-toned complexions. Not only was he dark brown, but he had very nonextreme looks: a normally round face, a typically short nose, eyes and lips that were neither large nor small. Plus he had nice, amply sized legs, an appetite like a country preacher, and his very chest expanded when he looked at Clarise, as if he were saying, "Right here, pretty baby, lay your head right here," meant she wouldn't have to worry about dying young like her mother did from the tainted, naked parts of lying men.

When the time came for Clarise to sneak out of the window on the Queen Street row house and spare her dear aunts and uncles the expense of a wedding, she wrote two letters. She'd had to write only two letters because she'd known no other family, no grandparents, no cousins. One letter she left in the shed where the aunts cured their ham; she thanked them for advising her so well. The other letter she propped next to the uncles' lead crystal sugar bowl in the center of the breakfast-room table; she wrote how much she'd miss their tapioca and begged them not to cry. Then she climbed out of the dining-room window into the alley that smelled of honeysuckle and bleach mixing well with Finch's Colgate aftershave.

Finch stood there wide-backed, flat-footed, trying not to sneeze. He lit up the alley he was beaming so, and patting his breast pocket that held their bus tickets to Elkton, Maryland, where the justice of the peace was, and then to Atlantic City to the Cliveden Hotel on Kentucky Avenue for their honeymoon.

THE aunts knew the very second Clarise snuck away from their home. Ness, the younger, softer sister, sat straight up in her bed when she heard the hushed giggles before they evaporated into the alley like blowing bubbles. She called across the room. "Til," she said. "Til, she's gone."

"We knew it was coming," Til said.

"But he's a poor man, Til."

"What colored man isn't?"

"Daddy wasn't."

"Daddy's dead. Whole breed of colored men like Daddy gone to glory. Probably looking down and shaking their heads at lesser versions of themselves that don't even own a pot to piss in."

"You think this Finch will do right by our girl, Til?"

"We did right by her."

"Lord, yes, we did."

"And she knows not to settle for less than what's she's used to."

"Pray, pray she knows it."

"Strong child."

"Well, well. Thank you, Sister, she is strong."

"And we got her inheritance stitched between the mattress springs should they really fall on hard times."

"I'm so thankful, Jesus."

"And our hacking knives stay sharp if he turns out to be the mistreating kind."

"You a mess, Til, a natural mess."

They laughed easy laughs, and then the air got stilted, as they both realized at the same instant it seemed the startling truth to Til's words: how Til had almost made two separate spheres out of Line 'Em Up Larry's face who'd lurked around after Clarise's mother died, insisting that the toddler Clarise was his child and he'd come to claim her, to take her to live with his sister, Vie, and him on Bainbridge Street.

Til told him he was either crazy or drunk. Anybody could look at Clarise and see she was no seed of his, black as he was, blacker than pitch tar, plus everybody knew his pecker had been crushed long before that short spell when he took up with Clarise's mother, when he jumped bad with the Irish during the union riots and they crashed him in his middle with a fifty-pound bag of sand, so he just better keep his black ass away from their house. He didn't heed Til, though. Came back again, talking about "my child, I'm here for my child, me and my sister, Vie, gonna raise my child." And Til told him to just wait right there, she was gonna split him in half. He waited. That became a family joke between the brothers and sisters. If they were talking in superlatives about how stupid somebody was, they'd sum it up with "He's stupid enough to wait in the living room while Til goes to get her sharpest hacking knife to split his head in two; in fact, if there's anybody else around, he organizes a line and claims his spot at the head." Line 'Em Up Larry survived, but that didn't stop two burly detectives from arresting Til and charging her with attempted murder, spurred on by Larry's sister, Vie, who boasted connections at City Hall, said she'd see Til under the jail. Til was found guilty but only slapped on the wrist with a suspended sentence since Larry's sister was only a low-level clerk down at Family Court.

"Ness," Til said, after they had both breathed and sighed and stirred up the bedroom air with remembrances of Til's fight to protect their baby niece, "you getting ready to cry, aren't you, Ness? I can hear it in your breathing."

"I am. Won't deny it. I'm just gonna miss our girl so."

"And you thinking about her mother, right, Ness?"

"How can I not think about Baby Sis at a time like this and the painful ending to her too-short life?"

"Clarise will have a better ending, Ness. But you go ahead then. Go ahead and cry. Just don't let Brother and Brother hear you. As it is, we gonna be wiping up their spilt tears for the next week once they realize our girl went and eloped."

"All right, Til. Stop talking then. Just let me cry, and while I'm crying, I'm gonna pray for the peace and love of their union, and for their prosperity; I'm praying real hard for their prosperity."

C LARISE'S aunt Ness wasn't the only one praying for their prosperity. Finch had moneymaking on his mind from the start of their holy matrimony. Clarise's type of beauty begged for mink and silk. But before he thought about such large-scale purchases, he knew he'd want to keep her in sheer, lacy nightgowns. He'd noticed right away after he'd carried her over the threshold of their honeymoon hotel on Kentucky Avenue in Atlantic City and she'd unpacked the quality tweed suitcase that belonged to the uncles, there was only one fancy nightgown. Lord have Mercy, he thought, she'll leave me for some other cat if I can't keep her in good lingerie. He could hardly concentrate on satisfying her appetites that night thinking about that nightgown. She'd teased him so, played peek-aboo and hide-and-seek with her one nightgown before she'd let him poke his fingers through the holes the lace made.

Finch just lay there staring at the ceiling that entire night while Clarise snored softly against his chest and lightly ground her teeth. Instead of counting sheep, Finch ticked off the mammoth hidden costs of having such a beautiful bride. In addition to nightgowns, there would be fine nylons, imported scents, luxurious skin creams, manicures, and pedicures, and even though he loved her hair when it went soft and bushy and looked like cotton candy, felt like it too when it bounced all up and down his chest to the rhythm of her body working his manhood like it had never been worked before, he knew she'd want to get that cotton candy hair pressed out on a regular basis, and not at someone's kitchen table either; she warranted the finest, full-service salons.

The list of expenses kept accumulating in Finch's head even until the morning, when Clarise woke glowing and chattering about that delicious ocean breeze sifting through the screen in the Kentucky Avenue hotel.

"Come on, Finch"—she giggled—"let's hurry and swim in the ocean early before the beach gets crowded and people let their untrained children stir up the sand in our faces and pee in the ocean and scatter wax paper from their bologna and cheese sandwiches all over the shoreline."

Mercy, Lord, he thought. He hadn't even gotten to children. Children would be a whole separate list. As it was already, he'd have to work night and day as a short-order cook at the Seventeenth-Street Deweys. But he couldn't work night and day. Surely Clarise would get bored waiting for him to come home to play peekaboo games with her nightgown.

He was so plagued with thoughts of some prosperous cat showering his exotic beauty of a bride with see-through lacy lingerie that his steps lumbered heavier than usual as they walked to the beach. Clarise tickled him and tried to entice him into a game of tag; she slapped his butt, blew into his ear, called him honeybunch, and jumped up and down like a squirrel as they walked. Finch hardly grunted. "Got things on my mind, pretty baby," he said.

"But the sun is overhead, the ocean's in our sight, the day is young, and so are we, Finch. What could possibly be so pressing on your mind?"

Before he could tell her that it was money, the type of money he'd need to treat her, to keep her, to do right by her as her man, a seagull released its creamy droppings right on Finch's hatless head. "What the fuck," he said as he patted his head and looked up, only to have the loose-boweled gull go again and again and again, substantial plops, until Finch had to cover his head and run around in circles.

Clarise was laughing and really hopping now. "Oh, Finch, it's glorious, it's the most wonderful thing. I knew it! I knew it! I was right. Thank you, Lord, I was so damned right."

"What the hell is so freaking wonderful about a nasty gull shitting on my head?" Finch asked, wiping his forehead furiously, trying to keep the shit from his eyes.

"It's luck, silly fool." Clarise continued to laugh. "Bird shit, just a dripping, on your head means prosperity. And look at you. You're covered in the shit. We're going to be rich, rich, I tell you, Finch. Filthy rich. So rich we'll move to a huge, brick, single heaven of a house. And that's what we'll call it, Finch. Heaven. We're on our way to Heaven, my wide-backed, flat-footed man." She wrapped her arms around his shoulders and kissed at his face, even where the milky omen of their prosperity dripped and ran.

Finch bought into the bird shit legend. After that it made sense for him to parlay what little he had left of his merchant marine final pay into his own enterprise. Cooking. He became a caterer.

This was 1950 in Philadelphia, and business was booming for

the wedding receptions, sweet sixteen parties, cotillions, graduation dances, golden anniversaries of Philadelphia's established, up-and-coming, and wannabe, well-to-do black folk. So Clarise named the business, Heavenly Caterers, and initially Finch managed it from their one-bedroom basement apartment on Ridge Avenue. He'd bake and fry and stew and broil and baste in the well-sized kitchen, then rent out a hall appropriate to the size of the event. Clarise would do the setting up, the coordinating of details; she had inherited the uncles' eye for mixing colors and knickknacks and lace and art. Plus with her heightened olfactory sense, which enabled her to almost see with her nose, she would go into a barren, dingy hall in some converted factory on Broad Street, stand in the middle of the room, and sniff. Then she'd tell Finch what color table linen, size doilies and bud vases, pattern of silverware, bloom of flowers, shape of servers, whether or not to use balloons, candles, party favors. Between Finch and Clarise the dowdiest of rooms were transformed into showplaces.

Within two years their reputation had caught on so that Finch had to turn down business. And their passbook savings account had grown exponentially, as had the contents of their spacious apartment, owing mostly to Finch's incessant gift giving.

"Not another nightgown," Clarise would say, and Finch would switch up, start bringing her panties instead.

"A person can only wear so many pair of panties in a lifetime," she'd say, and then it would be gold charms for her bracelets, stuffed teddy bears that said "To My True Love," bath crystals, singing jewelry boxes, ostrich feather hats, candleholders, glass paperweights with flowers inside.

"Finch, if you really do love me," she said finally, one Sunday evening after she and the aunts and uncles had just dined on his sumptuous roast duck over crab meat stuffing, and the uncles were sipping sherry from crystal cordial glasses, and admiring the life-sized ceramic Dalmatian with a solid gold dog tag, "you'll not step foot in some fine shop to bring me not another gift."

"But that's one of my greatest pleasures, pretty baby." Finch beamed, stood in the middle of the expansive apartment living room, rested his eyes on the aunts sitting straight-backed in the brocaded wing chairs. He was glad for the opportunity to make such pronouncements in front of the aunts, who he felt still looked at him undereyed as if they were waiting for him to misstep. "Deny me the privilege of showering you with gifts, and you might as well tell me never to cook again or feel the new grass under my feet out at Fairmount Park."

"Enough is enough, Finch. No more gifts until you buy us a house." Clarise stood too, tilted her chin coyly, held her hands behind her back, and swayed as if she held a secret in her hands.

"A house?" he asked, and looked around the room, at the knowing expression on everybody's lips and felt suddenly embarrassed that he was on the outside of their circle of understanding.

"A house, Finch." She held her resolve. "A great grand house that we'll call Heaven. It's time, Finch, it's time. A house," she said.

"Boy don't know yet, does he?" Til asked.

"Can't know," Ness chimed in.

"If he knew, he wouldn't be standing there scratching at his head like it's tic-infected," Til went on.

"Oh, for goodness' sakes." Clarise's tall uncle Blue stood from where he'd been perched on the brick ledge of the fireplace. "Tell the man, please, or I will. This fine cream sherry has my lips hot and ready to spill the beans."

"Either that or he'll cry," said short Uncle Show. "You know Brother can't take a sip of any kind of spirits without finding some reason to bawl all over the place."

"Clarise." Finch dragged her name out, and his eyes had that watery, pleading look that she never could resist.

"Oh, Finch, it's just that while you and the uncles were in the kitchen, the aunts pointed out that my hips are getting square. Do you know what that means? Means something has pushed the roundness of my hips into four corners."

"No, no, no, Clarise, you aren't sick, are you? I couldn't bear it—"

"A baby, Finch." Clarise rushed her words and opened her arms for Finch to lean into. "What else could it be? A baby."

"A baby?" Finch gushed, and his eyes watered for real as Clarise and he held each other and moved in a gentle, slow drag.

"Not the sharpest knife in the drawer, is he?" Ness whispered to Til as they watched Finch and Clarise sway slowly to their private beat.

"You said it, Sister." Til snickered. "Boy more like a spoon than a knife."

"Shish," Blue said from across the room. "Spoons are better than knives anyhow."

"That's right," Show echoed. "They don't cut, and they feed you well."

"I do believe Brother and Brother might have a point," Til said as Finch slowly spun Clarise in a turn and Til caught Clarise's eye and for the first time, and ever so slightly, nodded her approval of Finch. He was a good man, Til thought as she made a mental note to tell Clarise to keep his shoes pointing toward the bed, never toward the door, so no woman of the street would be able to talk him from his home.

THE thought of fatherhood made Finch dizzy and propelled him to find a suitable home. Of course he did, the grandest house his passbook savings account could afford, on a quiet, tree-lined street of impressive three-storied single homes where his neighbors drove new cars, spent old money, and politely snubbed Clarise and Finch. Not just because Finch and Clarise were black; these people after all were polite in a blue-blood sort of way, they had readily accepted a black doctor into their midst, and a professor from the university. So it was as much a matter of breeding as color. Finch after all was just a caterer. A glorified cook. Not a doctor, or lawyer, or banker, not even an undertaker or insurance agent for North

Carolina Mutual. A cook, an occupation that required the hands more than the head. No college, even though he spoke like the well-educated, thanks to his unabridged Webster's. But these neighbors tracked such things, plus they knew his money was new and crisp, hadn't yet been made old and prestigious on the passage down from one generation to the next.

Finch and Clarise were so ebullient over their house, which sent echoes ricocheting when they talked to one another because the ceilings were so tall, that they laughed off their neighbors' petite how-are-you waves that could have been shooing a fly, the dearth of invitations to the barbecues, the hat shows, the pool parties. So what if their reception into the thin edges of this upper-crust neighborhood was less than the open-armed, welcome-basket, come-in-and-let-me-pour-you-coffee type of entry they'd hoped for. They were too buoyant, too round with happiness especially now with the birth of their dark-eyed princess, Shern. They had such immense affection for each other, and the demand was bulging for the culinary and visual talents of Heavenly Caterers, that some days they looked at each other across their expansive Formica table in the breakfast room, and Finch would wink and start to chant that Heaven must be like this.

Heaven. That's what Clarise and Finch named their home. The welcome mat that should have said "Welcome" said "Heaven." The towels that should have been monogrammed maybe "Clarise" and "Finch" were instead monogrammed "Heaven." Even the brass plate on the bottom of the mailbox right under the address said in fine, thin script "Heaven."

Clarise drew on the uncles' lessons when she set to decorating their heaven of a house. From the porch to the yard, the shrubbery to the specially designed trash cans that Finch set out on Thursday nights, even the most unobservant passersby could detect the air of good taste wafting from that house as surely as they could smell the vanilla and butter when Finch was baking cakes. So much so that the molasses-drenched snobbery of the people on that block slowly turned to reluctant acceptance especially as Shern started to grow; she was such a smart, gorgeous child, and of course the mothers on that block liked for their perfect daughters to mix with similarly endowed girls. By the time Clarise gave birth to their second daughter, Victoria, the neighbors were asking Finch for recipes, Clarise for advice on china patterns. They even dropped by with pink teddy bears when Clarise and Finch brought their third child, Bliss, home, especially when they'd heard that the child had a head full of golden hair.

And Shern, Victoria, and Bliss were growing into nice, non-snobbish girls despite the opulence of their lifestyle: the little-girl dress-up tea parties in their sun-drenched playroom, the anklet socks with crocheted embroidery, lavish birthday celebrations complete with pony rides for all their guests, summer camp in the Poconos, and a twelve-foot spruce in their grand center hall at Christmastime. Although Shern was moody at times, and Victoria tended toward the serious, and Bliss had the aunts' penchant for quick, hard-hitting insults, they minded Clarise, whom they adored and who doted on them like a momma cat. "My girls this" and "my girls that" were the center of all her conversations with the neighbors, the patrons of Heavenly Caterers, even the bishop at the AME church she'd joined. Finch rarely lifted his voice higher than a coo to the girls; they were his little darlings, and he made them brownies from scratch every Tuesday night. No matter how large-scale a food preparation job he was on, it halted on Tuesday nights so that his girls would have their favorite brownies, fresh and hot with walnuts, to dunk in their milk. And of course the aunts and uncles visited weekly, the aunts reminding the girls to hold their backs straight, the uncles sneaking them pieces of their homemade butterscotch candies.

Such was the fine cloth of a world of Clarise and Finch, Shern, Victoria, and Bliss. But then in 1965 came the pulled thread, then the snag, finally the stitches that came undone, loop by loop, row by row, until their perfect storybook world unraveled completely right on that old-money block in the house called Heaven.

* * *

It was early morning, in January 1965, and daylight was tapping on the window to Finch's kitchen; he liked to call it his cook's studio since it was separated from the rest of their house by a terrace and a garage like an artist's studio. This morning he'd come in through the tunnel that ran underground and used to hide slaves and was connected to the rest of the house through a crawl space in the basement. It was a lot to go through just to avoid walking outside, especially after he still had to go out on the side of the kitchen that faced the woods, hose himself down from the dust he'd picked up on the way over. "Oh, go away, daybreak," he muttered as he flung his hands against the window. "I don't want to entertain you right now."

He covered three dozen chicken cutlets with his orange marinade and then checked the temperature on his oven, which he'd just gotten the year before from a restaurant supply store. "Hate to use all this oven for such a paltry amount," he said to the wide kitchen air that was swathed in the daybreak that had come on in and taken a seat despite Finch's reluctance to be social.

He pushed the baking pan into the oven, and almost instantly the sweet, acid aroma of his prizewinning orange marinade billowed through the kitchen. He took a seat at the table across from the daybreak, ran his fingers along the gullies his knives had made over the years in his oak cook's table; he looked for recent cut marks, there weren't many, he knew, lately he'd been able to do all of his cutting on the board that fit over the sink.

He sat there breathing deliberately, waiting until he could detect the scent of pepper through the orange, his cue to turn the cutlets. But instead a whiff of something like fresh grass rushed into the kitchen, and he looked up, and there Clarise stood, still in her robe and slippers, her hair straight and brushed back, giving a show to that face that had melted him all those years ago.

"I hope you're garnishing with parsley," she said as she slid inside the door, shook the daylight from the other chair, and sat down at the table. "You know green goes with orange; please, no purple cabbage this time like you used for the Wellingtons' party. Green, when you marinate in orange, your garnish must be green."

"I was going to use green, I'll have you know," Finch said, agitated, wanting to spend the beginning of this day with himself and his cutlets. "And please don't start in with me about colors so early. First the daybreak comes rushing in, and now you." He went to the refrigerator, pushed the colander of cut purple cabbage to the back, pulled out a brown paper bag with parsley leaves hanging out.

"Well, my flat-footed man, you'd have a better chance of keeping the daylight from coming in here than me. And what's got your dander up anyhow?" She ran her finger along the inside of the bowl where the marinade had been and licked the orange drippings from her finger.

"Tired, couldn't sleep; all night I was up." He arranged the parsley on his cook's table, spreading it wide so that it would take up more space on the table.

"Couldn't sleep? Why not?" she asked into the bowl as she sopped up another good fingerful of marinade from the inside of the bowl.

"If you must know, it was you grinding your teeth in your sleep. I was up all night listening to you grind your teeth. Have you ever heard yourself? Ghastly sound, so very irritating."

"Well, silly man, why didn't you wake me and tell me to stop?" she retorted, licking her lips and making a smacking sound.

"You know you die when you fall asleep." He reached for his vegetable knife from the knife block. "A bull chasing a matador could crash through the front window and there wouldn't be a peep from you, except of course for your teeth thrashing about, going at it with each other."

"Well, what are you doing up all night, listening to my teeth anyhow? Something on your mind, Finch?"

"Always something on my mind. I'm a grown Negro man with

a business and a family to care for and keep in style; don't you think I should have things on my mind?" He cut the leafy heads from the parsley and looked on the wall for his smaller colander. He remembered it was in the refrigerator filled with purple cabbage.

"Money's on your mind, right, Finch? Worried that we don't have enough to make it, right?"

"We have enough to make it."

"For today, Finch, when it's bright and sunny, like this room is now. What about tomorrow, when it rains?"

They'd had this conversation many times over the years. And usually Finch would hit Clarise with a saying, something about the perils of worrying about tomorrow. This time it was "Eat, drink, and be merry, for tomorrow you die." He shouted to be heard above the water gushing over the colander of parsley. "And I do have substantial life insurance for when that day comes."

Clarise raised her voice now too. Took the stance the aunts would take when they were teaching her how to hold her own: hands on her hips, legs slightly parted, head pushed way forward of her neck. "You sound like a got-damned fool," she said. "Don't you realize that the dodo bird went extinct because it didn't concern itself with tomorrow?"

He let the parsley fall back in the sink, shook the water from his hands, went to the drawer on the side of his cook's studio where he kept his contracts, pulled out the passbook savings account from PSFS and turned it to the balance page and flashed it in her face. He thought about something else he could quote, noticed the hand-painted lilies on her silk robe. Paraphrased Matthew then. "Consider the lilies of the field; they neither toil nor spin."

"You are not some flower, Finch, nor am I," she said as she snatched the bankbook from his hand.

"But even Solomon in all his splendor was not so richly clothed." Finch talked right over her.

Clarise studied the balance page. She was half satisfied that they could make it in the short term anyhow.

Finch held his breath while she peered at the bankbook. He could almost smell the lilies on her robe they looked so real. He lived for Clarise. Even though he'd gladly lay his life down for his darling daughters, it was for Clarise that his lungs took in air. He saw her dusty grey eyes soften. He wiped his hands against his apron, took her head against his expansive shoulder. "Clarise, you are so wrong," he said. "You are in fact a flower, my pretty baby flower, more precious to me than a whole field of lilies." He mashed his chin against her hair, which had gone from straight to fluffy while they argued, meant it was going to rain later. "So what if you kept me up all night grinding your teeth?"

"Awl, Finch," she gushed, "you are my dodo bird, the only one who was smart enough to stay alive."

They swayed against each other, telling love jokes and laughing softly, the daylight trying to get between them, trying to separate them so they'd have to talk real talk some more. Finch pushed the daylight away, told it to go sit its ass back down at the table. Told himself not to worry.

Finch was worried, though. A deep-down belly kind of worry that cut his appetite so that he hardly tasted his cooking anymore by dunking his finger in his gravies, and glazes, and juices from his meats. Clarise could taste his worry too: His pot pies were salty; the texture on the skin of his lambs was tough; the brown, crunchy head on his baked macaroni and cheese was thinner now; even the glaze on his yams, which used to shine like liquid crystal, was duller, grayer.

It was the lure of the catering chains. Lyndon Johnson had signed the Civil Rights Act, the last bastions of Jim Crow had buckled everywhere, and black people were flocking to J&A's, Mc-Closkey's, Bain's, to get their catering needs met. They still enlisted Finch for the teenage birthday parties, the Saturday afternoon club meetings, the private tea at somebody's home. But they answered freedom's call for the volume events where Finch used to turn a regular and substantial profit: the 200-guest wedding reception, the railroad retirement party to feed 150, the golden anniversary that was covered in the *Tribune* and would have given some ink to Heavenly Caterers. Those major accounts abandoned Finch, went instead with the display advertisers in the yellow pages that promised, "We'll cater to all your needs, your place or ours."

When someone mentioned the elegant affair they'd attended downtown, Finch would grunt, "Don't dare talk to me about some established caterer who's doing nothing but robbing people with god-awful potato salad and inattentive service."

"But, Finch," they'd say, "this is progress for our people."

Finch would grunt again and rock back and forth on his heels. "You want to know progress for our people," he'd boom. "Progress for our people won't be had until that giant white man that all you silly Negroes run to spend your money with like he's God on earth starts coming to the likes of me to spend his. Or," he'd snort, "when that Mayor Tate hires Heavenly Caterers to do his inaugural ball."

F<small>INCH</small> got increasingly more despondent as he started chipping away at the exterior of their charmed lives. There would be no pony rides at Bliss's eleventh birthday party, and summer for the girls would be spent at a day camp in the city. Last year's Easter garb would have to do, and his plan to install one more six-jet stove in his cook's studio would go on ice for now. It wouldn't be enough; had to admit it to himself and the daybreak every morning when he started his food preparations and the daylight rushed in and hit him over the head, forced him to see that his passbook savings account was flattening out like a tire with a slow leak.

He thought about redirecting his business, maybe apply for a small business loan; that was certainly more appealing than accepting money from the aunts and uncles. How much like a speck of dust he'd felt the night before, right after one of his lavish Sunday dinners, an eye roast, pecan string beans, potato salad, and a side of chitterlings because the aunts and Clarise loved them so, and the aunts and uncles cornered him in his kitchen, all four of them, under the guise of checking out his new paring knives. Til told him that they had money; their daddy, who'd been born a free man even though it was before the Emancipation, had left them land. And Clarise had mentioned he wasn't doing that big fraternity ball that he'd done every year that attracted thousands; they didn't mean to insult his manhood by implying that he couldn't carry his family in style, but the Negro has it hard, they'd said. Let them help, they'd insisted, please let them help.

But of course Finch was insulted, told them as politely as he could that there was no need to accept their offer, even accidentally nicked his thumb as he turned his paring knife over when he said it. Because he did need help, a quick infusion of funds just until he could concoct a plan for redirecting his business.

And now it hit him as he sat in his cook's studio sipping coffee and making small talk with the daybreak about his years at sea and how he'd envy the lone fishermen as they'd cast their nets, working for no one but themselves. Crabbing. He could rent his second cousin's boat and go crabbing. He'd secure a hall for himself this time, call it a crab feast. He'd steam them, mash them, and fry them in batter and oil, bake them, barbecue them, toss them in salads. He'd take out an ad in the *Tribune;* he'd leave flyers at churches; he'd make it a monthly thing, maybe weekly if it really took off. He got excited the more he imagined the potential for success. He wouldn't say anything to anybody right now, not even Clarise, especially with the seesaw her moods seemed to be riding on lately. He'd surprise her with the prospect when he was certain of its success; his lungs expanded at the thought of her face going wild with excitement, looking even more exotic when he presented her with his idea, wrapped up in good thorough planning like a diamond in a velvet pouch. Crabbing. He'd go out at least once and see the potential for the catch. Maybe even Tuesday he'd go. He'd watch Clarise's hair for signs of the weather; then he'd pack his hip boots and head for the Maryland shore.

Clarise had her own plans. She'd mentioned to her doctor at her yearly physical that her nerves had been affected by the financial fluctuations in Finch's business. He'd prescribed Elavil, small doses, and advised Clarise to take up knitting, or crocheting, or some similarly calming hobby. She did. Would even hum while she knitted. Used the finest wools and an inventive knit and purl cross-stitch to weave together all kinds of hats and scarves for the girls. She was quickly approaching the point where she was ready to start showing her work to department stores, maybe bring in enough to buy shetland and angoras in bulk, turn enough of a profit to put some black ink onto the pages of Finch's savings account passbook. Her heart tore a little whenever she'd hear the weight of Finch's flat feet lumbering into the bedroom, trying not to wake her, whistling, she knew, just in case she was awake. But even his whistling was a lower pitch, the notes sagging in the bedroom air, trying to stay afloat. She was more determined now that she'd buy the wool, work her fingers in fast weaving motions, mix colors, like she'd been taught by the uncles; stay strong, straight-backed, like she'd learned from the aunts. But that Tuesday night happened first.

THE girls were at their seats at the oversized Formica table in the breakfast room. They had just finished watching *Petticoat Junction,* and Shern, the oldest, thirteen-year-old gorgeous child with the dark, liquid eyes, argued with Bliss, the eleven-year-old baby with the golden hair. Their dispute this time, these two always disagreed, was over who the prettiest daughter on that TV show was. Victoria disinvolved herself in their argument. Victoria, who was twelve, was in the middle not only in order of birth but in all things it seemed: her opinions, her appearance, her height, but not her ability to modulate disagreements between her older and younger sisters; in that, she knew, she excelled. But this Tuesday night she let them go at it. One had just told the other she was a blind bat and looked like a bat too, with beady eyes and leathery skin. Victoria didn't even know who said it to whom; she was too plugged into her mother right now, feeling Clarise's extreme edginess as if she were connected to her mother through an electric cord.

Clarise walked into the breakfast room with the comb and brush and grease and a half dozen sponge rollers nestled in her pink mesh hair care caddie. And Victoria could no longer stand the jolts shooting through her stomach every time she focused on her mother. "Is something the matter, Mommie?" she asked finally as Clarise tilted Victoria's chin so that she could wind her bang around a hair roller.

Clarise dipped her finger into the jar of Dixie Peach hair pomade and smoothed it over Victoria's bang. "Sniff," Clarise said.

"Sniff?" Victoria asked, and then breathed in deeply through her nose. "Sniff what?"

"Exactly my point," Clarise said. "There's nothing. Nothing to smell but the sweetness of this Dixie Peach hair grease." Clarise moved across the table to do Bliss's bang. Both Bliss and Shern had stopped arguing, and all three were starkly silent, the perplexity of their mother's words hanging over the breakfast room.

"Nothing, just nothing," Clarise continued to mutter.

"Huh?" Bliss asked.

"Don't say 'Huh,' " Clarise snapped. She yanked on Bliss's hair when she said it. "Say, 'Excuse me, please, I didn't understand you.' "

"Excuse me, please, I didn't understand you." Bliss rubbed her scalp where her mother had just yanked her head and started to cry. "I'm sorry, Mommie."

"Okay, okay, don't cry, my darling." Clarise rubbed Bliss's scalp and kissed her forehead. "Mommie didn't mean to hurt you, but you must speak correct English, and you must learn to read the signs."

"Signs?" All three girls looked at their mother and hardly breathed as if she were about to explain to them the meaning of life on earth.

"Where are the brownies?" Clarise shouted it and banged the table.

They stared at Clarise with frightened circle eyes and were quiet as deer until Victoria smacked herself on the forehead with the revelation that this was Tuesday night, and their mother was not talking in some kind of code but actually meant brownies.

"Hey, where are the brownies?" Victoria asked. "It is Tuesday night after all."

"And we don't smell the brownies, right, Mommie? Isn't that what you meant when you told Tori to sniff?" Bliss asked.

"You mean, Daddy's not in his studio making them?" Shern asked. Clarise was rolling Shern's hair around a curler now, and Shern wished she had a thousand more to do. Her mother's hands were so warm and hard against her forehead, her fingers dancing on her forehead as she locked the curler in place. She just wanted the feel of her mother's fingers to dull the sharp breaths of worry catching in her throat. "Does that mean something's terribly wrong, Mommie?" Shern asked.

"Is something wrong with Daddy?" Bliss whined.

"My girls are so bright," Clarise said. "I've been blessed with such smart, geniuslike girls."

"What is it, Mommie? We can handle it, whatever it is. Please tell us what's wrong with Daddy," Victoria begged. "Where is he anyhow? I was sure he was in his studio." Victoria let a sob slip through even though she wanted to be strong and mature amid this dark cloud of a revelation that was hanging over the gold-candled chandelier in the kitchen and getting ready to fall on their heads.

"Please tell us, Mommie." Bliss got up from her seat and jumped up and down. "Please, Mommie, please. Tell us what's wrong with Daddy."

"Is it really bad?" Victoria cried openly now despite her attempts to act mature.

"It is something terrible, isn't it?" Shern neither cried nor begged. She sat up straight as a board and stared at her mother, trying to let her emotions neither out nor in. She just wanted not to feel, as she watched her mother's face, her beautiful, exotic face, go from pale to flushed to a blankness that looked like grief.

"Now I smell the sea," Clarise said as she stared into the darkening breakfast room. "It's an oily smell tinged with the sweet, sour scent of your father's breath."

A<small>T</small> that instant Finch's breath was mixing with the sea as he clung to the side of the crabbing boat that had just spilled his catch—his brainchildren that were going to redirect his business, his precious crabs—and him into the sea's demanding arms. He'd stayed out too long, he now realized. "Be back by sunset," his second cousin had warned. "This sea does a strange thing at sunset, and my boat seen better days." But the catch had been so substantial: the crabs had just climbed into his net as if they were saying, "Take me, Finch. I'll be a part of your all-you-can-eat buffet." He was so excited and laughing and counting the money to be made as he hauled in net after net he didn't even notice that the yellow was washing to red in the back of the sky. And when he did notice the red in the sky, he still assured himself that he could make it from the shallow waters of the shoreline through the deeper canal to get to the other side of the shore, where even more crabs were waiting to help him redirect his business. But suddenly, right after his cousin's boat went into a spin midway through the canal like a tub toy headed for the drain, he noticed the sky was hazy-purple on its way to a deeper blue, and his crabs were climbing, not spilling from the boat, and he was too. And now he flogged about, trying to wrestle his life from the sea.

The sea of course was stronger, a bully and a show-off. It wrenched the crabbing boat from Finch like a spoiled child snatching back a favorite toy, chanting, "Mine, mine, mine."

"Oh, fuck you then," Finch hollered out.

The sea laughed in his face, hit him with waves that were like tufted, braided ropes, over and over until he could feel welts unzipping along his back, his face. He started to curse the sea even more: "cocksucker, prick, son of a motherfucking bitch." Then he realized he was going to die. He'd never been a religious man, but he didn't want to die with some profane word curling around his tongue. He started to quote a Scripture, something about faith or possibilities. Then a hymn came to his mind; he'd just heard it the other Sunday at the Children's Day program where Shern was the MC—something about a tempest and raging billows tossing high. He laughed out loud at the appropriateness of the song as the sea continued to spit in his face. He was drowning, he thought, and laughing. Now he realized he was treading water more slowly because the sea had clamped hundred-pound weights in his hands. Now he begged the sea for his life. "I have a wife who needs me, and my girls, three beautiful, well-behaved, perfect girls. Please, dear sea, wonderful, kind, beautiful, magnificent sea, please let me have my life. Please don't snatch my life!"

He tried to remember what he'd learned about drowning all those years he'd spent on ships. Since he was twelve and had run away from home and lied about his age to get passage on that first ship as a sand spreader and worked his way up to pot scrubber until he finally made it to assistant cook, the conversation among the kitchen help often turned to shipwreck stories. They'd say things like "You better pray that the sea is a pretty woman 'cause you sure getting fucked if you find yourself out in it." But what he remembered right now was the night Deaf-and-Dumb Leaned-Over Johnson cleared his throat and spoke the first words anybody on that ship had heard pass his lips. "I survived the *Titanic*," Johnson said, his speech slow, almost slurred. "Wasn't on no lifeboat either, wasn't no such thing as a lifeboat for the colored help. But I survived 'cause I just give in to the sea." Finch remembered how Johnson had turned to look at him, as if he were talking to only him; he was an old man, had to be past seventy, but his skin was the smoothest black he'd ever seen, the whites of his eyes brighter than the North Star, almost a crazed look to his eyes they were shining so. "Boy," he said to Finch—he straightened his back leaned over from the years heaped on it, and suddenly he towered over Finch—"if the sea ever catch you in its belly, just give up the fight. Just give in to the deep. And if you not raised too much hell in your life, if you not filled with too much devilment, the sea might just carry you back to its top, let you rest on its palm whiles you can catch your breath."

So Finch let go. The fight was leaving his body anyhow, and he'd never been a strong swimmer, too much weight in his legs. And the wave coming at him now was the kind that would separate a man's head from his neck. He threw his hands up in surrender; he let his muscles go slack. "Take me deep," he whispered.

The wave taking him over now was like velvet: its softness made him cry, made him think of Clarise's hair, Shern's chin, Victoria's manner, Bliss's laugh, the sherry he'd pour the uncles on Sunday nights, Til's fox-foot collar, the sound of Ness's name. He thought he should see his life as he tumbled head over knees toward the center of the sea: the South Carolina lean-to where he was born, his mother, who died birthing him, shouldn't she appear right now with wings and a halo reaching for him to enter into eternity, his brothers, who'd all left home before he was born, who probably never even knew his name, shouldn't the faces come to him in death that never did in life? And where was Clarise's face? Could he just see her face one more time. How cruel that he should die and not see his beautiful bride pass before his eyes, even if he couldn't see his girls—Clarise. Where was Clarise? He jolted to, grabbed at the water in one final tug, one last try to live. But the water was slick, oily, too soft. It went through his hands like spilled milk, and now he really did let go.

It had been a month since the closed-casket memorial service for Finch; the casket had to be closed because there was no body to fill it, just his Ferragamo handmade shoes and the gray wool suit that Clarise used to insist he wear when he garnished with pink.

She placed his unabridged Websters in the center of the casket because Finch had been a self-made man and relied on that dictionary so that he could approach prospective clients and dazzle them by describing his food with words like "delectable," "succulent," "palatable," "pithy," "scrumptious." Plus she wanted the casket to have a little weight to it because Finch had been such a substantial man.

Now it was twenty-nine days later; she knew it was twenty-nine days because the aunts had stressed that she couldn't wash the sheets on which Finch had last slept for twenty-eight days. The smell of those sheets had brought her comfort over the past month, the way the creamy sweet of her cold cream blended perfectly with the Royal Crown Finch rubbed nightly in his scalp. But last night she hadn't been able to fall asleep clutching Finch's pillow and taking in the scent of his hair pomade because the aunts had come over and stripped the bed themselves the day before. They'd come over every day since Finch had been declared missing and presumed dead. The uncles concocted desserts that begged up fleeting smiles from the girls, while the aunts propped Clarise between the two of them, taking turns squeezing the nape of her neck, helping her hold her head up when the girls were in the room; they cried less when they could look on their mother's face.

Clarise was fading in and out still, which of course everyone blamed on her grief. Her pastor from the AME church stopped by once a week and told her things like "Joy cometh in the morning"; her best friend from high school called her daily with conversations that they'd had twenty years before, trying in vain to make Clarise laugh; Finch's florist sent her a single red rose three, sometimes four times a week; the aunts brewed her tea, chamomile, spearmint, licorice. Everyone had their own prescription to save her from her grief. All to no avail. Because it wasn't just her grief that was taking her over. It was the medicine.

This was 1965, and Elavil was being dispensed like lemon drops. And even though the drug had been a balm during the first days after Finch turned up missing, when Clarise's emotions were oozing and running like pus from a picked-at scab, after Finch was declared dead, her doctor increased the dosage so she wouldn't be devoured by her grief. He didn't realize, though, that Clarise had a sensitivity to the drug; probably the same thing in her brain that gave her such a heightened sense of smell rebelled against the chemical rockabys. Now her senses were dimming on and off like a short-circuited night-light, so much so that she could barely manage to do the one thing that calmed her, knit.

This morning she tried. She wrapped the loop of yarn around the pointed end of the knitting needle, and then that navy haze dropped over her that always fell right after she took her morning pill. It was irritating, that damned haze, especially when it bunched up between her wrists and got tangled and she could barely work her knitting needles because of it. She was determined to knit through it, though. She pushed one needle between the looped thread, wrapped the thread around, and easily slid the finished stitch to the other needle, over and over. She was working up a steady clicking to the needles that sounded like a song; it had been so many days since she'd been able to do this. She completed one row, a second, a third. She used bright purple thread, too bright maybe because her eyes were starting to sting, and now tear, and that haze was dropping, so that all she could do was sit there and hold her needles until it lifted.

It wasn't lifting. She blinked her eyes, trying to blink the haze from her eyes. Her vision cleared enough for her to drag across the room to get her sewing box, lift out her sharpest shears, and snip away at that navy haze wrapped around her hands, tangling up her yarns. She did. Parts of the navy were especially dense, and she had to grip and bear down hard with the scissors to get through it. Until the haze played a cruel trick, retreated suddenly, and it was the skin around her wrist that she sliced.

She didn't even feel it. Wouldn't even have known had it not been for the expression on Shern's face when she came into her room to kiss her good-bye on her way to school, and she stood there in the archway of her mother's bedroom door with such a horrified expression as if a scream had frozen itself on her face. And Clarise asked her what was wrong. "Talk to Mommie and tell me what is it," she said with a tongue so heavy that it seemed to her it took hours to get the words out.

But all Shern could do was point to Clarise's lap. It was only then that Clarise realized how that deceitful haze had duped her as she looked down and saw her wrists lying loosely in her lap, gaping quietly, spilling their contents like red satin ribbons unfurling gently to the floor.

W<small>HEN</small> Til answered the phone to Shern's broken, barely recognizable voice and she and Ness and Blue and Show hailed a cab to Chestnut Hill and rushed in on the house already emptied by the emergency crew, and the next-door neighbor told them what hospital, and they barrelled in on the emergency room, pleading: for information, for the girls, they were told they were too late.

Not too late for Clarise. Clarise would live, the hospital told them. She was under a thirty-day court-ordered commitment on her way right now to the Pennsylvania Institute for the Mentally Ill. All attempted suicides were handled this way. But they were too late for the girls. Children's Services had already claimed them, had someone from Family Court retreive the girls. "Hysterical," the aunts and uncles were told. "As you can imagine, those girls were hysterical."

So Til sent Blue and Show back to Clarise's house, to unspill Clarise's blood if they could, but at least to remake the house into a place where the girls could return without the images of what had just run very far awry that morning. Too far awry even for Til and Ness to fathom. They shook their heads right now and tried to still their breathing as they sat facing each other huddled in a brown-aired room at 1801 Vine Street waiting to see the case manager assigned to the girls.

"Family Court, case managers, attempted suicides, I feel like I'm stuck in a bad dream that's not adding up to anything that looks like sense. Just doesn't add up, Ness," Til said, seeing and not seeing the American flag standing behind a counter and between a door to an inner office and a wall where Lydon Johnson peered down from a scalloped gold frame. "Just doesn't fit in with everything I know about Clarise's constitution; she's just not the kind to try to take her own life, just not, no way, just not."

"I agree with you, Sister," Ness said as she reached across to help Til pull her coat off her shoulders. She let her fingers rest on the fox-foot collar. "Remember how Clarise loved this collar when she was a little thing, used to call it her pet."

"Do tell, she surely did." Til sighed and then laughed and said, "All the children had some kind of relationship with this collar: Shern would try to feed it; that little Victoria would run, scared it was gonna come off the coat and bite her; and little Bliss would threaten to beat the collar up for her sister."

"What you talking about?" Ness laughed too as she undid the buttons on her own coat. "Remember when Blue grabbed the coat out of your hands and threw it on the floor and told Bliss to go ahead and beat it up, stomp it to bits, he told her."

"He sure did with his old silly self, probably had been sipping sherry when he did it, my good coat too."

"And you let her do it too. You remember that part?"

"I do." Til smiled. "Some of my best times been spent at Clarise and Finch's on Sunday nights. Lord have mercy, and now Finch is gone and Clarise—mnh, I can't figure, Ness, I just can't figure. I do believe she was gonna come back to herself."

"She was, I believe it too."

"She was gonna get over Finch. It was gonna take her time, but she was gonna do it for the daughters."

"And still can, Sister. This is just a temporary setback, I do believe. We'll collect the daughters and help them and Brother and Brother and ourselves too; we'll all get through this, Sister."

"You're nothing but right, Ness. The disturbing thing for me right now is that we have to sit here and wait for some case manager to make a—a what did they call it, a determination? Determination of what is my question."

"Mine too, Sister. Now I definitely agree with you on how absurd that is. I mean, after all we're the only known living blood relatives those daughters can lay claim to."

"So why is my stomach flopping around like a tuna caught in a net over the fact that we even have to sit here and wait like this, like we're applying for a job selling secondhand TVs?"

The door next to the wall propping the American flag and under the Lyndon Johnson glossy opened, and Til looked beyond Ness's furrowed brow and felt her heart tear. "Ness, this is a bad dream, it's very bad, don't turn around and look behind you, just talk to me, Ness, talk to me calm, talk to me sure."

"I'm right here with you, Sister. Now you just breathe in and out deeply a few times. Whatever it is can't be made better if you throw a fit, and by the looks on your face you're headed in that direction."

"Ness, haven't we tried to live right?"

"We have."

"Never hurt anybody unless it was to protect ourselves or something belonging to us."

"Say it true, Sister. Say it true."

"Use only the purest ingredients in our soaps, even been good stewards over the land Daddy left in our charge."

"Well, well, well, Sister, you know what you talking about now, earning enough leasing fees on that land to keep us in stead for all our natural-born days should the soap business dry up."

"Don't complain much either, take each day as it comes, like the Word instructs us to."

"What you leading up to, Sister? Come on with it now."

"We send our tithing envelopes even when we don't make it to the service."

"Sister, Sister, I'm trying to stay with you, but you seeing something right now that's got your face fixed like Satan himself is standing behind my head. You might as well as go on and tell me, 'cause you getting ready to explode anyhow. Tell me right now, Sister, tell me slow and soft and easy."

"Ness, it's that old, spiteful woman. The case manager for the daughters. It's that fat-assed, pipe-mouthed, venom-spewing, Line 'Em Up Larry's spiteful sister, Vie."

Til's voice went higher and louder with each description of Vie. Ness reached across and put her hands on Til's knees because now they were going up and down too.

Then Vie shouted across the room, "You can call me what you want, but you're a convicted felon, attempted murder, remember, Til, and I'm not placing those girls with you."

It seemed to Ness as if the room were moving; it always seemed that way when Til was about to throw a fit. She was a solidly constructed woman, and even now in her sixties she had more muscle mass than fat. Til stood, and Ness did too and grabbed her, to hold her, to talk to her, to calm her down. But Til slipped through Ness's grasp like lard.

Now Til was at the counter, banging at it over and over. "You have no right holding a grudge against me over what happened more than thirty years ago," she yelled. "Everybody knew your brother's pecker was smashed so no way could he be Clarise's father, but he kept coming around like some kind of psycho, I was forced to go upside his head. Now you better just turn those girls over to my sister and me or I'm gonna do the same thing to you I did to Larry."

Vie pressed the security buzzer, laughed out loud in Til's face, and started backing up toward the door under Lyndon Johnson. "I'm not holding no grudge," she said, "but I am upholding the law. And as a convicted felon you are unfit, just unfit for those girls to be placed with."

A crowd had formed in the room, curiosity seekers walking through the corridor. Even Lyndon Johnson leaned as if to see what the commotion was.

Ness picked up Til's coat, which had fallen to the floor. She squeezed the fox-foot collar to her chest. This was bad, very bad. She tried to hold on to her tears and move faster than the police who had just run through the door, dispersed the crowd, and were now heading with determination toward her ranting sister, Til.

Part Two

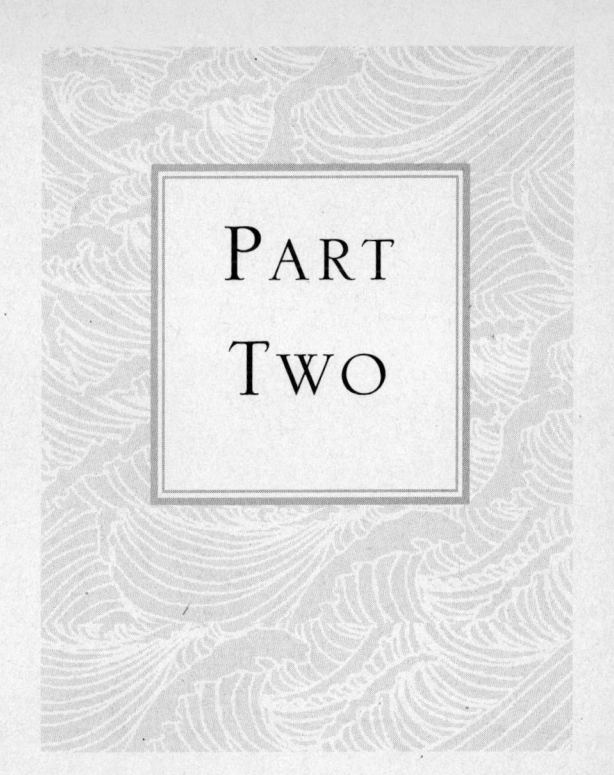

2

THE sun was hanging way back in the sky all feisty and red over Sixtieth Street; it could have been on a different hemisphere but was really just on the other side of town from where Clarise and Finch's heaven of a house stood. It was afternoon on a chilly Saturday, and the doings were at their height. People flitted in and out of their usual Saturday stop-bys: Baron's Meat and Poultry, Connie's Cards 'n' Gifts, Luke's Good as New Shoe Repair. They were an eclectic mix. Girlfriends called to each other through the throngs of foot traffic, "Hey now, we got to talk." Men breezed by other men, slapped hands, said things like "My main man, what you know good?" Bow-tied Muslims waved their newspapers with urgent gestures. "Free your minds," they called; their voices commingling with the high-pitched humming sounds of tambourine-clapping sanctified women in long skirts and little hats doing a holy dance at the bus stop. The blind man held out his tin cup and jostled with the Jehovah's Witnesses over prime standing space at the foot of the el. And all through here, the tunes of the Impressions floated from the outturned speakers at the Imperial Skating Rink; they lent smooth cha-cha–able rhythms to the mix as they crooned that everything was all right.

Then Ramona, the saucer-eyed, butter-toned West Philly head turner, emerged from Miss D's beauty parlor, where she'd just gotten a hard press, blond streaks, and a French roll tucked up high and neat with fifty hairpins. She caught the "yeah yeah" rhythm of the Impressions' song, but she didn't sway or finger pop; she carried too much pent-up anger for such outwardly fanciful shows of pleasure. She did smirk at the fireball of a sun, though, which looked to her like a hot-behind woman calling on her lover, the night, to come on and blanket her. She liked to imagine how the sun must be undressing herself for the night right now because such imaginings disrupted the predictability about her own life: her Lit Brothers paycheck down to the penny where she worked in the bargain basement as the assistant buyer; the songs her gospel choir sang every Second Sunday; the catcalls of "Hey, foxy lady," whenever she walked by the opened door of the Swank Club; more foster children arriving from the state for her mother to raise temporarily, like the three Vie was getting ready to drop off. Three girls. Ramona especially hated the girls.

She made quick loops through the assemblages of foot traffic on this five-block commercial stretch that fringed a middling-type neighborhood of the not rich, not poor, but sometimes broke till payday; where the consistent salute of the row houses was comforting to the mostly black folks who lived there and made them feel communal and blessed that they owned these patches of property to refinance to send their children to a teachers' college. Ramona felt neither communal nor blessed, so she avoided conversation with the men who'd want to flirt, the women who'd want to gossip, the children who were never cute to her.

She looked straight ahead as she walked. She felt as she imagined the sun did right now: itching for the night to come, needing to break the routine, be blanketed herself after her hardworking week.

Except that Ramona didn't have the expanse of the sky to put on her seductress dance, only the tiny row house on Addison Street where she lived with Mae, her mother, who had a lazy eye and who made her living by taking in foster children from the state. Nor was the one who Ramona would beckon as powerful as the night. Tyrone. Nice enough, seemed devoted to her, but lacked a city slickness she had come to expect in her men.

She walked fast, deliberately, trying to get what she needed from Sixtieth Street and make it home in time for her appointment with Vie to receive this new crop of foster children being dropped off. For once Ramona wished her mother would be there—these three girls would most likely be severely traumatized, and Ramona never knew what to do about the traumatized—but her mother, Mae, had gone to see about her ailing sister in Buffalo, so Ramona was left not only to cook and clean and otherwise care for the girls but also to be a pillow for them to cry into when their grief came down. That part she just couldn't do, especially for the girls.

She turned into Darlene's hosiery, where they were throwing in a garter belt with the purchase of six pair of nylons. She chose the black garter belt from among the inducements Darlene offered and managed a hurried "uh-huh" and "just fine" to Darlene's queries about Mae.

"Hear she's gone to Buffalo to see after her sister," Darlene said. "Keeping her in prayer, you tell her that; tell her I'm holding her Playtex Eighteen Hour stretch too. Don't forget now, Ramona. Just came in in that beige color she wanted. A month from Tuesday she'll be back, right? You minding the foster kids, for her, huh? Better her than me taking that ride; I'd rather walk through Dead Block at twilight and deal with the ghost of Donald Booker than suffer through ten hours on a Trailways bus."

Ramona didn't interrupt Darlene as she went on to talk about Donald Booker, the bad seed white boy who had disappeared in the park almost twenty years ago, and to say there'd been another sighting earlier that day. Ramona hated ghost stories, and this one made her chest go tight. She rushed to get to the door as Darlene's voice ushered her out, and she left clutching her box of smoke-colored hose. Even though her mother always told her those dark stockings on her light legs looked whorish. "Get the cinnamon-colored; that's the shade a girl who purports to be a Christian like you should be wearing," Mae always said. Ramona shook off her mother's voice about the color of stockings. Least she could do was show off her legs in the shade she wanted, especially after being saddled with grief-stricken girls until Mae got back.

She passed the five-and-dime where the window was done up in an oversized box of Jean Naté toilet water. "The scent for all of his senses," the sign read. The bright yellow box stopped Ramona, made her back up to gaze in the five-and-dime's window. She fingered the change from her stockings, which she'd dropped into her coat pocket. "A dollar and nine cents," the sign seemed to whisper, "splash on this, and he'll be all over you for a well-spent dollar nine."

The streetlamp in front of the five-and-dime popped on, and Ramona shrugged off the whispered enticements of the Jean Naté. What was the sense in eating into next week's bus fare just to make herself irresistible to Tyrone when she was only going to have to sneak him up to her tiny bedroom? Piece of car he drove barely had a back seat, and surely he couldn't afford a room at a drive-in motel, much less a lavish suite somewhere downtown where Ramona thought she belonged.

The March wind was starting to gurgle and belch on Sixtieth Street, and Ramona pulled her coat collar up around her ears. She was glad she'd worn her good trench coat with the genuine suede trim; she always wore her good clothes when she got her hair done on Sixtieth Street lest the loud-talking women in the shop think she was needy. They knew she made a half-decent living as the assistant buyer in Lit Brothers bargain basement, and she didn't want anybody to guess her real financial nonworth, how Mae was always siphoning her money, talking her out of generous bits of her pay week after week while Ramona watched in horror as her hard-worked-for dollars slipped through her own fingers into Mae's card-playing hands like Johnson's baby oil. So Ramona wore her good trench coat with the genuine suede trim in order to cover up for Mae.

Ramona straightened her back and brushed at her new French roll. She turned from the five-and-dime window and made her way toward the Sun Ray drugstore on the corner. Decided if the sun could do her thing with the night so boldly, she could certainly stop at the Sun Ray, treat herself to a Coke, sit at the counter, and listen to the els go by. She hoped she wouldn't run into any of the gospel choir, who'd surely want to talk. She wanted instead to try to think about Tyrone. Wanted to try yet again to summon up those tingling feelings that glittered that she thought she should have for Tyrone. Except every time she tried to think about Tyrone in the dreamy-eyed way appropriate for a woman allowing herself to fall in love, she'd end up sighing to herself, the way she guessed the sun would have sighed had she not been able to beckon the night; it wasn't Tyrone's face she'd see at all. It was a face more formed, hardened, lined in ways that stirred Ramona's passions. She felt cheap and common when she thought about that face in such a gushing, silky way. It was Tyrone's father's face. Ever since she was a teenager and would giggle to her best friend Grace how fine she thought Perry was, he'd had that effect on her. And Grace would tell her he was too old, old enough to be her father, and what did her father look like anyhow because on *The Edge of Night* somebody was in love with an older man and it turned out just to be a need for a father figure? But Ramona never knew her father; some high-yellow sailor who came and went with the ships at the navy yard was all she knew, so she told Grace that couldn't be it because Perry was brown as a chocolate snap cookie, and probably as sweet.

She shifted on the stool and nestled her body against the frame of the stool, which was padded and covered in red vinyl, and ignored the conversation bursting around her so that she could chase away thoughts of the father and try with everything in her to fall into mink-lined thoughts about Tyrone. She drew hard on her straw and swallowed a gulp of Coke. The cola was sweet and strong and fizzed all the way up into her head and threatened to push back out through her nostrils. There it was again, Perry's face instead of Tyrone's, all etched with lines that were gullies of entrenched manhood, signs of hard living that now that she was in her twenties Ramona knew often made tender lovers.

She shook the image of Perry again, now she had to. The whistle that still blew at five as if it had people to dismiss was sounding at the abandoned bread factory. It was almost time for her meeting with Vie; she had to go.

The plastic chair covering kept wanting to talk as Ramona listened to Vie going on and on about the blowout down at the office she'd had over the placement of the three foster girls waiting in the car. Vie was a big-busted, big-hipped woman and was sweating on the couch, even though it felt like wintertime outside, and squirming and forcing the air under the plastic to sigh and squeak almost right on cue so that Ramona didn't even have to utter "unhunh," and "mn," and "is that so?"

"Imagine, Ramona," Vie said, casting her large arms up and down, and looked to Ramona as if she were getting ready to do some Boardwalk-type dance like the cool jerk or Mickey's monkey. "That old Til gonna threaten me and I'm on official time, talking about I better let her have those girls or she gonna do to me what she did to my brother all those years ago. Oh, yes, she did. So you know what I did: I had them hold her over. Oh, yes, I did. And I got a restraining order put on her, all of them in that house; they are not to try to contact those girls long as they're under the jurisdiction of the court unless I say so, okay. First of all, she can't have the girls 'cause she's a convicted felon, and we can't be forced to place any child with a convicted felon that's not their natural parents."

Ramona was half listening to Vie now. She already knew the story of Larry getting his head darn near split in two trying to claim somebody's baby girl as his own; that story had followed him from downtown up to West Philly, where Vie and her brother moved shortly after Ramona and Mae. Ramona didn't blame the woman who'd cut him; everybody knew Larry had lost the workings to his manhood during the union riots. Still, every other weekend, even now, Ramona would hear about Larry beating somebody up in some club even though he was well into his fifties. Shipshop shape, though, since he worked out regularly at the boxing gym on Pine Street; rumor was that he'd even sparred for Sonny Liston in his prime. Ramona reasoned he had to, forced to go through life with a smashed dick like that, had to prove his manhood in other ways.

Now Vie was talking about how hard she'd had to work to rise from general clerk to case manager, thirty years it took her, plus had to put herself through community college to get her associate's degree, and she was damned if she was gonna undignify her position and allow those girls to go with that convicted felon Til. "I mean those girls darn near watched their mother bleed to death, do you get my point, Ramona?"

Ramona nodded and listened to the plastic chair covering clacking under Vie as she shifted around on the couch.

"Furthermore," Vie went on, "even if she didn't have a record from what she did to my brother all those years ago, I still have serious concerns about their lifestyle, all of them in that house, serious concerns."

"Lifestyle? What about their lifestyle?" Ramona asked, her focus back to what Vie was saying. "Do they drink and smoke and gamble?" Ramona thought about Mae's persistent card playing when she asked it.

"No, actually there are some, well, some gender identity issues, oh, yes, there are—"

"Wait a minute, are you saying that they're funny?" Ramona interrupted. "That those girls can't go with their natural kin because the aunts or uncles might be funny?"

"I'm not saying it's anything I can prove, okay, Ramona, but come on, all of them in that house never been married—"

"Me neither, Vie. I'm a single woman."

"Now, Ramona, your womanhood ain't never come into question, okay—"

"You single too, Vie."

"Look, yeah, I'm single, but ain't a damned thing wrong with me. Okay. All I'm saying is that as case manager I can use my discretion, and if Til and the rest of that brew really want those girls, they gonna have to go before a judge, oh, yes, they will, and trust me, with the backlog, hmh, they'll be a long time getting a hearing with a judge, oh, yes, they will."

"Yeah, but, Vie, they're the natural kin to those girls." Now Ramona shifted, and the plastic covering her chair started to moan and groan. "I mean, if not them, don't they have any other natural family that could take them in?" She asked it even though she knew Mae would have never asked such a question, wouldn't want to compete with any natural family for the dollars that constantly flowed through there, payment for the children's upkeep, and for Mae's time and bother.

"Nope, no other natural family." Vie crossed her arms over her chest. "Near as we can tell, Finch, the father, was a merchant marine until he married Clarise, and we haven't been able to track down any of his relatives in the immediate vicinity. And we certainly not about to go searching through every lean-to down South, especially not for a temporary living situation." She sat up along the edge of the couch. "You acting like you don't want this placement, Ramona. I mean, I talked to Mae in Buffalo this morning, and she was near ecstactic about the placement—"

"No, no, no. Of course she—we want the placement. It's just when they're so traumatized . . . and you know my mother won't be back for a month—but no, of course we want the placement."

"I mean, your mother is one of the best, darn near perfect record in foster care, oh, yes, she does. Her name stays at the top of the list, and your name too as her legal substitute."

Ramona mashed her body harder into the chair and the plastic did a humph. She knew it wasn't so much Mae's perfect record in foster care that kept her name at the top of the list, but more Mae's ability to get the vote out on election day and keep her ward leader drained and satisfied. "How long you think they'll be here?" she asked.

Vie pushed against the coffee table to hoist herself up. "The mother's under a court-imposed commitment, at least for forty-five days until she gets evaluated again."

She went on to describe the girls, told Ramona she was going to love them, such pretty girls. "The oldest has eyes like a china doll, and the youngest, oh, Ramona, cutest little round face with a deep cleft in her chin. Plus they're smart, nice, you know; they're the type who'll probably go to the library on Saturdays instead of sneaking under the el turnstiles to go downtown to shoplift from McCrory's, nothing like that last brew you-all had here that made all those phone calls long distance all over the country."

"What you talking 'bout? Had to put a lock on the phone that I use to this day," Ramona said, not really needing to know much else about the girls. She had already read about them in the *Tribune* when their daddy turned up missing. Knew they were raised privileged, lived in Chestnut Hill, thirteen, twelve, eleven. All she wanted to know right now was what kind of hair did the girls have; was it as long and thick as it looked in the newspaper picture? But she couldn't ask Vie such a thing, was sure that Vie wouldn't be even able to begin to fathom how many Saturday mornings she'd lost blistering her fingers in a smoke-filled kitchen while she pressed some foster girl's thick-ass hair. Ramona patted her own hair along the sides of her blond-tinged French roll.

"That hair looking good," Vie said as she stood, and Ramona could have sworn she heard the plastic covering sigh out a hallelujah. "Can't nobody do a hard press like Miss D. Even though mine won't hold a press these days, sweat too much with this personal summer I'm going through, but you won't know nothing about that for at least the next twenty years.

"I'm having the girls' former school send the paperwork over to Sayre Junior High so you won't have to bother with that detail." She lowered her voice. "Tuition seriously lapsed at their private school, oh, yes, it had, so they may not have been going back there even if this tragedy hadn't befallen them." She waved the air in front of her face again. "Let me show them in, Ramona, and start bringing in their things." She looked around the living room, large for a row house on a small street, and Ramona followed her eyes, from the mantelpiece, where her prom pictures and high school diploma were nestled in the Woolworth's gold-tone frames, to the magazine rack, where the *Ebony*s, *Jet*s, and *Philly Talk*s were arranged in sized order. Her Bible was perfectly centered on the speckless coffee table, and even the plastic runner covering the wall-to-wall carpet gleamed. She was glad she'd spent her morning cleaning, and with Mae out of town she'd had to do it only once and not two or three times picking up after the messes Mae left.

"I sure am grateful you and your mother keep such an orderly house," Vie said as if she'd just heard Ramona's thoughts. "Not many houses I could just show up at with three children and everything be right in place to just take them in."

Ramona accepted the compliment with a nod. Then she said "shit" loudly, three times in a row after Vie was out of the front door. Once for each girl, because Mae wouldn't be back for a month from Tuesday, and even though Ramona had always been the primary caretaker in terms of the cooking and cleaning, and laundry, and making sure the children stayed well groomed, it was Mae who did the sweet talking, who could calm down the most agitated of children by wrapping her words in honey like she was making pigs in a blanket. Ramona just didn't have that sweet-talking part in her, would barely say good morning to the steady streams of children who'd floated in and out of here over the years. Wouldn't know how to say a kind word to them if she wanted to. She'd never wanted to. She didn't now.

* * *

"Look at all this. How we supposed to get this heavy-ass trunk up the stairs?" Ramona said to Shern, Victoria, and Bliss. But she actually said it to the trunk because she wasn't even looking at the girls. Hadn't looked at them really in the whole ten minutes they'd been here. That was always the hardest part for her, looking at the fosters when they walked through that door for the first time, when their faces were still coated with the hell they'd been delivered from, evenly spread and matte over their faces like fresh paint. So she looked all around their faces, concentrated on their bodies instead. She noticed that they were slight-built girls, even under the high-quality plaid wool coats. The older two starting to bud out a little, the youngest still round with baby fat, all three of them soft-figured, wouldn't be much help with the trunk. She decided she'd wait for Tyrone to help her with the trunk.

She went to the closet and pulled out three hangers just so she could do something besides stand there and not look at them. "You the oldest, so you in charge of jackets and coats," she said to Shern as she handed her the hangers. "Maybe you had live-in help or just day help where you came from, but I'm the only help around here, and my wages aren't too damned good, so the least you can do is hang up your own coats."

Ramona's words fell on Shern's unacclimated ears with a smashing sound, like glass milk bottles against a chain-link fence. Shern looked at her sisters to make sure they weren't crying again, and then she scanned the living room, which was thimble-sized compared to their real home. She felt dizzy now when she thought about her real home. She took the hangers from Ramona and tried to tie her stomach like it was a kerchief, hoping it would contain the creamed corn she'd nibbled at when the social worker stopped them at Horn & Hardart's and insisted that they put something in their stomachs.

"Put your hats in your pockets," Ramona said as she watched the older two pull the hats from their heads. Odd-looking hats; she'd never seen a cross-stitch like that, all mixed up with no particular pattern, but it worked well in the hats. Now she was looking at their hair. "Damn," she muttered under her breath; it was as thick as it looked in the *Tribune* photo.

"My mother tells us to put our hats in our sleeves, so our pockets won't get stretched out of shape." It was Bliss talking, pouting, looking up at Ramona like she was nobody she had to listen to.

Ramona looked at Bliss standing back on her heels, basing up at her as if she were her age. She had her mouth all formed to snap at Bliss, to say to Bliss, "Your mother's in the crazy house, so what does she know?" But then she heard Mae's voice in her head telling to mind her meanness. So she tucked what Mae called her meanness in the palm of her hand, closed her fist over it to keep it contained for now, and didn't talk about their mother. She did stoop to Bliss's eye level, though. "I don't care where you stick them as long as I don't see them all over the closet floor." She pulled Bliss's hat from her head. "Doesn't this go in your sleeve?" She emphasized the "sleeve" and then shoved the hat in Bliss's hand. She noticed Bliss's hair was light brown and not as thick as her sisters'. She would have to be the one with soft hair, she thought, the one I'd most like to slip and catch with the hot comb right around the tip of her ear. There was her meanness again; she clenched her fist tighter, trying to hold it in.

Victoria watched the bad current zipping through the living room between Ramona and Bliss, and she immediately slid into her peacemaker's stance. "Bliss, come on and give Shern your coat," she said with urgency. She knew Bliss would readily trade insults with Ramona, and she was afraid that Ramona might land her palm right across Bliss's mouth. Already Ramona seemed to be opening and closing her hand like she was nervous or, worse yet, trying to restrain herself. "Come on, Bliss," she said again, and tugged on her shoulder.

Then she turned to Ramona. She wanted to tell her please to excuse Bliss, that sometimes Bliss spoke without thinking, that Bliss was the baby, though, and a little spoiled and didn't mean any harm. But now Victoria was looking at Ramona's face, and she couldn't talk. She was so struck by Ramona's face, the soft beauty just overflowing from Ramona's face. She wondered how such harsh, ugly words could come from that face. She cleared her throat. "Um," she said, and then she remembered her mother's caution about starting a sentence with "um." "People will see your brown skin and hear you say 'um' and automatically think you're stupid," her mother used to say. "You just don't have the luxury of starting your sentences like that." So Victoria pulled back the "um," and now she had Ramona's attention, and all she could do was stare at Ramona. Now her jaw was locked, and she couldn't say anything since she'd gone and thought about her mother; she just looked at Ramona and started to cry.

"Come on, Tore, don't cry." Bliss wrapped her arm around Victoria's neck. "And you don't have to take up for me, I know that's what you were getting ready to do, but Mommie did always tell us not to stuff our hats in our coat pockets, and I'm not going against what Mommie says for anybody." She rolled her eyes at Ramona and then pulled her coat off her shoulder.

"Furthermore"—Bliss directed her words at Ramona again—"my aunt Til, and aunt Ness, and uncle Blue, and uncle Show are coming for us anyhow." Bliss curled her coat around her arm as she spoke. "So we're not even going to be here long enough for anything to drop on your old closet floor. And my aunt Til doesn't play, especially when it comes to my sisters and me." Bliss continued to pout.

"I don't play either." Ramona tried to hold her meanness in her balled fist, but it seeped out between her fingers. Now she just opened her hand and let it take her over. "And you can tell your aunt Til I said so—that is, if you can find whatever jail they threw her in when she tried to jump bad down at the courthouse. Furthermore, the judge fixed it so none of your strange-assed people can try to contact you. And if you try to contact them, you'll be the cause of never seeing them again. Now what your little fresh mouth got to say about that?" Ramona stopped. Wished she had held her meanness and not said the part about jail. She could tell by the way Bliss was twirling her coat around her arms that the child was more afraid than she was fresh.

Bliss's coat was almost a ball now, and she mashed it against her stomach. "You're lying," she shouted up at Ramona. "My aunt Til isn't in jail. She's on her way here to get us, isn't she, Shern? Isn't that what you just told me when we were waiting in the car?"

Shern didn't answer Bliss. She gently pulled the balled-up coat from Bliss's arms without looking in her face.

"Shern, isn't that what you said? You said it! You promised me that Aunt Til was on her way here to get us."

Shern could feel the kerchief in her stomach starting to loosen, threatening to come undone. She had promised Bliss that the aunts would be coming for them shortly. Even though the fat social worker had told them they'd be living here for the next six weeks or so, Shern had whispered otherwise to her sisters. She'd had to. She'd needed to tell them, and herself, something so they'd stop crying. And now she wanted to cry all over again, hearing this dark news about her aunt Til. She swallowed hard, but the kerchief in her stomach wasn't going to stay tied. She felt it open completely now, one end, then the next, and the creamed corn and whatever else she hadn't eaten that day spilled out of the kerchief. She didn't even have time to gag. Now she was standing there feeling it seep down the front of her white cotton blouse. She put her hands under her mouth, trying to catch it; now she was gagging, and in between trying to ask where the bathroom was.

"Oh, shit, damn," Ramona said when she saw it. "Run, go to the kitchen sink, hurry up, and try to stay on the plastic runner. My mother just had this overpriced carpet installed. Shit!"

Shern ran back to the kitchen with Bliss and Victoria at her heels. She spit and gagged into the sink, and her sisters patted her back, and Victoria was crying, "I want Mommie." Then they all three were crying and moaning, "Mommie, Mommie," and hugging one another in a circle.

Ramona stood in the kitchen doorway, just watching them. For the thousandth time that day she wished Mae were here, and she never wished for Mae to be here. Most of her wishing had to do with Mae not being here, sometimes even wishing Mae dead. But at least Mae would know how to respond to this kind of outpouring. Ramona didn't. She only knew what to do or say with the fosters when they misstepped, when she had to threaten to kick ass. She couldn't even playact a response to girls crying because they missed their mother.

"Wash your hands good, and rinse your mouth out with warm water," she called into their circle. "I'll look through your many bags and find you a top to change into. Your room is the one in the back, the three of you sharing the one room, of course."

They quieted down and now were just whimpering.

"After you clean yourself up," Ramona went on, "you and your sisters might want to put your coats and hats back on and go outside, there a few kids your ages live on the block, or you might want to just go for a walk, see what the neighborhood's like. Fresh air might do you all some good."

That was it, the best Ramona could do in the here and now. She went to the shed kitchen to get the mop and bucket so she could clean up Shern's grief trailing from the living room into the kitchen. She pulled on her rubber gloves and walked back through the kitchen, where the girls were sniffing and making the air in the kitchen heavy with their sighs. She hurried through the kitchen back into the living room. She sighed now too and knelt to start cleaning the plastic runner. At least this part she understood.

3

THEY didn't hold Til long. She begged the pardon of the sheriff. Told him what she'd been through that morning seeing her niece's bedroom bloodied like that. The threats to the case manager were idle, she said. Just a temporary fit of madness caused by her trauma. She'd just wanted to watch over her niece's babies, is all.

So the sheriff let her go, told her a sitting judge would have to hear her plea to overturn the case manager's decision. She should get a lawyer, he said, and she should make sure she adhered to the restraining order and not try to make contact with the children because that order had been signed by a judge and a judge would never reverse a case manager's call in favor of someone who violated one of his rulings. Not that Til could try to see them. She had no idea where they'd been placed. Right now she thanked God that she at least knew where Clarise was; at least she and Ness and Blue and Show had the powerful motivator of rushing to the bedside of the niece they had raised to force them to pull themselves together.

* * *

Clarise knew it was the aunts and uncles even before they turned the corner into her room. She could smell the honey and coconut soap that Til and Ness made by hand and sold mail order four times a year. She wanted to be able to smile, to blow them a kiss, wanted especially to let them know that it wasn't her wrists she'd tried to slash that morning, just that navy blue haze that had gotten in the way of her yarns. But the clear fluid dripping down the plastic tubing into the largest vein in her arm had a clamp on all her body parts. She couldn't even stick her tongue out to lick around the corners of her mouth that were so dry they were cracking.

Her uncle Blue noticed. As soon as he stood over her, looking formless around the edges because her eyesight was blurred, and she smelled the cedar that meant he was wearing his chesterfield coat because he kept it hanging in his cedar chifforobe, she heard him say, "My goodness, is there any ice around here? Look at her poor mouth. Aren't they watching her?"

Show was at his side. "Hey, darling," he said. "They told us we can only stay five minutes. Yeah, that mouth does look a little parched."

"Move, Blue, let me see." Ness pushed her way in between Blue and Show. "Awl, look at our baby, you gonna be okay, Clarise, you gonna pull through this, yes, you are."

"Here's the ice." Til's voice was behind the other three. Clarise guessed that she was trying to be the strong one, and if she looked at Clarise right now, arms bandaged almost up to her elbows, flat in this bed with the sides raised like she was an infant in a crib, her attempts at being strong would fade into hushed sobs like the ones starting to rise up from her uncle Show.

Blue scooped a fingerful of ice chips from a Styrofoam cup handed to him by Til and rubbed them around Clarise's mouth. How good the ice felt, how cool as it melted into the hot, cracked skin around the corners of her mouth. She wanted to say thank you, not just for the ice but for the tough and tender love they'd always wrapped around her. Blue's eyes were filled up now and getting ready to run a river; she could tell because she could see glimmering light where his eyes should be. Til could too because she nudged him out of the way.

"Need some petroleum jelly on those lips," Til said as she looked in Clarise's face and gently smeared Vaseline around her mouth, especially where her skin was cracking. "Now that doctor out there said you probably can't talk because of the medicine they've got you on; he said you may not even be able to hear us—that is, make sense of what we're saying—but I personally think he's the one not making sense, and I do believe you can understand me. So I want you to listen good and do what I tell you; you've always minded in the past, so don't you dare start disobeying now. Now I want you to reach way down deep inside of yourself, as deep as you can go; I want you to grab a hold of the rafter you find there. Oh, yes, you got one, everybody does. You just don't realize it until your life goes liquid on you and rises above your head and you forced to search for something to get you to dry land. Grab that rafter, Clarise. Hold on. You got strong arms, Clarise, hold on. You got to let your grieving take its course, got to let Finch go. He's already gone, you got to let him go. I know you and he were so close you breathed in sync, and now your breaths are heavy and sad, pushing into the air single file. But you still got a whole lot of life left in you, a whole lot of living to be done, a whole lot of years of helping those daughters grow into women, so you hold on. Hold on tight, and hold on sure. We're gonna reel you into the riverbank, get you onto solid ground, but baby, you got to hold on."

They were all standing over her now. Ness was humming softly and rhythmically to the rise and fall of Til's words. The uncles punctuated what Til said with loud, soupy sniffles. And Clarise tried with everything in her to unclamp her mouth, to tell them she would hold on, for the girls, for them, for the memory of her beloved Finch. But her mouth wouldn't move, no words would form, and now they were putting on their coats to leave.

They took turns leaning into the prison of a bed to kiss her good-bye. First Blue, then Show, then Ness, then Til. Til's foxfoot coat collar stroked her face, and she was flooded with memories of her childhood, and how that collar was her pet because the aunts didn't believe in live animals roaming freely through the house and wouldn't let her have a cat or dog. And when everyone was asleep, Til would tiptoe into her bedroom and put the coat around her just so with the collar right against her cheek. Clarise was trying to say "pet," was hollering it in her head, trying to force the word through her mouth. This time Show noticed.

"What's she trying to say, Til? Look how wild her eyes are getting. She's trying to talk, Til."

"She's not hurting, is she?" Blue asked, leaning in to look on her face. "Dear God, please don't let her be in pain."

"She's not hurting," Ness said with confidence. "And, Sister, I do believe you know what she wants."

Til did. She unbuttoned her coat and eased it from her arms. She arranged it over Clarise so that the collar was against her cheek. "Hold on, Clarise," she said again as Blue put his chesterfield around Til's shoulders, and Clarise thought she was seeing something she'd never seen before. A single tear pressed from the corner of Til's eye and glinted in perfect form against her cheek.

4

THE aunts and uncles did hire a lawyer, who strongly reiterated the sheriff's caution about trying to intercede in the placement of the girls. He looked right at Til when he said it, repeated himself three or four times when Til wouldn't meet his gaze. Then his words went straight to Til's heart when he said she could jeopardize the possibility of ever having a relationship with those girls, God forbid. If Clarise were not to recover fully, he said, the restraining order could stay in effect, and those girls could remain in foster care until they were adopted permanently or turned eighteen, whichever happened first. Ness grabbed Til's hand when he said it; the uncles sucked their breaths sharply and swallowed their screams. And Til dismissed her plan of maybe hiring a detective to find those girls so that she could meet them after school, or at the movies, or the library, spend an hour or two a week with them, make sure they were being treated well, adjusting emotionally; nobody would have to know, she'd reasoned;

the girls would certainly never tell. But this lawyer's cautionary words made a small hole in her heart, and she let her plan sift through the hole for now and busied herself instead helping Clarise to come back.

They all did over the next month. Kept themselves from violating the judge's ruling and tracking down the girls by immersing themselves in Clarise's recovery. They did everything but lift Clarise up and rock her as if she were a newborn. They met the start of visiting hours at her bedside, combed her hair, massaged her scalp. Told her how strong she was. They hummed her favorite songs, rubbed olive oil between her fingers that always seemed dry. Told her how strong she was. They brought her yarns and knitting needles and put them in the top of her closet as an incentive, repeated stories that made her laugh when she was a child. Told her how strong she was. They squeezed each second out of those visiting hours until they were practically thrown out and Til would say, "Wait, wait, one last thing I got to do." Then she'd cover Clarise with her fox-foot—collared coat.

And Clarise was responding. The tube that had dripped that immobilizing fluid into her arms had been removed, so she was sitting up for longer periods during the day, talking in short phrases, but at least she was talking. And asking, all the time asking, about her girls. Smiled weakly when the aunts and uncles lied to her, told her the girls were doing fine, that they sent their love, underage, though, so they couldn't visit. "Ah, but, Clarise, they truly send their love."

AND the girls had sent their love over that month, through their constant thinking about their mother, longing for her, praying for her recovery and that they would soon be returned to her and their real home. And even if not that, at least that they could go and live with their aunts and uncles. Because the month in that Addison Street row house with Ramona and the girls was like a cheap leather coat, stiff, letting in the cold when it should be giving off warmth, cracking from the least bit of moisture, patched together with so many seams too easy to come undone.

And the girls were coming undone. Ramona listened to them cry themselves to sleep just about every night. When they weren't crying, they were quiet, withdrawn, at least in Ramona's presence, seeming not to want to have anything to do with Ramona. Just as well, Ramona thought, she was herself too occupied. There was breakfast to cook, and their bangs, which needed hot curling before they went to school and she went to her own day job at Lit Brothers bargain basement. There was dinner and dishes, making their lunch for the next day. There was laundry, that cart she despised, which she lugged to the Laundromat overflowing now with three girls bathing and going through towels as if the towels were Kleenex. There was Tyrone, her sweet country-boy boyfriend, who came by most evenings, trying to beg his way into her bedroom, who'd taken a liking to the girls, though, and sometimes occupied them playing crazy eights or hangman or tic-tac-toe. There was just too much to do, Ramona told herself, to spend time trying to think of ways to draw those girls out. So she listened to them cry and in between did what little she could to distract them from themselves. "Go outside and get some fresh air," she'd tell them, or, "Go do your homework," or "Turn the TV on low," or "Get down on your knees and say your prayers before you go to sleep for the night." But she didn't try to draw them out, didn't really want to carry on real conversation, even as she watched their personalities sneak out during lapses in their outward shows of grief.

She could see that the youngest, Bliss, was combative, smart-mouthed, spunky, though; Ramona was sure she'd heard Bliss laugh at least once since they'd been there. Victoria hadn't laughed, but she had the mildest manner of the three, always trying to keep peace between those other two. Shern was the most complicated for Ramona to figure, the moodiest, with pitch-black eyes that gave her an intense look. Ramona had to acknowledge the child had beautiful eyes, not that she would ever say such a thing to Shern, too much against her grain to compliment a foster child.

Plus Ramona hadn't been able to get beyond the apparent opulence the girls had been accustomed to. Most of the foster children came with a modest amount, a brown shopping bag full; some came with the price tag still affixed to what they carried where the social workers had to stop at John Bargain's just so they could come with something. But Shern, Victoria, and Bliss had come with a loaded trunk and the mind-sets that didn't understand a thing about stretching the havings, making do until payday. So Ramona was sure an air of superiority was hiding behind Shern's steely dark eyes. It caused her to speak to all three of the girls in short snippets and usually in a voice that was the texture of burlap.

She spoke to them in that voice right now as the girls stood in the dining room, high-quality wool plaid coats on, and Shern declared that she and her sisters were going to the library.

"Are you asking me or telling me?" Ramona snapped.

"She means, Can we go?" Peacemaking Victoria rushed her words like a tide coming in. "Didn't you, Shern? Tell Ramona that's what you meant. Can we, I mean, is it okay if we go to the library?"

"I want her to ask me." Ramona made herself peer into Shern's eyes.

Shern was just standing there looking at Ramona, though, as if she were forcing Ramona to take in her eyes.

"I want her to ask me," Ramona said again, anger seeping into her words. "Ask me, don't tell me." She had her hand on her hip now and was leaning into Shern's face.

Shern's eyes went beyond Ramona's stormy face over to the buffet cart and a brass-tone fruit bowl filled with plastic pears and bananas. She clamped her lips and stared at the plastic fruit and thought about how much she despised the taste of bananas.

The dining room was bright with the morning sun and swathed in an unsettled quiet. The quiet held, like a plane that's circling because it can't get clearance to land. Victoria couldn't tolerate the quiet. To her the quiet was a prelude to disaster, like Ramona hitting Shern, hurting her; she was getting near hysterical over the thought. "Shern!" Victoria dragged her sister's name along on a breath that was getting ready to cry. "Why is Shern doing this?" she whined, making waves in the dining-room air, her voice was shaking so.

Bliss jabbed her finger in the air. "I don't see what the big deal is. My gosh, she's telling her where we're going."

Victoria couldn't hold it. Told Bliss just to shut up. Then she yelled, "Shern, just ask her, ask her, just ask her, Shern." Her yelling did unlock the air between Shern and Ramona. Ramona eased back from Shern's face a bit.

Shern coughed a few times. They both looked at Victoria through the dining-room air. "May my sisters and I go to the library." Shern said it quickly, startled the air as she said it; she still said it as a declarative, though. All she did really was add the "may" because there was certainly no questioning tone to her voice.

It was enough for Ramona. "Don't let the sunfall beat you back here, you understand me?" she commanded.

"Okay, Ramona," Victoria said, out of breath from yelling so. "How do we get there?"

Ramona walked out of the dining room without answering. She had to. She had to gather clothes together for the Laundromat. Plus she would have called Shern a little bitch, stashing on her, challenging her like that. She might have even grabbed her by her throat.

"Oh, forget her," Ramona could hear Bliss saying. "How hard can it be to find the library?"

THEY did find the library, stopped to ask the mailman if they were headed in the right direction. Stayed there all that Saturday, except when they got hungry and ventured to the corner of Baltimore Avenue for soft pretzels topped with mustard, then back to the library, where the tall windows reminded them of the windows at their real home. They lost themselves in the stacks of books in the young adult section. Checked out two books apiece—*Little Women, Nancy Drew, Uncle Tom's Cabin*—then lied when the librarian asked them what they were doing so far from home according to the address on their library cards. "Just visiting friends," Shern said. She figured they'd suffered enough all month at the Sayre Junior High School when it caught on that they were daughters to the famous dead caterer, Finch, and his almost dead wife, Clarise, and they were forced to endure the whispers behind their backs and the pitying looks in the teachers' eyes. Shern hated that school. Some days she couldn't decide which was worse: Mae's house, where Ramona was always cursing under her breath, or the school, where she looked straight ahead whether she was in class or walking through the crowded, sweaty hallways to avoid conversation. She'd hold her water the entire school day so she wouldn't have to venture into the bathroom, where, on the one and only day she'd gone in there, the bad girls smoked cigarettes by an open window and looked her up and down and called her snobby bitch. They asked her if she thought she was cute or something walking around in her real mohair sweaters and fur-lined boots. Shern didn't answer, turned around, and walked back out more angry than afraid, even when she heard them saying to her back that if they weren't in the middle of a smoke they would have kicked her stuck-up ass. Victoria seemed to be faring only a little better at the school. Her fearfulness over getting beaten up, "moved on," as the people here called it, made her smile all the time, and say "excuse me, please," if she brushed up against someone, and look people in the face lest she get called names like Shern. Bliss, though, wasn't afraid at all, smiled only when she felt like it, adopted the hand-on-hip, roll-around-neck stance of the bad girls, imitated the teachers when their backs were turned, and acquired a small following of friends who'd lap up her inflated stories about what it was like to grow up rich. In any event, Shern reasoned this librarian would be one less curiosity seeker they'd have to put up with, even though he seemed sincere enough, took time to draw Shern a little map when she kept the lie going and asked him which bus routes did he suggest they take back home. And then they started back to Mae and Ramona's and got lost for real.

It was the sun. It looked delicious in the sky to these girls who'd just been lulled momentarily by the fantasy lands of the books they'd read. The sun was like a glob of butter melting in a pan to make hot fudge or some other warm sweet thing that the uncles used to surprise and delight them with. They just needed the sweet brightness to stroke their foreheads for a while, so they walked toward the sun, headed west, even though Shern knew they were going wrong; she counted blocks so that when they were ready to turn around and have the sun at their backs, she'd know just how far they had to go.

They were quiet as they walked, no one was crying; their crying had gotten so unpredictable, like brushfires that start out of nowhere and go until they burn themselves out. For the moment the sun diminished the need to cry, and they were suspended in time and could forget that until last month they lived in a grand single home on an old-money block inhabited by professors from the university and a prominent black doctor and banker and that they were accustomed to ribeye steak, crystal chandeliers, and velvet ribbons for their hair. For the moment they could push from their consciousness that their father, a self-made man who'd amassed his fortune without college, had turned up dead, and their beautiful mother had had a breakdown.

As they watched the sun ooze and drip yellow down the sky, they were just three girls walking, big-legged, brown-skinned anonymous girls with velvety bangs, perfect teeth, and pile-lined good wool coats. Their thick-soled shoes hit the concrete in sync and echoed in a rhythm that was like a chant. The air did a welcoming hum through the branches and the budding leaves, and even the trees seemed to bend on the block where they now walked, like doormen bowing and extending their arms. There were no distractions here, no cars, no houses, no storefronts, no peddlers, not even other walkers. Just the girls, and a park across the street that was conceited and bragged out its ability to turn green in the spring, and a closed-down bread factory on the side where they walked that still scented the air with a hint of butter and flour and yeast when it was breezy out.

For the moment this was their block, and they reveled in its emptiness. They didn't know, though, that this stretch where they now walked was always deserted this time of day, solely because of the superstitions of people who'd lived here for a while and who'd dubbed this block Dead Block.

And since they didn't know, when they saw a figure in the park across the street climbing up the underside of a slope in the ground, tall and lean in a plaid trench coat and gray fedora, they just viewed him as an object of curiosity rather than one of fear.

They were oblivious to the haunting legend of Dead Block: that eighteen years before, Donald Booker, a neighborhood boy, a white boy, had vanished in this block of the park, around the time of the great changeover, when the whites began moving away from this neighborhood in a massive tidal wave, as the blacks rode the wave and rushed in behind them, eagerly filling the spaces as if they were playing Monopoly and landing on Park Place. The Bookers had resisted the influx, would call out, "Nigger, go home," to the backs of the newcomers, write it out in chalk on the pavements in front of their homes, would even sit around on Saturday nights, talk about the crosses they should build, the brand kerosene they should use. But then their own personal tragedy hit; their twelve-year-old disappeared, last seen on the block where the girls now walked. "Like the block just swallowed poor Donald Booker up," the neighbors canted, even though while he was in their midst, most—black and white alike—readily consented that Donald Booker was a bad seed, incorrigible, disrespectful, meanspirited, vulgar, shoplifting, hate-spewing. . . . But after he turned up missing and became "poor Donald Booker," at least a half dozen dogs and cats were said to have vanished from here around the time of day when the sun was hanging way back in the sky. Brand-new

Corvette Stingrays and Mustangs stalled in this block as the day got tangled with the night, and even the birds lay low until the nightfall was complete. A once-prolific bread factory had to close up and relocate a few years ago. Taxes in the city too high, was the official word. But rumor had it that the shift that started at four-thirty refused to report in the winter until after the transition from sun to moon was finished. But since the girls knew nothing about the strangeness Dead Block was said to evoke in people and things this time of day, they took the man only as someone out walking, trying to beat the night and get to where he lived, until he jaunted across the street, straight toward them, and tipped his hat slightly and smiled.

"Cold as shit out here today, little ladies," he said.

The girls closed in the spaces between them and repositioned the books they carried so they could link arms in a huddle. "Stupid old man," Bliss said. "Probably drunk. Go on, man, get," she warned. "Or I'll tell our daddy to shoot your ass off."

Shern pushed her elbow into Bliss's side. Told her not to talk to him. "Just walk normally," she insisted.

The tall dark man kept pace with the girls and threw his head back and laughed a bellow of a laugh. "You wouldn't do that, would you? You wouldn't tell your daddy to shoot my ass off. For one thing, your daddy's dead." He stilled his laugh and now had a mocked softness to his voice. "Plus I'm your own flesh and blood."

"You don't know us," Victoria said tenuously, more a question than a declaration. She was walking on the end closest to the man, and the scent of pinecones and burned wood seemed to rise from his clothes in jagged bolts. It was acrid and went right to her head and made her feel dizzy and confused.

"Are you crazy talking to him?" Shern yanked Victoria's arm.

"But he might know something—"

"Shush!" Shern cut her off. "He's crazy, he's drunk, whatever."

"But maybe he knows the aunts and uncles if he knows us," Victoria half wailed. "Maybe he can tell them where we are; they must not know where we are since we've been here a whole month and they haven't tried to see us."

"It's the courts that are keeping them from us." Shern yanked Victoria's arm again, and Victoria cried out. "Now, do you want this drunk-up old man following us all over the place? We talk to him and he'll think he's making sense and we'll never get rid of him."

The stranger continued to talk in uninterrupted streams. "Yeah, I'm your own flesh and blood, yes, I am. Sad child that doesn't know their own line. You part of my line, directly descended from me."

"Wait a minute." Bliss stopped suddenly. "I know who you are."

Shern and Victoria stopped too. "Don't talk to him, Bliss, just don't," Shern yelled in her sister's ear.

"Look, though, look." Bliss pointed wildly. "He's the man who tried to take Mommie from the aunts and uncles. See the scar where Aunt Til went upside his head."

They all three looked at him, at the thick beige scar running down his forehead that looked like steak gristle. They were startled and mesmerized to see the subject of so many Sunday night dinners standing right in front of them.

"She was my child, my baby girl." He moved in closer to the girls. His voice went to a lower tone. "I'm Larry. Girl, I know you know me; look at you, you the spitting image of me. I'm your granddaddy. Come give me a hug."

"My aunt Til said you couldn't have fathered my mother because you don't have a pecker." Bliss spit the words out right before Shern grabbed her from behind and covered her mouth and tried to drag her away.

"Lies! They told you lies! She was mine, and so are you." He opened his arms toward the girls. "Now come give me a hug. Come on, you with the dimple in your chin, you first."

He lurched forward, and all three girls turned at the same instant and started to run, galloping, determined runs. They quickly put space between themselves and Larry. But right then Victoria tripped over a slither of a hole in the grainy concrete and fell. She fell hard. She cried and spit bloody fragments of teeth and curled on her side and clutched at her knee, which felt as if it had just splattered like grade A extra large eggs hitting a concrete floor.

"Victoria, oh, my God, Victoria," Shern screamed in a panic as she let her library books drop so she could help her sister run away.

"Oh, no, you're bleeding, Tori," yelped Bliss as she spun around in fast circles.

Shern hoisted Victoria up and half dragged, half pulled her to the doorway of the abandoned bread factory. She propped her up at the bottom of three short steps. "You're okay, you're okay," she whispered over and over to try to calm Victoria and herself.

Larry was where they were now, still calling for a hug, still chanting, "Lies, lies, they told you lies." The air around him had turned filmy and rippled with his voice as the wind rose and the sun fell and his words dipped and peaked with the wind and mixed with the deserted block and the sound of flapping as every wren in the park, it seemed, was roused at that instant and took flight. Even the sun had gone from butter drips to a red bruise in the sky and was chilling and especially affected Victoria and looked like the ribbon of blood that circled her mother's wrist that morning last month.

Victoria could no longer tolerate Larry's words, or the pine and wood smell coming off his clothes and hitting her nose like pinpricks, or the red-tinged sky. She started to scream hysterically. "Make him stop! Please make him go away!"

Bliss ran right in front of him and stomped her foot like she was trying to make an alley cat run. "Stop saying that, you old crazy, just stop it." She rolled her neck around like the bad girls at school when they talked back to the teacher. "You're not our grandfather. You're not!"

He did stop then and flashed his eyes. His eyes looked amber from the reflection of the waning sun and froze Bliss where she stood.

The commotion in the air outside his bedroom window woke

Mister from his nap, and he sat straight up all at once in his bed, actually his cot, his bedroom window actually the window on the lower level of the abandoned bread factory. His home was actually the bread factory where he'd lived since 1961, a reformed man of the streets struggling with a habit and an attitude and three different varieties of VD. The habit he kicked cold turkey over four days of chills and sweats and vomiting and cramps after his young wife moved everything out of their apartment when he'd gone to cash his veteran's check, which used to take two, three days sometimes to cash. The VD was cured from VA-dispensed penicillin. The attitude took care of itself, dissipated over months of living alone down here in the cozy corner of the bread factory in relative grand luxury considering some of the foxholes he'd known since he'd also served in the Korean War. He'd feed the squirrels through the window down here and reflect on aspects of the human condition ranging from the existence of God to capitalism to race relations to whether Smitty or Schaffer made the best hoagies. Now he was wide-awake and on alert; he always woke alert, another habit he'd picked up in Korea. He moved to the window and cupped his hands against his face and peered out. Then he grabbed his heavy black coat and ran outside and around the corner to where the girls were.

Shern saw him first. She said a silent thank-you when she saw him. His face was dark brown and wide, and his eyes hung low and looked sad as if someone were pulling on the skin beneath his eyes. He had a flat-footed walk that reminded her of how her father used to walk. The sad eyes and the archless feet made her think she could trust him, and even the air got still as he approached; the acrid scent of pine and wood yielded to the butter-tinged aroma of rising bread.

"Get away from them gals," he yelled to Larry.

Larry had just picked Bliss up and was trying to kiss her cheek, while Shern kicked and punched at him and Bliss tried to claw his face. Victoria hobbled from the sidelines, screaming, "Please, God, make him go away."

"Hey, Larry, you old crazy fool," Mister called, "put that little gal down, put her down, I say."

"You the crazy one," Larry yelled back. "You ain't even got enough sense to live in a house, living in an abandoned factory and you calling me crazy."

"I'll tell you what, though," Mister shot back, "I bet I got a baseball bat in there with your name all over it, don't make me go whip it out."

Larry turned to look at Mister directly.

"Oh, yes, I will, try me, just try me."

Larry coughed a low-pitched cough that sounded like a lion's growl. "But these my grandkids. Look at them, look just like me."

"Am not!" Bliss gave Larry one final kick and wrenched herself free while he and Mister argued. She and Shern each grabbed Victoria under the arms and ran like hell to get back to Mae's.

5

FIVE minutes bled into ten to fifteen to an hour. Ramona turned the knob on the gas stove to lower the flame under the hot dogs and baked beans. She went into the living room yet again straight to the window and watched the night and the wind shaking hands on the front porch. No girls yet. Didn't matter how turned around they must have gotten trying to find their way to and from the library, they were an hour late. What a whipping she wanted to give them for making her worry like this, like the kind she'd been raised on: an ironing cord strapping right around the meaty part of her calf until red welts came up in a pattern that would have been beautiful were it not against skin. That's what those girls needed in her mind; that's what the whole band of fosters had needed over the years. The ones taken from their parents by the courts, the ones given up on, the truants, the orphans, the runaways.

She went back in the kitchen and lifted the lid from the pot and counted the hot dogs, which looked like logs turning over in red-dirt mud. Mae always told her that it was bad luck to count food; she counted now for spite. Two apiece, that was it; she dared one of them to ask for the extras.

She wiped at her sweater and folded the edges along the waist of her Wranglers and went back into the living room and looked out the window for signs of those three. Nothing, just the dark porch air.

She lifted the cover on the boxy hi-fi stereo. Her stack of Sam Cooke 45s were already disked up and sitting on the spindle, waiting to fall. She flicked the lever and sat on the velvet ottoman and waited for the stereo to go through its rotations. The ottoman was the only piece of sitting-on furniture in the room that wasn't swathed in custom-made plastic covers. The covers were seam-stitched in royal blue thread; Mae insisted that they match the carpet. Ramona tried not to look at the royal blue–bordered chair covers. Tried not to remind herself how much money Mae squandered. Mae had even taken to calling Lit Brothers furniture department, pretended to be Ramona, and ordered nightstands, lamps, face-sized mirrors. When Ramona challenged her shortened paycheck with the bony-necked accountant, said she'd only charged a Maybelline face powder and a tube of lipstick that week, and the accounting person came down on the selling floor and pulled Ramona from a customer who was just about to purchase a half dozen Hawaiian print shirts and showed Ramona the order sheet for a nightstand and lamp and mirror, Ramona had feigned a lapse in memory, focused on the bones jutting out in the accountant's neck, and said yes, she'd ordered the nightstand and lamp and mirror but she didn't think the deductions would start until the following week. She was too embarrassed to let anyone know her own mother had such tangled, knotted ways, that she could be so mean and devious to her only natural child.

The stereo clicked loudly, and then Sam Cooke's voice rushed in like a mushroom of air that wrapped Ramona up, and for an instant she felt like she was riding on the music, floating, like Sam Cooke's voice was floating through the room as he sang about the change that was going to come, and for an instant it didn't matter that she was almost to her mid-twenties, unmarried, barely able to save two quarters to move from this house filled with plastic slipcovered furniture and child after child showing up for her to have to help her mother raise.

She sang out loud that a change has got to come and danced herself around the room in wide circles until footsteps on the porch startled her away from the music and dropped her with a jolt. "It's about fucking time," she muttered as she ran to the front door and snatched it open, ready to grab Shern, Victoria, and Bliss into the house one at a time by the throat. It wasn't the girls, though. It was Tyrone, grinning sheepishly and shivering against the wind.

"My lucky day," she said, voice tinted with sarcasm, "you're early, and they're late."

"I'm not here yet for our—you know, our date." His face broke into an apologetic grin. "Me and my pops was just riding through here, my doggone car broke down again—"

"Your car went again?" She wanted to scream it.

"Yeah, bad plugs, I think. Anyhow Pops picked me up—"

"Your car went again." This time she sighed it, resignedly. She looked beyond him to the black-on-black '65 deuce and a quarter parked in front of the door. "I thought you said your father was with you. No one in that car." Her breath caught in the top of her throat at the thought of his father.

He let the opened storm door rest against his back. He touched his finger lightly to her lips. "If you let me, I'm trying to tell you my pops had to stop in 'cross the street at Miss Hettie's, had to drop off a printing job. So I figured I'd ring your bell and steal a kiss from my baby doll."

He whispered it and smiled and ran his finger through her hair. "Nice," he said, "so soft, brings out your cheekbones swept up like that too."

Ramona jerked her head and pulled his hand from her hair. "Please, I just got it done this afternoon, and you ready to mess it up already."

"No, I'll wait till tonight to mess it up." He winked.

"Yeah, well, where we going tonight besides here?" She folded her arms across her chest and tapped her foot impatiently.

"Well," he stammered, "thought you were the only one minding those girls till your mother gets back on Tuesday. How we going anywhere when you have to baby-sit them?"

"That oldest one is thirteen," she said, now tapping her fingers across her arm to the same impatient rhythm of her feet. "Shit, I was taking care of a whole roomful of foster kids by the time I was thirteen, cooking and cleaning for them too. So if you had a plan of a nice evening for you and me, that oldest one is more than grown enough to stay here for a few hours and watch those other two. I guess that's why we ain't been nowhere decent the past month, you feigning it off on me having to watch those girls. Well, consider yourself on notice, I don't have to spend every waking minute with them, okay?"

"Well, I didn't know." Tyrone's eyebrows receded to the space on his forehead they always found when he was embarrassed. "That's why I haven't planned anything, you know, you seem so preoccupied with those girls."

"Those brats. I'm not hardly preoccupied with those spoiled little rich girls. Mhn. Thought I was gonna have to slap that oldest dead in her mouth this morning. And now they're late, like they think they're old enough to run the streets after dark."

"They don't seem like the type to be out-and-out defiant, Mona. I've gotten to know them kind of well playing tic-tac-toe and checkers with them. Maybe they got lost or something. But I'm sure you've told them how to get from point A to B around here."

Ramona felt her stomach drop a little when he said that. "I've told them what they need to hear." She stopped so her words could stay angry, so her guilt and worry over the girls being late wouldn't poke holes in her voice and sift through the anger and come out with her words.

He looked beyond her into the living room. Now Sam Cooke was singing "You Send Me," and the muscles in his arms twitched at the thought of holding Ramona in a close grinding slow drag. He pulled the collar up on his corduroy jacket. "It's cold out here, baby," he whispered.

"Well, they dressed warm, I made sure of that, all the coats they came here with got put to some use today. I've never seen kids come with so many extra coats, three coats apiece, not counting the suede jackets. Such excess," she said, shaking her head and sucking in the air through her teeth.

He rubbed his hands up and down her arms. "Come on, let's get you out of this cold doorway." He was whispering again. "Can't have my baby catching no draft."

"No, I'm just catching hell, saddled with these kids by myself their first month here. And the breaking-in period with any of them is always the hardest. And these three are particularly grief-stricken." She backed into the doorway, fixing her eyes on Tyrone's father's car. Then it was just the closed front door she saw as he pushed it to, then his tan corduroy jacket as he pulled her in close and tried to mash his mouth against hers. She shook herself from him and walked toward the kitchen.

Tyrone tried to hold his good nature against her mood. He'd come to know this side of Ramona that was like splintered wood. Sometimes he wished that she were more like the other women who just blossomed when they were around him. Big smiles, sometimes even a fullness would come up in their eyes and make them appear serious and intense, like if he were to just tap them, their passions would break through in bubbling rivers. He reasoned that Ramona didn't have to gush like sap oozing from some maple in the spring; she was too beautiful for that, he told himself over and over, with her saucy eyes and healthy legs and fleshy lips. He told himself that now as he watched her walk away.

"Where you say your daddy went?" she asked again. "Maybe he can give me a ride around the block to see if I see traces of those three." She talked quickly, hoping to mask the excitement in her voice over riding with his father. "Dummies probably did get turned around. Before they left from here this morning, I told them specifically to be back here before the sun fall." She said all this with her back to him.

"I don't know how long Pops is gonna be; Miss Hettie's probably going through the printing he did line by line. How 'bout if you and me walk and see if we see them?" He caught up with her back and let his hands rest along the side of her hips; her Wranglers were stiff, and he rubbed his hands along the curve of her hips and felt an uncoiling of his essence that was so forceful it surprised him. "I'll ring Miss Hettie's bell and tell my pops to go on home without me. That way we can walk as long as we need to. We can snuggle against the wind too." He tried to nestle his chin against her shoulder.

Ramona yanked his hands from her hips and jerked her shoulder upward against his chin. She thought she heard his teeth snap together. "I don't want to walk." The words burst through her lips with much more force than she'd intended and sputtered now through the room like a balloon that's losing its air and flying and falling fast and unpredictably. "If I had wanted to walk, I would have already walked, okay. I want to ride. I'll be glad when you can piece together enough money to buy a car that runs longer than a day. I mean, even if you had planned something for this evening, we gonna have to be jumping on and off buses like poor people, and it's all cold out." She stopped and exhaled and turned to look at him. "Plus I need you to stay here, I mean, if you think your father'll take me to go look for them. Won't nobody be here to let them in if you go too. So I was gonna ask you to do that."

"Oh, you was gonna ask me to do that?" He stood in the center of the room, watching the balloon fly until it landed at his feet, his arms hung, his eyebrows down now to that lower spot they went to when he was hurt.

"Is that a lot to ask?" She said it softer. She could see how low his eyebrows were. That's what she'd first noticed about him, when the women's contingent of the gospel choir clacked about this new, fine guy, Perry the printer's son, up from Virginia to live with his father, "tall and muscle-bound," they'd said; "slim waist; wide, straight back; good hair; grin that opens his face and softens the hard line of his nose. Girl, Ramona, you got to see him," they'd said; "coloring that's like a purple-brown; mix that with someone light like you, girl, y'all would have some pretty babies," they'd insisted. But it was his eyebrows that caught Ramona and made her think that for once she could settle into an honest relationship. They were coal black and thick and had their own life the way they dipped and bowed and punctuated in the most genuine way whatever else his face was showing. Now they looked to her as if they wanted to drop to the floor.

"Look"—she walked toward him—"the sooner those brats get here, the sooner I can lose this attitude you the only one here to absorb. You do want me to lose this attitude?" She widened her eyes and fixed them on him. The muscles in her face loosened; she let her hips go in an exaggerated side-to-side swing. "Don't you, baby? Don't you want me to lose this attitude so I can be nice to you?"

Sam Cooke was at the end of the song. Tyrone was pudding now, and he knew it. He cleared his throat and licked his lips, which were dry. He moved like a robot. "I'll go get my pops; then I'll come back here and wait to let them in."

Ramona watched him leave. She smoothed at the edges of her French roll, which were soft and silky straight.

6

Tʜᴇʏ landed on the porch, three piles of plaid wool, like they'd just fallen from the sky. First Bliss, then Shern, then Victoria came limping and crying. All the way back to Mae's they talked about what could have happened: Suppose Larry had had a weapon, suppose Victoria had fallen on her head instead of her knee, suppose Larry was the type to take a young girl back in the woods of the park and do nasty things to her, suppose this, suppose that. They scared themselves so with their own imaginings that they ran as hard and fast as they could, pulling Victoria as she half ran, half hopped. The cold air in their chests had them gasping and wheezing, their undershirts soaked from perspiring, and the porch at the house they hated was such the unlikely welcome sight that they collapsed on it and heaved and coughed while their hearts settled some. Such was the scene when Tyrone clicked the switch to turn on the porch light to the house Mae and Ramona shared.

"Hey," Tyrone said, walking into the bright light of the porch.

"I was hoping that was y'all. It's about time. Ramona's out looking for you. Her jaws all tight over y'all being so late." He stooped and lightly tugged the tassels on Shern's hat.

Shern slowly unfolded herself from the porch floor and sat up and jostled Bliss and reached beyond her to nudge Victoria. Victoria started to sob fresh all over again.

He walked over to where Victoria was. His eye went to the bloodstain seeping through the knee of Victoria's brown corduroy pants. "Awl, man. You're hurt? What you do? Let's get you in the house." He picked Victoria up and carried her into the house.

Being lifted and cradled like that reminded Victoria of the way her father used to carry her when she'd fall asleep in the rec room. She'd keep her eyes shut tight and nestle in her father's arms, fearing that if he knew she was awake, he might make her walk on her own. She kept her eyes opened now. It didn't matter if Tyrone tried to make her walk on her own, she wouldn't be able to. Maybe hop. Crawl on her good leg maybe. But the pain in her hurt knee pulsed like the neon sign at the House of Hong Kong in Chinatown, where their father would take them for dinner. She imagined the bright orange letters pulsing on and off, on and off; her knee hurt less when she pictured it that way.

Tyrone let her go softly onto the couch. She sat up so her bent knee wouldn't touch the plastic covering on the couch. She didn't want to be the one to give Ramona reason for irritation; blood on the stiff plastic furniture, Victoria was sure, would be a serious offense. Tyrone moved the brass urn that held the powdered blue artificial carnations to the other side of the coffee table so that Victoria could stretch her leg out on the table. He told her that he had been a Boy Scout, so his first-aid training should come back to him. He laughed, hoping Victoria would laugh too.

She didn't; she winced and let out a cracked moan as she tried to straighten out her knee. She closed her eyes, hoping for the neon sign.

Bliss and Shern pushed through the front door.

"This old crazy man talking about he was our grandfather came out of the park and chased us and made Tori fall," Bliss said to Tyrone, and then barreled past Tyrone to get to her sister. She flopped on the floor at Victoria's feet. She blew on Victoria's knee. "Does that make it feel better? When Mommie used to blow on my cuts, they would feel better." She leaned her head against the leg of the couch and said soothing words to Victoria.

"Wait a minute, what happened? Somebody chased you? Who chased you?" Tyrone asked as he moved the velvet ottoman in front of the couch where Victoria was. He sat on the ottoman and slowly started folding the bottom of Victoria's corduroys up to get to the hurt part of her leg.

Bliss was rushing her words telling him what happened while Shern busied herself at the closet hanging her coat. "Whoa, slow down, Bliss," he said. "You talking faster than I can listen; you know I'm a slow-talking country boy." And then he got quiet when he had Victoria's pants leg up, exposing the rawness, the red and pink and yellow that used to be smooth brown skin. He told Shern then that she had to be his assistant, told her what supplies to bring him, while Victoria tried not to holler out as the pulsing to the neon light faded and left just a steady glaring orange that was moving in circles down her leg.

"Just hang on, Tori," Tyrone said in his softest voice.

Shern tried not to hear his tone of voice. She'd heard him use that tone before, when Ramona and Tyrone's night sounds sifted through the walls and Ramona would be complaining about them, and Tyrone would try to settle Ramona down. "Well, how do you think they feel, Mona?" he'd asked in a voice that would have felt like lamb's wool to Shern's ears if she didn't hate everything about this house so.

She ran to do Tyrone's bidding, and Bliss went on with the details of how Larry had made Victoria fall. When Shern got back in the room with the first-aid supplies, Bliss was telling Tyrone how Larry had chased them right to the steps of the closed-down factory and snatched her up and tried to kiss her cheek. Tyrone's fists were clenched, and his jaw was going back and forth, and Shern was surprised that he could look so mean.

He started cleaning Victoria's sore, and she made hard, sucking sounds. They were otherwise quiet as he worked; he had to be quiet, or he would have used profanity about Larry. He knew Larry from around West Philly, would see him walking especially at night if Tyrone ventured down to do some barhopping on Fifty-second Street; he'd never liked Larry's haughtiness, the way he'd loud-talk people since he knew he was a decent enough boxer. Tyrone had half listened to Ramona recant the story told to her by Vie about the blowup over the girls' temporary living arrangement. He was just now making the connection between Larry and the girls, how their mother had been the object of Larry's delusions of fatherhood. And now his crazy ass was extending that delusion to these girls, who couldn't even call on their aunt Til to split his head once again. So right now he had to be silent as he worked, while Shern handed him peroxide, then gauze, then cut tape into strips, while Bliss squeezed her sister's hand. He had to swallow hard and push his anger into a ball in his throat and concentrate on dressing Victoria's knee.

When he was finished with the knee and sat back and wiped the sweat that glistened on his forehead, Bliss broke the silence.

"Why you want to be with Ramona?" she asked. "She's all mean and do. And two-faced. You're too nice for her."

Shern looked down at her fingernails. For once she was glad to hear one of Bliss's inappropriate comments.

"Wait a minute, you not being fair, Bliss," Tyrone said. "Ramona's sweet."

Victoria moaned when he said that.

"Well, she is in her own way when you get to know her. Y'all just haven't been here long enough to see her good side; she got a real sweetness about her. All right," he conceded, "she can be a little, you know, a little snippy sometimes."

"Sometimes?" Bliss said. "Try every time she breathes."

"Or maybe we're just missing her good side when we blink." Shern looked directly at Tyrone when she said it.

Victoria made a sound that was a half laugh, half grunt. "That was pretty good, Shern." She whispered it and shifted her leg and tried again not to holler out.

Tyrone got up from the ottoman and sat in the chair across from the couch and let a smile tickle his throat and diffuse the anger over Larry that had formed there. He tried not to picture Shern blinking and missing Ramona's good side or he would have surely laughed out loud. Ramona was his lady; he couldn't be joking about her to these young sisters, who apparently couldn't see what a man could see, what he saw whenever Ramona fixed her saucer eyes on him. He leaned against the back of the chair. The royal blue seam of the custom-made plastic covers scratched his neck and he leaned forward.

That's when he noticed how swollen Victoria's mouth was. "Awl, man," he said again in that voice that was making Shern feel warm and confused, "you hit your mouth too. Let's see your teeth." He walked back over to the couch and leaned down and gently pushed against her teeth. "Whew, it's looks like the root is still good and attached to your gum, but you chipped a corner, right there. Let me get you some ice for the swelling."

Right then Ramona burst through the door and moved into the living room like a flash of light popping on an Instamatic camera.

"Where the hell y'all been?" she demanded. "Didn't I tell you to be here before it got dark out, huh? I said, 'Don't let the night beat you here,' didn't I? And don't be looking at me like I'm the one wrong; you're wrong." She tore off her coat and threw it on the chair. She moved to Shern and jabbed her finger in her chest. "Wrong, wrong, wrong."

Shern and Victoria sat stunned, the color gone from their faces, mouths dropped. Shern pulled her head way back into her chest like a turtle trying to go into its shell. She was so unaccustomed to anybody stabbing her in the chest with a finger like that she didn't even know how to react.

Victoria just looked down. Because she knew if she looked at Ramona, she'd see again how beautiful Ramona was, a soft, liquid beauty, and she'd wonder how anyone with such soft beauty could act so brittle all the time. She thought that if she had just a hint of Ramona's beauty, she'd just float on air all the time. So she wouldn't have to feel like she was crazy, imagining being a floating beauty in the midst of Ramona's tirade, she just looked down.

Bliss didn't look down, though. She jumped up from where she sat at Victoria's feet. "You better get out of my sister's face," she yelled up at Ramona. "We're not afraid of you in your old cheap hairdo. We're just polite."

"Polite." Ramona shrieked and wagged her finger at Bliss, who would have appeared comic if Ramona weren't so angry. She turned again to Shern. "You, you go in the shed and bring me the ironing cord. I'm gonna give y'all what your privileged behinds been needing all your lives."

"Hey, hey, hey, Mona, baby doll," Tyrone said, walking into the room with ice for Victoria's mouth. "No need for no whipping in here. Is it now, baby doll?" He went to Ramona and kissed her cheek.

Shern's eyes darkened some when he did that, and Bliss stomped back to the couch and sat down. The plastic covering exhaled loudly.

"I'm trying to discipline them," Ramona almost snarled at Tyrone. "They gotta listen and do what I tell them to do."

"Awl, Mona, she's hurt for God's sake." Tyrone motioned to Victoria and then handed her the ice. "Just dab that against your lips," he said.

Ramona looked at Victoria for the first time good since she'd been back in the house. She rarely looked at Victoria, the quietest, the plainest of the three. She was always looking at that youngest, Bliss, arguing back at her, threatening to slap her dead in her mouth. And Shern, that oldest with those eyes, who had a maturity about her that Ramona didn't trust, she had to look at her to make sure the child didn't have a pair of scissors aimed at her back. But

Victoria was mostly compliant; she didn't even argue with those other two like that bad-assed Bliss. Ramona suddenly felt a twinge of something other than intense dislike for Victoria, not just because the child was hurt but because she was, well, good.

"What the hell happened to you?" she asked Victoria in a softer tone, not a nice tone, but at least the steel was gone from her tone.

"I—I fell." Victoria tried to swallow the suds in her voice.

"And she chipped her teeth." Bliss puffed out the words as if they could knock Ramona over. "So you and your momma gonna have to put out the money to get them fixed. Aren't they, Shern?"

Ramona ignored Bliss this time. "You think she need to go to the hospital?" she asked Tyrone. "Shit, who feels like sitting up in some emergency room all night, a Saturday night at that?"

"I don't think so," Tyrone said. "Least not for the knee, can't be stitched 'cause all the skin has been rubbed off, more like a burn than a cut. Got to be kept cleaned, though. If it gets infected, mnh, won't be pretty. She will need a dentist for that chipped tooth."

"Damn. Just what I need, for Mae to come back here Tuesday to a hurt foster child," Ramona said under her breath.

"Don't let that ice water drip on the carpet," she said to Victoria as she picked up her coat from the chair and went to the closet to hang it. It was her good coat, the one with the suede trimming. She'd worn it so Tyrone's father, Perry, would be impressed. Not that he'd noticed. Ramona had been so nervous once she'd slid into the supple-feeling front seat of the new-smelling deuce and a quarter, and since it was a rare thing for a man to make her feel nervous, she just stared straight ahead or out the passenger side window looking for the girls. She gave one-word replies to his gentlemanly attempts at small talk, the "How's the job? How's your mother?" type conversation. Finally she was able to pull her eyes from the window and concentrate on him instead of the fast pace of her heart thumping under her good coat. She gasped silently when she noticed the hair curling around the thick gold band of his watch as he reached across her lap to get his cigarettes from the glove compartment. Thought she would melt from the sound of his voice as he sang along with Johnny Hartman something about you are too beautiful, and I am a fool for beauty. Knew then what he'd probably been doing at Miss Hettie's, could tell by the drained, satisfied tone to his voice and the way he was leaned back in the car, faraway-looking smile turning his mouth up; scent rising off of him was like he had just showered with Palmolive Gold soap. So she just looked out the window, thinking about how much she hated Miss Hettie and hoping she'd see the girls so she could jump out of the car before her nervousness showed through.

Tyrone was trying to tell Ramona how Larry had bothered the girls on Dead Block, of all places, how something was gonna have to be done about him, he was gonna have to be reported or something, and anyhow, hadn't she warned them about being on Dead Block around midday? he asked.

She told him nothing could be done about Larry, that Larry's sister, Vie, kept Mae with a decent income streaming through there by making sure that children were placed with Mae. Plus, she said, waving him away, she'd have to hear about it later; she had to get their dinner. She walked into the kitchen away from their voices. Bliss was telling him they'd left their library books all on the ground where they'd fallen. Tyrone said he'd walk up Dead Block on his way home and see if he could find the books. Then Ramona could hardly hear him as his voice dipped to a low, smooth rumble, and he told Victoria she was going to be just fine. And then Bliss's voice blaring, asking him what was Dead Block anyhow.

Ramona didn't want to hear about Dead Block. Already she was getting that prickly feeling in her spine that always moved to her chest and felt like a slab of granite rising in her chest every time she thought about Dead Block and that missing white boy, Donald Booker. So no, she hadn't told them about Dead Block; she hadn't even told them how to get to the library.

She went to the stove and turned on under the hot dogs and baked beans. The sauce around the baked beans was erupting in bubbles. She stirred around in the pot and poked holes in the molasses that was separating from the sauce and glazing over. She thought about how Victoria's face looked just then, scrunched up in pain. She counted the hot dogs again. If Tyrone stayed for dinner, there would be two extra. "That hurt one could have the extra two," she said to the pot and the stove and the molasses-scented kitchen air.

7

TYRONE did stay for dinner and made much over the hot dogs and beans, said he hadn't eaten that well in the months since he'd left his mother's table. Ramona told him to shut the hell up, he was lying, and he knew it.

"If I'm lying, I'm flying," he said. "And my feet are on the ground."

Bliss laughed then, said all the kids in her class used that line. Even Victoria smiled some, despite her newly chipped tooth. Shern didn't smile, but the ice in her glare melted a bit. The house seemed larger with Tyrone there. The air was wider, less constricted. It felt like the animosity between Ramona and the girls had more room to spread out and, in so doing, dilute. They were looser; Ramona sighed less when Tyrone was in the room. And Bliss was especially affected, latching on to his humor, even laughing openly and loudly at his jokes.

Tyrone stayed late Saturday night. At first Ramona thought he was just waiting for those three to go to sleep so he could scoop her up and carry her to bed. But after he'd taught Bliss cutthroat pinochle, and rechecked the dressing on Victoria's knee, and tried in vain to get Shern to talk, he got up to leave. "Not proper, Mona," he said to the question mark in her eyes. "Your room so close to theirs, they might hear our—you know, our sounds. Nice girls, Mona, let's not offend them in that way."

Then Ramona asked him why now, he hadn't resisted staying before. With all the other fosters he'd begged to stay as soon as they went to bed and Mae left to gamble at her Saturday night card party. What was so different about now?

"They were just shadows before now," he said, "you know, blurs, and now they're in focus, you know, real people. I wouldn't be able to be with you with all my heart and soul the way I want to be with you if I'm worrying 'bout them hearing, you know what I'm saying, baby doll?"

Ramona didn't push. She was relieved. She was reminded too much of her failings lying with Tyrone in that tight bedroom, sometimes not even feeling his manhood as he tried to touch her in places that should make her back arch. Instead she'd be preoccupied with the faded pink roses drooping on the wallpaper; the roses seemed so worn out, tired, like she was always tired, like if she stared at them hard enough, the petals might fall from the roses right off of the wall and cover her as if she were dead. She once thought that she would be a model, but her legs were too big, her hips too wide, and though her hips and legs caused much lip licking among the men when she walked down Sixtieth Street, they wouldn't work on the runway or magazine ad, the talent scout had told her, but had she considered being a pinup girl for *Philly Talk* or centerfold for *Jet,* and he knew someone shooting movies, you know, male-type movies, he'd said. After that she buried the dream of being a model under the pink roses on the wall, even under the cream-colored background of the wallpaper, and was relieved this Saturday night just to linger over a good-night kiss at the door.

* * *

Plus Tyrone had other plans for the balance of this Saturday night. He had already walked through the shimmering darkness of Dead Block like he'd promised Bliss that he would, saw no sign of their library books, though. And then as he left the intense quiet of Dead Block and headed down a neat street of massive row homes and uniformly clipped hedges toward the noisesomeness of the hub of West Philly's late-night frivolity, he saw a tall dark figure about to pass him on the street, and right after he said, "What's up, my man," and got a quick head nod for a reply, and he saw the fat slice of wrinkled beige skin running down the otherwise pitch-black forehead, he knew it was Larry. He felt his anger rise up in him now like it had as he'd cleaned Victoria's wound and Bliss described the feel of Larry's lips against her cheek. Now his words were rising out of him too, and he was calling to Larry's back, "Hey, man, hey, you, Larry."

"Yeah? You speaking to me?" Larry turned around and pushed his hands deep into the pockets of his trench coat.

"Yeah, I am. You better stay away from those young girls you damned near molested on Dead Block this afternoon."

"Yeah? And you better get the fuck out of my face." Larry started walking toward Tyrone.

Tyrone knew not to back up, knew to keep facing Larry, keep his eyes on Larry's hands; country though he was, basic rules of a fight transcended geography. "I ain't in your face yet, you deranged old dirty old man," he said as he watched Larry's hands slowly come up from his pocket. Just don't have a weapon, he thought. I think I can take you down if you don't have a weapon.

"Those my grandkids, motherfucker, and you ain't got a damned thing to do with them." His hands came up empty.

"They nothing to you, fool. And I'm gonna have your crazy ass locked up if I hear about you going near them again. That is once I finish scrubbing the street with your dim-witted ass."

Their voices were menacingly thick, pushing through this residential stretch. So much so that three porch lights came on in a row, followed by voices that bounced down to the pavement and kept Tyrone and Larry apart.

"Who's out there?" came from the middle porch.

"I don't know who"—from the next porch over—"but whoever it is I'm not having this. I'm calling the cops."

"Or throw a bucket of hot water over them"—from the third. "They want to act like animals, treat them that way. Thugs like that what's taking this neighborhood down."

"Sorry to have disturbed y'all, madams," Tyrone called over the hedges to get to the porch lights. "I'm just gonna be on my way. If this other, uh, man hangs around, though, I would definitely call the cops." He half laughed when he said it and then turned his back on Larry; he could now since Larry's hands had come up empty.

Tyrone wondered what could make a man try to claim children that were no way his. He shook his head about it and then shook Larry from his mind completely as he turned the corner to where he intended to be, under the boastful lights and the begging-for-love music wrapping around the Strip, Fifty-second Street, where the bustling shopping district by day was transformed to a different kind of shopping under the black velvet air. People here weren't interested in Shapiro's shoes or Peter Pan dresses for their little girls. Even though they were paying good money for lighter feet and pretty young things. The five-and-dime was locked and chained, but dime bags of green weed were in plentiful supply. And even though the gold shop had closed at six, liquid gold flowed freely for a price at a leather-clad bar or linen-draped table, under red and blue lights or candle flickers, at Coupe De Ville, Jamaica Inn, the Pony Tail, Mr. Silks, the Aqua Lounge. A young man could step inside any door after nine on the Strip and admire himself in the mirrored walls, maybe talk a little trash to some tightly dressed, false eyelash–batting perimenopausal divorcée. He might catch up with Milt Jackson playing the vibes at one spot or be met at another by a jukebox blaring Smokey Robinson and the Miracles calling for "More Love." Or he might just do like Tyrone and stand on the sidewalk, because even that pulsed and gave off heat.

Except Tyrone wasn't looking for heat. Nor trash-talking, nor liquid gold, dime bags, or pretty young things. Even though he'd sampled all the Strip's offerings during the year he'd been here— small samplings because he still loved the Lord. But his real reason for being on this corner of Fifty-second and Walnut, his cotton shirt collar on the outside of his windbreaker jacket, struggling against the bristle in the March air to light a Pall Mall cigarette, leaning, as if he'd been leaning on corners on the Strip all his life, was for a confirmation of his manhood.

His mother had moved him from Philadelphia when he was three back to the uppity section of Virginia where she was from, a furious move precipitated by Perry's infidelities. He'd acquired the nickname Mama's boy, growing up. Even when Perry would go down to Virginia to try to see him, try to take him out for a pop or an ice-cream cone, Tyrone would cry that he wanted his mother to come too. And Perry got so frustrated after a couple of years of three, four times a year trying to spend some time with his son and being met with Tyrone's cries for his mother and his ex-wife's satisfied, smug expression that he stopped trying to see him altogether. His father should have kept coming, Tyrone reasoned. One or two more years and he would have passed through that mommie-attachment stage. But a year ago Tyrone left Virginia for Philadelphia. Closed his eyes and took a hatchet to the too thick cord binding him to his overly protective mother, who, even though he was in his twenties, had tried to keep him from finally establishing a relationship with Perry (he was a teenager before he realized that his father's name wasn't "two-timing no-good louse").

So as he finished his cigarette and smashed the butt on the ground outside Brick's after-hours spot and stepped inside the blue air that rippled with perfumed sweat and laughter, adjusting his eyes to the smoky dimness, the rest of him to the cloud of heat that fell heavily once he was all the way inside, he knew that he wasn't here entirely to satisfy a thrill for the nightlife on the Strip. He was here mostly for his father.

"You got to pay to play, daddy." An oversized outstretched palm rose to his eye level even before the door closed behind him.

"No problem, bud," he said, trying to thin his accent. He reached into his pocket and pulled up a five-dollar bill. "Does this cover it?"

"Covers it." The palm closed over the money and then extended itself, ushering Tyrone deeper into the club's dimness.

Tyrone had not been here before, but he had heard his father mention it to his patrons who frequented the Strip. "My lady, Hettie, don't like me in there," he remembered his father saying. "Those foxes in there hungry."

Tyrone would try to get in on the conversations when he'd hear his father talking like that. He'd say something like "Yeah, Pops, they hungry, hunh?" But instead of a sly smile shared between men, he'd see a smirk on his father's face that seemed to say that he was just a vulnerable country bumpkin only a knot away from his mother's apron strings. And then the smirk would darken on his father's face, turn to a look of parental worry when Tyrone would drop the names of his favorite spots on Fifty-second Street. "You outta your league down there, Ty," Perry would say. "Even I watch my back on the Strip, and I cut my eyeteeth in places like that."

This place was packed. Tyrone had to angle himself sideways to get to the bar, where he ordered a Ballantine and nibbled at the beer nuts. He took a long swallow from the brown bottle and looked around the club. He wanted to remember the details, the table by the window where a mound of fried shrimp and crab cakes attracted really hungry foxes, the corner off to the side where couples did the bob and the cha-cha to the Four Tops crooning "Baby, I Need Your Loving," the card game going on in the back; he could tell it was a card game by the high-roller look to the men getting the nod to go on back by the substantial bouncers. The sounds of laughter mixed with the music and booming conversations swirled around his head as if a flock of giggling, cursing geese circled overhead. He wanted to be able to drop the details on Perry tomorrow, wanted to let him know that yet another Saturday night had come and gone and he had handled himself on the Strip. He turned and looked around him; he had taken Perry's warning seriously about watching his back, but the figure approaching him now, squeezing between the cigarette-smoking, fried shrimp–eating, hand-slapping bouquet of partyers made him straighten his back and adjust his shirt collar over his windbreaker jacket. She had a creamy brown face framed by a startling yellow headband that pushed her Afro back into a puff of hair and gave her a look of regality. Sizable gold hoops dropped from her ears, her neck, all along her tight black shell, her arms; even a gold-hooped chain belt hung around her black and yellow–striped hipster skirt. She made an opening through the clump of loud talkers that separated her from the bar and was now walking, no, it seemed to Tyrone, floating right toward him.

She lowered her eyes, a subtle way of saying hello, he realized, as he tried to match it with his own brand of cool. But the sensation taking him over now would not be subdued and turned his mouth up into a smile so wide he was embarrassed.

"Hey, young blood," she whispered into his ear, and he felt as though the caramel-shaded frosted lipstick she wore coated her words and melted to a warm sweetness in his ear.

"You of age, young blood, in case they start carding in here tonight?"

"I got more than a card to prove my age, baby. But how about if I start by offering you a drink?" He tried to keep a point on the ends of his words so that his drawl wouldn't creep through.

"Scotch and soda," she said to the bartender, who was now standing right in front of where Tyrone sat.

"Another Ballantine," Tyrone said as he put a five-dollar bill on the bar and got down from the stool so that she could sit. He edged his body in next to her and smiled and lifted one eyebrow slightly. He hoped she could see it through the blue air; he'd come to know the effect his eyebrows had on women. Even though it still caught him by surprise when a beautiful woman responded to him with passion-tinged breathlessness. It certainly had with Ramona. Right after their first date, when they'd taken the subway over to North Philly to the Uptown to see Sam and Dave, Martha and the Vandellas, the Delfonics, after they got off the el, tired and hoarse from the audience participation those shows evoked, he offered to give her a tour of his father's printshop. She'd seemed mildly impressed as he told her how he worked such and such printer, and mixed colors, and spread ink. And when they were getting ready to go, he raised his eyebrow, not as an overture, more just asking, so what do you think? She was all over him then; her lips covered his face, his neck, almost popping the buttons on his shirt, trying to get to his bare chest. He pushed Ramona from his mind now. She hadn't come on to him like that since.

The bartender placed their drinks; she clinked her glass against his beer bottle and then drained it. He tapped his finger against the bar to the beat of the music and pretended not to be shocked at the speed at which she emptied her glass.

"Okay, young blood, so you were gonna prove your age." She swiveled the stool so that she was talking right in his face. He thought he could smell her lipstick. "What you proving with? A wedding band? A rap sheet? Couple of kids maybe? A draft notice? Hunh? All the cute ones dragging some kind of weight that they proving their age with. What's your ball and chain say?"

"Whoa, baby. Can you at least tell me your name before you go off into a dissertation on such a, excuse the pun, baby, but such a weighty topic?"

"Mnh, dissertation, huh? Candy, my name's Candy. And you been to college, I see. You cute, and you smart. Now ain't no doubt in my mind that some little young chick done already nailed you."

"Ain't a nail been hammered that can't be pried, uh, Candy?"

His drawl slipped through as he decided not to comment on how sweet she must be with a name like Candy.

"My, my, my, and from the country too."

"Yeah, they grow them strong where I'm from, Candy." He smiled again.

"And hard?"

"Hard and soft, baby."

"Give me your hand, young blood, let me touch your flesh and make sure I didn't just dream you up. And order me another scotch and soda. You just might be coming home with me tonight."

He motioned the bartender, pointed to her glass, and she grabbed for his hand and squeezed it, and he couldn't hold his smile and got embarrassed again as it took over his face. He knew he wasn't going home with her; he was after all committed to Ramona. But what a story he'd have for Perry in the morning. He'd describe the yellow headband, the chain belt, the hipster skirt, the frosted lipstick; he'd say, "Yeah, Pops, I could have had one of the hungry foxes you always talking 'bout at Brick's after-hours spot, but Ramona's more than enough woman for me." She was asking him now if he ever dropped acid since he'd been a college man.

"Naw, that's a white boy thing," he said. "I went to a black school, Virginia Union." He noticed the bartender set yet another fresh drink in front of her. Damn, he thought, she was on number three, and that was his last money on the bar. What was left? A dollar. He thought about what he could do. Excuse himself to go to the men's room and then slip on out. Let her keep drinking and then feel for his wallet and pretend he'd been robbed. Or just come clean. Say something like "Hey, baby, your unquenchable thirst broke the bank."

He was about to do just that when he felt a rough tap on his shoulder. He realized then he'd violated a primary rule of hanging on the Strip. He'd turned his back on the door.

"You the country motherfucker that threatened me over talking to my own granddaughters?"

Tyrone hunched his shoulder and turned slowly. He could smell the whiskey on Larry's hot breath as it hit the side of his face. What had been a crowded space around the bar receded like a puddle of water evaporating from the center and left an empty circle around Larry and Tyrone. Tyrone was directly in front of Larry now, staring at the beige-colored scar on his forehead.

"Come on, you corn-fed nigger." Larry thumbed the lapels of his trench coat. "I'll teach you to get involved with matters between blood."

"Awl, Larry, leave him 'lone," Candy called from the bar.

"It's all right, baby, I got this," Tyrone said.

"I'm afraid you don't." It was one of the bouncers who'd been guarding the entrance to the card game. "Y'all gots to take it to the street."

"Awl, let em fight," a high-pitched voice called from the circle's edges.

"Yeah, it's gonna be quick and dirty anyhow"—from deeper in the circle that had grown four deep around. "Ole Larry sparred for Sonny Liston. I would put a Lincoln on him, but I know ain't a motherfucker in here dumb enough to put their money on the young boy."

"Naw, break it up"—from the other side of the circle. A big man, almost as big as the bouncer, wearing a red, black, and green dashiki, pushed his way through the thickening edges of the circle. "That's why the black man on this continent is still enslaved. We're waging war on each other instead of against the white slave master who wants to see us poison ourselves with their alcohol and drugs."

"Shut the fuck up," somebody called from the back of the circle.

"Yeah, didn't I just sit over here and watch you down a fifth of the white man's poison?"

"And smacked his lips and asked for more."

"Take that shit back to Africa. Shit, I came to party."

"Wait a minute, y'all, the brother got a point."

"Yeah, the point his hair is shaped in that needs to meet the barber's shears."

The red, black, and green dashiki walked to the center of the circle and planted himself between Tyrone and Larry. He directed himself to Larry. "You ought to be ashamed of yourself. You old enough to be his father, ought to be teaching him about the struggles of peoples of African descent all over the world, and all you can do is call him out for a fight."

"Hey, man, fuck you." Larry started to swing at the dashiki, but the bouncer caught his fist, told him both he and dashiki had to go right this second, or he was gonna signal for his posse. He opened the door. Dashiki half pushed Larry into the outside sounds of the Strip.

Tyrone was surprised at the rate his heart thumped in his throat right now as Candy ran her hands up and down his back, told him he was not only cute and smart, but brave too. "Larry's a serious boxer, plus all the people he knows in here," she said, "you could have put that good-looking face of yours in serious jeopardy."

Perry knew that too. He'd been sitting in a dark corner of the club, sipping vodka and stroking the arm of the woman sitting in his lap. Saw Tyrone come in, gawking as if he were a first-time tourist to New York amazed by the skyscrapers. He didn't want to make his son feel like he couldn't handle himself; he sensed he had that effect on Tyrone. So he kissed the shoulder of the woman he was with, laughed and clapped as the dancers did the bop and watusi, and tried not to keep watch over his son at the bar. Then he saw Candy walk by, knew she was working tonight because she always wore that yellow headband when she did her night job of coming on to the men at the bar, getting them to buy her drink after drink of scotch and soda that the bartender knew to fill only with soda, plus it kept the men at the bar keeping up with her, ordering drinks of their own. He whispered to Candy that he needed a favor for old times' sakes, then pointed out Tyrone. He had just settled back down to kiss the arm of the woman he was with, whose name he could not remember, when Dashiki approached him and asked him if he could speak to him about the plight of black men. Then the voices got loud at the bar, the rest of the club silent, and Perry almost threw the woman from his lap as he jumped up to see about his son. He told Dashiki if he was for real about saving the lives of black men, take this ten-dollar bill as paternal gratitude for saving the life of that young man with his shirt collar sitting on the outside of his windbreaker jacket.

Candy could feel Tyrone's fast breaths as she rubbed her hand up and down his back. She glanced at her watch; it was after two, and the club was still packed. This had been a good night; she knew that the 50 percent of the take at the bar that her conversation and soda guzzling brought in was at least forty dollars tonight. Not a bad take, and she didn't even have to be touched. But suddenly she wanted to be touched. Not by the likes of Perry, who filled this bar every weekend, wives or steady women waiting up for them to finally creep home, waiting for that hello kiss so they could confirm their sugary lies. Tonight she really did want this young blood to touch her with his honesty, his fear, his newness to the life on the Strip.

She pulled off her yellow headband and wrapped it around her wrist, and then squeezed his neck and pulled his neck down to whisper in his ear, "Come on, young blood, I'm feeling shaky after what almost went down. Come on home with me tonight, baby; help me settle down. Please. Please."

Tyrone tried to get his breaths to flow one into the other the way they were supposed to. His lungs wouldn't cooperate. So he had to concentrate on his breathing. Told himself that's why he couldn't ponder over his love for Ramona right now. Nor could he try to figure out why, as committed as he claimed to be to Ramona, he leaned down and kissed Candy on the lips and then allowed her to take him on home.

8

Sunday, and Ramona was up early making salt pork and egg sandwiches for those three girls. She was muttering, like she usually muttered when she did her foster care chores. Right now she muttered about the too thick slices of salt pork, how that slab could have gone much farther if Marty at Baron's meat market had just sliced it thin like she'd asked. Then Tyrone rang the doorbell decked out in his go-to-church clothes, his Florsheim shoes and his father's good black suit. And after he followed her back into the kitchen going on and on about how good that meat smelled frying, Ramona recognized the suit as his father's suit. She had watched his father, Perry, walk his smooth walk in that suit when he was a pallbearer for Mae's cousin. She wished it were Perry in the suit right now standing in front of her. She asked Tyrone then if it was a new suit; she didn't want him knowing she'd studied his father so.

Tyrone responded to the way her face filled up at that instant, the way he rarely saw it fill up. He didn't know that the way her cheeks seemed engorged right then and the way her lips parted, showing the tip of her tongue, had everything to do with that suit, with his father in that suit. And since he thought that filled-up look was for him, and since also he was feeling guilty that he didn't feel more guilty about having allowed Candy's gusts of passion to spin him around like a rudderless ship the night before until he spun into a pinnacle that widened and covered him like a deep, deep river, he took Ramona's face in his hands, told her that if she wanted it to be a new suit, it could be, whatever she wanted, if he could make it happen, he would.

He was still kissing her, a thirsty openmouthed kiss, when Bliss barreled into the kitchen.

"Did anybody call you in here?" Ramona snapped at Bliss as she pushed Tyrone from her and smoothed at her flowered duster, and didn't have a chance to think about what was different about Tyrone's mouth.

"Boss suit," Bliss said to Tyrone, ignoring Ramona. "Let me know when you ready to get creamed again in pinochle."

Tyrone cleared his throat. His eyebrows were embarrassed. "Well, don't you look like the little princess," he said as he adjusted his tie.

Bliss did a half curtsy and rolled her eyes at Ramona. She was dressed for church in the clothes Ramona had laid out for her on the banister the night before: her red wool jumper with the drop waist and her white cotton blouse with the lacy, pleated collar that matched her white lacy leotards. Ramona didn't even want to imagine how much the leotards cost. "Take your fresh-assed self into the living room and sit on the couch until I call you," she said to Bliss. "Those other two better get the hell down here or they gonna be leaving outta here hungry, and it won't be my fault; I'm doing my job and cooking the damned food. Even though I don't know how that hurt one's gonna walk to church," Ramona said half to herself and half to Tyrone after Bliss went back in the front room.

Tyrone rubbed his hands up and down Ramona's arms. "Mona, baby doll, she does have a name, you know." He put his hands gently on her lips. "Repeat after me," he said, "Vic-tor-ria. Her name is Victoria." He kissed her before she could respond.

Shern walked into the kitchen then. She didn't have a bounce to her step, like Bliss. She did have on a mid-heel, though. The last pair of shoes her mother had bought her, her first pair that didn't have a corrective arch support. Ramona looked at Shern in the grown-looking shoes; she rolled her eyes back in her head and sucked the air through her teeth. She decided against commenting on the womanish shoes; the Empire-waist green velvet dress was girlish enough to hide her developing bustline and offset the shoes. "You and that fresh-assed Bliss need to put a towel around your shoulders, so I can hot-curl your bangs," she said to Shern. "You first, come on before I put the eggs on. And you both use the same towel, y'all don't have any appreciation whatsoever for towels needing to be washed."

By the time Ramona finished with Shern's black-as-black-velvet bangs, and was wrapping Bliss's light-brown hair around the steaming curling iron, and complaining about how damned much hair they had, both long and thick, a terrible combination for whoever was charged with its upkeep, Victoria limped into the room. Her dress was chocolate brown suede, her collar beige like her textured nylon over-the-knee socks, except her legs were bare above her mid-calf.

"Why you got your socks pushed all the way down like that? Aren't they over the knee? Don't you know how they supposed to go?" Ramona half barked as she blew at the steam coming off the hot curlers and clicked the handles to loosen them. She unfurled Bliss's hair and put the curlers down on a half-burned dish towel and then combed out Bliss's bang and fingered it into a perfect barrel shape. "You finished," she said to the top of Bliss's head. "Put the towel in the shed, and go back in and sit on the couch with your sister. And don't turn on the TV all loud, I don't like no whole lot of noise around me on Sunday morning."

She turned back to Victoria. "So you were telling me why you got those socks bunched all down around your calf like that."

Victoria swallowed hard and tried to choke down the remnants of the sobs she'd let loose in the bathroom while she ran the water so no one would hear. She forced herself to look at Ramona. "It'll hurt to pull these socks up past my sore."

Ramona's eyes tried to stay stern but softened when she looked at Victoria, just a hint, but it was enough for Victoria to notice and take a deep breath and continue talking.

"So I folded my socks down so they still look neat." She struggled to keep her eyes on Ramona's face. "But if my coat rubs against my sore, that might not feel too good either."

"Tyrone," Ramona half pleaded, "could you check her knee?"

Tyrone came into the kitchen from where he had just been in the living room telling jokes to Bliss. "Sure I will, baby doll," he said. "In fact, I noticed she's limping. Probably doesn't need to be taking that four-block walk to church."

Ramona agreed with a sigh as she spread bread out on a plate and commenced to cover the slices with scrambled eggs and salt pork. "Yeah, well, my luck, if I leave her here by herself, she'll fall and break her neck. Then I'll really have some explaining to do when Mae gets back in here on Tuesday. I sure as hell hope her limp is gone by Tuesday."

Tyrone cringed when she said the part about Victoria falling and breaking her neck. "I'll walk Bliss and Shern to church," he offered. "You can stay in and keep an eye on Victoria. Will that make you feel better?"

"As a matter of fact, it will," Ramona said. "My choir's singing at the night service, so I won't even feel guilty about missing this morning since I have to go tonight. And with you with those other two, there's no excuse for them getting lost or scared by someone like crazy Larry." She smirked when she said that.

"Yeah, baby doll, we need to talk about Larry. Something's got to be done about him, almost had a run-in with him myself last night; we almost came to blows right over on Chestnut Street."

"What you doing over on Chestnut Street?" Ramona was pouring juice into glasses when she asked it, and paused and put the pitcher down and looked at Tyrone.

"I uh, I had just walked through Dead Block to see if I could find their books." Tyrone tugged playfully on the thick barrette holding the end of Victoria's braid in place.

"Yeah, but even going through Dead Block, Chestnut's way outta your way, isn't it?" Ramona was still looking at Tyrone, trying to read his eyebrows, which appeared unusually stilted against his forehead.

"Yeah, but I just felt like walking, clearing my head, and like I was saying, you might have to file some kind of complaint about that Larry, he can't be walking around like he got rights to those girls and he's no relation to them, none at all."

"Well, he's probably harmless." Ramona sighed as she resumed pouring juice, told herself it was morning light casting a glow on Tyrone's eyebrows and making them look different. "Plus Larry's sister calls the shots about what children go where, you know; we need to stay on halfway good terms with her."

She was finished pouring juice and then started arranging silverware and napkins as she called into the living room, "Get on in here and eat." And to Victoria she said, "You might as well take the socks all the way off, and change out of that good dress. You staying in with me this morning."

V<small>ICTORIA</small> spent the Sunday morning in with Ramona. They faced each other at the oblong Formica kitchen table as they ate salt pork and egg sandwiches; Ramona languished over her brewed coffee; Victoria sipped at her Ovaltine and milk. Neither spoke—Victoria because she was quiet by nature, Ramona, because there was no need to chastise or otherwise insult the child right now—so they listened to each other's slurping sounds and the crackle of the March wind hitting the kitchen window.

Plus Ramona was preoccupied with Tyrone's mouth. She knew

men, had been experiencing them in all varieties since she was sixteen. She knew their arms, their backs, the calves of their legs. But she especially knew their mouths. And Tyrone's mouth was polite, the way it lightly touched hers and almost asked for permission before parting her lips with his tongue. But this morning his mouth had been powerful, confident, the way it came at her wide open and mashed against her lips like it was going to swallow her lips. She only knew one thing that could change a man's mouth like that. She remembered then how his eyebrows looked pasted on his forehead when he told her why he was on Chestnut Street; it wasn't the morning light, like she'd tried to convince herself; his eyebrows were guilty-looking. The very thought of Tyrone lying to her, maybe even running around on her caused such a thick slab of emotion to bear down on her that wasn't even anger—she would expect to feel the how-dare-he kind of rage—but this mass of feeling falling heavy all around her like humid Philadelphia air before a rainstorm in July was a sadness so dense that it caught her off guard. She hadn't realized that her feelings for him were that solidly strong.

She shook the image of his mouth from her head and forced herself to focus her eyes on the here and now, the coffee she was sipping, the red and white vinyl place mat, the Abbott's dairy calendar on the wall behind Victoria's head, Victoria holding her salt pork and egg sandwich—struggling to eat.

"Does your mouth hurt?" Ramona asked as she watched Victoria bite her sandwich using her side teeth instead of the ones in the front.

"Just a little." Victoria lied. She so hated appearing hurt and needy and helpless. And right now her lips felt puffy and hot; her gums above her two front teeth throbbed even as she bit down with her side teeth. She cleared her throat and shifted in her seat and stared at the stalk of breakfast meat hanging out over the white bread and scrambled eggs. She broke the salt pork off. The eggs would be easier to chew. She tried to bite down using her front teeth. The throbbing spread and raced even up through her nose. She held the eggs in her mouth and glanced up at Ramona.

Ramona watched her intently. She couldn't believe that the child was acting like she was fine when it was so obvious the pain she was having chewing the soft scrambled eggs. "Why you lying?" Ramona said it more than asked it as she put her coffee cup down. "I can see you hurting." She got up from her side of the oblong table and went to Victoria's side. She put her thumb against Victoria's chin and held a napkin under her mouth. "Spit the eggs out 'fore you swallow them without chewing and choke to death. Then I don't even know how I'll be able to face my mother when she gets back in here from Buffalo on Tuesday."

Victoria did as she was told and spit the half-chewed eggs into the napkin. Ramona's thumb was warm against her chin as she moved it down to open Victoria's mouth. Victoria's mother always used to touch her chin right before she kissed her hello or goodnight or good-bye. She hadn't felt a thumb against her chin for a stretch of time that seemed so far gone she sometimes wondered if she'd dreamed her life before now, if maybe she had always lived here with Ramona.

"How come you don't have a cleft in your chin like your baby sister?" Ramona peered into Victoria's mouth as she talked. "They say a cleft is where the angels kissed you. I can't even imagine nobody's angel ever getting close enough to that smart-mouthed youngest sister of yours, that Bliss; shit, her bad ass would scare away the boldest of angels. You about the only one out of the three of y'all that deserves a cleft in the chin, and look at you; you ain't even got the sense to tell someone you hurting." She tilted Victoria's face. "Your gums looking mighty puffy. Let me mix you some warm salt and water for you to soak your gums in."

Victoria thought she felt Ramona squeeze her chin affectionately before she pulled her thumb away. She couldn't tell if Ramona really had or if she'd just imagined it because she'd wanted Ramona to do what her own mother used to. She was certain now, though, that Ramona had a softness about her that was as smooth and rich as her mother's velvet evening purse. She'd sensed it from their first day here but couldn't say it to Bliss and Shern, they hated Ramona so, and neither of her sisters had ever been able to pick up the shades in someone's character like Victoria could. She always reasoned it was her plainness that gave her her greater insight. She wasn't always responding to a litany of compliments like Shern with the dark, liquid eyes—"Where she get those Indian eyes?" people always asked about Shern; "gorgeous, just gorgeous," they'd say—or like Bliss with the light brown hair and that snappy say-anything way about her that charmed people so. "Mnh, isn't she nice," is all they ever said about Victoria, at least in her mind. So since her energy wasn't constantly stirred up saying thank you about her eyes or the color of her hair, she was freed up to see things in other people that her sisters could not, like now, the goodness about Ramona that was hidden way beyond her teeth sucking and threats of whipping their butts with the ironing cord.

Ramona mixed the warm salt and water and let Victoria rinse her mouth out in the kitchen sink. "I'm only letting you do this here 'cause you probably can't get up the steps good; otherwise you got no business spitting in this kitchen sink, you hear me?"

Victoria nodded and then spit. She could feel granules of salt separating from the warm water and sticking to her gums. She wondered if the salt would eat through her gums the way the salt had eaten through the concrete on their front steps the year of the big ice storm. "Damn salt," their father had cursed as he'd surveyed the smooth pebblestones peeking through the concrete. She imagined that's how her teeth looked now, eaten away like their steps that year.

"Leave your glass in the sink when you done. I got to get in the shed and get the laundry ready for me to drag out to the Laundromat tomorrow evening."

Victoria held a gulp of salt and water in her mouth as she watched Ramona walk away. Ramona's button-down duster was navy with bright yellow tulips. Victoria thought the tulips too overpowering for the navy. Small white daisies would have looked better. A hint of lace is better than a twelve-inch ream, her mother used to say when she'd tell them that they'd always know when someone wasn't used to much because they'd overdo. Victoria could tell by the overdone tulips that Ramona wasn't used to much. Suddenly she felt sorry for Ramona that the tulips were too big and Ramona didn't even know it.

She spit the water and salt in the sink and then limped into the shed behind Ramona. She heard Ramona complaining to the overflowing basket of dirty clothes and winced when she heard her say, "Little rich bitches." She cleared her throat behind Ramona.

"What the hell you doing in here?" Ramona turned sharply, pulled her mind from Tyrone's mouth again, and grabbed at her chest. "You scared the shit out of me. Go back on in and sit down and get off of that leg."

Victoria just stood there at first, tasting the salt that lingered on her tongue and watching Ramona clutching at her duster, the overdone yellow tulips seeming to spill out through her fist. She was struck by her beauty again, and she had to look away. "Can I help you do something?" she asked, putting her voice toward the small block of light coming in through the shed window.

"What you gonna help me do and you can't even walk?" Ramona answered.

Victoria forced herself again to look at Ramona, at the brittle outline of her otherwise soft face. "I just thought I could help you do something," she said, her voice strong considering the pulsing of the salt settling into her gums. "You're always so—so busy cleaning and everything, I just thought . . ." Her voice trailed off as she turned away again toward the light of the window.

Ramona pointed her face at Victoria as if the child had just called her some heinous, filthy name. "What did you just say?"

"I just thought—I just—"

"You don't want to help me"—Ramona mocked Victoria in a slurred voice—"and please stop looking at me like that, just stop it."

Victoria's eyes were smoky with tears.

Ramona could no longer stand the benevolence of that face staring at her, or the storm of feelings in her chest, or how tight the shed was with the overflowing basket of dirty clothes. And now it was as if she could see all the fosters who'd ever lived there prance before her view. Even that big, ugly sixteen-year-old boy who everyone said was half retarded who'd snuck into her bed when she was twelve, and was pawing and biting all over her, and at first she thought she was dreaming, so she just lay there trying to wake herself up until she smelled the Glover's Mange that Mae had rubbed in his scalp so his hair would grow. And that mixed with the sound of elastic snapping against her skin as he tried to get her pajama bottoms down, and the feel of his mouth against her breasts jolted her, and she realized then she wasn't dreaming, and she hollered out for her mother, and Mae ran in and saw what almost happened. She told him to pack his paper bag, he was leaving in the morning, and then she sent Ramona for the ironing cord, stripped her, and whipped her like she was trying to make a racehorse run. Told her it was her fault, she had probably been smiling up at the boy, shaking her butt in front of him, pressing up against him when nobody was looking, little heifer, she knew the boy was backwards, hadn't she caused it to happen? Mae asked her that night as she whipped her and told her it was all her fault.

Ramona could almost feel the skin on her back blister even now standing here in this shed when she thought about how Mae had beat her that night. She looked around the tiny shed for something to distract her from the cloud of feelings rising in her chest. Nothing. Just the overflowing basket of dirty clothes, and the small square of a window, and Victoria's face, looking up at her now; it was small too, and needy, a niceness about it.

So right then she did the only thing she could do. She slapped Victoria's face right across her already swollen mouth. She slapped her as if she were every foster child who'd ever crossed the threshold into Mae's house. She slapped Victoria's face as if with that slap she could erase every situation that would have a child taken from its real home and placed with Mae. She slapped her so hard her own hand stung and now throbbed. Then she grabbed Victoria to her, almost buried her in the bright yellow tulips of her duster; she pressed the child's head to her chest and gently pummeled her back. Her feelings were so conflicted, like jagged lightning bolts popping through the clouds in her chest, she didn't even know what to say. She just held Victoria to her and listened to her cry.

Part Three

9

CLARISE was trying to come back to her right mind as she sat in her room at the Pennsylvania Institute. The aunts and uncles had just left her bedside this Sunday morning, and now they headed for church, like they had every Sunday for the past month. Clarise turned her chair toward the window so that when they walked through the courtyard, she would be able to see them. She tried to remember what she had wanted to think about while they massaged her hands this morning, but that pinging had kept firing in her brain and felt as if small pebbles were exploding, as if bath oil beads were bursting and oozing their contents, coating her brain until her thoughts were squishy and sopping and she couldn't even hold on to them. The pinging was always a prelude to that navy-blue haze that would drop over her, confusing her so that she couldn't tell where the haze ended and her own body began—like that morning last month when she sliced at her wrists and wound up here.

And now the pinging was especially irritating because it was interrupting that something that she needed to be figuring out, a revelation that had come to her and then retreated, the way her thoughts did her sometimes, as if her thoughts were playing a child's game of tag, calling out to her, "Catch me if you can."

She'd noticed, though, that her thoughts took a seat in her brain when she first woke up, hung around some so she could mull over them. But right after her morning medication her thoughts turned to vagabonds, drifting in and out like aimless smoke until the smoke darkened to that blue haze. So this morning she had taken only one of her pills, hoping to forestall that thick navy haze. The other pill she slipped inside the generous tuck around her pillowcase; she would take it later, she told herself as she inhaled deeply to try to remember the burst of insight she just had. Nothing was coming to her though. Just the smell of White-All shoe polish that her nurse used every morning in the utility room next door; she'd hear her walking down the hall in her street shoes, she guessed, while she left her nurse's shoes there to dry.

She sighed deeply since she couldn't remember, decided to think about her Finch and all the questions still unanswered about the way he vanished. She squeezed her eyes shut and was seeing the hastily written note that Finch had left on her bureau, probably the last note he penned before he disappeared. After Clarise had calmed Shern, Victoria, and Bliss that Tuesday when both Finch and his "steady Eddie" Tuesday night brownies were absent from the house, and she'd knelt with the girls while they said their prayers at the sides of their beds—"Please, God," let our daddy be okay," they'd prayed—Clarise had stumbled, choking on her pent-up tears, into her bedroom. There, right in the center of her dresser, a corner of the paper pressed beneath her velvet-lined wooden jewelry box that played "Sincerely" when it was opened, was Finch's note. "My darling Clarise," it said, "I've gone crabbing in the luscious salty waters right off of the Maryland shore. Here is the recipe for the brownies that our precious daughters devour so. Feel free to substitute pecans for walnuts. All my love, your Finch."

He had in fact gone down to the Maryland shore, Clarise was

certain. And he had rented the crabbing boat from his second cousin Harel. Harel had produced a mimeographed copy of the receipt, had turned it over to the Maryland police investigating the boating accident. Apparently Finch had netted a good catch too; crabs still clung to the floor of the boat when it washed ashore. The police and the coast guard could not say for certain what made Finch take the small, rickety boat into deeper waters. They surmised he was trying to make it across the inlet to the other side of the shoreline, also known for copious crab catches, when the storm came up and the boat capsized. It must have happened suddenly because Finch wasn't wearing a life jacket even though Clarise always thought him to be no better than a moderate swimmer.

Now as she sat at the window, waiting to see the aunts and uncles walk through the courtyard, she wondered why he'd left the note upstairs on her bureau. Why not in the breakfast room on the tack board or in his office, where he listed the schedule of halls she'd need to check out, even in the dining room on the fancy notepad next to the phone?

Then there was the passbook for the savings account. He'd always kept it in the top drawer of his chest right next to the thin nylon socks he wore to church. Suddenly it was in the bureau drawer where Clarise stored her lacy French-cut bras, the ones she'd wear when the girls were at their Scout meetings on Friday nights and she'd primp into his studio, where Finch was preparing the food for some lavish Saturday event, and she'd have her top unbuttoned, two, three buttons down, and just the hint of her flesh pushing itself up through the lace did as much for Finch as if she'd paraded in there butt naked. He'd work the dials on the stove then, like a pilot putting his craft on automatic, and turn his attention to Clarise, who'd unwrap her nature all over him and whine and hiss and coo so until Finch was singing opera by the time he got back to his stove.

Now she thought about the passbook too, couldn't figure why he'd moved it from his sock drawer and placed it with her good bras instead. It had taken her almost a week to find it; with Finch missing and presumed dead, she had no reason to dress her breasts so. But on the day of his memorial service—they couldn't call it a funeral because there was no body to lower into the ground—she needed a black bra since she was in mourning and would be dressed in black from the netting around her hat to the supersheer nylon hose, and her only black bras were lacy and in her good bra drawer. That's when she'd found the bankbook. That's also when the haze started to darken her world. As if it weren't already dark enough because of her grief, which was so tight around her she couldn't poke a hole in it with her sharpest nail. Finch after all had been her only love since she was sweet sixteen. They'd even breathed in sync, as her aunt Til reminded her when she'd tell her it was okay to grieve. Even when Finch interrupted his breaths to snort occasionally, Clarise would anticipate, would hold her own breath for the count of three; then both their chests would rise again and fall to their own syncopated beat. Now the air around her moaned in grief for this sad solo of a breath that should be a duet.

Her grief, though, had a naturalness about it; it was smoky and foggy and still let in light. But the haze that began to fall right about the same time that she'd found the bankbook was dripping navy, slowly at first, as her doctor increased the prescription for her nerves in small degrees, until there was just the blue. So by the time the insurance policy surfaced, the one that was above and beyond the substantial whole life policy Finch had left, the one that the aunts had found between the mattress and box spring after they'd stripped down the bed on the twenty-eighth day, the haze was falling and lifting so often that Clarise couldn't tell if she was blinking erratically, or if the blinds in her room were opening and shutting on their own, or if the daylight was obliterated behind the night only to return again a few minutes later.

She pulled her mind from the haze and her Finch because the aunts and uncles had just emerged into the courtyard under her window. They walked four across, her uncle Blue tall and graceful in his black and tweed chesterfield, and next to him Til with the perfectly straight back, then Ness tipping along in her high-heel boots holding on to Show's arm, and Show in a ten-gallon top hat to give himself some height. She pressed her fingers to her lips when she saw them and blew a kiss through the chain-link screen covering the window. How blessed she felt to have them in her life. She was about to close her eyes and whisper a prayer of gratitude, but right then she let out a small scream instead. Suddenly she remembered what revelation had tried to come to her earlier as the aunts massaged her hands. It did come to her now, tiptoed into her head, sat in a facing chair, tapped on her knee, said, "Here I am." She screamed louder now. It had nothing to do with the flickering haze or her Finch, but everything to do with her girls. They weren't with the aunts and uncles. My God, my God, why hadn't she seen it before? They'd never been with them, the whole month she'd been locked away in this crazy house. Wouldn't the aunts have made sure she talked to the girls on the phone had they been tucked away safely in their Queen Street row house? And if she knew her Uncle Blue, he surely would have snuck Shern in, told the guard she was a young-looking sixteen. At the very least they would have stood the girls in the courtyard under her window so they could blow one another kisses through the chain-link screen. Where were her girls? "My God!" She was hollering out loud now. "My girls, my girls, where are my girls?" She banged against the chain-link screen to try to get the aunts and uncles to hear her, to turn around, to explain to her what had happened to Shern and Victoria and Bliss. She jumped up from the chair, lifted the chair and threw it against the window, picked it up and threw it again. She felt helpless, hopeless, she had to know about her girls.

The nurse was in the room now; she could smell the White-All shoe polish. A whole host of people were in the room; she didn't even need to turn around to confirm it, their various scents were so crowding the air at her back. And now she was in their clutches, two, four, six, eight sets of hands had her, all talking fast, demanding so many milligrams of this, liters of that, and then the puncture in her buttock, and she could feel it streaming all around her, except now it was tighter than a haze and darker than navy; it was thick like gumbo and black as pitch tar and completely surrounded her. She couldn't see through it, or hear through it, or even smell through it, except for the tiniest pinhole that let in a ray of ether that went straight to her nose and kept her hanging on. And of course she couldn't have known that her status in this mental hospital came up for review that following day. It had been a month. They couldn't hold her longer than this without her permission. Unless of course she demonstrated that she would pose a danger to herself or others if she were released. Then they could hold her, could even restrict her visitors in fourteen-day allotments. Which of course now they were going to do.

10

THAT Addison Street row house was calm for a change. More than quiet, it was actually absent of the bitterness that usually kept the air there unsettled. The air had a snug feel now, like a contented child falling off to sleep, like Victoria, all cried out and napping on Ramona's bed.

Ramona hadn't been able to summon the right words to apologize to Victoria for slapping her, didn't know how to explain to the child that for fifteen years she'd seen fosters come and go, she'd washed their clothes, cleaned their dirt rings from the tub, combed their hair, sometimes even wiped the remnants from their diarrhea-stricken behinds; never ever had even one of them offered to move even a plate from the table; Mae spoiled them that way. And it was actually easier for Ramona because she never had to worry about getting too close or feeling too sorry watching their childhoods wrinkle and sag as they were shuttled in and out of the temporary, tenuous haven of Mae's, Mae's house often just a stop-off between the hell they were leaving and the one they would return to. She could douse them all with her hatred while Mae forced her to wait on them hand and foot. But now this one had dared to step out of the mold and offer to help, even poked around in the bitterness and stirred up other than the hate that Ramona felt for every child who'd come through there. She didn't know how to explain any of it to Victoria or how to say she was sorry. But everything she did from that moment on said, "I'm sorry." When she held Victoria to her like she thought a mother would, even though Ramona really couldn't know what a mother's hold felt like, she was saying, "I'm sorry." And when she gently dabbed Victoria's lips with ice, she was saying, "I'm sorry." And when she let Victoria in her room while she did her nails—she never let the fosters in her room—she was saying, "I'm sorry." And when Victoria fell asleep propped up in the bed and Ramona slid her shoes from her feet and covered her over with her good woolen satin-trimmed blanket, she was saying, "I'm sorry." Now, as Victoria slept, as Ramona crept about, gingerly removing her navy and gold choir robe from the plastic bag, deciding if she needed to give it a steam iron, the air in the house this Sunday almost had a redemptive feel.

Even though Mae couldn't feel it as she stumbled through the front door.

M<small>AE</small> was back from Buffalo like gangbusters, two days early, Sunday instead of Tuesday. She had traveled back to Philadelphia with Addison, the eighteen-year-old delinquent son of her ailing sister slung over her arm like he was a good leather purse. She'd had to sneak him out of Buffalo under the cover of night so the daddy of the poor teen he'd gotten pregnant wouldn't shoot him. "He's gonna kill me," Addison had cried in his aunt Mae's arms. "It ain't even been proven that it's mine, and her old man is sitting in his car right in front of this door with his pistol cocked, and I know he's gonna try to shoot me dead."

Mae told him to throw some things in a paper bag; they would leave through the kitchen and down the alleyway, bound for Philly that very night to the street whose name he bore.

This nephew, Addison, was Mae's favorite child in all the world, partly because he was born in her living room back in 1947. She'd just had a major win at a high-stakes poker game, and that, plus what she got from the sale of her tiny ace, deuce, tre on Mole Street, allowed her to buy her dream house on Addison Street: three bedrooms, a porch, a yard, and a concrete basement. She was the first black person to claim that block of Addison Street as home. With her five-year-old cupid doll daughter, Ramona, to help, she kept her mortgage current by taking care of the children of her white neighbors, until the day she unwrinkled the piece of paper one of her charges was using as a toy ball, and she read the bold-lettered flyer that said, "Have you seen your new neighbor? Now is the time to act. Because once the influx has taken hold, the value of your house will plummet. With 25 years in the real estate business, we can sell your home at an attractive price in under 60 days. We urge you to act—Now!"

Mae was so incensed that she was being used to bust the block in that way that she told each mother she could no longer take care of her bad-assed children, and don't even be thinking about asking her to clean their houses. So she cleaned her own house and loved her little dream house all the more. She taught Ramona how to clean, even how to shine the windows with newspaper and vinegar. She'd show them who the unclean were and how to raise a child. So she took to spanking Ramona too, whenever she misstepped, and even when she didn't; just as a preventive, she'd smack her soundly around the meaty part of her legs with the ironing cord until she saw the welts that let her know she had gotten her good.

But even with her immaculate little dream house, and well-behaved cupid doll daughter, Mae needed income to keep her mortgage current. So she sought out something half days with the city so she wouldn't have to pay a baby-sitter to watch Ramona when she got in from school. When the city job didn't materialize, she waited tables at night after she put Ramona to bed, but she couldn't tolerate all those hours on her feet. So she settled on just parlaying what scrapings together she had left from the sale of her Mole Street house into future earnings at the card table. She'd always been lucky when she sat down to spread her cards; looked like her father, and as the old folks said, "Girl look like her father always have luck with money, when she look like her mother, money slide between her fingers like a clump of melting lard, but that Mae, Lord have mercy, look just like her daddy even down to that lazy eye she got. Can't nobody whip her at cards when she lay that lazy eye on them."

So she played cards to pay her bills: bid whisk, pinochle, spades, poker, five hundred gin rummy, tunk; she'd play anything that had a wager attached. And though she was winning handsomely, card playing too had its drawbacks. She had to go all the way downtown to Clara Jane's to play, and sometimes people paid her her winnings in ways that were not immediately negotiable: a handmade lace tablecloth; a bond that couldn't be redeemed for two more years; a free hack for a month to take her to and from grocery shopping. Then one night, perched at the card table downtown in Clara Jane's basement, tired and low, her lazy eye drooping so much that she couldn't hold on to her good poker face, the game so intense people had even stopped talking stuff about each other's mommas, a child came up on Mae from behind and wiped her sticky fingers on her neck. It shocked Mae because she knew Clara Jane was childless. "Lord have mercy, Clara Jane, where in the hell this child come from, scaring the mess outta me like this, got me almost ready to expose my hand?" Then Clara Jane told Mae that was her foster; child had been turned over to the state because her mother couldn't do for her. She got monthly upkeep money for the child, plus a little extra payment for her own time and bother. "Just go on down to City Hall and put your name on the list," Clara Jane told Mae. "And it will sure help if you know someone who'll skip over the names in front of yours in order to get to your name first."

So Mae went down to City Hall the first thing Monday morning, getting her name put on the list. And last thing Monday night she was up at the ward headquarters, in the back office, rocking back and forth on the lap of the ward leader, making sure some worker would get the directive to skip over all the names in front of hers even though she was a single head of household, in order to get to her name first.

Near the end of her first year in that house, after a half dozen foster children had come and gone and helped her keep her mortgage up-to-date, and she gave out pamphlets and sample ballots for her ward leader on election day to make sure her name stayed on the top of that list, her pregnant sister, Martha, came to stay, just until Martha's husband was done his stint in the army. And then Martha's husband, Albert, came. And he stayed, just until he could get his work situation together. Then the baby came, right on the living-room floor before the yellow cab could get there, or even the red car. The baby came, and Mae helped birth him, and she named him Addison for the street.

And Addison was always her favorite child because whenever she looked at him and his sly little grin, she'd think about his father, Albert, and his sly grin, and the way Albert's sly grin would come up at night, after a couple of beers, after Martha was asleep, after Mae would come down in the shed kitchen, where Albert had taken to sleeping after Martha had gotten so outrageously large with that baby in her womb. "Oops," Mae would say, and blush through her cheeks and quickly cup her hands over the sheerest part of her negligee, even though the hand cupping exposed more than the negligee did. "I'd forgotten you'd taken to sleeping down here in this old cramped little shed. I had the taste for some cling peaches, and I believe I have a can of split ripe ones in heavy syrup right thereabouts on that shelf, right above that nail where you done hung your pants."

And Albert would look at her with her hands cupped, pushing up her womanhood like she was offering it up to nurse a newborn, and the sly grin would come up, and he'd figure since there was no newborn to oblige, he might as well, and later they'd share split cling peaches in heavy syrup from the can.

So Mae had to bring Addison back to Philly to save his life, her favorite child in all the world, born to her sister in the living room of Mae's dream house, where he'd slid out looking red and sly just like his dad.

"R<small>AMONA</small>," Mae called up the stairs from where she stood in the middle of the living room, her bags surrounding her where she just let them lay where she'd dropped them. Her black and gray tweed coat was dropping off the back of her shoulder, her flowered scarf over her red wig was slightly crooked, and her lazy eye, the left one, which drooped and seemed to stare straight ahead, was more pronounced now; it always drooped more when she was tired. And tired she was after that long bus ride from Buffalo, after carrying the heavy bags to get on the el, then the waiting for the G bus, then trying to keep up with Addison and his long, fast steps. She was almost sweating, even as the cold March air was rushing in the opened door behind her and wrapping her up. She stood in the middle of the floor now and called for her only natural child.

"Ramona," she said again, "get on down here and help me with my bags, please, Lord Jesus, am I ever tired."

"Ma'am?" Ramona called from upstairs. "You here already?" Then her voice got closer as she ran down the steps; she gripped the banister so she wouldn't slip and fall down the blue-bordered plastic runner that protected the new carpet hugging the stairs.

"What happened? Is Auntie better? Why you back today instead of Tuesday?" she asked as she walked straight past Mae to push the front door shut.

"Lord Jesus, child, quit with the questions and help me outta this coat. So tired I can't hardly stand up." Then a smile crossed her lips, and she said, "That Addison got such long, quick legs, my, has that boy grown, couldn't hardly keep up with him after we got off the G bus."

"Addison!" Ramona shrieked, stopping like stone with Mae only half out of her coat.

Mae shook her arms impatiently. "The coat, child, just get me outta this coat; then we can talk about Addison." She pulled one arm out, then the other, used to Ramona helping her in this way. Then she tilted her head so Ramona could untie the scarf under her chin. "Yeah, my baby boy, Addison," she said as Ramona tried to work the knot out. "I told him to go on and stop off at Smitty's and play the jukebox or the pinball machine and relax hisself for a bit. Poor child been through a lot. Little heifer gets herself in a family way and then try to pin it on him. So I told him come on back to Philadelphia with me, ain't nobody gonna hurt him or be saddling him with something they can't even prove he did."

"For how long?" Ramona asked, blowing her words out at Mae's neck as she pulled and tugged at the scarf's ends.

"Till that situation with that little hot-in-the-behind child blows over. Can't rightly say just how long that'll take. We'll see, maybe through the summer."

"Through the summer!" Ramona's jaws were pushed way out, and her voice was shaking, as was the scarf that she'd finally untied from Mae's head; it was hanging loosely in her hands and going up and down with her hands. "And where's he supposed to sleep? The summer is three, four months away. And what about school? His dumb behind needs to be in school somewhere. I swear, I really don't believe this, I just don't believe this."

The scarf was really going now in Ramona's hands, and Mae snatched the scarf from her. "Don't you be shaking this scarf in my face like you taunting me." She squinted her eyes at Ramona, and the lazy one shut completely.

Ramona looked away. "Well, did you at least think about where he's supposed to sleep?" Her tone was lower, but the shaking was still there. "I mean, you know those three girls are here now and they got a room, I got a piece of a room, and you got a room." She swallowed hard so she wouldn't cry. Another person for her to have to pick up after, do laundry for, cook for. Plus he was cocky and trifling and stupid.

"He'll sleep back in the shed," Mae said as she walked to the couch and sank into it. "I'll put that little cot up for him that we used to use all those years ago when his daddy stayed here. He'll be just fine." The plastic covering snorted, and Mae extended her feet. "Please help your mother out of these shoes, then hand me my slippers from outta that small overnighter bag."

Ramona complied and peeled the low-heeled, snug-fitting shoes from Mae's feet and let the shoes hit the floor in thuds.

Mae sighed and flexed her toes while Ramona went through her bag to find her slippers. "Where those new little girls?" Mae asked in a voice that sounded like it was ready for sleep. "What they like? Did they mind you all right? I know they did. Vie said they seem to be nice little things even if they do come from money."

Ramona was stone again. She had almost forgotten she was going to have to tell Mae about Victoria's fall, about her knee, the tooth chipped in the corner. She thought she'd have two more days. And now Mae was back two days early, hadn't even given the child enough time to heal.

"They at church," Ramona said into the overnight bag.

"Speak up, girl, what you over there mumbling about?"

Mae's head was resting against the back of the couch. Ramona wondered if the blue-stitched seam irritated Mae's neck like it did her own. She wished at that moment that it did, that it would scratch Mae's neck like the point of a straight pin.

"At church," Ramona almost shouted it. "Two of them anyhow."

"Why only two?" Mae shifted her head and nestled it deeper along the couch back. Her red wig was crooked, and Ramona fought the impulse to go straighten it out.

"One of them couldn't go, that middle one, fell yesterday and hurt her leg and chipped her tooth. She'll be fine, though. A little scrape." Ramona rushed her words all in one breath.

Mae sat up slowly. With the sun pouring in through the window and stopping as a wide slat of a beam just above her head, she looked like a red-hatted circus seal getting ready to do an alley-oop over a diving board. "What you mean, hurt herself?" Her words were deliberate. Her head went through the sunbeam and scattered it.

"Awl, Mae, it's just a little scrape; it's not like she's hurt bad." Ramona walked toward her mother with her powder blue slippers in her hands.

"Don't you know my livelihood depends on my perfect record with my fosters?" Mae barked. "I don't be turning back no damaged kids. How dare you let one of my fosters get hurt when you supposed to be minding them." She was sitting straight up. "Tell her to come here; let me see what harm you let happen while I'm away trying to tend to my sick baby sister. Sometimes you the most useless, inept person I've ever seen in all my born days. Call her down here, right now, I said."

But she didn't have to call her down. Victoria was already standing at the top of the steps. "Do you want me, Ramona?" she asked in a voice that had just awakened from a nap.

"It's Mae that want you, sugar." Mae softened her tone. "Come on here and let Mae meet that baby girl and see how that lil darling hurt herself."

Victoria held the banister and tried with everything in her to walk normally down the stairs. The blue-bordered plastic runner had almost tripped her earlier. She looked at Mae sitting there, her eye drooping, her wig crooked, scowling at Ramona. She looked shorter, meaner than she did on the picture propped next to the color glossy of President Kennedy inside the glass-cased china cabinet. Suddenly as her feet left the bottom step for the living-room floor, she was afraid of Mae, more afraid than she'd ever been of Ramona. She almost wanted to run to Ramona, to hide behind her tulip-laden duster. Her sisters, she knew, would never understand this sudden need she had for Ramona to shield her from Mae.

"How you fall, doll baby? Tell Mae what happened to you."

Victoria thought that she should keep her lips clamped shut to hide her chipped teeth. She pushed her voice through her barely opened lips. "I'm not that hurt."

"That's a mighty big dressing over your knee for you to be not that hurt. Come a little closer, and let Mae get a welcome hug and a good look at this doll baby."

Victoria took baby steps; she limped less that way. She tried to sift through the air in that room that was so confused right now it was hard for her to breathe. She understood that the appearance of her being hurt in front of Mae might be to Ramona's detriment. Though the exact dynamics of the situation between Ramona and Mae hovered just above her twelve-year-old understanding, she was certain that she needed to conceal the severity of her pain, like she had been concealing it from everyone, even Shern. And she rarely hid things from Shern. So she inched toward Mae, trying to make her steps strong and sure, battling now with the plastic runner that was too smooth for her slippered feet to grip. She saw red, then felt a burst of red through her hurt leg from the weight she was forcing it to bear. She thought her knee would explode if she didn't shift all her weight to her good leg. She wished for a rail at that instant, or a gate, or a cane. She started to sweat.

Mae studied the child inching toward her, her good eye fixed on the gauze and tape strips covering Victoria's knee. She knew the walk of children. They'd come to her from the state with all kinds of peculiar walks. She'd gotten them stricken with polio so that one limb was always curled or with joints dislocated where they'd been thrown against a wall; she'd gotten them brain-damaged from lead fumes so they staggered like drunks or with a bad case of rickets so they hopped when they walked. She knew how to look them over like she was doing a walk through on a house she would rent, knew how to point out their maladies to the social workers dropping them off and how to get it in writing witnessed and notarized that they had come to her less than perfect. She prided herself on turning her fosters back in a condition that was at least as good as how they'd come. And Vie had assured her when she'd called her in Buffalo that these girls were in perfect, absolutely flawless physical condition. But this child inching toward her had a less than perfect walk. Mae could see now that there was a persistent bend in the child's knee. The child was hurt, and try as she might not to let it show, it was a hurt that went all the way to the bone.

Ramona suspended her breath while Victoria walked to the couch where Mae sat. "See, Mae, it's not like she's all banged up or anything, just a little scrape, like I said."

"Don't you say a word more to me right now." Mae answered Ramona with a hiss, without even turning to look at her. She kept her stare fixed on Victoria's walk. "Me and you gonna get together about this all right, when it's just me and you." Her voice was low and steady, her words measured and controlled. She stretched her hands out to Victoria. "Come here, pudding." The syrup was back in her voice. "You don't have to feign like you're better than you are for Mae. Mae can see that lil darling done hurt herself."

Mae took Victoria's hand, and Victoria's first instinct was to wrench it back. She did at first.

"Lord, Lord, Lord, is your hand hurt too? Did that hurt you when I pulled your hand? You didn't say nothing to me about her hand, Ramona."

"It's fine." Victoria said it quickly and let her hand relax in Mae's. Mae's hands were calloused around the fingers, and Victoria thought they smelled of Clorox. She wanted to sit, to take the weight from her leg. Mae squeezed her hand and began massaging her arm up to her elbow. Victoria inched in to get all the way to the couch.

She sat, and Mae put her arms around her shoulder and squeezed her to her and coated her with her syrupy words. "Mae sure hopes that Ramona took care of this sweet little piece of caramel candy. Mae so sorry about that baby doll's situation that has her living here. But don't you worry, time's gonna fix it, and your momma's gonna get better too. Not today or tomorrow, but she will, I promise you that, buttercup."

Victoria's stomach started to spin, and she hoped she wouldn't have to vomit caught up in Mae's arms and the aura of Clorox that seemed to surround her.

Before she could vomit, the doorbell cut through the room.

Ramona ran to open it, relieved for the distraction. She saw Tyrone first, even though he was behind Bliss and Shern. He seemed taller, more acutely appealing; she felt the sadness bearing down.

Shern blew inside the door as if she'd been pushed. She ran straight up the stairs without even a hello to Victoria or even a quick glance at her sister to make sure she was okay, to make sure some harm hadn't visited her alone all morning with Ramona.

"Boy in Smitty's tapped her on the butt," Bliss whispered to Victoria as she walked past.

"What? What happened to her?" Mae sat forward, her wig so crooked now the tan-colored edges of the stocking cap she wore under her wig peeked through.

"Tell me what happened to her." Mae held Victoria even tighter, bracing herself.

"Boy came into Smitty's and bothered her," Tyrone said matter-of-factly. "Uh, Mae, thought you were gone till Tuesday, uh, Mae."

"Bothered her, how?" Mae ignored Tyrone's question. The more anxious she was to hear details, the tighter she clutched Victoria, who was squirming, trying to free herself from Mae's clasp.

"Oh, you're Mae," Bliss said, walking in closer, studying Mae as if she had just come upon an interesting rock or leaf on a nature walk.

"That would be me, cupcake. And look at you, aren't you adorable-looking like a piece of gingerbread with that light brown hair and the eyes to match? Now tell me what happened to your sister, doll face."

Tyrone and Bliss exchanged glances; neither spoke.

"Well, Tyrone," Mae said, her voice a full octave deeper now, "somebody better tell me something." She had both hands around Victoria now.

Victoria could hardly breathe caught up in Mae's arms, the air around Mae smelling like Clorox. Victoria felt like she was smothering in the bleachy air. "Tell her!" Victoria shouted as if the telling would save her own life. "Somebody please tell her what happened to Shern."

"Well." Bliss took a deep breath after the "well," and Victoria rolled her eyes up in her head knowing Bliss would do a long, too long explanation.

But Bliss was already caught up in the telling, starting with how they'd stopped at Smitty's after church and Tyrone was treating them to butterscotch Krimpets, and right when Tyrone went to the counter to pay Smitty, and Shern and Bliss stood peering into the glass case of two-for-penny candy—she listed the candy: chocolate-covered malted balls, red licorice sticks, spearmint jellies, strawberry cream-filled wafers—when they were pointing to the wafers, licking their lips at how good they looked, this boy bounced into the store like he owned it. "He went right to her, right over to my sister Shern and said, 'Hey, sweet baby,' right in her ear." Bliss lowered her voice in a near-perfect imitation. "And Shern jumped and said, 'Boy, you better get away from me.' Then he made this old nasty slurping sound right in her ear; I could hear it clear as day from where I was standing. And Shern jumped back and pushed him away. And he laughed this old nasty laugh and acted like he was walking away, just so Shern could turn back around and try to forget he was even in there, but then he did a double take, and he put his old nasty hand right on my sister's butt. You believe that? And I mean, he didn't just put it there; he had the nerve to squeeze it like he was playing in clay dough or something."

Ramona listened to Bliss describe the wretchedness of the boy. For the first time she was actually glad to hear Bliss's fresh mouth go on and on. Ramona knew the boy had to be Addison. Sounded just like the kind of asinine thing the likes of Addison would try right in the middle of a store filled with people.

"Oh, my poor things, my poor, poor, poor things." Mae gasped. She flung her arms in the air, finally freeing Victoria. Victoria fell against the back of the couch; she didn't even mind the irritation of the plastic chair covers. For the moment she could breathe again.

"My poor things are having a bad time this week." Mae went on. "I do declare I'm not gonna be able to leave town again. I leave here for a short trip on a mercy visit to my sister, and one poor little thing gets hurt and the other gets bothered. Thank the Lord I came back early like I did. Lord, Lord, Lord. What would I have come back to if I'd stayed till Tuesday like I'd planned?"

Ramona watched Mae's theatrics; she knew the children were commodities to Mae, as much as she called them pudding and doll baby; she knew Mae cared about their well-being only as long as there was payment from the state associated with their well-being. So now Ramona was itching to ask, couldn't wait to ask, even though she already knew, she asked it quickly, loudly, for her own satisfaction, she asked it. "What the boy look like?"

"Tall and skinny," Bliss blurted, "looked like someone who thought he was cute all his life. Big old hands. Ugh, I can't even imagine how my sister felt having those old nasty hands squeezing all over her like he was giving someone a massage or something. I mean, he squeezed her so hard her long dress coat went way up over the top of her knees."

"Bliss," Tyrone said quietly, "sh-h, I'm sure we all get the idea."

"Not unh," Bliss half whined, half shouted. "You get the idea because you were there, Tyrone. They weren't there, they don't know how disgusting it was. I'm just trying to make them see it."

"And you did a good job of describing it, sugarplum," Mae said to Bliss as she looked at her with her one good eye and smiled. "I sure don't hope I run into that no-count, no-home-trained, disrespectful hoodlum. I might be tempted to knock him into next week."

"Well, pick which day you want him to land on," Ramona said with a smirk. "Here he comes walking up the steps right now."

S{HERN} stayed up in the bedroom facedown on the twin bed with the pillow covering her head, still in the Empire-waist green velvet dress she'd worn to church. Bliss couldn't talk her into coming down for dinner, nor Victoria, even though she had at least responded to the sound of Victoria limping, pulled her head from under the pillow long enough to ask her how was her leg. Then retreated again where the only thing remotely comforting to her this Sunday afternoon was the feel of her own breaths under the dark tent the pillow made.

She relived the horror of the feel of that hand against her, and then the sound that drummed through her head, a screech, then a thundering bang that she felt in her chest, as if she'd just watched a car filled with every person she'd ever loved barrel into an eighteen-wheeler and explode. That's how she felt at Bliss's screech and then her proclamation, "That's him. That's the nasty good-for-nothing that squeezed my sister's butt."

And then Mae, saying, "You must be mistaken, young lady. That's my nephew, Addison, a fine young man he is. Gonna be living right here with us for the next few to several weeks."

The very thought of living under the same roof together, and a ball of yarn started spinning in the pit of her stomach. She'd have to pass him in the hall, see him across the dinner table, God forbid, go in the bathroom right after he came out. What if she were caught in the house with just him? What if he tried to touch her again? He might even go farther next time. Might try to take her the way her neighbor around the corner had been taken after the holiday party at the law firm where she'd interned over Christmas. "A disgrace the way they spoiled that child," her mother had said. "Slipped something in her drink. And now she's ruined. A real lady she was too." But this thing whom Mae had the nerve to call a fine young man might be brazen enough to try something with her head-on and staring her straight in her eyes.

Now even the feel of her breaths blowing back against her face had ceased to comfort her, and she tried not to think about the one thing that could still the spinning in her stomach right now, the sound of her mother's voice. She knew if she dwelled on her mother and the impossibility of hearing her voice, a piercing hurt would mix with the anger and humiliation she was feeling over that horrible boy's hand, and she might be thrown into a fit of hysterical crying that would be all-consuming. So she dwelt on the next best thing, her aunts and uncles.

Suddenly she just needed to hear one or the other of their voices. Needed a link to her life before now, needed it confirmed that what her life used to be wasn't just a smoky illusion. Suddenly she refused to ponder the consequences, Ramona's threats about jeopardizing the opportunity ever to see her aunts and uncles again if they made contact while the judge's order was in effect. Suddenly Shern, the oldest, the most patient, the one who impressed over and over to her sisters that it wouldn't be much longer, "any day now," she'd tell them, "just hold on, and before you know it, we'll be going back home," right now couldn't last another second without going back home, even if it was just going home in a sense through the telephone line.

She uncurled herself from the bed and stood and smoothed down her velvet dress. She wiped her face with her hands and then rubbed her hands through her hair; the thick wool of her hair easily absorbed the wetness of her tears in exchange for a slight greasy film. She walked across the bedroom, which was bathed in an orange afternoon sun, and eased the door open and listened for the downstairs sounds. They were eating dinner, she could hear metal against glass, Mae talking; she had an irritating voice, Shern thought, like a fingernail against a blackboard. Now Mae was laughing, sounded like Hettie from across the street was down there too. Good, Shern thought. Ramona's probably busy serving the meal. Just keep talking, keep laughing, please.

She crept through the hallway, which suddenly seemed long, as she tried to get to the telephone just inside Ramona's bedroom. How many times she'd seen that phone over the past month when she walked past Ramona's room. How many times she wanted to pick it up to scream out for her aunts and uncles to come and rescue them. But she had taken Ramona's threats to heart, plus the phone had a lock on it. She'd seen Ramona pull the key from the pocket to that ugly navy duster she always wore, the one with the huge hideous flowers. Ramona had even sent Shern for the key once when she was getting ready to use the phone in the kitchen and the lock was in. "You, oldest," she commanded, "go reach in my duster pocket that's folded at the foot of my bed and bring me down the key that's in there."

Shern's prayer now as she stepped inside Ramona's room was that Ramona didn't have the duster on. There was the phone right on the edge of the dresser right next to the door, there was that little cylinder right in the number one on the rotary so that the dial wouldn't spin beyond that little black tab, and there, thank God, on the foot of the bed was Ramona's ugly flowered duster.

Shern inched her fingers into the pocket, pulled up a stick of Doublemint gum, went to the other pocket, felt her fingers go weak as she wrapped them around the key and rushed to the phone. It took several tries to insert the key into the cylinder because her hands were slick from when she'd rubbed her hair and now they were sweating too. Finally she turned the key in the cylinder and pulled it out of the number one hole.

Her heart felt like thunderclaps in her chest as she dialed the number, and then she heard it, her uncle Blue say in his sherry-tinged voice, "Speak to me."

Just hearing his voice loosed a floodgate in her throat. She couldn't even say hello, just a moan came up from her throat, and then another one, and she had to cover her mouth so that they wouldn't hear her downstairs.

"Who is this, please? It's your dime, but it's my time, so spill it or chill it," her uncle Blue said.

She tried to speak, but just a huge bubble carrying a sob passed through her lips, and now she could hear her aunt Til in the background. "Who's that on the phone, Blue?"

And then Blue's voice got further away as he said, "Some uneducated fool playing on the phone, just breathing hard and saying nothing."

Then Shern whispered as loud as she could without shouting, "No, it's me, it's me, it's Shern." And now she was talking to a dial tone and staring in Ramona's face.

Perhaps it was the utterly defenseless, caught look on Shern's face; perhaps it was that Ramona too had felt violated in her life by some no-good man's groping hand; perhaps it was even Ramona's preoccupation with Tyrone's changed mouth that made her feel a misty blue kind of sadness that lent itself more to sighing than rage. Whatever the reason, Ramona didn't perform, didn't curse and holler, didn't hit Shern, didn't demand her to go from her room. She just took the phone from Shern's frozen hand and put it back on the receiver. Stretched open her palm, calmly told Shern, "Just drop the key right here, please." Then went to the closet to get her gold and blue choir robe, turned her back on Shern to give her a chance to leave the room.

11

RAMONA tried to push the petrified look on Shern's face from her mind later that night as she stood on the choir loft, decided she didn't even want to know who Shern was trying to call. She tried to chase Addison from her mind too, Mae, that row house, even Tyrone and his changed mouth. Tried to clear her mind so that she could throw her head back and sing the lead with her choir.

"We doing your song tonight, Ramona," her choir director had called into the changing room, where Ramona and all the other female choir members had crammed, jostling for space to pull their robes on and check their lipstick, straighten their wigs, fix their bangs, take their cash money from their purses and stick it in their bras.

"All right, now," Ella, the alto, boomed. "We ain't done your song in weeks, Ramona. I'm ready for you, girl."

"Oh, hush, girl," Ramona said, shooing Ella from the mirror so that she could smooth on her frosted peach-toned lipstick. "Ain't nothing but a song."

"I got your nothing but a song," said Beanie as she swept a single loose hair from Ramona's meticulous French roll into place. "The way you close your eyes and start to moan and carry on when you do that song, honey, honey, honey, I'm praying for you that all you thinking about is the Lord and you not having some blasphemous thoughts about that cute country boy you done snagged."

The changing room seemed to slant like a ship making a hard turn, they all laughed so hard.

"Beanie, that's your mind in that gutter," Ramona said. "Now shut the heck up and give me back my pressed powder before I tell everybody what you whispered to me last Third Sunday."

"Ooh, ooh, tell us, Ramona," the whole dressing room begged as if it were singing in a run.

"Watch yourself, Ramona." Beanie put her hands on her hips and feigned sternness.

"It ain't nothing, y'all"—Ramona tried to keep herself from laughing—"just that Beanie was telling me that Freddie, the usher, wears a toupee."

"Ooh, no, he doesn't," Ella said as she slapped Beanie on the back, "and how would our Beanie come to know this?"

"Came off in her hand," Ramona said, pressing tears from her eyes she was laughing so hard.

More room-slanting laughter.

"But wait, wait"—Ramona tried to catch her breath—"that ain't the funny part."

"Ramona, you know like I know you better save your lungs for the song you gotta sing," Beanie said.

"Beanie, tell it, please, y'all got to hear this," Ramona gasped.

"Awl, shucks, y'all." Beanie pushed her way to the center of the tight room. "Everybody knows Freddie is like my man now, okay. We christened our relationship 'bout a month ago."

"Unhuh," and "Yeah, we know," and "Okay, none of us in here is gonna put the moves on Freddie" floated through the changing room.

"So all I did last Third Sunday," Beanie went on, "was describe to my bigmouth sister in song, Ramona, over here how I was running my fingers through what I thought was his hair, you know, I'm into it, maybe I was pulling the man's hair a little rougher than I should have, and the toupee came off in my hand, scared me so bad, I thought I had pulled up my own body parts, like darn, is this man making me explode so much my own stuff is coming off?"

Now it was as if the ceiling had caved in on the close room. They laughed so hard they staggered into one another and fell all over the changing-room floor. Ramona laughed too, leaned up against the ledge under the mirror, arm pressed into her stomach; she laughed like she rarely did. In fact, it was only during these precious minutes when the women of the choir fused together in this tight closet of a room that she laughed like this. She had no girlfriends with whom she could laugh like this; her mean streak she knew would quickly alienate any woman who would seriously try to be her friend. So even though her choir members made overtures when she'd see one or the other on Sixtieth Street, the el, at Penn Fruit, or Miss D's beauty parlor, they'd call out, "Hey, girl, call me, we got to talk," Ramona never did call. She blamed it on her day job, tending to the fosters, trying to keep Mae off her back, spending nights with the man/men in her life, told herself that closeness between women was a frivolous endeavor that she would get around to one day when she could finally siphon off some free time. She really meant when she could sustain a decent attitude and keep her mean streak at bay. But during these segments when they changed in and out of their choir robes, sharing makeup and man stories, tucking one another's bra straps so they wouldn't show, knocking elbows and shoulders and behinds, Ramona felt loose, unfettered, like she rarely did.

But now she was standing on the choir loft, the giddiness she'd felt in the changing room was gone and her insides were locked again as she looked around the congregation and tried not to see the longtime married couples like Mr. and Mrs. John sitting right in her view, holding hands, Mrs. John elegantly middle-aged with her center city–coiffured hair, Mr. John glinting up at Ramona, vestiges of his and Ramona's passion-filled trysts hanging in his eyes. And seeing it in Mr. John's eyes made Ramona's own eyes turn inward and recall it for herself.

She was only nineteen when she'd tried it with him. She'd just been promoted to assistant buyer, and Mae had bragged about it all over West Philly, and people were stopping Ramona on the street to congratulate her. Then Mr. John pulled up in a rented Fleetwood, backseat strewn with a dozen long-stem roses and an ice bucket cooling off fifty-dollar champagne. "Get in, Miss Ramona," he said. "I'm going to introduce you to the high-class mature way of celebrating your notable accomplishment."

She was young and impressionable, so she got in the car, let him take her up to Belmont Plateau, where she'd been so many times, too many times before, with any one of countless boyfriends, they could have been the same they were so much alike, so young, greedy, fast. But Mr. John was at least twice her age, and she tingled at the way the gray in his hair almost sparkled as they watched the city lights come on through the tinted windows of the Fleetwood Cadillac. They sipped champagne as he whispered compliments to her success and her beauty and her brains. She giggled and cooed and blushed inside. His hands were strong and smooth inching up her thighs, his lips hot and coarse barely sliding down her throat, until his hands and lips met at her center and it was so easy, too easy for her to part herself and let him take her, over and over, on the supple leather of the oversized backseat. After that it was those hands and lips and his slow-moving manhood in the best suite at the Airport Motel, or the borrowed apartment of his richest friend, even the back room of the real estate office when his wife took the evening off. And then there was his generosity, the fifty-dollar bills he'd fold into her bra, twice, sometimes three times a month—"Don't want my baby to have to worry about lunch money," he'd say—the better-quality stockings he'd surprise her with, six, eight pair at a time. "Love looking at those big, pretty legs under this smooth silk," he'd croon. She'd go to get her hair done and get up out of the chair and reach for her purse and hear Miss D's voice whispering, ringing in her ear, "Your sugar daddy done already taken care of it, sweetheart. What kind of mojo you gone and put on that man anyhow? Shit, give me some of that. Let me whip it on my man." They were together the whole summer into the fall of 1960, discreet; she was very respectful of his wife, never left her fancy underwear around the office, like she'd heard some women did. Then one night, a big night, Mr. John had just gotten the deal to be the closing agent on the abandoned bread factory, could net him thousands in commissions if he could move it, they celebrated so hard at a suite at the Warwick, he'd gulped down water glass after water glass of Johnnie Walker Red, couldn't do anything but lie back and squeeze Ramona's finely pressed hair against his chest, talking drunk talk, slurring his words, getting raunchy, too raunchy, so raunchy that Ramona wanted to tell him to shut up because she knew he was about to say something that would turn her insides to ice from then on whenever she looked at him. He did too. Told her she was the best piece he'd ever had, and he'd had some good ass, he said. She was even better than that drooping-eyed Mae.

    She looked away from the Johns and tilted the microphone down and slightly away from her mouth so the sounds of her breathing wouldn't be amplified. At least she didn't have to vomit now when she thought about it, the way she'd vomited for a solid week after that night. Couldn't look at Mae for a time either. Not that she was jealous; she knew Mae would spread herself in a flash to negotiate payment of a debt, no difference to Mae between doing that and going under her bra to pull out a ten-dollar bill. It was just the knowledge that she and her very own mother had shared in the one thing that mothers and daughters should never share, even if her time with Mr. John had been spaced years from Mae's. For a while after that she couldn't even be with anyone she felt so dented and rusty inside. Like a silver-toned can that's dropped from up high so many times until even the dents turn a burnt-orange shade of roughness.

Now Mr. John was smiling, blew her a subtle kiss. She rolled her eyes and looked away. Looked instead at the pianist choir director, who was finishing up his prelude to the song; his graceful fingers flittered around the keys in a buildup that was not only gospel but classical, blues, and jazz. He nodded at Ramona, a nod filled with assurances that what was to come was very good indeed. Beanie reached over and tugged the generous pleat in Ramona's robe sleeve, an encouraging tug. Someone up in the balcony called out, "All right now, Ramona." And now Ramona felt propped up, protected, ensconced like she rarely did.

She listened for the spaces in the piano keys. Then she closed her eyes, closed her eyes on all her wrongdoing: on Mr. John and every other man she'd been with whom she had no rights to; on the profanity that slid off her tongue like butter; on the hatred she had for her own mother; the meanness she showed the children; the misdirected anger that had made her slap Victoria's innocent face. She closed her eyes and started to sing about, no, beg for peace.

She was midway through her song about a ship caught in a storm, had sung about the tempest raging, the billows tossing high, no shelter, and no help. And then those wavy lines that she always felt in her chest when she sang this song were moving through her chest. And she was at the part in the song when she was asking the Lord doesn't he care that she might perish. And the lines in her chest were trying to rise to the top and break through that block of granite that always came up too, sure as those lines did when she sang this song. When she was trying to get peace, whether she was trying finally to leave Mae's or let herself know honest love, that obstruction would come up, and her insides would go dark, all but obliterating those lines that were wavy and green like fresh-cut grass or a sapling of a girl child trying to live. Then she threw her head back, raised her hands toward the rafters, and in a voice so clouded with emotion that it was as if a fog had settled over the church and turned everything a silvery beautiful blue, she chanted, "Get up, Jesus," and the church went into a hollering, crying frenzy. Then the choir came in for the refrain, and their collected voices bounced up to the dome-shaped ceiling and hung there until they fell back on the congregation like rain. Ramona just listened to this part, caught her breath as they called for peace, be still, as they crescendoed. And it was always here, while she waited for her cue to rejoin the song, that Ramona's eyes welled up and the congregation stood on their feet, clapped their appreciation for her for allowing herself to become so Holy Spirit–filled that she had to cry while she sang. Except they didn't know that Ramona really cried because once again that block of granite had not succumbed to her cries for peace. Once again she'd gotten confirmation that the devil had such a lock on her insides that she would always be mean, deceitful, hate-filled. So she cried out loud and Beanie rubbed her back, and then she rejoined the choir, closed her eyes again on Mr. and Mrs. John, and sang about the peace she feared she would never have.

S HERN was wide-awake in this house she hated. It was after midnight, and the velvet bedroom air rippled with the night sounds: her sisters breathing, the occasional clank and hiss of the radiator, the wind spitting against the window. The sounds were tinged with a starkness as if she could see what she was hearing her senses heightened so. Her senses needed to be heightened, she reasoned, to keep her alert to when that devil-formed Addison was slinking around.

She thought about how she had botched her attempts at communicating with the aunts and uncles earlier. Told herself that it was probably for the better; they might have rushed right over there, gotten themselves in trouble. It would be better, she reasoned, if she went to them. She let the thought of telling Vie about Addison's violation twist and turn in her head, asking Vie, could they please go stay with their aunts and uncles until their mother was well. But in her mind it was Vie who was keeping her from the aunts and uncles. It was Vie who had assured them that they were going to love it here. It was Vie whose own brother had taunted them and made Victoria fall. Who knows where they'd end up should she complain to Vie? Might end up someplace worse than here. Was there even worse than here? She might be separated from her sisters; that would be worse than here.

She blew a tear-laden sigh into the dark bedroom air at the thought of being separated from Victoria and Bliss. Victoria stirred and whimpered and moaned groggily about her knee hurting so bad and then pressed her head against Shern's chin and was sound asleep again. Now Shern felt the sound of her sister's pain in her stomach too.

She drew herself up slowly from where she had been cupped into the twin bed the three sisters shared. Mae actually allowed them more room than the one bed; there was a twin bed next to the one on which they slept, and there was a hunter green velveteen sofa bed under the window. But the girls preferred being cramped to being separated through the night; they'd already lost both parents in a sense, so they locked their bodies into curves on that single bed that accommodated the three in a relatively fitful sleep.

But now Shern was wide-awake, listening to the night sounds, feeling them twirl in her stomach, and needing to go to the bathroom. But how could she go to the bathroom? The bathroom was at the other end of the hall. She was afraid to go, afraid that that Addison might be crouching in the shadows of the upstairs hall. She'd have to hold it until morning. Now there was a river between her legs at the thought of holding it until morning. She'd have to go now.

She wrapped herself in her lime green velour bathrobe and pulled the belt tight around her waist, the shawl collar close against her neck. The robe still smelled like the Bonwit Teller box it had come in, like the sweetness of the sample bath crystals that had been tucked into a silk purse in the corner of the box. "Ooh, Mommie," she'd said when she'd opened the box, "oooh, it's like something a grown lady would wear, ooh, I love it, Mommie." She pushed her hands into the oversized slit pockets of the soft, sweet-smelling robe. Her finger went straight through a hole in the pocket. Her mother had cut a small square of the fabric when Shern went to a sleep-over party at the home of a new friend. Clarise didn't know the people well enough to feel entirely comfortable, so she'd cut the square and put it under her pillow and told Shern to make sure that she slept in the robe that night so that she would return safely to her. Shern had laughed at her mother and called her silly and superstitious. Now she swallowed the cotton that came up in her throat at the thought of her mother. Wished she had a piece of her mother's robe that she could put under her pillow to make sure her mother was returned safely to her.

She pulled back the bedroom door ever so slowly. The hallway smelled like the barbecued chicken Ramona had cooked for dinner. She hoped the barbecued chicken smell wouldn't get into her robe; she didn't want to carry the smells of this house back with her when she finally returned to her real home.

She half skated, half slid down the hallway. The plastic runner covering the wall-to-wall carpeting was cool and slick against her bare feet. She held her breath until she was at the opened bathroom door, rushed in and closed the door, and quickly and firmly affixed the lock.

The bathroom was small and warm. A pink night-light softened the black-and-white ceramic tile, and Shern felt safe in here with the door good and locked. She sat on the toilet for a long while and listened to the sounds of the cellar heater hum and pulse through the radiator and mix with her own stomach growling. She hadn't eaten dinner, had stayed cloistered in that bedroom all afternoon after she'd bungled that phone call, tensed up, expecting

Ramona to rush in the room any minute and berate her the way she'd expected when Ramona caught her with the phone in her hand.

The radiator clanged, and Shern jumped; she settled back down when she realized it was just the heater shutting off. The bathroom went silent. That's when another sound came into focus. A quiet and dark sound. She squinted, as if the squinting could help her hear. The way she'd squint when she'd heard Ramona's bed creaking and Tyrone's muffled breaths, which seemed to sift through the walls and land sharp and hard against her ears and made her feel nauseated and clammy, and warm and confused. This sound she heard now didn't come from Ramona's room, though; this sound came from the basement straight up through the radiator, it seemed. She could almost taste the dust on her tongue as she tried to picture the basement filled with all of Mae's retired furniture, couches and end tables and lamps turned sideways or upside down to take up less room because there were so many pieces down there, much of it looking practically new. She wondered why Mae seemed to replace her furniture so often. Her own mother had prided herself on the mahogany china closet that had been the uncles', the handmade cedar chest that had been the aunts'. "Junk, they make such junk now," her mother would say, and turn up her aquiline nose as she fingered a mass-produced vase, or lamp, or bookend.

Then Shern heard the sounds again. As if the air in the basement were being chewed and spit. She could make out the words, horrible words, now they were piercingly clear. She could hear Victoria's name, so now she had to listen as Mae called Ramona a worthless, whoring hussy.

"Let that child fall and hurt herself, I should knock the living shit out of you."

Crying. "I'm moving from here. I'm not putting up with you anymore and your deranged self."

"You just try it. I don't know where in the hell you think you going where you can live as cheaply as you do here."

"Cheaply! All the money I give you."

"You don't give me shit."

"And all I do for you around here."

"You don't do shit."

"All the money you gamble away."

A slap.

"Hit me again, here."

"And what you gonna do, you gonna hit your mother back, huh? You just try it and I'll have Bernie put your ass under the jail, you worthless, mean, no-good hussy."

"If I am worthless, if I am mean, you made me that way."

"Awl, get outta my face, go cock your legs open for that little ol poor country boy you saddled up with. That's why you let that little girl get hurt like that. Go on and get out of my face before I hit you in your mouth this time. Disrespecting me, you—you."

"You just a crazy miserable old lady."

A slap.

Sobbing. "You just wait and see, I'm getting outta here, just wait and see." Footsteps on the stairs. The plastic on the couch in the living room screaming, then settling to a low, steady moan.

Shern jumped up from the toilet and slid along the plastic hallway runner back into the bedroom. She closed the door and leaned against the door to catch her breath. She undid her soft lime green robe and tossed it on the other bed and squeezed back into the bed her sisters shared. She burrowed her head in her arms and prayed for morning to find them back in their real home, prayed that she was caught in a nightmare that she hadn't been able to wake from. She didn't know, though, that there had been another Donald Booker sighting on Dead Block that evening. That Hettie had hollered across Addison Street to Mae, "Hear that evil spirit of that missing white boy was kicking up in the park again and now the Lawsons can't find their German shepherd puppy." And that whenever there was a Donald Booker sighting, which happened five, six times a year and was never, ever substantiated, an agitation between Mae and Ramona would sprout up like a well-fertilized weed and cause such consternation, arguments, even fights sometimes worse than the one they'd just had. All Shern knew was that the bad air between Mae and Ramona might spread to her sisters and her, might cause Mae to slap at them.

Her chest was on fire. She got up again and grabbed her lime green robe and wrapped herself in it. She climbed back in bed, nestled her head under the robe's collar, and pushed her finger through the hole in the pocket her mother had cut. She clamped her eyes shut and swallowed her sobs as she thought about the sound of her uncle Blue's voice earlier that day. Eventually she fell back to sleep dreaming about the aunts and uncles.

12

BLUE'S sherry-induced euphoria of Sunday afternoon had lifted this Monday morning, and now his clear head told him he had hung up the phone too fast. He stood next to Til as she mixed around in the steaming pot of linseed and coconut oils for the next batch of soap they were readying.

Til didn't even have to turn to look at him to see something was wrong. Blue was the closest to her in age, and from the time they were children, whenever he stood right next to her not saying anything, just weighing down the air with his sighs, she knew something had bothered him so deeply he was getting ready to cry. "What's the matter, Blue?" she asked, pausing over the huge pot to reverse the direction she stirred. "Hangover wrapping around you like a spider's web?"

"For your information my mind's quite clear, thank you."

"Well, what then? Don't tell me you and Show didn't finish fashioning the molds. Now, you're the ones who insisted on doing ovals instead of squares this year, so it's up to you to have those molds ready when the tallow is."

"Molds done, Til. Coconut flecks heaped in a mound ready to be pinched into the honey, cellophane wrappings measured and cut, Ness and Show just counted them out, two thousand, right?"

"So if everything's in order"—Til stopped stirring and looked directly at Blue—"why does the air all around you feel like it's wearing steel-plated boots?"

Blue couldn't hold it. Started crying like he was five years old. "I can't believe what I did, Til, Til, I feel so bad."

Til banged her wooden ladle against the side of the stove. "Stop crying, Blue. Now toughen up and tell me what you did."

Ness and Show were standing in the kitchen doorway. Show carried the vat of honey for mixing with the tallow, set it on the floor next to the stove, reached into his back pocket, and pulled out his white cotton handkerchief, which he handed to Blue.

"What did he do, Sister?" Ness asked as she stood over the pot and sniffed. "My, my, my, Sister, that coconut smells heavenly; I do think we should go up on the price twenty-five cents a bar this year."

"Next year, Ness. Catalog's already out with the price, and you know that white man that stamps his name on our soap is not budging a penny from his profit to add to ours."

Blue honked into the handkerchief and called attention back to himself. "My world is crashing in on me over what I've done, and all you two can do is talk profits."

"When you ready to pull yourself together and straighten your backbone and talk without a quivering to your voice, I'll listen," Til said. And to Show: "That honey's ready to be sprinkled with the coconut flecks, isn't it? Let's have as much out of the way as possible so we can meet the beginning of visitors' hours at Clarise's bedside, especially after her relapse."

"Lord, Lord, Lord, and she was doing so well too." Ness sighed.

Blue cried openly again at the mention of Clarise's name. He leaned his bent elbow on Show's shoulder. "Brother, Brother, I can tell you what I've done, can't I?"

"Speak to me, Blue," Show said. "You've got both my ears."

"Brother, I think I hung the phone up right in the ear of one of the daughters."

"What!" all three shouted in unison.

Til went to Blue and pulled him from Show's shoulder, reached up and put her hands on his forearms, shook him. "Look me in the eye and talk to me. Talk me true, talk me now."

"Lord, please talk to her," Ness chimed in.

"Yesterday afternoon, when the phone rang and I answered, and I thought it was some pervert just breathing hard and moaning into the phone—"

"When I asked you who was on the phone?"

"Yes, yes, yes. I hung up, just banged it down on the receiver. Didn't give it another thought until I woke this morning with the daughters on my mind and my chest riddled with guilt."

"What makes you so sure it was one of the daughters?" Til asked. She stared off into the smoke the boiling soap made. She moved her hands from Blue's arms and rubbed her own as if she'd just caught a chill.

"Does anybody ever ring this phone on a Sunday? Think about it," Blue said, putting his hand to his forehead. "Since Finch's tragedy has that phone rang once on a Sunday afternoon?"

"Brother has a point," Ness said.

"Damn good point," Show added.

"And this morning, as I lay in bed and tried to catch my breath over what I'd done, I realized that I heard her voice as the phone was on the way down. She was saying—she was saying, 'It's me, it's me.'" He hung his head in his hands and sobbed.

"It was Shern?" Til asked.

Blue nodded from his hands.

"It was Shern," Til said to Ness and Show as if they hadn't also seen Blue's head going up and down in his hands. "Distraught too, or she would have spoken sooner. It was Shern."

"What we gonna do, Sister?" Ness asked as she squeezed her fingers and spun her hands in circles.

Til turned the flame down under the pot of boiling soap. "We gonna finish up this batch of soap. We gonna meet visiting hours at Clarise's bedside, we gonna pass some money down at Family Court and find out where they placed those girls, we gonna say fuck some motherfucking judge's ruling, we gonna go see about those girls."

Over that next week, while the aunts and uncles waited to hear news on the girls' whereabouts from a buggy-eyed clerk who said he had a friend whose cousin was married to Vie's assistant, they occupied themselves with their soap. That's all they could do. Clarise's visiting hours had been restricted again down to thirty minutes a day after her episode of mania the week before, and since they knew the importance of keeping the hands moving when the heart is standing still, they doubled their usual production of two thousand bars of soap to four.

Exotic-shaped ovals this soap was, cream-colored with golden patches where the honey had settled in clumps; white flecks of coconut in the honey looked like snowflakes; the coconut and honey scent with a hint of linseed oil drifted through the cellophane and heightened the exotic, tropical appearance of the soap. They wrapped all four thousand bars in clear cellophane. Sent it to the distributor, who would stamp it with a fancy gold label and his French-sounding name and pay them half of the $1.99 price listed in the catalog. Four times a year they did this, and their soap was always the first item to sell out from the catalog distributed to those who could afford $2 for a single bar of soap. Only the distributor knew the fine coconut-honey soap was made by a quartet of American blacks. But the aunts and uncles didn't mind the anonymity. They understood that maybe rice might sell with a black face attached to it, pancake mix for sure, but not soap, not in 1965, when Alabama and Mississippi were called the places where democracy doesn't apply to the Negro and cities in the North and East were prone to eruptions of race riots again in the summer.

So the aunts and uncles worked without recognition, lived quiet, modest lives on their soap profits, plus the money they earned from leasing their daddy's land. They spent their money on quality rather than show so their possessions could last a lifetime. And always, always, they put up a portion of their earnings for Clarise and the girls to inherit.

And now a week later they finally heard some news on the girls. It wasn't really news, though, more like an update that Vie had so many confidential stickers on the girls' paperwork that it would take at least another two days. And this information only after Til surprised the buggy-eyed clerk as he stepped out of his basement apartment on Broad Street, headed for the newsstand on the corner to buy a tripack of Old Original El Producto cigars. Til walked right up next to him, pushed her voice through the March wind right into his pointed ears, and said, "Either I get their whereabouts, or my money back, or your forehead mounds out to twice its size on a permanent basis."

Til agreed to wait two more days. This was Monday morning, Wednesday, she insisted. She'd better know what she needed to know by Wednesday.

This Monday morning was a vulture for Ramona. A barnyard buzzard. Circling, ready to swoop down and pick at those parts of herself that had died over the weekend, a snatch of her spirit, a fleck of her ambition, little fragments of her soul. She was even dressed in black this morning, ready to go to her job at Lit Brothers bargain basement. She and Mae had fought all week long. Over money: Ramona confronted Mae about calling the store and charging things against her paycheck; Mae told Ramona to look at it as going toward the rent she should be paying. Over Addison: Ramona insisted that he go out and at least bag groceries at the Penn

Fruit, offer to walk people home and carry their bags, at least make a couple of dollars a day in tips instead of lying around the house all day, eating all the food, burning electricity running the television all the time; Mae said he'd been through a trauma in Buffalo, he needed time to clear his head. Over Larry: He'd followed the girls home from school one day last week, and Ramona was beginning to agree with what Tyrone had said after the first time it happened, that he might need to be reported; Mae slapped Ramona then, told her don't be quoting that poor little old country boy to her, who was gonna pay her bills if Vie stopped placing children with her?

This most recent fight over Larry happened the night before, and Ramona's jaw was still sore this Monday morning as she studied the skirt of her black knit set and then thought about what those girls would have for breakfast. She gently dabbed her skirt with a piece of rolled-up masking tape to pick off the lint and decided they would have cereal. She was careful with her appearance, meticulous. Even though she couldn't afford to shop the upper levels, she doted on her acrylics like they were cashmere, her nylon blends like they were silk. She squinted to make sure she'd gotten all the lint. But it was dark in here for 7:00 A.M.

She rolled the shades all the way up in the kitchen, trying to get some natural sunlight in there; she even went into the living room and dining room to roll up shades. Then she remembered the shed door right off the kitchen was closed. Her dose of morning light came through that window in the shed. But now Addison was sleeping there.

She pushed the door open anyhow and tugged on the shade string and let it go quickly. The shade unwrapped to the top of the window with a bang. The noise and the sudden onslaught of light woke Addison, and he sat up, his face fixed in a confused scowl. "Whoa, cuz, what's your problems, why you gonna insult me with such a rude wake-up? I mean, damn, cuz, I ain't been here but a week, and this is how you gonna treat me."

"Time for anything big and dumb as you to have his lazy ass

up." Ramona went back and sat at the kitchen table and tilted her face to catch the light streaming in from the shed. "If you not interested in any kind of school, the least you can do is get up and go out and try to find a piece of a job to help pay for your room and board around here."

"You mean, I gots to pay for this shit." He wrapped his torso in the sheet he had slept under and picked his Wranglers up from the floor. He rifled in his pocket and lifted out a rumpled soft pack of Winston filter tips. He leaned back after he had lit one and inhaled and smiled.

Ramona ignored him and sipped at her coffee and thanked God she had her job to go to.

"Aren't you gonna ask me what I'm smiling 'bout, cuz?" Addison's voice cut into her thoughts.

"I'm not asking you shit," she said, and turned her back on the shed and sipped at her coffee.

"I'll tell you anyhow. I was just thinking 'bout the hot time I had last night with this foxy little chick from Sayre school."

"Sayre's a junior high school, you stupid asshole." She said it in an unaffected voice and got up to set out cereal bowls for those three.

"So?"

"So, that means she can't be more than thirteen or fourteen."

"Hmh. STP all right."

"What?"

"STP. You know sweet tender pus—"

"I'm not listening to this." Ramona banged the last bowl on the table and turned her AM radio up high. "You're a cruel imitation of a human being. I hope somebody's father really does shoot you right through the balls."

"Well, it won't be yours, huh, cuz? Seeing as how you don't even know who he is."

Ramona cringed when he said that and started running tap water full blast in her coffee cup, trying to blot out Addison's voice. "I can't hear you, fool." She shouted it over and over as she sponged out her cup and set it on the drainer next to the sink. She snatched open the silverware drawer and picked up a handful of forks and spoons and threw them back down, once, twice, before she took out three spoons to set on the table next to the bowls. That's when she turned around and saw Mae standing there just watching her with a steady expression like she was waiting for a traffic light to turn green.

"Cut the foolishness, and bring me my coffee, would you, please?" Mae said as she plopped in the chair at the head of the table. "And turn that radio down. That dumb DJ Georgie Woods can't find nothing better to say than 'Ladies, y'all got your girdles on?'"

Addison came out of the shed laughing. He had his Wranglers on now, and he went to Mae and kissed her cheek. "Morning, aunts," he said. Then he turned to Ramona as she set a cup of coffee down in front of Mae. "I'll have one of those, cuz."

"You'll get it yourself," Ramona said, her voice markedly lower. She went back to the cabinet and took down a box of shredded wheat and tore open the white waxy pouch with her teeth. She placed a biscuit in each bowl, taking her time. She knew Mae was watching her, the way she always did after they had a blowup, studying her, waiting to see if she acted differently. She never had. She didn't now.

"Oh, so you gonna leave me hanging on the coffee, cuz," Addison said, oblivious to the tension between those two.

Mae slapped Addison playfully on the behind. "Let her get those girls their breakfast first and tell me how did little old cot been sleeping my nephew."

Addison stretched and pulled at the air and said, "Actually, Aunt Mae, I don't think that cot has the support it used to have; In fact, I was noticing you got some pretty all right couches in the basement down there—"

"Don't have to say another word," Mae said, smiling up at Addison, almost wanting to rub his straight, silky hair the way she would when he was much younger. "Go right down there right now and pick the one you want and move it on up to the shed."

He was out of the kitchen before the words were from her mouth good and it was just Mae and Ramona once again, and Georgie Woods blaring through the radio, "Ladies, it's Monday morning. Y'all got your girdles on?"

"I thought I told you to turn that mess off." Mae made slurping sounds as she drank her coffee.

Ramona didn't move toward the radio though. She busied herself mixing powdered orange juice crystals and water. The spoon hit the inside of the glass pitcher in rapid clanks as she put all of her force into the stirring.

There was a commercial on now about Carolina Rice, and Mae tapped her fingers to the beat. "Ramona, I was thinking . . . I got the taste for some fish tonight. Why don't you stop when you come off the el and pick us up some butterfish. Can't nobody fry up some butterfish like you. Tell them to leave the heads on this time, too."

"I can't cook tonight." Ramona said it matter of factly as she poured the juice into three short glasses.

"What you mean you can't cook tonight?"

"I won't be here."

Mae took a long, loud slurp of coffee and then put her cup down slowly, making sure its base fit exactly in the circle in the saucer. She smoothed her hand over the scarf that covered her head full of small sponge rollers. She let her hand come to rest at the nape of her neck. She fingered the collar to her robe. "And where might you be?" She asked it quickly, like a fast whisper.

"My choir's singing out tonight, at a revival," she lied.

"And we're supposed to do what for dinner?"

"You could have hoagies, you could have cheese steaks, you could have Chinese food." She poured sugar from a five-pound bag into the crystal sugar dish. "You could cook." It came out unintended, just oozed out like wet noodles sliding through a colander when the holes are too large.

Mae's lazy eye shot way open as if she were amused. "I could. I could also knit you scarves like those girls' poor crazy mother; hear tell when they went in that house to bring her out there were big old skeins of yarn all over the place, all tangled up, half-done pieces of hats and sweaters strewn all around, big old bruised hole in her hand from the knitting needles. So yeah, I could cook, and I could take up knitting too, but I ain't doing neither." She drained her cup in a noisy swallow. "Pour me more coffee, would you, please?"

Mae sat back quite satisfied with herself as Ramona turned to pour her coffee. She was looking at Ramona's back now and was struck by Ramona's figure in that black knit. She was often struck by Ramona's figure: the long, slender neck, the straight shoulders, the tiny waist, the perfect curve to her hips, the healthy legs with the well-defined calves. She so hated her own squatty, short-necked, short-waisted, thin-legged frame. Hated it so much she'd never hung a full-length mirror in that house. The only full-length mirror was in Ramona's room, the rest of the house had only squares and ovals for looking at the face. She didn't mind her own face much, not a bad face for a woman in her forties; even if her right eye drooped, she thought she had a well-built nose and a nice straight mouth, not a full mouth like Ramona's mouth, but she knew how to use her mouth to its best advantage, got everything she needed from her ward leader by putting her mouth to its best use.

But now she was looking at Ramona's face as Ramona set her coffee down. Now that child had a face, especially with her hair done up in that French roll, blond streaks to highlight it, the black against her light skin, the gray-toned eye shadow making her saucer eyes appear deeper inset than they already were, even the way the orange-red frosted lipstick was painted on that perfectly full mouth. She resisted telling Ramona what a fine young woman she was, spoil a child when you compliment them too much, she knew that. And once she started with the compliments she might end up all the way back there when Ramona was a cute little cuddly girl in her light blue cotton blouse and new maroon oxford school shoes and loved nothing better than the sight of her mother. No sense in dredging up the past and everything that went with the past by complimenting her at this stage in her life.

"Before you leave outta here, tell me one thing, please," Mae asked instead. "Why do you insist on wearing those black stockings on your legs? I've told you before they make you look like you trying to be a whore, either that or like you trying to hide the fact that you're yellow. Which is it?"

Used to Mae's rhetorical insults, Ramona didn't answer; she was busy thinking about what Mae had said about those girls' mother, wondering how Victoria felt watching her mother go crazy like that. And now she was thinking about Victoria's knee, about how she was still limping when she'd passed her in the hallway this morning. She sliced up bananas over the three bowls of shredded wheat. "I think that middle one needs to go to the doctor," she said into the bowls.

"What you mumbling about, girl? Speak up." Georgie's voice was coming through the radio again. "Especially if you insist on listening to all that mess all loud, you got to speak up."

"That middle one, the hurt one—"

"You mean, the one you let get hurt."

"She needs to see a doctor," Ramona shouted it.

"When did you notice, hawkeye?"

"Pus still draining, she's still limping, and it's been more than a week since she fell. Not good, might be infected."

"Well, Ramona, isn't that exactly the point I was trying to make with you after it happened, that the child was hurt? You know I hate to be cursing and carrying on, acting like a maniac around here, but your ineptness brings that out in me."

Ramona flinched and rubbed her tongue inside her jaw. "I know my mouth is still sore from last night. You just better be glad it's not swollen or I was gonna have to call out sick from work today, and we get docked two days for calling out on a Monday."

"No, darling"—Mae slurped her coffee again and paused to swallow and let out a small belch—"you just better be glad it's not swollen."

"So you gonna take her to the clinic?" Ramona asked, shrugging off Mae's last comment, just wanting to get Victoria's medical needs met so she could get the hell out of here and go to work. "I would, but like I just said, I can't call out from my job on a Monday."

"I will, I will. Ain't no sense in me trying to hide the fact that the child got hurt, the child is hurt, I know hurt in children when I come across it. I'm just gonna have to fill out those thousand forms and document it. So before you walk out of that door, leave enough money on the table for hoagies for dinner since you won't be here to cook and I got to spend what little I got at the clinic on that child you let get hurt."

Now Stevie Wonder was blowing "Fingertips" on the harmonica and Addison danced his way back into the kitchen. Mae let out a little hoot and clapped her hands to the rhythm of his dancing feet. "Get it, Addison." She laughed. She pushed herself up from the table and danced a few steps with him. "My boy," she said, "go on with your bad self." She reached out and grabbed Ramona's arm. "Come on, Ramona, dance with your momma and your cousin. You know you can dance us both under the table with your pretty self."

Ramona pulled her arm from Mae's, not a jerk but still a determined pull. This is as close as Mae would come to apologizing. Ramona knew that. No matter. She wouldn't have to feel anything but relief when she could leave here finally. A good belch after a bad meal that wouldn't go down right is what it would feel like to leave. Another few months for her to have her finances right, and she would be able to do it, finally, run away across town to that apartment building in Germantown, the one that looked like it was sitting in the middle of the woods with its abundance of southern-exposed one-bedrooms, the one she was going to see tonight. She hoped she could go all the way through with leaving this time. Each time she'd come this close it seemed a rock was placed in her path, then the rock in her chest that wouldn't let her breathe, then her feet would go to cement, and she'd be plastered there, stuck in that house with the fosters winding in and out, and the new couch always coming, and Mae with her mean ways and incessant mother-cloaked demands.

Addison was dipping and twirling all through the kitchen, and Ramona had to dodge his waving hands or she would have surely been hit.

She went into the living room to get her coat from the closet and called up the stairs for those three to hurry up so they could have breakfast. "And don't dump the whole sugar dish in your cereal," she said.

"Yes, Ramona," she heard Victoria answer. She almost wanted to wait for them to get down the stairs, wanted to look on Victoria's sad, lean face for a minute before she left. Addison and Mae were still laughing and dancing in the kitchen. It was time for her to get to work. Time for her to pretend she empathized with her coworkers' complaints about having to come to work on Mondays. She left two dollars on the coffee table for their hoagie dinner. "Lord, thank you for this piece of a job that I can go to today," she whispered as she stepped out into the sun and walked quickly up the street, headed for the el that would take her to work.

Because she really did love her job, especially when no one called out sick and she wasn't pulled down on the selling floor. She preferred working with merchandise over people. She developed feelings for the items that ended up in her department: the low-budget, cheaper knockoffs of originals, picked over by buyers from all over the world, then rejected. The selling floor in the half-lit basement was the last stop before they were finally discarded, donated maybe to some famous charity for the tax write-off, but no longer on display, no longer having a shot at being chosen.

Tyrone hadn't come back over the night before. Even though Ramona had whispered that Mae was going out to play cards, why didn't he come and keep her company after she got back from the night service where her choir was singing and after those girls went to bed? He declined, though. Said he had to be up early to start running a big four-color job, the church program covers for Palm Sunday. Ramona almost asked him then what her name was. She held her tongue, though. Had heard too many men complain to her over the years about their nagging, suspicious wives or other lovers. She shook her head even now thinking about it as she turned the corner off Addison Street. They'd be laying up with her with their pants down and complaining because they had suspicious wives. Her consolation was that Tyrone was honest enough, and they'd been together for almost nine months; he wouldn't be able to lie for long and look her right in her face. At least she hoped. She decided she wouldn't confront him just yet, she'd try to wait it out; a confession rising up out of his own guilt was better than one dragged out by a confrontation. And maybe he wouldn't even confess; maybe he'd be so bothered if she didn't get in the way of his guilt and just allowed it to fester, maybe he'd just stop. She put Tyrone from her mind as headed for the el, she walked past Perry's printshop. She looked straight ahead so she wouldn't be tempted to look in the two-way mirror that stretched along the side of the building. Undoubtedly some man would see her and call across the street all loud, "Hey, sugar, you looking good." Or else Perry might be in the shop looking out at her. She quickened her pace at the thought of Perry, trying to outwalk that warm, silky feeling she always got when she thought about him, even now as she was wanting to cry over the wandering attentions of his son. She started up the el steps thinking about how she'd never wanted to cry over a man before.

13

PERRY pulled the shade up on his two-way mirror that took up a side of his printshop and squinted from the suddenness of the light rushing in. Just he and Tyrone in the shop this Monday and the color glossies of JFK, LBJ, and Martin Luther King looking down on them. Tyrone was in the back of the shop greasing down the press, and Perry was at his window; he always started his day at this window, watching the early birds of West Philly rush by. Sometimes they'd stop in front of his mirror, forgetting or not knowing that people inside could see out. And sometimes Perry had to look away, out of respect, like when the women lifted their skirts, maybe to knot the tops of their stockings to hold them at mid-thigh. Other times he'd get a comedy routine as people primped and tilted their hats, or straightened their ties, blended their rouge, or put spit to their eyebrows.

Right now he watched Ramona hurry past like he watched her hurry past every morning at seven forty-five. He instinctively straightened his back and sucked in his gut when she walked by.

She never stopped to check herself in his window mirror, though. She was hard and soft, all right, just like his second wife. Soft look to her that fooled a man, made him think she was the embraceable type, the type that would purr and coo and call him papa. Then turn to steel like his second wife would, have a man's balls dragging the ground, she would get so mean.

He felt sorry for his son that he had fallen for such a hard and soft woman. Tried to tell him, "Man, don't let that beauty blind you. Better to have a less perfect-looking woman who knows how to smile." Tyrone had given him that insulted look, though. Like how dare he try to tell him whom to love. Perry didn't push. He was really just getting reacquainted with the boy. So he didn't want their views on women to come between them at this tender, redevelopmental stage of their father-son two-step. And at least Ramona seemed like a decent enough woman, took pride in her appearance, hardworking, consistent; he couldn't remember not seeing her on the other side of his two-way mirror rounding this same corner every morning for the past five or six years. Seven forty-five, like clockwork. They had that in common, Perry and Ramona, they were both consistent. Not like that night owl Candy, whom Tyrone had left the bar with Saturday night a week ago. Even though Perry had all but set it up by asking Candy to keep an eye on his son, Perry had gotten an unexpected twinge, a tightness in his stomach that he told himself was not envy as he watched Candy take off her yellow headband and then Tyrone lean down and kiss her. Shit, he thought, it wasn't like he and Candy had ever had anything heavy between them. Just some drinks, some talk, some laughs, some pleasures, and that had been more than a decade ago. It's just that when Tyrone took Candy's hand and walked out of that bar, he wasn't gawking. He looked strong to Perry, young and strong, and sure of himself.

"Yo, son, your lady just walked past," Perry said to chase away that twinge that he had convinced himself was not envy. "Yo, Ty," he said again. This time he yelled to be heard over the hum and grunt of the press starting up. "Miss Ramona just turned the corner."

He could see that Tyrone was grinning even from the back. His shoulders got wider suddenly, and his neck tilted. Boy got to learn how not to let his feelings spill all out through his muscles like that, Perry thought. That was his main regret over not having had a greater hand in his raising him, boy never learned the ways of city men, how to hold his face like stone even if he was melting inside.

Tyrone was at the window with Perry now. His whole body grinning. "Where is she, Pops? I don't see her. Which way she go?"

"She gone, boy. Already turned the corner. You should get here early every morning; she walks past every morning the same time. See, you let her keep you up half the night, and then she still gets on up and out to work, and you all drained, dragging in here after nine."

Tyrone didn't tell him that Ramona wasn't the one who'd kept him up last night. "Did she look in just now?"

"Wouldn't matter. How many times I got to tell you? You can see out, but can't no one see in, two-way mirror, Tyrone."

"Yeah, yeah, I forgot. She's fine, ain't she, Pops?"

"You doing it, son." Perry and Tyrone slapped hands, and Perry resisted the urge to lecture. Hell, she was fine. He couldn't deny that.

Tyrone went back to spreading ink over the press, he hummed a few bars of "My Girl" until the press went so loud that he could no longer hear himself. Then he just held the rhythm in his head and sang it in his head, one bar he sang for Ramona because he truly loved her, the next for Candy because he loved the way she drew him out and held on to his explosion all the way until that last spark had fizzled into a tiny red dot. Not even Ramona held on like that. He'd been drawn back to Candy's lair again every night since that Saturday night they met—it was more like a lair than an apartment, with fake animal skins covering the couch, chairs, most of the walls; candles burning in every room; smoked mirrors on the walls that were absent the leopard and tiger prints—and he was going to see her again tonight, and tomorrow. He couldn't help himself. He'd start the day off planning to spend time with Ramona, and Candy would call, rather, purr in his ear, "Please, please come see me tonight. Young blood." She was so attentive to him too, from the crown of his head to the soles of his feet; no part of him escaped her attention, which was soft and thick and warm and creamy. He couldn't pass it up. Would just have to think of some excuse for Ramona about tonight, and tomorrow. He smiled inside; he really felt like a man now, having to think up a lie to tell his main lady so he could spend some time with the one on the side.

He watched the inked pages run through the press so he could settle himself down. Thinking about Candy was gonna have his pants bulging for real in a minute. He concentrated on the pages running through the press, each page sharper than the last until the color and the clarity would be up to Perry's high standards. Tyrone liked running the press. Liked the notion that he was a craftsman like his father. Also liked this feeling of having a woman on the side. Was so secure in his manhood now he didn't even feel the need to brag to his father about the whirlwind week he'd had with Candy.

These blank reams he was sending through the press were becoming bulletin covers for the Palm Sunday service at his and Ramona's church. A flowing white robe surrounded by emerald green palms and pink-centered lilies splashed out on the finished page. Four-color process was a challenge, though; he was studying the lilies, deciding if he needed to spread a bit more red ink to get a deeper pink. He almost didn't hear Perry again. This time telling him that his maybe future mother-in-law was walking past.

"Your momma gonna have to send up some strong southern prayers to protect you from that Mae woman if you and Ramona should ever decide to tie the knot," Perry said as they both looked out the window now. "She's a tough gambling woman, all right. I don't know where she pulls the nurturing from to take care of all those foster kids always coming and going. And that eye, look at it, damn, son, don't you shake in your shoes a little when she fixes that eye on you?"

Tyrone would have laughed, but Victoria was with Mae, limping, hopping actually, her hurt leg bent so she looked like a bona fide cripple. Tyrone's eyebrows dipped way low in concern.

"I'm only messing with you, boy," Perry said as he noticed his son's face, almost stricken-looking.

"Naw, naw." Tyrone waved his hand. "That's not it." And then he was out of the door calling first to Victoria and then to Mae.

Victoria heard him first, so unaccustomed to anyone calling her name on these strange streets. She stopped, glad to stop and lean on the side of the building that housed Perry's printshop and rest her good leg for a second, and then really glad when she saw it was Tyrone saying her name.

Mae walked a few paces before she looked around and realized that Victoria wasn't at her side. "What you stop for, pudding?" she called.

"It's Tyrone." Victoria pointed to Tyrone rushing toward them.

"Your leg's still bothering you that much?" he asked, his face so worried-looking Mae thought there was something else amiss as she walked back to where they were.

"You shouldn't be walking on that leg if it's still hurting that much." He was right next to Victoria now, and his voice and his face softened. "Where you headed anyhow? Why you not going to school today? Where's your sisters?"

"I'm going to the clinic," she said, putting her tongue against her chipped tooth and almost smiling. She was glad to be standing here with Tyrone next to her. The air got warm and spongy when he was around and dabbed at the pain and fear that was usually like silt clinging to her skin, absorbed the silt for a moment and her skin could breathe.

"You shouldn't be walking on that leg." The concern in his voice made it crack, and he cleared his throat and lightly tugged at the pompoms swinging from her hand-knitted cap. "You should be riding."

"Mae doesn't have a car. Ramona doesn't either." Her voice was low and dragging because she was tired and the slower she talked, the longer she could lean on the side of the building while Tyrone cleaned the air.

"I know," he said as he lifted the pile-lined collar to her coat and pulled it up around her neck. It was the only thing he could think to do, hearing how slow her words were falling and thinking it was the pain in her knee coming out in her words. "But couldn't she have gotten a ride or even a cab?"

Now Mae was where they were; she heard the part about the cab. "Lord, Lord, Lord!" she exclaimed before Tyrone could speak to her directly. "Do you know how much they charge you just for sitting in the cab? The meter jumps to sixty-five cents soon as you close the door, and then got the nerve to click every few seconds after that. Lord, no, I can't afford no cab all the way down to Philadelphia General, especially not when the el's right here." She pulled at the ends of her head scarf tied in a bow under her chin and tucked them under the velvet collar of her tweed chesterfield. The coat used to be Ramona's, but Mae had commandeered it, had it shortened, had the buttons moved over to accommodate her wider frame.

Tyrone noticed how off-centered the buttons were, and suddenly that angered him as much as watching Victoria being forced to walk. "Well, how she gonna get up and down those el steps? Looks to me like she can barely walk on the level ground."

"We don't have a choice, now do we?" Mae switched to her proper voice, the one she used for the caseworkers and judges. She pulled Victoria to her and squeezed her shoulder. "I'm explaining to you that I don't have money for a cab. I mean, we're on our way to see about her leg, what else can I do? I mean, I'm doing the best I can. Now maybe your daddy wants to loan you his big fine brand-new deuce and a quarter since I don't think you have much of a car to drive, least every time I see you, you seem to be walking, so unless you willing to go one better than my best and give us a ride, in your daddy's car, of course—"

Tyrone held up his finger to stop Mae, thinking what nerve this stump of a woman had, squirting him with insults, scowling up at him with her one good eye, when he was only looking out for Victoria's well-being. He cringed at the thought that the likes of Mae had mothered his baby doll, Ramona. But since she was Ramona's mother, his good raising kicked in, and he put lead to his tongue and instead reached under his printer's apron to get to his pants pocket.

Mae watched him pull up a modest wad of bills. She licked her lips; it was unconscious, and when she realized she was doing it, she put her hand to her mouth and pretended to yawn.

"This ought to get you down to PGH and back in a cab," he said as he peeled off four one-dollar bills and handed them to Mae.

Mae took the money quickly. Her first thought was of tripling those four singles at the table tonight at Clara Jane's. She let the thought go in the same flash as it had come. They'd at least have to take a cab there, especially with him standing right in front of them; he'd probably hail them a cab, which he was doing right now. Who asked him to be such a gentleman? she thought as she guided Victoria to the opened cab door. Well, at least she'd be able to save the two quarters she'd just pulled out for their ride on the el. And they still might take the el back home. Hell, it would be a gamble him finding out, but a scared bettor never wins; Mae knew that more than most people.

Tyrone helped Victoria into the cab, but when Mae started to get in, he pulled her arm, told her that he had been meaning to talk to her about Larry, that something needed to be done, maybe an official complaint to keep him away from those girls; he was crazy, might pose a real threat to their safety.

"Oh, no!" Mae pulled her arm from his hand. "I can't say nothing against Larry. Those foster kids are my livelihood, and his sister makes sure I always get a good supply." She squinted her good eye at Tyrone. "And I expect you won't be saying anything either."

"And how can you expect that?" Tyrone's head was pulled way back as if he were offended by Mae's breath.

"I hear you already had one run-in with Larry over at Brick's." Mae's voice went low, chilly. "Oh, yeah, I heard all about it. I got friends who play cards down there, told me you was with some fast woman in yellow; I told them they lying, though, 'cause I know Ramona's the only thing in a skirt you got eyes for. So we just gonna keep a closer watch over the girls so Larry can't get near them, and then we just gonna forget any of it ever happened." She tugged on the end of her flowered head scarf knotted under her chin and then climbed into the cab with Victoria.

Perry's voice hit Tyrone in the face as he walked back into the shop. "Damn, boy, the mother got you giving her money. I can see you helping out your girlfriend, but you'll never keep a dollar you start giving it up to Mae. Like feeding mice as much as that woman loves to play cards."

"I just gave her for a cab. That little girl, one of the fosters she takes care of, fell and hurt herself last week. She didn't need to try to be maneuvering no el steps."

"Mnh, you always had such a costly soft spot, boy?"

Tyrone was defensive now. The feeling was back that his city slickster father thought him a head-scratching, foot-shuffling country boy. And now with Mae's threat hanging, he was starting to feel like maybe he was in over his head. "It's no soft spot. I got to know those girls through Ramona, nice girls."

"That so?" Perry asked. He could hear the irritation in Tyrone's voice, so he egged him on to talk about them to hold him there for a minute so that he wouldn't go back to the press mad. A printer's emotions came out in his work, so Perry believed. "My lady friend, Hettie, says they come from a little money."

"Big money, Pops." His voice rose in degrees as he started to talk about the girls. "And now they've been thrown into this world that's got to feel like shark-infested waters when before now they were used to swimming with goldfish. I feel for them, that's all. That's the only reason I gave Mae for a cab." He waved the bulletin cover in front of Perry. "Do I need more red for the pink in the lilies, Pops?"

Perry lined paper against the straight edge of the cutter and pulled the handle on the cutter and sliced through the seventy-pound card stock. He really wanted Tyrone to keep talking about the girls now. Had the feeling that Tyrone was talking about himself as much as he was talking about those girls.

"I'll check the color in a minute, son. So how long you think those girls gonna be with Mae?" He lined more card stock on the cutter.

"Don't know. I guess when their mother's thinking comes back around and they let her out of the institute." He lifted a stack of the card stock from the side of the paper cutter. "Is this stack ready for the press, Pops?" he asked.

"Yeah, son. Cute little sad-faced girl just out there."

"You'd have a sad face too if you been through what they've been through." The irritation was back in his voice.

Perry paused to bring the straight edge down over the paper. The paper grunted as it was sliced in two. He ran his fingers over the edges of the fresh-cut paper. That had been a good, even cut; the edges were smooth. "Tell me this, Ty." He glanced at Tyrone, quickly, and then readied another stack of paper to cut. "Do you think those girls are scared, you know just walking through the streets in this part of the city since they're so unused to it?"

"That youngest ain't scared of too much," Tyrone said as he picked up a handful of the cut paper ends and threw them in the bin of scrap paper. He allowed a slight smile to turn his lips at the thought of Bliss. "That middle one, Victoria, yeah, she's definitely a little shy. The oldest is probably more afraid inside of that house." He thought for a second. "I don't think they're like trembling in their boots, but hell, they got to feel exposed, you know, unprotected. Like at any minute something could jump off that they're not prepared for." Tyrone thought about how unprepared he was for what Mae just said.

Perry watched Tyrone's face go from right there in the printshop to some rough, spiky place. Probably back to last weekend at Brick's after-hours spot. "Tyrone, I've been thinking." Perry stopped the paper cutter and looked directly at his son. How vulnerable and exposed he looked standing here in the ink-spotted printer's apron, his eyebrows raised, dark and thick and innocent against his smooth, maroon-toned skin. "I want to show you where I keep my piece."

"Your what?" Tyrone resisted the impulse to scratch his head.

"My piece, my pistol, my gun." Now Perry's voice was irritated.

"What do I need with your gun?" Tyrone did scratch his head now.

"Shit, what don't you need with it? Some rough cats hang out on Fifty-second Street after dark. And you travel solo a lot. You know, if you ever feeling threatened, out of your element, you know, my piece might help take the edge off—"

"You think I'm out of my element, don't you, Pops?"

"Come on, son, don't go getting all touchy. I watch my own back, and I was born and raised up through here."

"So that's why the sudden interest in those girls. You think I'm defenseless as they are, don't you? Admit it."

"Naw, naw, naw. Those girls are interesting; that's why I want to hear about them. I mean, they got one hell of a story; even Hettie talks about them. Plus you obviously attached, they even got you going in your pocket."

"Keep your gun, Dad, okay? I'm not exactly defenseless." He tossed another fistful of scraps into the bin. "I'm actually pretty good with my hands. Had you been around more when I was growing up you'd know that." He stomped toward the back of the shop where the press was. He'd figure out the pink for the lilies on his own.

"Don't you run that press while you mad, boy," Perry called behind him. "I mean it, I don't have no paper to be wasting on your emotions that you need to learn how to keep in check. You run that press now, mark my words, you gonna have to run it again.

"And need to tone down that accent a notch," Perry muttered, mad at himself too as he went back to cutting paper in front of his two-way mirror as pieces of this part of West Philly rushed on by.

14

SHERN and Bliss walked faster than normal on their way home from school. Even their conversations were jumpy and rushed. Partly because at every turn, at every black iron-gated alley, every clump of hedges tall enough for a man to hide behind, every corner house with an alcove down into the storefront basement entrance, they slowed, looked around themselves, then darted past making sure Larry wasn't jumping out, like he had last week, like a jack-in-the-box that would horrify these girls. Plus today Victoria wasn't walking in between her sisters since she'd gone to the clinic earlier with Mae, and Shern and Bliss could feel the spaces in their conversations that Victoria usually filled. When Shern said she'd been threatened again by that gang of girls who insisted that she thought she was cute, Bliss said they should organize their own gang and take them on. No Victoria to say that Shern should maybe smile once in a while, at least say hello back when people tried to be friendly, go to the vice principal about the threats. And when Bliss told Shern how the whole science class laughed when she whispered out, "Mrs. Potato Head," when her classmate walked to the front of the room and her feet flopped out of her loafers and showed holes in her socks around the heel, Shern said, "That's so corny." No Victoria to remind them how hurt their own mother used to tell them she would feel when she was teased about things she couldn't control. And now when they were at the corner of Addison Street and the holy girls who lived on the corner dangled their rope pleadingly, said they were trying to jump double Dutch but they needed somebody else to turn the rope, Bliss begged Shern, said it had been so long since she'd jumped, but Shern said, "No!" She had to go to the bathroom, and she didn't want to leave Bliss on the corner by herself. No Victoria to tell Shern to go ahead, she would wait while Bliss played rope.

Bliss continued to beg, though. "Please, Shern, I never have any fun, please let me stay and play rope."

Then Shern noticed the holy girls' mother on the porch looking down at her almost as if to say, "You can go. I'll keep an eye on your sister." Shern gave in then. Really didn't want to keep Bliss from the rope game, didn't want to hear Bliss's mouth about Shern never letting her have any fun. And Bliss was actually having fun; Shern could hear her laughing out loud as she started down the street to Mae's. At least one of them should have a few moments of fun.

She carried Bliss's book bag and her own; the two bags together were heavy, and she was panting by the time she got up on Mae's porch, and dancing too, she had to go to the bathroom so bad. She reached under her collar and retrieved the key around her neck and burst through the door just in time to shoot upstairs and make it to the bathroom. She went straight to the bedroom the three girls shared after that, peeped in, figured Victoria was napping. That's when the stillness in the house descended on her like a blue-black cloud bringing up a storm. Just those two twin beds with the beige-ribbed bedspreads, the plastic carnations in the clay pot on top of the radiator cover, the sinkable velveteen couch under the window, their footlocker in front of the couch as if it were a coffee table, with a bottle of peroxide and a spool of cotton gauze sitting in the center like they were crystal figurines. No Victoria, though. Mae and Victoria were not here.

She thought surely Mae and Victoria would be home from the clinic by now or she would have asked the holy girls on the corner if she could use their bathroom. She didn't realize, though, that Philadelphia General was not like the private doctor they usually saw in the mansion of a brick house that had been converted into a doctor's office, where the receptionist and nurse knew them by name because they'd had the same doctor since they were born and where their wait to get examined was never long. Had she realized where Victoria had to go—a reception room crowded with the hobbling, the bleeding, the fevered, severely infected, vomiting, burned, blistered, wheezing, and otherwise stricken, all needing to fill out a thousand forms to have their clinic cards validated just to wait in line for a seat at the table to explain their symptoms to a nurse's aide—she would have certainly known Victoria and Mae wouldn't be here by now, and she would have certainly not come in here alone.

She tiptoed to the top of the steps, was anchored by fear at the top of the steps. Until she crouched on her hands and knees and stretched her neck to see down into the living room. The living room appeared empty, and she traced the quickest path to the front door. Like a low flame zipping along a greased trail, she blazed down the steps, two, three at time, and was all but at the front door when Addison appeared as if he had just assembled himself from the wood of the door, as if his whole body had just been part of the wood fibers; he was right there in front of her, grabbing at her, laughing when she turned to run.

She ran straight to the back of the house, screaming and praying as she went, straight to the first door she saw. Her heart went from her feet to her head when she realized that it wasn't the back door. It was the door to the shed. And now her heart was beating wildly in her throat, trapped in her throat, like she was trapped in the shed. And she really didn't think that it would happen this soon.

It was only Monday afternoon, just a[s] Addison had slithered in here on his belly, and already he['d] [run] his tongue in and out, in and out, making circles arou[nd] his tall, spindly frame. He peeled her pile-lined plaid co[at] [off] [her] shoulders and pushed her up against the wall of the she[d] [under] the box of a window, chanting, "Sweet thang, sweet t[hang,] [when] you gonna give it up to Addison, sweet thang?" His b[reath] [was] hot against her face, and the remnants of cigarette smoke [stung] her eyes. Her eyes were red now and tearing.

"Please leave me alone, please." She cried and looked at the wooden planks of the shed floor. The planks had been painted a pea soup–colored green, and the color made her dizzy.

"Stop acting like such a nice girl, sweet thang. What you gonna give me, tell me, tell me, what you gonna give up to Addison?"

She let her whole body go in a loose sob. Rarely did she let her body go like that. Usually she held her muscles squeezed together. Even curled in bed with her sisters, she kept all parts of her contained and unspillable so the three would have enough space on that one twin bed. But this sob was so filled with resignation and pleading all of her muscles went slack all at once. She thought her bowels were going to break right there on the green wooden floor. "Please," she cried again. "Please leave me alone."

"I'll leave you alone, sweet thang, just tell me what you got for me. Just say it and you walk. Don't say it and I'm taking it. Huh? Huh? I don't hear you, sweet thang."

He leaned in to put his mouth against hers, and she spit. He threw his head back and laughed again. A torturous laugh to Shern. She squirmed and twisted her body, trying to unpin her arms.

"You got the moves, sweet thang. Awl, shucks, now, work it, baby, work it, baby. I'm coming to you, baby, you won't tell me what I need to hear, we goin' get naked, do the nasty, awl, yeah, awl, yeah."

She stopped squirming then. Got stock-still. Fixed her dark eyes right on his. "What do you want me to say?"

I can hear it coming off your tongue, just let it slide," he whispered. Her head stopped spinning once she said it. Her world stopped spinning as if she'd been on a merry-go-round now it was still and she could step on off. Step on off in what? she thought. Into a world where she walked around whispering such words. What would her mother think? What could her mother think? Her mother hadn't thought enough of her to stay well, to stay in her right mind so she could have been spared this situation that had her pinned up against this wall in this shed. She said it again. Pushed her face right up to Addison's and shouted it. "Pussy! Pussy! Pussy!" She said it as if through the saying her mother could hear, and to hear such a word formed in her perfect daughter's mouth, her mother might be shocked back to her right mind.

Addison was shocked. He let go of both her arms, stared at her quizzically as he did. "Damn, babes, you said that with so much fire I can't wait till next time, till we actually get to do it. Lessen you wants to do it right here and now, you sounding like you know what you talking 'bout."

He leaned in again as if to kiss her, and her arm went up like the arm of her vintage walkie-talkie doll that would just spring up for no reason, straight up like a missile, her arm reached for his eyes, caught a line of skin along his cheek instead.

"Awl," he hollered out, and grabbed at his face. "You little cock teaser. You little Goody Two-shoes bitch."

She pushed past him, straight through the house and out the front door down to the corner to where she'd left Bliss jumping rope.

She was shaking when she got to the corner and sat on the steps to catch her breath. Bliss had her coat off, it was on the ground next to the steps, and Shern picked it up and put it in her lap and watched Bliss in the middle of the rope, her hands and feet going in sync to the chant, "You can turn all around, you can touch the ground, you can tootifie, tootifie, side by side. Hands up, lady, lady, lay-dy; hands down, lady, lady, lay-dy." Bliss was still jumping, doing as the chant commanded; even when she touched the ground, she didn't miss. A circle of a crowd of other children was forming, and they were cheering Bliss on. Clapping and singing the rhyme, and in between, saying, "That girl can really jump. Go on, girl, with your bad self," they said.

"Who she anyhow?"

"She one of Miss Mae's fosters?"

"What grade she in?"

"Sixth, I think."

"She can sure jump."

"Yeah, yeah, that girl's all right with me, anybody can jump like that gotta be all right."

Shern just sat on the steps seeing and not seeing. Hearing and not hearing. She felt like she was falling inside herself, and if she did fall, she'd sink so deep she would never be able to climb outside herself again. She tried to focus on the color of the air, which was blue mixed with orange; the words and the beat of the rhyme; the smack of the rope hitting the concrete; Bliss's light-brown bang flopping against her forehead to the beat; even the scent of turnips and liver coming from the holy girls' house. She tried to hold on to everything outside herself because inside her there were no anchors, no poles for her to grab to keep her from drowning, just mud-filled rivers. And now she was up to her waist and now her neck, and she was going to suffocate inside herself if she went any deeper. She pulled Bliss's coat tighter to her; she balled it up against her stomach and tried not to remember her mother's gaping wrists, the bronze and black casket that carried her father's shoes, the scar on Larry's face, the sneer of her cigarette-smoking schoolmates who'd threatened to beat her up, the sound of the air in the basement when Mae cursed and hit Ramona, the green wooden floor of that shed, the feel of the word "pussy" sliding up her throat, Addison's tongue darting in and out, in and out. She couldn't breathe anymore, and she just gave up and started to sink. That's when she was pulled back by a hand against her arm; it was a thin, strong hand. It was the holy girls' mother's hand.

"Do you know Jesus?" the mother asked Shern.

Shern looked at her and squinted, but she could hardly see her because her sight was blurred. "Huh?" she said. She was confused and dizzy. She shook her head, trying to shake away the confusion. "Huh?" she said again.

"What a beautiful face you have. Do your insides match your beauty on the outside?"

"I—I, huh?" Shern was trying to say that she didn't know what she was asking her. That she was confused and dizzy and here and not here, that she was falling inside herself because the reality of her life was much too much for her, that she was only thirteen anyhow, so why was she even talking to her?

"Have you accepted Jesus as your personal Savior?"

Shern wanted to answer her, wanted to have to think and talk right now, anything to save her from herself. But she had been warned about the fanatical by her mother. "They take religion to the extremes, let it get in the way of the life God really intended for them," her mother used to say.

"What life did God intend for them?" Shern would ask her mother.

"Prosperity," her mother would say. "They walk around proud of being poor, talking about being poor is righteous. Like it's a sin to have money, mnh, don't ever let anyone tell you that it's a sin to have money," her mother would say.

Shern's vision was starting to clear, and the holy woman's face was right in front of her. She was dark and thin, even her hair was thin and pulled back in a tight bun, and Shern could see traces of her scalp along the sides of her hair. Her eyes were shining, and Shern thought that the whites of her eyes were whiter than any she'd ever seen.

"Do you know the Lord loves you?" the woman was asking her now.

Shern struggled to concentrate, to form an answer. "Huh?" she said again. She looked at this unprosperous holy woman with the dark skin and thin hands. She wondered if the woman was about to tell her she was a sinner because her parents had money. She wouldn't allow that. She'd just get up from the steps and grab Bliss from the rope and go. She could hear the woman now talking about Satan. How Satan makes people ugly on the inside, makes the heart an inhospitable place for the Lord. Shern thought about how inhospitable that Addison Street house was.

"Is your heart a place where the Lord would want to take up residence, child?" The holy woman had her hand back on Shern's arm. "Do you want me to pray with you right now to evict Satan from your heart?"

Shern didn't want to pray this holy woman's prayer. She had her focus back completely, and now she just wanted to go.

"Do you? Do you, child?" The woman's voice was louder and more insistent. "Do you want me to pray with you right now, right now, I say?"

"I have to go. I'm sorry, I can't pray with you." Shern stood up from the steps and called to Bliss and held up her coat. "We have to go. Come on, Bliss, right now."

She walked away from the steps toward the game of rope. Somebody else was jumping in the center, and Bliss was off to the side, surrounded by a group of cute girls. Shern waved Bliss's coat in her face. "I said we have to go."

"Just five more minutes, Shern, please." Bliss jumped up and down. "I just want to get one more turn, please, Shern."

"Please, Shern, let her have one more turn." The cute girls were a chorus surrounding Shern, jumping up and down, giggling. "Please, Shern, please, Shern."

Shern glanced back at the steps at the holy woman. She was sitting straight and still on the steps, her eyes clamped, her head bowed, her hands a temple in her lap. Only her lips moved.

"Don't pay any attention to her," Bliss said, and then she lowered her voice. "My friends said she stinks."

"She does stink," one of the cute girls said.

"But her daughters have the best rope on the block," said another.

"Please, Shern, just five minutes," Bliss continued to beg. Shern wondered how Bliss couldn't see what she had just been through, that she'd almost been pinned to that shed kitchen floor and forced wide open, that she'd almost drowned inside her own thoughts, that she was confused and starting to whirl around in that dark space again. And Bliss couldn't see it, couldn't see beyond her bratty desires to jump double Dutch. Victoria would have been able to see it. As soon as she ran up the street, Victoria would have sensed her dread, would have left the rope game, politely told the girls that she had to go because her sister needed her. Now she wanted Victoria. Now she wished it were Bliss instead of Victoria at the clinic with a hurt leg.

She tried to answer Bliss, to tell her to stop being such a selfish brat, to put the rope down so they could go. But go where? Back to that house, to that shed. She formed her lips but couldn't form her words, and only a moan pushed through her lips.

Now Bliss did see it. "Shern," she yelled, almost frantically. "Shern, what's wrong? Why you acting like this? Talk to me, Shern."

"What's wrong, Shern?" the chorus of girls called.

"I—I want Victoria," is all she could say.

"Victoria?" one of the girls asked.

"Who's Victoria?" asked another.

"What she crying about?" asked a third.

Bliss reached up and pulled Shern's head to her shoulder. She patted her back in the center of the widening circle of neighborhood girls. "Victoria's our sister," Bliss whispered over her shoulder. "Fell and hurt her leg and had to go to the clinic."

"My sister fell last summer and broke her arm, and she's fine now," one of the girls said.

"My sister fell off her bike and had a concussion for a solid week, and you wouldn't even know it now," said another.

"Don't cry, Shern."

"She'll be okay, Shern."

The holy woman was praying out loud now. Shouting from the steps where Shern had just been. "Touch, Lord. In Your Holy Name, Lord. Touch. Touch."

The circle of girls moved in closer and collapsed around Bliss and Shern in the center. Shern was shaking, and one of the girls pulled a scarf from around her neck and handed it to Bliss. "She acting like she cold; wrap this around her neck."

Another offered a tam. "Cover her head; my grandmother says you can catch the grippe if your head gets too cold."

"Let's play squeeze the lemon," another called. "I'll bet we can keep her warm for real."

Shern was crying out loud now, a cathartic cry. The louder she cried, the tighter the girls moved in around her, propping her up, stroking her with their fatty words plump with urban adolescent wisdom. She could still hear the holy woman calling on the Lord to touch. And now she could hear the corner boys too, warming up for their evening of a cappella on the steps across the street. "Look at me," they sang. "I'm as helpless as a kitten up a tree."

Shern took it all in. The praying, the corner boys singing, the philosophizing from the warm, tight circle. She leaned completely on Bliss. Allowed her baby sister to take her weight while the circle of neighborhood girls propped them up.

15

RAMONA wouldn't be going to see the apartment tonight after all. The rental agent had just called her at her desk adjacent to the bargain basement stockroom. Told her that her credit hadn't gone through. Overloaded, he told her. All of her charge accounts meeting or surpassing the limit. Ramona protested. "I can afford it," she said. "Forty dollars a month is right in line with the income/expense ratio. Please, you've got to approve my application," she insisted. The rental agent listed off Ramona's creditors, and Ramona fought back tears as he did. It was her mother. Mae had apparently opened up charges all over the city in Ramona's name that Ramona knew nothing about. She hung up the phone and then banged her fist on the ink blotter that covered her desk. "I hate her!" she said out loud.

"What did you say, Ramona?" It was Cass, her orange-haired boss who managed the bargain basement. She turned the corner into Ramona's work area, pushing a wheeled rack filled with hanging flowered dusters.

"Oh, ugh, nothing. I just broke a nail, hate when that happens." Ramona kept her fist balled.

Cass smiled and nodded. "I'll leave this cart here, Ramona. These dusters need to go on the floor first thing in the morning to get ready for the sale starting Wednesday, especially since they're calling for a big storm tomorrow night."

Ramona got up and pushed the cart against the wall. "I'll get right on it," she said.

"No, Ramona, tomorrow morning's fine. I thought you were punching out an hour early today anyhow."

"Change of plans," Ramona said, and then started removing the dusters from the cart and hanging them on the pole just inside the stockroom door.

"Oh, go ahead and take the hour, Ramona. It's already approved. In fact, you know what, doll, you can take it with pay since those brass bangle bracelets you selected for the entrance bin sold out by the end of the lunchtime rush."

"They're gone?" Ramona asked. "I never made it back down to the selling floor once I packed the bin this morning."

"Sold out, doll. You've got one hell of an eye for what the bargain shopper wants. I just told the real estate guy who called to get a reference on your character and income potential that you would always have a future with Lit's."

Ramona stopped transferring the dusters from the wheeled cart to the bar and looked directly at Cass as if she hadn't heard right.

"I did, Ramona. I says to him, 'Listen now, Ramona is one beautiful, conscientious lady. She's not your ordinary run-of-the-mill Negro.'"

Ramona just stared at Cass, at the half-moon hazel brown eyebrows drawn against her forehead that sometimes made it hard for Ramona to read her because the eyebrows stayed still even as the rest of her face moved. She could tell even without the eyebrows, though, that Cass wasn't just joking around, and now she was embarrassed for them both. She turned her back and headed deeper into the stockroom, mumbling, "Excuse me, something just occurred to me that I need to check on back here."

"Really, Ramona." Cass followed Ramona just inside the stockroom door. "You really do your race proud. You're never late, never take off a Friday or a Monday, you don't steal, you know what I mean, Ramona. I told that apartment guy too. Listen, I says to him, when he was hemming and hawing about the effect renting to a Negro would have on the other tenants, 'You should be proud to have the likes of a fine Negro girl like Ramona wanting to rent from you,' I says."

Ramona wanted to sink to the floor, cover her face in the dusters, close her ears. She wanted to turn Cass's voice off. She wanted to explode. It was enough that Mae had thwarted her move; she didn't need to know that powers much larger than Mae were thwarting her too. And what could she do? This wasn't even Selma, where they were getting ready for the march. She could sit at the counter at Woolworth's, drink from the same fountain as her boss, and Mae had in fact driven her credit into the ground, so she couldn't even prove in a court of law that the apartment was denied her for other than legitimate reasons. Her eyes were burning. "Cass, I'm going to be a minute in here," she called out to the doorway. "And then I think I will take that hour. I'll see you in the morning. I'll get those dusters on the floor first thing."

Her nose was running when she got back to her desk, but she wouldn't let herself cry. She went to her bottom drawer and pulled out her purse, took out a token for the el ride home, swallowed hard. She didn't want to go home. She thought about where could she go. Out for a drink maybe, a light dinner. But with whom. Not Tyrone; he kept the shop open late during the week, more eye burning at the thought of Tyrone. She went for her address book. Whom could she call for a last-minute dinner date? Ran her finger up and down the pages, turning the pages. Not him. Married. Please, not him. Ugh, can't believe I spent time with him. She was almost through the book; she had to sit down at the realization that there was no one she could call at this moment. How limited her world had become, how limited, really, it had always been. How sad, my God, how very sad. The names and addresses were blurring on the page; she still wouldn't let herself cry.

Then she came upon Beanie's name. She stopped her finger at Beanie's name. It never occurred to her to call up the likes of Beanie, even though she was always promising Beanie that they were going to keep in touch between choir rehearsals. She dialed the number, dialed it quickly before she could talk herself out of it, and got suddenly shy when Beanie said, "Hello."

"Hi, Beanie, it's Ramona." Ramona forced the words out on her pent-up breaths.

"Hey, Ramona, girl, what you know good?"

"Nothing good, girl," Ramona said, and then wished she could call the words back.

"Uh-oh, what's wrong? Spill it, girl. That cute country boy starting to show his butt? Huh? The cute ones always do sooner or later, that's why I keeps me an ugly man. Toupee and all." She laughed a raucous laugh, and Ramona almost laughed too. Ramona wanted to laugh, then wanted to tell Beanie all about Tyrone's mouth, and how it had changed, wanted to tell her about the apartment falling through, and how much she hated Mae. She wanted to tell her to put a pot of coffee on, pull down that square-shaped bottle of Manischewitz grape concord, she was on the way over, and Lord have mercy, she didn't know what she needed more, the coffee or some wine. But she didn't know how to start, hadn't been friends with a woman since her friend Grace from high school went away to college. And now she was feeling her chest tighten, and she had to get off the phone before that block of granite came up and took over her chest.

"Ramona? You there?"

"Yeah, Beanie, I just wanted to make sure we had rehearsal Wednesday night, supposed to be a storm tomorrow night into Wednesday."

Beanie exaggerated a smacking sound. "Awl, shucks, girl, I

thought you was calling to talk. I'll call you if rehearsal's off, you know that. What you doing later? Me and a few of the girls going over to Sunny Honey's to have some wings, you want to come?"

Ramona twirled the token along the ink blotter on her desk. "Can't," she lied.

"All right, well, listen up, Ramona, and listen up good. I'm here if you need me, I mean that too, girl. All right?"

"Yeah, sure, Beanie. Got to run."

She hung up the phone and just sat at her desk playing with the token. The air was heavy around her, and now she truly missed Tyrone. Then it occurred to her just to go to the shop and visit him there. She was tired of waiting for him to come around anyhow. And now she wanted—needed—to be with him. That's what she would do, go straight to the shop and keep Tyrone company until he was ready to close.

She grabbed her coat and purse and punched her time card and headed for the el. Now she couldn't wait to get there, and the el ride was seeming to take forever. She tried to drive the el herself with her stomach and her breaths, rushing it, but the more impatient she became, the slower the clickety-clack of the wheels against the tracks seemed. Finally, once the el screeched and grunted and sighed to a stop at Sixtieth Street, she pushed past the throngs of people to get through the doors. She ran down the steps, zooming in and out between the slower walkers, and then across the street. She couldn't wait to tell Tyrone about the apartment, about Mae; she'd never told anyone about Mae before. Maybe she'd cry. For sure he'd take her in his arms. She was at the door. She glanced back across the street at the clock atop the el platform advertising Morton's salt that said, "When It Rains It Pours." Almost six. Good, Perry would be gone. She turned the doorknob and pushed the door. The door pushed back. She jangled the knob. It wasn't turning. She knocked on the door, looked for the sign that said be right back. That's when she saw it, right in the bottom corner of the window, resting against the manila-colored window shade. The small red and white sign said CLOSED.

· 1 8 8 ·

"Where the fuck is he?" she said out loud. She walked on down the street feeling like a zombie because she didn't know what to feel. This kind of anger toward a man was new for her. She'd feigned it plenty of times, stroked their egos and pretended she was having a jealous rage even though deep down she didn't give a shit. But now she really was angry, and hurt, and disappointed, and humiliated, and sad, she was very, very sad. She counted the days since they'd been together, before Victoria had fallen and hurt her leg; damn, that was well over a week.

She walked faster to do something with all the feelings spinning like a multicolored windmill until it was spinning so fast and all the colors washed together that she couldn't tell where one started and the other ended. She was right in front of Sunny Honey now. She could almost hear Beanie's laughter. She walked on past Sunny Honey and was in the next block, and then she couldn't explain it, but she turned around suddenly and started to run, could feel a snag opening up in her stockings and rushing up her calf she was running so fast, she'd have to put her shoes in the shop, she thought as she felt the rubber tip on her high heel give and she could hear her heel scraping the cement as she ran. She was back in front of Sunny Honey. She didn't stop to let herself think or she would have surely stopped herself. She busted through the door, followed the sound of Beanie's laughter to a booth in the back. Just stood there breathing hard until Beanie looked up.

"Hey, girl." Beanie jumped up to hug Ramona. "I'm so glad you decided to come."

Ramona didn't hug Beanie back. She just stood there with her arms hanging, her purse dangling from her wrist. She did let her head go on Beanie's shoulder, though. And then she couldn't even help herself. She just allowed her head to rest on Beanie's shoulder. Now she let herself cry.

16

CLARISE was on the way back. More than a week since she'd gone hysterical over the girls, and her thinking was shimmering like an icicle catching the sun and making rainbows as it melts. The haze had lifted. Once she'd come back to awareness from that powerful injection they'd given her that Sunday afternoon, and realized that her first thoughts in the mornings were clear as spring water, and as the day progressed they went to cloudy, to mud, she finally made the connection that it was the Elavil pills. So she stopped taking the pills whenever she could. Only when they stood right over her, handed her water, and watched her swallow did she take the pills. Otherwise, especially if it was the morning shift nurse, who always rushed through Clarise's room in her street shoes while her nurse's shoes sat in the utility room sopping up the White-All shoe polish, Clarise would hold the pills in her hands, wrap them in the napkin on her breakfast tray, and leave them to go out with the garbage.

Now it was Monday evening, and she sat in the patients' lounge, knitting and figuring things out. She tried to keep a blank look to her eyes the way she guessed someone's eyes would look who was actually swallowing all the pills handed her in the pleated paper container. She didn't even allow her reaction to show as Emma, the silver-blue haired woman who occupied the room next to Clarise's, began pointing wildly at the window in the patients' lounge and flailing her arms up and down, saying that the moon was falling out of the sky and it was headed straight for the window. About once a week Emma spotted such catastrophes on the way to happening and the staff would be called to arms, rushing from whatever else they were doing to restrain Emma, get her back to her room, shoot her up with a stream of narcotics that had her smiling and nodding for days after. Clarise had taken note of the beatific expression on Emma's face before she emerged from her smiling and nodding state of mind. She would imitate that expression later this evening during her session with the psychiatrist; maybe he'd okay her full visiting privileges again. She had missed the aunts' and uncles' daylong stays, which had been reduced down to fifteen minutes twice a day after her ranting session the week before. And she certainly understood why the aunts and uncles had lied to her about the girls, knew that the wall separating the aunts and uncles from the girls must have been impenetrable or surely her aunt Til would have knocked it down by now with her sledgehammer will. So she didn't waste her clarity of thought bemoaning what was done and for the moment unchangeable. Nor did she try to guess where the girls might be. Of course they were alive, well too, she told herself. By law they couldn't withold drastic information about the girls from their own mother, she was sure of that. Plus, if she dwelled too much on the dearth of information she had about their whereabouts, she feared she'd drive herself right into another fit of hysteria and they'd shoot her full of that liquid that caused that black, gumbo-textured screen to fall all around her that let in only a pinhole of ether. So right now as she clicked her knitting needles which sounded melodious even against the backdrop of Emma's screams about the moon falling, resounding through the hallway as Emma was being carried back to her room, Clarise counted the rows of knit and purl stitches she had to do yet before her bright purple shawl was completed. She yawned and settled back deeper in the chair and calmly knitted while she planned her escape.

Clarise wasn't the only one planning an escape. Shern was too. Right now she was in the small bedroom at Mae's, undoing the catch on the trunk to pull out extra leotards and sweaters because an unseasonal March snowstorm had been forecast. It was just past one in the morning, and she felt unclasped for a change, a range of motion in her muscles and her feelings that was unusual for her in this house. She had moved the small table lamp to the floor to cast just a smattering of light from down low to guide her fast-moving hands, and suddenly the light shooting upward rounded the hard, angular lines of that room and opened it up some. Victoria and Bliss were snoring lightly, and their rhythmic breaths were settling to her as she worked as quickly and quietly as she could. She was judicious about what she packed; they would need to move like lightning through the night air, and she didn't want them to be too loaded down. Plus she and Bliss would need to take turns helping Victoria, she was still limping so.

"Just a little infection," Mae had said that afternoon when she'd finally gotten in after that el ride from the clinic with Victoria hobbling behind her. "The doctor gave her penicillin pills and said she's got to keep that leg elevated at night." Mae had fixed her lazy eye on Shern as she gave the doctor's report. "So I'm trusting you to do that, dumpling." She had squeezed Shern's chin when she said it. "You girls not gonna be able to sleep all huddled on that one little bed with your sister needing to keep that leg raised, okay, sugarplum?"

Victoria had protested when Shern tucked her into the other twin bed. Said that she wanted to sleep with Shern and Bliss. Shern had consoled her, though, persuaded her by reminding her how close the beds were in that tiny room. "All you have to do is stretch good and you'll be able to touch me in the other bed."

Now Shern was lining up their shoes in front of the velvet green couch; she laid a sock on each shoe. She almost started humming, the way she'd hum at home when she did some big-sisterly-type thing, like match three pair of ribbons for their hair, or spoon out the ice cream into the three bowls that she lined up neatly on the counter, or get their Sunday School money from their mother's purse, three quarters that she'd place one each on top of their Sunday gloves. She stopped herself from humming here, too incongruent a thing to do in this house. She couldn't stop the electricity in her bones, though. She was excited to be getting ready to steal away from here. They would take the bus that stopped at Sixtieth Street at 2:00 A.M. to three blocks from the aunts and uncles. She had planned it out so well too, without a mention to Bliss and Victoria. Just like how she hadn't mentioned to them Addison's violation earlier that afternoon, when he'd trapped her in that shed.

She put a sweater and pair of corduroy pants for each of them on the green couch right above the shoes and socks. She wanted the clothes they would put on shortly to be organized so that they could get dressed while they argued. She knew they would argue. Especially she and Bliss. She had actually considered letting them in on her plan earlier as they got ready for bed and even as they took turns crying the way they still cried some nights before they fell asleep. She didn't. Thought it best to wake them quickly, tell them to be quiet and put the clothes on. Perhaps in their fogginess they might not even protest.

She started with Bliss.

"Go where?" Bliss said it so loudly Shern had to cup her hand over her mouth.

"To the aunts and uncles!" Shern put her mouth to Bliss's ear and pushed the words in as hard as she could.

"We can't just leave here," Bliss said as she struggled with Shern to uncover her mouth. She grabbed a bit of the skin of Shern's palm and held it between her teeth.

"Ouch, you didn't have to bite me," Shern snarled.

"Well, you didn't have to try to smother me."

"Keep your voice down then, or I will smother you for real. Now get up and get dressed while I help Victoria get up."

"You must didn't hear me." Bliss flung her legs over the side of the bed and sat up and attempted to whisper. "We can't just leave here. They'll find us; then they'll tag us runaways; they might even throw us in the Youth Study Center."

Shern had considered that possibility. But she had to take the risk now while she could still walk from here with her knees facing forward, before Addison forced her knees apart and left her waddling in circles like a confused, violated duck. "By the time they find us," she said forcefully, "Mommie will be better and we'll be back home."

Shern could see even through the light of the low-sitting lamp that Bliss's eyes were brimming over in disbelief that Shern had concocted such a plan.

"And how are we supposed to get there, Einstein?" Bliss had heard Mae use that expression with Ramona. She thought it was funny then; it wasn't funny now.

"On the bus."

"The bus?"

"Yes, the bus. I have my milk money from the past month wrapped up in a sock under the mattress. I called the PTC from the phone booth on the corner while you were jumping rope. The last bus that takes us within two blocks of the aunts and uncles leaves at two A.M."

"And where we supposed to catch this bus?"

"On Sixtieth Street."

"And how are we supposed to get out of this house with nobody knowing?"

"That's why we have to go now. Ramona's asleep, Mae's out gambling, and who knows where that—that—" She couldn't say his name or even utter a substitute for his name. She looked at her hands through the lamplight. "We just have to hurry."

"And how's Tore supposed to run? I'm sure you figured out in all of your figuring that we'll probably have to do some running."

"We'll just have to help her." She moved to the bed where Victoria was curved except for her hurt leg, which looked straight and stiff resting atop one of the pillows from the green velvet couch. "Victoria." She sat on the side of the bed and whispered into Victoria's ear. "Come on, wake up, and be very quiet."

"Wha—" Victoria sat straight up and then grimaced and stretched to bring her leg down from the pillow. She let out a small moan.

"Unhunh," Bliss said. "She's really gonna be able to tiptoe on out of here tonight quietly. I guess she'll be able to leap over tall buildings in a single bounce too, huh, Shern?"

Shern reached over to the other bed and punched Bliss on the shoulder with all the strength she could call. "Just stop being so contrary," she almost yelled. "And stop saying 'huh' and 'unhunh.' That's why Mommie almost yanked your head off that Tuesday night."

Bliss starting crying. "You didn't have to hit me," she said. "And you didn't have to hurt my feelings reminding me of that night. You're mean, Shern, just plain old mean."

"Tiptoe out of here?" Victoria was sitting with both feet on the floor now, and she leaned her weight on her hands. "What's going on?"

"Go ahead." Bliss sniffed. "Tell her about your brilliant scheme to run away from here."

"Run away?" It was Victoria's turn to look at Shern in disbelief. "Run away to where? How? Run away?"

"Thank you, Tore." Bliss stood in front of Shern with her arms folded. "That was exactly my question. But big sister here has this grand idea that we can get out of here unnoticed and make it to Sixtieth Street to get on a bus that's supposed to take us to the aunts and uncles."

"Shern, are you serious?" Victoria asked it without the sarcasm.

"Does it look like I'm playing?"

"You might as well be playing," Bliss said as she went over and sat on the bed next to Shern. "I think it's a stupid idea, and you're dumb and stupid for suggesting it."

"I don't know, Shern," Victoria said slowly. "It might not be the best idea. I mean, what about when they come looking for us, have you thought about that part of it?"

"Yes, I thought about that part of it. I've thought about every part of it, from getting on the bus to how much I want to feel Aunt Til's arms around me. I mean, I have everything packed and all organized. Do you think I would have suggested it if I'd thought it wouldn't work or if it was like we could be harmed?" Shern's voice shook as she looked from one sister to the other staring at her through the light coming from the floor like she was a lunatic or, worse, a fool. She wasn't a fool. She thought she was being the oldest, the decision maker, the action taker. She was proud of herself, had even felt a fragment of something that approached happiness in this house as she'd arranged for their escape. And now they were staring at her and just snatching her swatch of happiness right from her. Didn't they know what would happen to her if she stayed? Didn't they even care? Bliss had her buddy Tyrone; Victoria and Ramona were like girlfriends. Whom did she have? Mae with her drooping eye? Addison with his snake of a thing that he couldn't wait to ram inside her? She hated both Victoria and Bliss right now. Was so angry at their selfishness that she just wanted to mash her hands into both of their staring, disbelieving faces.

"Then don't go, you little selfish bitches." She cried the words out and picked up the neatly packed double-handled shopping bag and dumped it on the floor by the green velvet couch.

"Oh, no, you didn't." Bliss ran up behind Shern and grabbed the back of the neckline of Shern's lace-trimmed flannel pajama top. "I know you, Miss perfect-grammared, never curses, gonna-remind-someone-what-Mommie-said-about-them, didn't just call us bitches."

Shern pulled away from Bliss, and the lacy neckline of her pajama top made a searing sound as it ripped along the back. "See what you did." Shern turned around and knocked Bliss to the floor right on top of the bag of dumped-over clothes.

Bliss kicked up at Shern again and again, and then Shern was all over her, and they were both kicking up the dark air in that bedroom and making slapping sounds and saying "ouch" and "you bitch" this and "you bitch" that.

Victoria tried to get to them, to break it up. She was crying now too. "Stop it. Have you gone crazy? Just stop it." Before she could hobble to where they were, a rush of bright yellow light pushed into the room like a missile landing and fell right over Shern and Bliss.

Ramona was behind the light as she pushed the door all the way opened and walked in the room. "What the hell is happening in here?" she said. She clicked the switch on the wall, and the low lamplight retreated completely under the beds. She ran straight to Victoria, who was sobbing in the middle of the room, pointing to her sisters, crying, "Make them stop, Ramona. Please make them stop fighting."

"Wait, wait, are you all right? Come on, first let's get you off of that leg," Ramona said as she guided Victoria back to the bed. "And they are gonna stop fighting, hell, yeah, they are. Because if they don't, I'll have to get in it, and if I have to get in it, both their behinds gonna be kicked to kingdom Kong."

Shern and Bliss sat up, breathing hard and irregularly. They looked at neither Ramona nor each other. Shern did look at the little travel clock that sat on the dresser. It was 1:45. They should be leaving out the door right now. She could feel the sound of a bus pounding through her ears. Her ears felt like they might explode. She picked herself up and staggered to the bed and flopped on it. She lay wide, not caring that there was not enough room for Bliss on that bed. She covered her head with the pillow and cried into the bed.

Bliss just sat on the floor, staring at the clothes that Shern had dumped. Her hair had come undone; even the sponge roller that held her bang in a curl had come out and hopped to the other side of the room.

Ramona bent down and picked the roller up and tossed it over to where Bliss sat. "Curl your bang back up, please," she said to Bliss. "And get those clothes up. How the hell they get out of the trunk anyhow? And put that lamp back on the table where it belongs. And then your fresh ass better go on back to sleep. And I better not catch you and your sister fighting no more. I wish I had a sister, and all you can do is pick with yours." She clicked off the ceiling light. "You sure you're all right, Victoria?" she said as she stood in the archway of the bedroom door.

Victoria sniffed out a yes, and Ramona closed the door and let the sisters have the dark bedroom air back to themselves.

Bliss was in a turmoil all that next day. Felt like she'd been spun around on the end of a lasso when her stomach was full. Shern wouldn't talk to her. Since their fight last night and all day into this evening. Not a "Good morning, Sister," or "Don't cross on the red." Not even a "Watch your mouth" when Bliss said "oh, fuck" just so she could get a reaction from Shern. Shern hadn't reacted. And now Bliss sat at the dining-room table and tried to get down a swallow of peas and rice and remembered how Shern sounded crying last night. While Bliss had tried to sleep on the green velvet couch because Shern wouldn't make room for her in the bed, Bliss had listened to Shern's cries pierce even through the pillow and the heavy bedroom air to stab against Bliss's ears like knife points. It was a sharper cry than even their first nights here, when they all three were yelping like newborn puppies that needed to nurse. But last night Shern's sounds were absent the "I want Mommie" kind of sob that had become typical for them and was familiar and almost comforting because it was born out of their longing for their parents and their home and was shared completely by the three. Shern's crying the night before had been incomprehensible to Bliss. As if Shern had swallowed a part of hell that

Bliss couldn't taste. It was such a dark, solitary kind of cry that the memory of it now was coating the peas and rice that Bliss held in her mouth like a gravy that's too thick. She felt like she needed to throw up.

She put her napkin to her mouth and spit the half-chewed food into her napkin and then looked around the table. It was just Mae and Victoria and Bliss there now. Ramona had eaten quickly and was up from the table, saying something about getting to the Laundromat before a storm hit. Addison wasn't even there, and Shern had come in from school, said she didn't feel well, and gone straight to bed. Bliss looked at the tablecloth to try to still her stomach. The tablecloth was white lace with a pink plastic lining; she thought that at least the lining would save the table underneath from the contents of her stomach should she vomit right now. She kept her eyes on the tablecloth and asked Mae if she could be excused.

"Sure, darling," Mae said, between slurping sounds as she gulped at hot tea and lemon. "Neither you nor that number one daughter had much of an appetite tonight. I hope you girls aren't filling your stomachs with too much candy during the day."

"No, ma'am," Bliss answered as she avoided Victoria's eyes that she knew were saying, "Please don't leave me down here with just Mae."

She rushed from the table as she heard Mae say to Victoria, "It's just you and me, buttercup, with Ramona headed to the Laundromat and those sisters of yours holed up in that bedroom. Why don't we play a game of pit-a-pat, doll baby?"

And then Bliss was upstairs and in the bedroom where Shern lay facing the radiator and the wall, still lying wide so that no one else could fit on that bed.

"Shern, are you awake?" she asked, quietly, tenuously, the spinning in her stomach slowing down now that she was away from that table and the peas and rice.

Shern didn't move, not even a twitch to acknowledge Bliss's presence in the room.

"Shern, please talk to me, I said I was sorry. As it is, you won the fight last night; if anybody should be mad, it should be me. But I'm not angry with you, Shern. Please." Bliss played with her fingers and dragged the "please" out like a child begging for a piece of a candy. She leaned over Shern's back to try to look in her face, knowing that Shern wouldn't be able to resist the pleading splashed all over Bliss's face.

Shern shrugged Bliss away from her shoulder as if she were trying to shake off a bad itch.

Bliss persisted. She squeezed her body in the bed behind Shern and wrapped her arms around her neck. "I won't let go until you talk to me. And you know I won't, Shern."

Still nothing from Shern.

"You'll just have to knock me off the bed when you're ready to get up," Bliss went on, "and even then I'm not going to hit you back. I'll just go nonviolent on you like the Reverend Doctor Martin Luther King, Junior." She carefully enunciated each syllable of his name the way her mother used to.

Bliss thought she heard her sister sigh, so she kept it going. "Then what you gonna do, Shern, turn a fire hose on me, while I'm laying on the floor where you knocked me, and I'm not even fighting back, then you gonna drag in that German shepherd that's always barking out back, you gonna let him loose on me and I'm not even fighting back, that's what you gonna have to do, Shern, 'cause I'm not moving until you talk to me."

The image of knocking Bliss down with a fire hose was suddenly funny to Shern. She didn't find it odd that she could be so despondent at this moment, so dread-filled at the thought of remaining in this house, and yet laugh. She did laugh then. It was a laugh that came from some deep place filled with light and air that she hadn't even known was part of her. Her whole body laughed as she thought about giving Bliss a good, hard hosing down. And then as quickly as it had come, the light- and air-filled laugh faded. And the image was no longer Bliss fighting a water hose, but Shern herself on the floor, and the hose was now Addison's thing aiming at her, getting closer and closer as his laugh filled her head. She gasped and started to cry. That same cry that frightened Bliss so because she didn't understand it.

"What is it, Sister?" Bliss whined, and tugged on Shern's neck. "I can't stand to hear you crying like this." Bliss's words started and stopped and rose and fell and were filled with tremors. She took a deep breath and held it in as long as she could and then let the breath explode through her half-pursed lips. "I'll go with you" came out with the breath, and she wished she could call it back, but Shern's crying had stopped, so she said it again. "I'll go with you, okay. I said it, okay. I'll go with you, I'll even help you convince Tore, okay. Just please don't cry like that anymore."

"You—you don't know what happened to me." Shern choked on the words, and Bliss could hardly understand her at first. She was half into the telling of it before Bliss did understand as Shern described how tight the air in that shed was as Addison had almost gotten her, almost done it to her. She told Bliss how his tongue looked like a snake's tongue darting in and out and how his breath burned her eyes as he'd tried to mash his body against hers in big circles. She sobbed the story out even down to how the word "pussy" felt exploding in her ears, and then later the sensation of falling inside herself when the holy woman pulled her back. Her only comfort, she told Bliss, came in planning their escape.

Bliss was like stone, she was listening so hard; she almost stopped breathing and even held her breath when Shern described Addison's tongue.

"We have to tell," she said when Shern stopped talking. "Tyrone would gladly kick his ass, Shern. We can't let him just get away with this. We have to tell."

"No, Bliss." Shern almost shouted it. "That's why I didn't want to say anything to anybody. They'll move us from here, and they might even separate us. I'd rather take it upon myself to move us. At least we'll be together, and at least we can see the aunts and uncles."

"But, Shern—"

"No, Bliss." This time Shern did shout it, and Bliss felt her sister's back tighten.

"Okay, okay." Bliss said quickly, not wanting to lose Shern again to the radiator and the wall. "Nobody." She took a long, sigh-filled breath and was quiet until she felt Shern's back loosen again. "When do we leave?" She asked it in a whisper and then cringed as she heard Shern say, "Tonight," they would leave tonight. The earlier spinning in her stomach stopped completely now and was replaced by a resolute fear that was taking her over in waves.

17

WHILE Shern and the reluctant Bliss were huddled in the bedroom, planning out their escape and trying to convince Victoria that they had to go, Ramona dragged the shopping cart filled with dirty clothes against the wind. This was Tuesday and not even her regular night to do this, but a big storm was forecast for later, and it might be three, four days before the sidewalks were clear enough to get the wheeled cart through, and the dirty clothes basket was always overflowing with those three girls going through towels as if they were Kleenex.

She felt so poor wheeling the cart those three long blocks to the Laundromat. Most working people had a washer these days, even if it wasn't a semiautomatic washer, even if they were sending the clothes though the wringer and then hanging clothes on the line to dry. She'd tried to talk Mae into getting a washer last month instead of that overpriced royal blue wall-to-wall carpet. But even though she usually dreaded and despised this walk, right now she hummed "My Guy" and laughed when she got to the part: "I'm sticking to my guy like a stamp to a letter."

Last night at Sunny Honey had almost transformed Ramona. After she'd wet Beanie's shoulders with her tears, and apologized for leaving a stain on her white polyester blouse, and Beanie said, "Oh, here, Ramona, get the other side, so at least I'll match," Ramona laughed the chest-vibrating laugh that she usually reserved for the choir changing room in the basement of the church. Then she told them about Tyrone. She held on to the part about hating Mae, but she let loose with Tyrone. Told them when she noticed his mouth change, how scarce he'd been, how she felt when she came upon the closed shop. Told them how honest he was otherwise; she couldn't fathom what had gotten into him; she wasn't used to this, just wasn't.

Then, after they'd listened intently, echoing her words with heartfelt "mnh-hm," "know what you saying now, girl," "oh, yeah, I been there too," Beanie said it sounded to her like some experienced hussy had the man's nose open. Told Ramona she should fight for him, because all the emotions she'd just described signaled head over heels in love. Told her she should buy some sexy lingerie, even spring for a bottle of wine, then call him up and whisper in his ear what she was gonna put on, and then how she was gonna take it off as soon as he rented them a fancy room somewhere for the weekend. Told her she was more than equipped to go up against whoever the scampy bitch was who taking advantage of Tyrone's honest country ways. Ramona had winced when Beanie said "scampy bitch." She winced right now as she dragged the cart. She wondered how often a bunch of girlfriends sat around a basket of chicken wings and said similar things about her.

She tried to shake the thought, difficult to do because now she was walking past Mr. John in his real estate office. There he stood at the window, peeping through his venetian blinds, his mouth formed as if to say, "You don't have to pull that cart, baby. I'll pay your Lit Brothers' salary plus buy you a Maytag." She turned away and walked around to the other side of the laundry cart so she could switch hands that she pulled the cart with, give her right arm a rest and pull with her left.

She pushed her free hand into her pocket and tried to forget about Mr. John and asked out loud when the month of March was going to show its lamb side. She could use a pair of gloves right now like those girls' mother knitted. She'd never seen a stitch like that, a cross knit and purl that didn't let the cold through. That mother must love the shit out of those girls, she thought. She wondered how it must feel to be so loved. She felt a stirring in her chest, as if she had known that kind of motherly love once, a long time ago; every now and then she would get such a stirring, try to figure out what it meant, but then a block of granite would come up in her chest and make her feel like she was suffocating. It did now.

Mr. John had come out of his office now and was calling out Ramona's name. Now she did turn around. "You might as well go back in your office and go about your business," she yelled against the wind.

Times like this, when her mistakes called out her name as she tried to go on with her life, she understood why she missed Tyrone so. Sometimes the way Tyrone's face went open and submissive when he looked at her made her feel so pure inside, even if he was usually broke and couldn't keep a car running for longer than a day. The honesty that hung around his eyebrows when they dipped in a smile for her was sometimes enough to replace the candlelit, white linen–draped tables where they never dined.

She was almost to the Laundromat, and in the next block, just beyond the cyclone fenced–in hedges that surrounded her church building, she could see the orange and blue sign that said PERRY'S PRINTSHOP. Suddenly she needed to see Tyrone right now. She couldn't wait for this weekend, she needed to have Tyrone's pretty country boy eyes melt when he looked at her. Needed to have the sight of his eyebrows take away that dented, rusty feeling.

Damn, she thought, she really did have a well of feelings for Tyrone that right now were bubbling to the surface and threatening to spill over. And that rarely happened. He was usually the one making the first moves, pulling on her, begging. And even then sometimes her meanness would get harder than his manhood, and she'd deny him. But this evening she decided she would let her feelings for him spill over. Already the brimming that was starting deep in her softness was warm and silky, made her step up her pace, heavy cart and all, so she could throw the clothes in the extra-large-capacity washer, set it to long wash, and run up the street to see if Tyrone was still at the shop.

Her footsteps took on a new rhythm once she'd stuffed the dirty clothes in the washer and was back outside. Now the wind was at her back as she walked beyond the church and was right across the street from the printshop. She couldn't tell because of the two-way mirror that took up the whole storefront whether or not the shop was still open. She just knew that it was well after 5:00, and she knew before Tyrone moved to Philadelphia, Perry closed up at 5:00 P.M. sharp. But Tyrone would stay late—at least until last night he would—keep the place opened until 8:00 or 9:00. They'd even used the double-length worktable on occasion and moved to the beat of Martha and the Vandellas singing "Heat Wave" pushing through the AM/FM transistor that Tyrone kept by the press. She thought about the last time they'd used that table. Asked him what was the table's real intended use. "For spreading out work on," he'd said innocently, and then they'd both broken up in laughter as she'd smoothed at her blouse and he stepped back into his shoes.

She was excited at the thought of coming on to Tyrone for a change. She'd ask him if his spreading-out table was clear, purse her lips, lick her finger, and touch it to his cheek. She was at the door to the printshop now, and even her ungloved hands, which had gotten cold and stiff and sore from gripping the handles of that heavy cart, were warm and throbbed at the thought.

She turned the knob and the door opened easily and there Perry stood, like he'd been expecting her. She remembered his wall of a two-way mirror, knew that he'd probably been watching her since she'd turned the corner and stood across the street waiting for the light to change. She was embarrassed, Perry looking at her, eyebrows arched in a mild question mark as if he'd been able to read her thoughts about Tyrone and her on that table. She looked away, her blood pulsing in her ears.

"Is Tyrone around?" she asked the floor, and the orange-glowing space heater on the floor, and the printing press, and the sharp-edged paper cutter, because she certainly couldn't ask Perry, couldn't even look at him after he'd caught her face the one time it was filled up for his son, and now it was filled up for him, and if she looked at him, he might know that too.

"No, Miss Ramona," he said lightly. "You just missed him, said he was going past your house to check on that little one that hurt her leg. Then he needed to stop at Penn Fruit, supposed to be a storm through here tonight, and you know Ty's a country boy, so when you say storm to him, it means load up on the candles and the kerosene and some canned goods 'cause the power might be out for days." He laughed and glanced at his watch. "I should have been gone, I don't keep no late hours here, but Ty was trying so hard to get the colors right on those church bulletins, and he had to run them through one more time. I told him to go tend to his business, I'd wait and shut the press down. And of course"—he cleared his throat in an emphasized way that meant he was joking—"I knew the boy wanted some extra time so he could go check on his ladylove."

Ramona was trying to recover from the shock of finding Perry here instead of Tyrone, and now standing here in this printshop with just Perry and the space heater and the paper cutter and the long spreading-out table right in her view, right where she was looking now so that she wouldn't have to look at Perry. "I'm sorry, what did you say?" She looked at her fingernails after she asked it and coughed and put her hand to her mouth.

"I said I'm sure he had it in his plans to stop off and see his ladylove, and I don't mean your mother, Mae."

Ramona forced a laugh and wanted to say something like

"Thanks, tell him I stopped by." And then she wanted to turn around and leave the shop. And she would have been able to do it had she just focused on the straight edge of the cutter, or the orange lines humming in the space heater on the floor, even if she'd kept her eyes on the long table right behind where Perry stood, but she didn't. She looked up at that instant right into Perry's face.

The eyebrows were Tyrone's, but the rest of that face was years ahead of Tyrone, filled with those deep river lines that meant he had lived awhile, knew a little about the hard life. She looked at that face and all that that face meant. What did it mean? She hadn't figured it out. All she knew was that her mouth was dry and her hands were wet. The skin on her face was tight and hot, and she knew it was shadowed in red.

Perry was looking at her now, and his look was as strong as the lines in his face. He knew the look of women, and since he did know, he was surprised as he looked at Ramona now and saw that unmistakable look of roundness, like a rhododendron that swells itself shut right before the blossoms explode. He hadn't known. Damn. He couldn't acknowledge what he was seeing on her face, couldn't give rise to the desire that was in fact his own manhood rising, right now, catching him off center, like he hadn't been caught since he was a young man. And now he was a young man as he looked at her: He was Tyrone's age, and she was his woman. Damn, he thought, the Lord ain't supposed to put more on a mere man than he can stand; fine as she is, this just might be more than I can stand. Now he was ashamed at the thought. This was his son's lady. Not his brother's or uncle's or even best friend's. His son's.

Now he cleared his throat and forced a cough. Now he looked away from Ramona.

They did a cha-cha then, of pretending not to see what each was in fact seeing. Now they looked around everywhere in the printshop except at each other.

"Could you, um, tell Tyrone, um—"

"I'll tell um, Tyrone, um—"

"Um, thanks, um, Perry. See you later."

She was out of the door then. She almost stumbled across the street she was rushing so, to get back to the Laundromat, where she should have stayed in the first place, she told herself, so she'd be there to add fabric softener at the right time in the cycle, and the blue-in for extra whitening. Should have even gone back home in between cycles instead of trying to seduce Tyrone; should have dragged another load over, to make sure there was enough clean linen to last in case she couldn't get back to the Laundromat for a while, in case the pavements became impassable to that wheeled laundry cart should the storm hit.

18

THE storm hit. After midnight it started with pretty, twirling snowflakes that could have been pink-draped ballerinas, their fall to the earth was so full of grace. Until the wind lumbered in, a continuous blast of wind that was like a clumsy giant. Tripping all over itself, knocking everything in its path hard to the ground: tree branches, power lines, roof shingles, even the warmth in the air. And what it didn't knock down, it bumped into and pushed and sent flying, like trash cans, milk bottles, porch chairs, and now three big-legged, brown-skinned, richly bundled girls clinging to a light pole and to each other so that they wouldn't be blown away from where they stood, waiting, watching, praying for a bus that would take them to their aunts and uncles.

"There's no bus coming, Shern." Bliss yelled to be heard over the loud-talking giant of a wind. "We have to go back. Tell her, Tore. We have to go back to Mae's or we'll die out here."

"We do, Shern." Victoria tried to yell too, but her voice cracked so she pressed her head into the back of Shern's neck, forced her voice through the double-knitted scarf so it would get to her ears. "We're going to get frostbitten out here. Come on, Shern, we tried, okay, but it's not going to work this time."

Shern knew they were right. She had hoped that the bus was just late. Had reasoned that buses were often late. Weren't Mae and Ramona and even Tyrone always complaining about the so and so bus that didn't get to the bus stop until such and such a time? But this bus wasn't late. She peered down the street one more time just to make sure, no flickering bus lights, no car lights, for that matter. The only light came from the snowflakes, which were no longer ballerinas but spiked-heeled witches taunting them each time they landed against their flesh, just the snow and the girls and the vacuous stretch of frigid night air filled with the sounds of the lumbering giant wind.

Shern loosed her arms from the pole, called around her to tell Victoria to keep herself wrapped tightly against her back, told her to tell Bliss to do the same. They left the bus stop then, looking like three girls playing choo-choo train the way Victoria was linked to Shern's back and Bliss was linked to Victoria's. They all had their heads down, even Shern, who was trying to be their guide. But Shern could look up only in short glimpses, the witches' heels were so assaultive against her face driven by the giant wind.

And when she did look up, the entire neighborhood had taken on such a snow-draped sameness that it seemed they were struggling against the wind up the same block over and over again. She lost count. Had they turned at the second corner or the third? Should she now go right or left? If she turned up this street, at least the wind would be at her back, and then she could turn right at the next corner. She was confused. She kept moving, though. She had to keep moving, even as she could feel Victoria behind her, dragging her leg; what she must be going through with that hurt leg. Now she could hear Bliss crying, sobbing. "We're gonna die, oh, sweet Jesus, we're gonna die." She wanted to tell Bliss to stop hollering like that, to save her breath, to keep her head buried in Victoria's back so her tears wouldn't freeze to her face. But she couldn't yell out. She was too tired. Too lost. Too defeated. They would have to stop. They would just have to walk up on somebodys porch and ring the bell, bang on the door, break through the window, if need be. She raised her head a little to look for a house. There were no houses. Nothing but trees. The trees looked so warm and beautiful under their white, satiny blankets, and for a second she wanted to curl up under the blanket too. But then the wind giant's thumb went right to her chin, tilted her chin back so that she had to look all the way up, moved the rest of its massive body through the snow witches' spiked heels, cleared the air so she could focus.

Now she did cry out. Wasn't that the beginning of the park across the street? And wasn't this building adjacent to where they stood right now the abandoned bread factory? And now the corner where they stood, wasn't this the foot of the block where Victoria had fallen? Shern couldn't believe it. She had walked them in the wrong direction all right. She had walked them back to Dead Block.

She felt like she was falling again, the same way she'd felt the day before as she'd sat on the holy woman's steps. This time the sinking was in her chest, pulling her down, persuading her to give up, to lay her sisters in the snow and then cover them with her own body so she could die first. She was too depleted to fight the sinking, should have just given up that morning when she'd found her mother with her wrists separating from her hands. Then she wouldn't have had to endure the social workers, Mae's, that shed; she could be curled up with her mother right now, both labeled mentally ill. Her knees started to bend, her back curved, her chin pressed against the knot in her double-knitted scarf. She could feel Victoria's weight, so heavy against her back now, Victoria's arms hugging her waist, trying to hoist her up, trying not to let her sink. But she knew Victoria's leg must be ready to give out. Poor Victoria, she rarely complained; that had always been her strength—and her weakness. She should rest now; they all should rest. She could even feel her faith leaving her body in rapid exhalations of the frigid air. Her knees were bent completely; she barely felt them touch the snow through her double-layered leotards and wide-wale corduroy pants. She just wanted to lie on her side, to curl up under the fluffy white blanket, and finally to go to sleep.

But the wind kept her from sleep, stroked her face over and over with snow-laden breaths. She lifted her gloved hands to her face, to shield her face from the persistent wind-driven snowflakes. Then she felt Bliss's voice against her face; her voice was hot and round with hysteria. "Shern, get up. What are you doing? My God, my God. Get up! Let's pull her up, Tore; she'll freeze to death just kneeling in the snow like that. Come on, Shern, get up! Get up! Get up!"

Candlelight flickered deep inside the bread factory as if the tiny flame itself could hear Bliss's cries. Mister held his flame to the window and got excited when he saw it was those three little gals from last Saturday. He'd known since the day that middle one fell that those gals would be back. It wasn't just the library books that they'd left on the sidewalk right by his front door, the books he'd dusted every day and kept out of the sun so that the pages wouldn't yellow; it was their eyes, like the eyes on the Korean girls who had seen their villages bombed. That's why he hadn't pushed when they refused his offers of help. One thing he'd learned in his hours of sweet solitude down here was that there was rarely a need to push; it was the gentle wave that inched farthest inland. So as excited as he was to see the three girls outside his bedroom window, which had once been the lower vestibule to the bread factory, he contained himself. He pulled his pants over his long johns and threw on his orange and gray plaid flannel shirt. He grabbed his coat from the hall closet, actually the pantry where the day-old bread had been kept for resale when his home was still a bread factory. He went around to his terrace, to the side door that would open right where they were standing.

That's when Shern felt his voice against her face. Thought at first she was already dead and this was the voice of Jesus it felt so warm and soft against her face. "Come on, child. Let's get you in where it's warm. Tempest rising out here. Yeah. Let's go in. Come on, child. Let's go in. Yeah."

19

At first Ramona thought that it was the spanking sound of the metal trash can rolling around in the yard that jolted her awake, but then she realized all at once that it was the stillness from the girls' room seeping through the walls and covering her like a shroud. She sat straight up in her bed, almost gasping for breath. The bedroom air was gray and pink from the outside clouds billowing through her window and mixing with her pink-bulbed night-lamp. It had snowed. She could see the snow-laden branches on the backyard tree that was the center of her bedroom window. Maybe that's why the quiet was so unsettling and going right to her chest; the storm had hit after all.

No, that wasn't it. It did have to do with those girls. She had become accustomed to emerging from her morning dreams to their sounds, whether it was muffled cries, or Bliss and Shern arguing, or the three whispering, or even just their rustling around on the bed and causing the springs to creak. But this morning there were no sounds sifting through the wall, just a rigor mortis–type stillness, as if even the air in the room were locked into place.

She jumped out of her bed, pounded her feet to the floor, fists balled, face fixed like someone ready to do battle. She punched her arms through the air down the short stretch of hallway to get next door to those girls' room. She just stood there after she threw open the door, and then she was assaulted by the emptiness in the room, as if the emptiness were an oversized hand that slapped her repeatedly in the face. She turned her head to and fro, trying to shake off the emptiness, cursing it, and yelling for the girls as she did.

She ran through the house, then, snatching open doors and then banging them shut. She called out their names as she ran. "Bliss, Shern, Victoria, don't pull this shit on me." She was sweating and shaking and gasping. "Where the hell are you?" she shouted. She went out on the front porch; the only footsteps interrupting the fresh coat of snow were her own. She looked up and down the block in its gray and white stillness, moved like a flooding stream back through the house, then down into the basement, even looked under the furniture down there. She burst through the door to Addison's bedroom in the shed, yanked the blanket from him just to make sure. Finally she went into Mae's room. She stilled her shaking by the time she stood at the foot of Mae's bed, Mae's ward leader, Bernie, nestled under the sheet against Mae, snoring with his mouth open. The gray outside air rushing through the venetian blinds made the scene on the bed appear like a black-and-white movie on a cheap TV.

Mae sat up all at once. "Who's that?" she asked squinting through the gray air. "Ramona, is that you? What's wrong with you busting through my door without announcing yourself? I ought to knock the living shit out of you." She pulled the bed sheet over to cover herself and, in so doing, left Bernie exposed.

"They're gone," Ramona said. She looked away from Mae, preferring to look at the naked mass of the ward leader than watch Mae try to cover her breast, then her thigh, then her breast again. "The girls, they're gone, they're gone, gone."

"What you mean, gone? What the fuck you let happen to those girls?"

Bernie snorted and shook himself awake and let out a small scream seeing himself exposed like that. He grabbed the edge of the sheet wrapped around Mae, and they played tug-of-war with the sheet, leaving them both half naked.

Ramona turned her back on them and talked to the wall. She threw her voice against the wall as if her voice were a sledgehammer and she needed to crack through the wall. "Gone, gone, they're gone," she said. "I looked everywhere. They're gone."

There was a small knock on Mae's door, and Addison edged the door open and stepped lightly into Mae's bedroom, asking, "Everything okay, aunts?" He looked at Ramona quizzically, facing the wall. "You on punishment, cuz? Looks like all you need is a dunce's hat." He laughed and then looked at the bed, at Mae and her ward leader fighting over the larger piece of sheet. "Awl, damn," he said, covering his eyes and backing out of the bedroom. "Shit."

Bernie huffed and puffed and threw up his hands and didn't even try to cover himself anymore. He jumped off the bed and grabbed his pants from the chair and did cover his front with the pants. He bounded out of the room and slammed the bathroom door shut. Mae propped herself up in the bed to sitting and leaned her back against her headboard, fully covered with the sheet now, looking as if she were waiting to be served breakfast in bed. "Ramona," she said calmly, "I think you got some explaining to do."

"Me?" Ramona's voice screeched, and she turned back to face Mae, to glare at her, to tell her once and for all that she was a sad excuse for a foster mother and an even more pathetic natural one. But Mae's expression was so steady, like the face she put on at the card table when it was time to raise or fold, her drooping eye blinking out of sync with her good one, that Ramona swallowed the rest of her words, and only air was left in her mouth, which she huffed at Mae, and then stomped out of Mae's bedroom. She ran back to the girls' bedroom to survey it again, maybe get some clues. Wasn't kidnapping a possibility? Weren't their parents rich? Maybe she should hunt for a ransom note. She let the thought go as quickly as it had come. Kidnapping wasn't a possibility. She was sure. Nor did she need to go in that room to find out why they'd left. The whys were running all through that house. Starting with Addison, she thought, and his dick that was where his brain should be, and Mae with her sweet-sounding words that were like cotton candy, no insides to her words at all, just puffs of sugar-coated air. Even herself. She didn't want to begin to see her own behavior, hear her own words, which had been filled with venom for the girls. Even after she had allowed Victoria to get close to that part of her she'd kept buried and covered with granite, she would still use her words to slap around Bliss and Shern every chance she got. Especially Shern.

The closed bedroom door stopped her thoughts about Shern. Now she was flooded with the image of the girls curled up in that twin bed. Now she hoped that maybe she just thought the beds were empty, that she'd woke in a fog and gone in there before her eyes were working right. "Please let them be here," she whispered against logic, praying now that she wouldn't have to pick up the phone to call the police to report them missing. She opened the door lightly. She would have to call the police. The bed was empty. They were gone.

She went back into the girls' room to wait for the police to come. The massive gray cloud had gotten comfortable with this day and was all leaned back in the sky and only allowing a thread of the early-morning pink to push through the window. The pink settled in the bedroom and illuminated what the girls had left behind. The beds appeared freshly made, and Ramona almost choked on the thought that those girls were the type who took the time to make up the bed they'd slept in even as they were preparing to run away. Their trunk was still there; their book bags were piled neatly in the corner; they'd even left shoes behind, lined up in size order and peeking from under the spread. She got down on her knees and searched under the beds for their fur-lined boots. Good, there was a hole under the bed where the boots usually stood; at least their feet may have stayed dry and warm through the night.

Shern's lime green velvet bathrobe was folded at the foot of the bed, and Ramona picked it up and felt around in the pockets, for what she didn't know. The pockets were empty, and she held the robe up to straighten it out and fold it down again. She was struck then by the feel of the robe, the way the soft lush threads were warm under her fingers as they yielded to her press and then surrounded her fingers and held them there. She'd never owned anything where the richness permeated every fiber. Even the way the robe smelled, a light sweetness to it, like lavender with a touch of mint, not like the heavy perfume she wore that she bought on special that sometimes reminded her of how a funeral parlor smelled.

She imagined Shern and her mother shopping for the robe together. Maybe they'd just had lunch in the Crystal Room at John Wanamaker's and then taken the escalator down to the fourth floor, where the sales manager of the fine lingerie department waited on them personally, offered them tea and cookies, and then they sat in the dainty parlor chairs and sipped tea from real china as they waited for the robe to be boxed and wrapped. Ramona was sure that they filled the time with warm chatter, Shern's mother telling Shern things a girl becoming a woman should know.

Ramona put the robe on and tied the belt around her waist. She lifted the shawl collar up around her chin and breathed in the gentle puffs of lavender and mint rising from the robe like a morning fog. She looked at herself in the mirror in that soft, rich robe. People were always telling her how pretty she was, and some days, right after she'd gotten her hair done and had on a good blouse and her thin gold-tone hoop earrings, she could see that she was pretty. But she'd never felt it. Couldn't even dream up what pretty would feel like. Except standing in this tight bedroom looking at herself in the mirror in this sweet-smelling robe, the collar pulled up Loretta Young style, she began to sense how pretty must feel, how pretty Shern must have felt every time she put on that robe.

She tilted her chin and gently pushed her hands into the slit pockets and swayed back and forth in the robe. She could almost hear what Shern must have heard from her mother, hard and soft words about how to live. Courage and dignity wrapped up in her words like spiced apples tucked inside a strip of dough. She imagined that as Shern sat there holding the china cup, she must have felt a rising in her chest that went way beyond just feelings of physical beauty. A line of strength and determination rising up in her like a flag being raised the likes of which had allowed Shern to pack up her sisters and break away from Mae's.

Damn, she thought, Shern had gotten out, accomplished in a single month what Ramona hadn't accomplished in a decade. Now Ramona was sorry she'd called the police. She wanted to shout instead, "You go on, Shern. You take God with you, girl, and you just go on. You got out, Shern. You got out."

She wrapped herself tighter in the robe, tried to nestle her head under the collar, took in the air under the robe that was green like the robe, and soft and sweet. She could feel that stirring in her chest again, a stem of something green like a sapling trying to grow around a rock to get some sun. This time the sapling was stronger than usual, more persistent, but there was the granite, the rock, with mean, jagged edges. The rock was taking over her chest again like it always did when she tried to think about it. She gasped, felt like she was choking. She would just have to choke; she had to let herself remember, swathed in the green of the robe as she was. And then it came. She didn't even have to force the remembrance. The granite exploded into tiny bits of sand; then the remembrance just poured out in front of her and moved along on the gray, cloudy air.

E<small>VEN</small> the air in the park was green that day. Blades of grass and tree leaves and shrubbery and stems trumpeted their deepest shades of green because these were the last days of summer and the air swept it all up and dripped color on Ramona and she got a smile in her stomach as she and Mae got closer to the park.

Ramona was five and on her way home from her first day of afternoon kindergarten. She held tightly to Mae's hand as they jaywalked to get across the street to the park. "My teacher says only cross on the green," Ramona blurted as Mae half dragged her across the street before the cars rushed down. "She said a car could hit you and then you would be dead."

"Tell your teacher to kiss my ass," Mae said absentmindedly, and then laughed. "No, don't tell her I said that, lil darling. She's right, we should be crossing on the green, we should be crossing at the corner too. But I got things on my mind. Now you asked me to bring you to the park, okay. We're at the park. Good and empty this time of day, too. Glad I picked you up early so we got this spot in the park all to ourselves. I'm gonna sit right here on this bench and do some heavy thinking while you go play. And stay in my eyesight while you do, you hear me. And please, please don't scuff up your new school shoes."

Ramona jumped up and down and pulled her hand from Mae's. "Okay, Mommie," she called behind her as she ran down a slope of grass straight to the swing. She hoisted herself up on the wooden seat and grabbed the chain links in her tiny hands. She mashed her feet against the earth for her takeoff into what always felt like heaven to her, flying through the green park air, the air whistling in her ears, the aroma of bread baking in the factory across the street going right to her head, making her head feel lighter, the sight of the tree leaves from up high, the sun dancing under her chin as she threw her head back and laughed out loud. She kicked her legs out, then in, then out, until she got the shrill in her stomach that told her she was going high enough, so she eased back on the motion of her legs to maintain the speed that was laughable and fun.

But this day she felt a push against her back just as she tried to slow down the swing. It was a heavy push against her small back, and it sent her up and through the air at the height that was scary. "Stop!" she screamed as she hunched her back to make the shrill in her stomach go away. She looked down and saw the baseball bat on the grass, knew it was that Donald Booker who was always bullying people, especially black people, with that bat. Had everyone at Sayre Junior High, where he sometimes showed up for class, terrorized with that bat.

"Stop it, Donald Booker, right now," she yelled. "I don't want to go that high."

But Donald Booker didn't stop. He pulled the swing back as far as he could and then with all of his force catapulted Ramona on the swing through the air. Ramona got a feeling in her stomach like she'd never had, like a scream filled with circles of white light. She almost felt it right now, standing in the bedroom wrapped in Shern's soft green robe. She had to sit down on the bed, had to lean forward so the feeling would stop, so she could finish remembering.

"Mommie, Mommie, help me," she'd screamed. She was coughing and choking and hollering out for Mae.

"Your momma ain't nothing but Bernie's nigger girl," Donald Booker sang, "Bernie's girl, Bernie's girl, your momma ain't nothing but Bernie's nigger girl from early in the morning."

"Help me, Mommie," Ramona cried. "Mommie! Mommie! Mommie!"

"You no-good bastard," she heard her mother yell frantically from far away. "You leave her alone right now, right now, or I swear I'll fuck you up." Mae's voice got closer as she yelled, and then she was right there almost talking in Ramona's ear.

"Mommie, Mommie," she sobbed, as she felt Mae grab the chain link of the swing arm and hold it still so Ramona could get down. "He was scaring me, Mommie, and making me go too high in the swing." She fell into Mae's arms and rested her head against her chest, which smelled like fresh-cut grass.

"He's not gonna bother you anymore, lil darling, Mommie's here," Mae said as she held Ramona to her and mashed her chin into the top of her head.

Ramona had forgotten that Mae used to do that, hold her tight like that. She took her hand from the pocket of the soft lime green robe and rubbed it through her hair. She could almost feel Mae's chin there the way it must have felt all those years ago, moving up and down against Ramona's head as she told Donald Booker about his bad-assed self.

"Go on, you juvenile delinquent boy, and get home where you belong before I do to you what your momma should 'ave been doing," she said, still holding Ramona tightly. "Big as you are and you ain't got nothing better to do than to pick with babies."

Donald Booker poked his thin lips at Mae. He was as tall as Mae, and Ramona was almost afraid for her mother as he stared in Mae's face like he was grown too. "Awl, shut up, Bernie's nigger girl," he huffed.

"Wh-what did you say to me, you heathenistic son of a bitch?" Mae unwound her arms from Ramona, stooped down lower to whisper in Ramona's ear, stretched and reached for the baseball bat as she did. "You go start on up the slope, lil darling. I'll be right there."

Ramona clung tighter to Mae; she didn't want to leave her. Donald Booker's chest was swelled up like he was ready to do something to Mae, spit in her face or lift his foot to kick at her. But Mae gave Ramona a hard and soft shove. "Go on, lil darling," she said, "just stand under that wide tree with the big arms; the arms will protect you till I get up there."

Ramona started up the slope, reluctantly. She could hear Mae telling Donald Booker that he needed a lesson taught to him. By the time she got to the top of the hill and was standing under the tree she couldn't hear anything they were saying, as if the woods around the bottom of the park were gobbling up their sounds. She could see Donald Booker's mouth moving, his face getting redder and closer and closer to her mother's face, his shoulders going back and forth like he was putting up his dukes. Then his hand stretched way back and came forward right toward Mae's face. Ramona started running back down the slope, hollering, "You better not hit my mother, you better leave my mother alone." She saw his hand stopped in midair by the bat, sent flying way over his shoulder. Then she saw his head go back too, just like his hand had. She was close enough to hear the crack of the bat against his head, and now she could hear Mae too. "Threaten me, will you, or any part of me, I'll teach your no-good ass a lesson you'll never forget. Get up, you grown, you gonna jump at me, get on up, and finish what you started."

But Donald Booker didn't get up. Even when Mae leaned down over him, and shook him, and slapped at his face, he didn't get up. With Mae stooping over him as she was, all Ramona could see were his dirty canvas sneakers. Then Mae stood, and Ramona could see his head, how odd his head looked. Not just that it was swollen, but the way it was arched, as if he were getting ready to do a backward flip, as if his head and neck didn't belong to the same body.

Ramona pulled her hands from the pocket of the soft green robe. She knitted and unknitted her fingers in quick movements that made her knuckles click, much the same way Mae clicked her knuckles that afternoon. Her drooping eye was just about shut tight, and her voice shook as she spoke. "Ramona," she said, "this don't look good, not good at all." She picked up the handle of the bat and wiped it in the pleats of her belted sundress and let it fall down the hem of her dress into the grass. "Him being a white boy and all, Lord, no. This is serious, very, very serious."

She reached for Ramona's hand. "You and me gonna walk out of the park, and this never happened, you hear me." Her voice shook less the more she talked.

"Huh?" Ramona asked.

"Don't talk, just listen," she said as she looked all around them. "We wasn't at the park today. We took the long way home from your school because I had the taste for some fish from the fish store on Market Street. But we didn't go into the fish store because once we got there I didn't like the smell of the fish sitting on ice in the barrel outside, so we came on home. Now that's all we did this afternoon. The rest never happened."

"What never happened, Mommie?"

"Ramona, are you messing with me or what? Now, this is important. I'm trying to get you to understand that this afternoon never happened. We wasn't at the park today, Ramona. You don't see Donald Booker back there laying in the grass."

Ramona was trying to understand what Mae was saying. She turned around to look back at Donald Booker. She gasped. "He's not laying in the grass, Mommie. Look, he's getting up. Now he's walking like a drunk man further in the woods. He has his bat too, Mommie. Look."

"I'm not looking back there. And don't you either." She yanked Ramona's hand. "Might turn into a pillar of salt looking back there. Ain't no way that boy got up."

"Yes, he did, he got up, Mommie, honest he did. Just look and see for yourself." Ramona felt Mae's hand clap hard against her mouth in a way that Mae had never slapped her before. It was such a forceful slap that it seemed as if night fell all at once and she could no longer see the green or smell the bread, and now she was cold too.

"Shut up! We weren't here. We went for fish. We took the long way home. We'll never speak about this again as long as we live. And there ain't no way that boy got up. Just ain't no way. Now say it. Say what we did today."

"We went for fish." Ramona pushed the words through her mouth, which was already beginning to swell. "You changed your mind. We took the long way home." She sobbed the rest of it out. She was dizzy and confused as she felt her lips puff up. She waited for Mae to tell her not to cry, to call her lil darling. But Mae never did, not the whole walk home. It was a long, silent walk as Ramona kept licking her lips, nursing them, trying to get rid of the puffy, burning feeling, grabbing for her mother's hands. Mae would hold her hand for a second or two and then drop it, suddenly, as if she'd just remembered something she'd forgotten.

And when they got home that evening and Ramona said that

she was hungry, Mae told her to make herself a sandwich for dinner, and later, to take her bath on her own, to roll up her own bangs, to lay out her own clothes for the next day of school, to learn to say her prayers by herself. And Ramona, obedient child that she was, did everything Mae told her to, including the most important thing: She forgot.

20

Ness, Blue, and Show made a circle around Til as she talked on the phone with the buggy-eyed clerk giving her news about the girls. "Addison Street, hunh? Mae? Ramona? No, I'm not writing it down; Bic can't invent a ballpoint pen that could scrawl out what you just told me and make it more indelible on paper than it is on my heart right now." She hung up the phone. "We going to West Philly," she said. "Addison Street. We gonna talk to some one named Mae or her legal substitute, her daughter, Ramona. Gonna find out what caused Shern to have to call here and moan into the phone line. Gonna call that scary-assed lawyer too. Put him on alert. Tell him that if I don't like what I see, he might have to come and bail me out of jail later on today."

"I'll call a yellow cab, Sister," Ness said, stroking Til's arms to try to keep her calm.

"I'll line the boots up in the vestibule," said Show. "We surely won't have a merry time walking down those steps."

"Maybe one of the neighborhood kids will come by to shovel," said Blue. "I'll go down in the basement and bring up the shovel, leave it out front since we don't have time to heave ho at snow right now."

"Any excuse to get down in that basement to your stash of sherry, huh, Blue?" Til smirked.

"Actually we do have time," Ness called as she waved the phone. "Hour and a half delay on getting a cab delivered to our door due to the storm."

"Go get the shovel, Blue." Til sighed. "I'll do it. My muscles jumping all over the place at the thought of getting ready to see those girls, I got to move around right now. You go have yourself your nip; have one for me too. Just be standing straight and tall in an hour and a half so we can get right in the cab when it comes."

21

Addison blinked hard to shut out the gray sky barrelling in through the living-room window and almost blinding him. He hated morning. Had grown up spending most mornings trying to stay asleep. But this morning he was up thanks to the commotion in Mae's bedroom over those girls being gone. Little Miss Goody Two-shoes done run away, and now I don't have any amusement when I'm bored, he said to himself as he pulled the string to draw the shade down some at the living-room window. Can't wink at her no more and watch her cower, or try to touch her half-girl, half-woman parts and get off on her hysteria.

He went to the closet to get his jacket, figured he'd rather slip and slide down the snow-covered block than be here to listen to the rumbling now coming from overhead in Mae's bedroom. He wanted to spit when he thought about it. Bad enough he'd had to listen to the joker hollering half the night, he hadn't even had the decency to leave before the sun got up so Addison wouldn't have had to catch him trying to cover his ass. He was mad at his aunt too, a rare thing, just for letting him see her like that. She was his mother's sister all right, he thought, shaking his head, trying not to remember the times he'd seen his mother scrambling to cover her own bareness.

He stuffed his arms into his fleece-lined bomber jacket, decided he'd walk the streets and see what he could get into, maybe hang in front of Smitty's and wait for him to open, play a little pinball. He was at the door, and right before he opened it he saw the police out front. He immediately knew they were police because they were in a '65 Impala. The detectives in Buffalo drove the same car. Plus they had that unmistakable cops' head, more forehead than dome. Usually that type car, those shaped heads would send him into a panic, have him running through the house for a back door, or a side window that dropped into an alley, even a crawl space where he could squeeze his tall, thin frame and elude them. But he'd been on relatively good behavior here, only shoplifted twice, a silver-toned cigarette lighter and a pack of Top paper; at both stores he'd escaped notice. No, these cops weren't here for him this time. So he didn't have to run through the house and find an exit into the alley. He could open the front door for a change, invite them in, offer them a seat, call them sir. He was getting amused at the prospect. His boys back home would never believe that he'd played good host to the police in the middle of his aunt's living room.

But right then he heard Mae and her all-night company coming down the stairs. They were arguing coming down the stairs, and Addison walked back to his bedroom, muttering curse words to himself; this joker was intent on ruining his day, first by being naked in his aunt's bed, now by getting in the way of Addison having a little fun playing nice boy for the cops.

He pulled his shed door to and then cracked it a bit, just so he could peep into the living room and make sure the joker didn't try any fast moves with his aunt, loud as he was talking. He could see the half-dressed white man standing in the living room, buttoning his shirt as he yelled at Mae, "Now, Mae, they're limits to what I can do. I'm not even gonna begin to promise I can keep this from being part of the public record. Missing children is a serious thing, a very serious thing."

"I thought you could do anything in this city," Mae said, shaking her finger up to Bernie's face. "Isn't that what you're always telling me, that you're such a fucking power broker? Now when I really need you to broker some power, you tell me it's too hard."

Bernie threw his shoes against the floor with such force that Addison almost flung his door open to tell Bernie just to hold up, don't be getting all carried away now. He didn't, though. He listened instead. "Now, Mae, every time you've needed something done it's the most important thing," Bernie said, stuffing his shirt into his pants. "Every time I've fixed the situation when your card house gets raided, or the kids report to their social worker that you're never here, that it's Ramona that's always here, or when you're late with your paperwork, even when you're not rightfully next in line to get more kids, I've always fixed it. Haven't I, Mae? But missing children, Mae, I'm sorry, I'm just sorry."

"Yeah, well, I'm sorry too, motherfucker," Mae said, and Addison had to cover his mouth or he would have shouted, "Go ahead and tell him about himself, Aunt Mae."

Mae wouldn't have heard him, though. She was like a typhoon blowing and spitting.

"Dammit, now, Mae, it's missing children. I can't touch that—"

"Well, don't try to touch this, you whore-making son of a bitch."

Mae lifted her housecoat. Now Addison did turn away, out of respect. The doorbell sounded, and Addison jumped. He reminded himself again that the police weren't here for him. He closed his door all the way shut, until just a minute later it burst open frantically, Bernie standing there, red-faced and sweating. "Wrong door, my man," Addison said, matter-of-factly. "If you're trying to find an alley to run through, you want the next door over."

22

Ramona curled herself tighter in a ball on the girls' bed still snuggled in Shern's robe. She rocked and moaned and pressed her knees into her stomach to still the grief spinning there. She missed her mother. Had missed her since that day in the park when Donald Booker spoiled it for them. All those years of not being held and rocked and kissed good-night. Keeping her ears perched, waiting to be called lil darling. Waiting. All the time waiting. She reasoned that was why she hadn't been able to leave. Why her feet would go to cement whenever she thought about walking out of that door for good. Why she would get a twinge that would propel her into grand irritation whenever someone mentioned how Donald Booker disappeared. Not a trace of him. Not his dirty sneakers, not his mean bat. Just vanished, they'd say.

What must her mother have gone through, knowing she killed that boy? Her blood must have gone to ice water every time she looked at me, Ramona thought, probably all the time waiting to see if I remembered. Probably why she treated me like she hated me all these years. Probably did hate me, probaby incapable of love, having to keep that day buried in her heart like that.

This she said out loud as she unfurled herself from the bed. She fluffed the pillow, but a sag persisted in its center. "Guess you done had it with daughters mashing their faces into you of late, crying 'cause they miss their mothers," she said to the pillow.

She heard the doorbell then, smelled boot polish. Knew it was the police. She smoothed the robe out, tied the belt tighter around her waist, folded the collar down the way she'd seen Shern wear it. She started down the hallway to go to the bathroom to wash her tear-stained face. Then she would go downstairs to tell the police what they needed to know.

Mae ushered the police into the living room and sat quickly. She had to sit quickly, her knees were bending so. She was wearing one of Ramona's better dusters; she'd taken it from Ramona's room last night because she knew that Bernie was staying. But last night she had the barrel-shaped wooden buttons unfastened almost to her waist. She had them fastened up to the collar now, even had the drawstring at the top tied around her neck; she wanted to appear pious.

The sound of the plastic chair covering breathing under her weight as she sat on the couch startled her, and she jumped. She rarely sat on the couch or even in the living room, for that matter. Her usual seat was at the dining-room table; she'd always been more comfortable with a table around her because a table was a prelude for a card game. But she wasn't inviting these trench coat–wearing detectives into her dining room. She'd worked too hard for nearly the past two decades to keep them out of her house altogether, kept at bay in all that time the shadowy fear of this moment, detective police in her house, asking her questions.

She breathed in and out, slowly, trying to quell the thumping in her chest. She didn't want to appear nervous; do that, and they'd really go to snooping, she thought. Start to dredging up the present and the past, making the two blend so you wouldn't be able to tell one from the other.

She cleared her throat. "Have a sit down."

She was sure she saw them look at each other before they both replied, "No, thanks," and, "That's okay." Had she said it wrong? she wondered. Something in her voice make them think she had something to hide. She glanced from one to the other. They were both tall, beefy, one silver-haired, the other just about bald. One was leaning on the banister that led up the stairs; the other stood in the center of the room, his coat pushed back, showing the silver handcuffs hanging from his pants pocket. A trail of dirty water sat on top of the plastic carpet runner where they'd tracked in melting snow. Mae was usually particular about her carpet. Had threatened people with their lives over not wiping their feet before tracking through on her new carpet. But now she just sat and watched the water trail off the runner and seep into the carpet fibers. She figured she'd need to keep her wits about her should they try to mess with her mind; she wouldn't waste her good thinking rebuking them for bringing melted snow into the house.

"Pictures?" the silver-haired one asked.

Mae cleared her throat again. She told herself to stop clearing her throat. "Ugh, Vie, the case manager, I'm sure she has pictures."

"Describe them, please." The bald-headed one said this and flipped open a top-spiraled bound notebook. "And also, if you know what they were wearing, that would be real helpful."

Suddenly Mae couldn't remember a single item of clothing those girls owned. She couldn't even remember the color of their everyday coats. "Funny what you remember at a time like this," she said.

"Excuse me," the bald one said.

Mae looked at him with his pen poised over his pad. She'd expected a tape recorder. Didn't the police use a tape recorder on *Perry Mason* when they thought they were close to a confession? What confession? The girls! She let the words burst in her head. They were here for the girls, not for her, not for Donald Booker. "I'm just saying I don't remember what they might be wearing.

That's all. And of all times, this time when they done turned up missing, I should remember."

She thought she heard the silver-haired one clear his throat as if he were signaling his partner. Probably getting ready to ask me what was I doing eighteen years ago that September afternoon, she thought. She decided then that she'd call them out on it, shit, who did they think they were messing with? Didn't they know that some of the best card sharks in the city had tried to mess with her mind and lost? "Look," she said. This time she deliberately didn't clear her throat. "Don't act like I'm saying something strange or acting strange. I see the way you and your bald-headed partner signaling each other like I got something to hide." She looked from one to the other. Let her drooping eye blink out of sync with her good one the way she'd always do at the top of her game. "I mean I could tell you what my only child was wearing in September some eighteen years ago. A navy pleated skirt, sky blue nylon knee-highs, a sky blue cotton blouse, and her new maroon oxfords from Shapiro's. Now. I can tell you that, okay. And I can't tell you what those girls was wearing yesterday. Is that so strange? Well, if you think that's strange, all I got to say is fuck you and your mommas."

"They got on plaid fleece-lined coats." Ramona's voice was calm and efficient floating down the stairs. "And their pictures were just in the *Tribune* when their daddy turned up missing a couple of months ago. I have that issue; I'll get it for you."

Now the two beefy men did clear their throats and look at each other and at Mae. "Your mother's tough," the silver-haired one said.

"Yes, siree." The bald one half laughed, "Why she got to bring our mommas into it?"

"Um, the shock, you know the girls missing." Ramona pushed the robe sleeves up on her arms and then smoothed at the back of her French roll. "She has a perfect record in foster care, you know. Isn't that right, Mommie?"

Mae was just staring straight ahead, fighting to focus on the police, on Ramona, on the melted snow seeping into her new wall-to-wall. But Ramona had just called her Mommie, hadn't called her Mommie in almost two decades. Mae's focus was distracted at the sound of that word. And the air in the living room was going quickly from gray to green.

"Um, come with me, please." Ramona rushed her words to the police when she noticed Mae just staring into space like that. Even guided the silver-haired one by the elbow, curled her fingers to the bald head, "Come, come," she said. "I can show you the girls' room just the way they left it. I'll bring you the newspaper with their picture in it. Coffee? Or water? Anything I can get for you? Um, please don't mind my mother; you can't imagine the shock for someone with a perfect record in foster care like hers."

They both pulled their attention from Mae. Ramona almost breathed out her great relief. She was almost pushing the silver-haired one up the steps, curling her fingers almost frantically for the bald head to follow. And she would have had them too. Would have closed the door on them in the girls' room while she ran back to help Mae get reoriented. But right then Mae cleared her throat. It was such an impervious sound, and they all three stopped where they were. "Damn!" Ramona said under her breath.

"I had on my fancy yellow sundress." Mae's voice was strained, weak. "I'm not a pretty woman, you know, not like my child over there, but I always felt so pretty in that sundress. So I put that dress on to pick Ramona up in, since it was the first day of school, so that the other children would think I looked nice too and maybe then they wouldn't tease Ramona about the way my eye has a tendency to droop."

"Mommie, you're talking silly." Ramona forced a laugh. "Please, detectives, the girls' room."

The bald head motioned for Ramona to be quiet. "The girls." He drew it out, spoke very slowly as if he were talking to the hearing-impaired. "What happened to the girls? Did you do something to the girls, Mae? This is important, and you have to tell us if you did."

"That boy's sneakers were dirty." Mae continued in the same weak voice. "Which was unusual for the first day of school because everybody wore their best shoes the first day. I could only conclude that his mother wasn't taking good care of him, must not have been any grandmother or aunt around either, not even a good preacher or deacon's wife to take an interest in the boy to make sure he had good shoes to start school in."

"Mommie—" Ramona's voice was pleading.

"I always made sure Ramona had good shoes on her feet. Everything I did back then was for Ramona. Mostly. Even when I took a man to bed, I was measuring him up to see what I could persuade him to buy for her, a new bike, some skates, a pink Hula Hoop. God knows I loved that child, that lil darling of mine—"

"The girls, Mae." The bald head cut her off. "What did you do to the girls? Why are they missing, Mae?"

"No, you wanted her to talk, let her talk," Ramona snapped at him, at the same time melting inside hearing Mae say what she just had.

Mae jerked to then. All of a sudden. Ramona taking up for her like was just odd enough to bring her back. She jumped up from the couch, pointed at the bald head. "What the fuck you keep talking 'bout those girls for? What I'm talking about don't have a thing to do with those girls. They ran away. Why you think you was called in? To find them. So why don't you go on and do just that?"

"Well, what were you talking about?" The silver-haired voice was smooth, persuading. "Who had dirty sneakers on, Mae? Tell us, please tell us."

"I'm talking about what I remember and what I don't, okay. I remember everything about my child's first day of school, okay. And I don't remember what those girls were wearing yesterday. So why the fuck don't you do your job and go find them? Find them! It snowed last night, and they're out there in it. Dammit. Fucking find them!"

Ramona let her pent-up breaths out. Tried not to smile. Tried not to blush with pride over her mother, her mean, conniving, loose, foulmouthed wizard of a mother whom she couldn't wait to start learning how to love all over again.

23

THE girls slept through the rest of the storm on Mister's couch and looked like dominoes leaning toward a fall: Bliss half sitting against Victoria, Victoria half sitting against Shern, Shern with her head nestled in her elbows against the arm of the couch. Victoria woke first. She woke all at once with her heart beating in her ears; she couldn't have slept for more than an hour, she thought. She sat straight up and let out a small moan. Shern's back had been an uncomfortably hard pillow, and now she had a crick in her neck. Plus her knee had gone through the night unelevated and was throbbing again like it hadn't throbbed since she'd started on the penicillin. She hoped Shern had remembered to pack her medicine.

She looked down, was half covered over with a big black coat; she guessed it was Mister's coat and pushed it over onto Bliss; she was warm enough since she'd slept in all of her clothes except for her plaid pile-lined coat. Her sisters had done the same. Shern had even slept in her gloves. She still had one on; the other she had stuffed into the pocket of the big black coat that had been their blanket. Victoria noticed the incongruity of the purple knitted glove peeking from the pocket of the oversized man's wool coat.

Gray air poured in through the tall windows and the skylight, and now Victoria could see the room absent the shadows that had been everywhere in here last night, riding up and down the ceiling and the walls whenever Mister moved around the room with that candle flickering under the frosted glass globe. The makeshift coffee table in front of the couch where they'd slept was just that, two crates with a slab of wood on top, not the child-sized coffin, as it appeared to Victoria last night after her sisters had fallen asleep and she was wide-awake staring around the room, afraid to go to sleep, afraid some horrible tragedy would happen to them if she allowed herself to close her eyes on the room. The two overstuffed armchairs catty-corner to the couch were only chairs, not attack dogs waiting for a cue from Mister, the six odd-shaped cannon against the wall were actually their boots, taken off at Mister's persuasion so that they wouldn't catch pneumonia sleeping in furlined leather boots. Even Mister looked less threatening to Victoria under the gray daylight as he ambled into the room still wearing the orange and gray flannel shirt he'd worn the night before; he carried a small pot in one hand, three bowls in the other.

"Ah, you're up, huh, middle one. Just in time for a bowl of hot cereal. Yeah. You like hot cereal?" He lined the bowls up quietly on the purple and gold scarved table and spooned up smooth clumps of Cream of Wheat into the three bowls.

"Yeah, glad you gals came by and graced my little home here. Not a bad home, I must say, cool in the summer 'cause the ceilings so high, warm in the winter thanks to my potbelly stove over there."

He spoke softly, slowly. Surrounded with so much silence down here, he knew the power of a human voice. A steady tone of voice could sop up fear like a sponge, no matter what words were being spoken, just the connections of somebody's breaths shaped and formed through their vocal cords, mixing with another's ears going from the brain eventually to the heart, to calm it. So he kept his voice hushed and low; he let his words run together but in an unhurried way like a continuous, languishing hum.

"Nice amenities down here too," he went on. "Running water, yeah. City didn't shut the water off after the place reverted to them, too expensive to bleed the pipes in this old huge factory, so my man, Real Estate John, asked me to come in once a week and let the water run in the winter so the pipes wouldn't freeze. I did him one better. I run it every day. Moved on in here and found this to be my best home yet. And I've lived in some good places, let me tell you. Yeah."

Victoria didn't say anything except for a whispered "Is that so?" Now that they'd lived through the night, Victoria was irritated, a strange thing for the usually understanding, compliant, peacemaking middle sister. But the sore on her leg was itching, and she had to go to the bathroom, and she was sorry she'd allowed her sisters to talk her away from Mae's.

Mister opened miniature packets of granulated sugar and sprinkled the sugar over the cereal. The sugar sparkled under the early gray air falling in through the skylight and gave the sugar a pinkish hue. He went back into the other room and returned shortly with a container of powder and a glass of water. "I don't think I want any," Victoria said, as she watched the smoke rising off the cereal and realized that she was in fact hungry. But to gobble down the cereal this instant would make Mister feel good, and right now she was tired of making other people feel good. "I can't eat hot cereal without milk anyhow," she said.

She shifted on the couch, trying to sit up straighter without moving her leg too abruptly. She stood so she could straighten out her knee, ask to use the bathroom, but the sudden weight on her hurt leg felt like a burst of thunder had exploded in her leg and fizzled into red-hot filings that radiated up and down from her knee and now settled into a stream of pain that was beyond red; she couldn't even give this pain a color, it was so hot and searing moving up and down her leg. She cried out and fell back deeper into the couch, and then she just cried and begged for relief from the colorless pain.

Shern and Bliss both woke, clutching their chests, hollering, "What is it? What is it?"

"Oh, my God, are you okay, Tore?" First Bliss asked it.

Then Shern: "Oh no, it's not your leg again, is it? Darn! No! Don't tell me it's gotten that bad all over again."

Then Mister: "Shs, let's take a look. Is it still an open wound?"

They made a circle around Victoria as she writhed in pain on the couch.

"It is my knee." Victoria panted the words out and then started to cry. "I hope you remembered my medicine, Shern, I just hope you did. The infection can't heal without the medicine. The doctor said it specifically. You did bring it, didn't you, Shern? Please tell me that you brought it."

"Now, now, now," Mister cut in with that slow, steady tone. "What kind of medicine you talking about?"

"Her penicillin," Shern said. "I can't believe I forgot it. How could I have forgotten it? I knew how important it was too. I'm sorry, Victoria, I was so careful and organized too. Oh, God, oh, God."

"You forgot it? What do you mean, you forgot it?" Victoria sat forward on the couch, her lean face pointed like a knife at Shern. "We have to go back, we have to. Come on, let's go back so I can take my medicine." She tried to stand again, but the thunderbolt pain crackled through her leg and forced her down, and she leaned back against the arm of the couch and cried.

"Take it easy, now, middle one," Mister said slowly. "Let me go out back and get some ice in case if it's swelling." He was out of the room, and Shern sat down on the couch, deflated.

"Looks like we have to go back, Shern." Bliss tried to sound sober, but the excitement about going back to Mae's crept through her words. "I mean, I know I promised I would leave with you, and I really did keep my promise, we did leave, but Tore has to have her medicine. Don't you agree? You have to agree that's the most important thing right now?"

Shern put her hands on her head and jumped up from the couch and then jumped up and down. "Oh, God, I do have to go back there. I don't want to, I don't. We're so close to getting to the aunts and uncles too. We're just a bus ride away. Oh, God! What else can I do? I'll have to go back there and get the penicillin for Victoria." Shern spoke in fast circles, her voice getting higher in degrees. "I'll have to sneak in, oh, no, how can I sneak in? Everybody's probably up by now."

"They probably already called the police by now too," Bliss said, a smugness to her tone.

"Shut up, Bliss, just shut up and let me think!" Shern shouted and waved her hands around.

"There's nothing to think about; we just shouldn't have left." Bliss jumped up at Shern.

"Stop it!" Victoria covered her ears and screamed. "Stop it! Stop it! Please, just stop it." Then she startled the gray air in the room and startled herself even more when she began to call for her father.

"Daddy, Daddy, I want my daddy," she cried.

Then Bliss sobbed too. "I just want to feel his thumb on my forehead the way he used to do when I was sick."

And Shern joined in. "He would know what to do about Victoria's penicillin; he would even know where to get more."

They wrapped their arms around one another in a circle, Bliss and Shern holding their hurt sister up.

"Wait, little gals, I know where to get penicillin," Mister blurted into their circle. "My main man Smitty get me any kind of medicine I need. Of course I don't need much these days, yeah. Not like the old days. Stay put, little gals, I'll be right back; half hour is all I need. If it starts getting a little chilly in here, put a couple more pieces of wood under that black stove there, heat this room back up. But I'll be back in time before it gets cold, yeah. I'm gonna put this ice in the bathroom bowl; if that knee is swollen, hold the ice close to it. When I get back, we'll figure out whether you gals going home or whatever you gonna do. Yeah. Eat the cereal while it's hot, little gals. Mister be right back. Right back. Yeah." He grabbed his coat from the couch that had served the girls as a blanket and was out of the room, his footsteps echoing down the hallway as he left, Shern's purple glove peeking through the slit his pocket made.

The aroma of baking bread was stronger in here this morning after Mister left, intoxicating. The girls' crying lost its erratic, cutting quality, and they settled down to whimpers and then sniffs. Even Victoria's leg warmed, and the icy stabs of pain turned to a bearable pulsing. They went back to the couch and moved the makeshift table in closer so that Victoria could prop her leg. They fed one another tastes of the steaming cereal that went right to their stomachs and felt like sunlight. They huddled against one another and fell back asleep as they waited for Mister to return.

24

THE news of the girls missing spread through West Philly like lava oozing down a mountainside. This was burning, hot news: that Mae, who bragged about her perfect record in foster care, had lost three children at once. The news dripped and ran into the next block of Addison Street, around the corner, onto Osage, Pine, Spruce, Locust. Taking the routes where the news best flowed—through the basement corner stores like Mr. Ben's, famous for his barrels of sour dill pickles; Schaffer's, who made twenty-cent hoagies with salad dressing instead of mayo; Jeff Coats, who sold for a nickel packets of Nescafé coffee that restaurants gave for free; Lassister, where the children stopped on the way home from Sunday school to buy penny candy with the money they should have put into church. And once the corner stores got the news, the lava was like molten dust, falling on the coats of the people in and out of the corner stores, taken back out in the streets to the hairdressers, the cleaners, the meat store, the Laundromat, the printer—Perry's printshop, where Perry shut down his press once he heard, knew something must have happened when he hadn't seen that fine Ramona rush past his window the way she did every workday at seven forty-five.

He didn't even pause to call Tyrone to wake him up but did pause just long enough to undo his ink-stained apron, change into his black and white dress shirt, which he was going to wear later when he went to pick Hettie up, rub down his mustache with a dab of Murray's, splash on a little skin bracer, and pop a crystal mint Life Saver in his mouth. He locked up the shop and jumped in his deuce and a quarter, on his way to Addison Street, his heart thumping wildly in his chest, to see what he could do to help find those little lost girls.

R<small>AMONA</small> was praying for a ten-minute hole in the stream of activity so that she could lose herself in a hot tub of water and still her thoughts, which were whirling around like a last dance at the prom. Mae had left with the police to ride around for possible sightings and then to the station house to file an official report. Addison was probably somewhere trying to turn somebody's daughter out, Ramona figured. So now would be perfect. But then the phone kept ringing, a dozen more times at least; she could have been running a tape the way she was saying the same thing over and over: "Yeah. Looks like they ran away, thanks for the offer, yes, please call, any sign at all of them, please call."

People she hadn't seen in years stopped by, asking to look at a picture, to hear a description so they'd know should they spot the missing trio. A group of neighborhood girls came past, even had the holy girls with them, said they weren't going to school, they were going to help find those three. Asked if they could tie their double Dutch rope in a bow and hang it on the front door until the girls were found. Ramona had to swallow hard then; she had been so busy responding, reacting to the whole neighborhood's consumption of the missing girls, coupled with her own stark remembrance, she'd not focused on the girls themselves, that they could be in need, maybe even in real danger. She was like the next of kin the morning after the death, bustling so, tending to details, she'd forgotten about the heaviness in her own chest, the lump in her throat, the pulsing, the persistent pulsing in her head.

Finally, after she thanked the girls and closed the door, a quiet descended on the house. She paused then: no phone, no doorbell. Now she could take her bath. She ran the water as hot as she could stand it. So hot that her skin blushed its red undertones. She leaned back in the tub and closed her eyes and squeezed the hot water through her washcloth around her neck and her shoulders until her neck throbbed steady like a reverberating drum. She was perspiring and tasting her sweat, which dripped down her face around her lips. The air in the bathroom was white with steam, and she reached through the steam to the silver-toned faucet to turn the hot water back on full blast, lest the water in the tub cool. She held her foot under the running water, forced herself to hold it there until her foot sprang back of its own volition from the assaultive stream of heat. Then she just sat there and felt the new water get hotter in ripples, until the ripples moved through the layers in her skin, until she was ready to cry out. She stood then and yanked on the black chain to the skylight, pulled it all the way down and the cold gray air rushed in. The air was wet too, and it popped and sizzled along her skin like water dancing in a hot skillet. It found her open pores, as usual, closed them so tightly that her skin beaded up. This is how she always bathed, hot to cold, gaping wide open to nothing out, nothing in. From the time she was five and Mae made her bathe that first night on her own this is how she'd done it. Except this morning the cold couldn't reach all the way, couldn't close those parts that the hot water hadn't opened, couldn't make her skin bead up at the part of her where the soft, sweet-smelling robe had touched. Way, way under her skin, way deep, way deep.

*　*　*

PERRY had second thoughts once he rang the bell to the house Mae and Ramona shared. He kept telling himself that he was doing a proper thing, stopping by to offer his assistance. But now he was chewing on the inside of his jaw because he hadn't called Tyrone to wake him so he could know about the news of the girls missing too; maybe they could have both come here together. That would have really been proper, he thought. He considered running across the street to see if his lady, Hettie, was home, bring her over with him, but now the door was opening, and there Ramona stood, looking like butter that was softening on a counter to make a cake, as if her soft beauty would just melt and drip all between his fingers if he were to stroke her face right now.

"Miss Ramona," he said, and then looked back around him across the street, hoping maybe Hettie was coming or going through her front door.

"Yes? Perry, oh, hi," she said. And then, watching him turn around, asked, "What is it? Is that Tyrone with you?"

"Oh, ugh, no. Thought I heard somebody call my name." Perry turned back around, and his eye caught the jump rope tied in a bow hanging from the wreath nail at the top of the door. "Now that's different," he said. "Your idea?"

"Neighborhood girls. I was so touched—" Her voice cracked and she put her hand to her mouth.

"Uh, listen," he said quickly, rushing to fill the gulf of air before she started to cry, "I just heard about the girls being missing and all, and I just came by to offer my assistance. Anything, anything at all you need, Ramona, please don't hesitate—" Now he stopped abruptly; he was looking at her face again, and her face was filled up the way it had been the other night when she'd come into the shop. "Anything." Now he was whispering. It was an involuntary kind of whisper that always came up from his throat when he was talking to a woman who was causing his manhood to stir.

"Actually, now that you mention it, Perry, we could use some flyers."

"You know, I was thinking that exact thing," he lied. He'd had no such thought, could kick himself now for not having had the thought, for not being the one to say, "Let me do a run of flyers to help find the girls."

"We'd sure appreciate it," she said. She hesitated and then pushed the door wide open. "Come in, Perry, please. I don't mean to leave you standing out there; it's still half cold out. I—I just didn't know if you were coming for a visit or just to, you know, I hate to say 'pay your respects,' it's not like somebody died, I just feel almost, you know—" Her voice cracked again.

Perry covered her hand over the doorknob with his own. "I wouldn't mind visiting for a minute, Miss Ramona, 'specially if you getting ready to cry; we can't have you doing that, at least not alone. Nothing worse than a beautiful woman crying alone." He tried to keep the whisper from taking over his normal voice, but it was no use; his voice was so low it was like he should have had his mouth to her ear. And now he realized that his hand was covering hers; he pulled his hand back as if he had just touched a hot iron. He wished Tyrone weren't such a late sleeper. Should have had his ass up and at the shop first thing this morning so he would've gotten the news same time as me, he thought. He should already be here. Should be sitting on the couch and saying, "Hey, Pops," when I walk through the damned door.

Ramona was looking down at the porch floor, had been looking there since Perry said the part about a beautiful woman. She wished she had put on another sweater. This sweater was not only berry red, not only tight across her chest, but short too; meant the print of her hips was showing through her Wranglers. But then she reasoned it wasn't like she knew he was coming, wasn't like she'd said, "What's the most revealing outfit I can put on today because Perry's gonna drop by out of the blue?"

She ushered him into the living room, trying to walk her stilted walk, the one she reserved for walking past corners filled with gold-toothed, processed-haired men who'd call out, "Hey baby, what's yo number?" Not that Perry was uncouth; she just didn't want him to think she was coming on to him.

"You have pictures of the girls you can spare just for today?" he asked as he stepped into the living room, unable to keep his eyes off of her sweater, then her Wranglers, then back to her sweater again, before letting his eyes fall on her face. "I'll make sure you get them back once I run the job."

"Mnhnh. All I have is the one that was in the *Tribune*. Please, have a seat, rest your jacket; I'll go get the newspaper."

He folded his jacket along the arm of the couch and then sat down to the plastic chair cover's clatter. He sat back against the couch and crossed his ankle over his knee and let his arm hang casually from his knee.

Ramona came back into the room with the newspaper. She sat next to him, close enough so that they could share in their view of the paper, close enough so that she could tell that both he and Tyrone wore Aqua Di Silva aftershave.

"Mnh, this picture probably won't reproduce too well," he said as he held one edge of the paper while she held the other. "They sure are cute little girls too."

"Nice girls too," she said, and then stared off into the gray air of the living room. "All three of them, very nice girls."

"What you think happened? I mean, why you think they ran away? You do think they ran away, don't you? I mean, you don't think they were kidnapped or anything like that, do you?"

Her eyes clouded up. "They ran away, I'm sure of it."

"To get back to their mother?"

"Yeah, plus they hated it here, especially hated me." She let the edge of the newspaper fall. Her hands had suddenly gone to ice, and she rubbed them together like she was trying to get a fire to start.

"Hated you? Naw. Impossible." Perry breathed as he shifted on the couch, angled his body so that he faced her, draped his arm along the top of the couch just above her shoulder. "I doubt anybody could hate you."

"You don't know me."

"What you talking 'bout? I been watching you walk past my shop every workday since you started down there at Lit Brothers. I know what I see."

"What do you see?"

He cleared his throat. He could feel his voice dipping way low again. "What do I see? Mnh, I see a hardworking, responsible, respectable, good daughter of a young lady."

"That ain't all you see."

"Yeah, it is. Swear it is."

"Watch yourself, you know it was lightning out in that storm last night."

He laughed, and when he did, his hand fell lower along the couch back and touched her shoulder.

"You don't see that I'm a moody bitch? That's what people say about me behind my back; a few even told me to my face. I'm not even saying it's false rumor. You know, sometimes I just don't feel like being bothered with people."

He started singing a song about a moody woman and tapped his hand on her shoulder to the beat.

"Oh, stop," she said, and relaxed her shoulder under his arm.

"No, really, Miss Ramona, I don't feel that way about you, that you're a horrible person."

"What do you feel?"

"What do I feel? Honestly?" He looked at her breaths rising and falling against the sweater. "Mnh." He let his thumb touch the back of her neck, then up to smooth his fingers over her French roll. "What I feel right now I shouldn't be feeling."

"Well, then stop yourself from feeling it," she said quickly, talking to herself as much as to Perry, the skin on her neck melting from his thumb touch.

"Ooh, but, Miss Ramona," he said, his arm wrapping around her shoulder, pulling her in closer, "it's—it's strong, you know; caught me by surprise how strong it is. I didn't even realize it was there, you know, these feelings I have for you until you came in the shop the other night and your face was showing what I guess I been feeling all along. You know, every time I saw you walk past my shop I was feeling it, I just couldn't admit it to myself." The more he talked, the more the fullness of her eyes drew him in, until he could smell his own breath echoing from her face back to his; his breath tinged with the scent of crystal mint Life Saver tucked in the corner of his jaw. "Mnh," he said again. "Why don't you tell me what you feeling, Miss Ramona?"

Ramona just wanted to touch the lines on his face, those rivers of entrenched manhood that excited her so, that were close enough now for her to breathe on. "I'll tell you what I feel," she said.

"What? Miss Ramona. Tell me. What?" His voice was dragging against the carpet; his mouth was at her mouth; his fingers were against her chin. He could feel his manhood throbbing all the way up in his head, pushing his logic to the smallest corner of his brain. Right now he had no logic, nor a conscience, nor a son, all he had was the tremendous calling to feel her melting-butter-type beauty drip between his fingers. "Talk to me, Miss Ramona, tell me what you feel, what you feel, baby? Huh? Tell me." His mouth was wide open and covering her lips. Her lips were thick and soft, and he thought he would explode from the feel of them inside his mouth. "What you feel, baby?" he asked again, moaning it from the back of his throat, running his fingers along her chin down her neck, trekking across her tight berry red sweater.

And had this been yesterday she would have matched his fingers with her own, would have touched those lines in his face, pulled his chin down, parted his lips with her own. Had this been yesterday she would have led his hands all over that sweater, then under it, until his head was mashing into her chest and she was pulling him up the stairs, back to her tiny bedroom, where the roses were faded on the wall.

But she knew more today. Knew she wasn't cheap and worthless, whorish, like she'd been called by Mae for as long as she could remember. Knew she deserved better than that nauseating shame cloud that would hang over her head after doing such a low-down thing as bedding her boyfriend's father. Knew she could acknowledge how her flesh was hypersensitive right now, standing at attention because she wanted Perry so bad. And it didn't have to go further than the acknowledgment. She could think it, she didn't have to do it, until the day would come when she didn't even have to think it.

Then she said it, right into his wide-open mouth that was trying to swallow her lips, almost shouted it so that it went straight to his head, where his throbbing was: "I'm in love with your son."

It was more effective than a slap or a bucket of ice water over his head. He sat back so sharply he unintentionally swallowed the crystal mint Life Saver. Then coughed a choking cough. Coughed so hard he had to stand up and walk around the room. Coughed so hard he shook some sense back into his own head. Now he was ashamed. So ashamed he couldn't even turn back around and look at her. Damn. Why was he even here? His lady lived right across the street. And if not her, there were a half a dozen women right here in West Philly he could swoon with a candlelit dinner and a stack of Delphonics forty-fives. But he was decent, tried not to run around once a lady emerged as his main squeeze. "Damn," he said out loud when he could stop himself from coughing. "Ramona, I'm sorry, I'm so so sorry. I swear to God, I don't know what got into me." Still unable to look at her, he walked to the window. "I just came to offer to do the flyers." He looked at his dress shirt, could smell his own cologne. "Damn," he said again. "I'm honored that you love my son. He's a good man, and you a good woman, Ramona, God knows you are." He focused on the plastic chair cover as he walked across the room to get his jacket. "I'll call my man down there at the *Trib* and see if I can get ahold of the original picture of those girls. Tell Tyrone what you want the flyer to say, you know, when they were last seen, that kind of thing." He cleared his throat. "I'm going on 'cross the street and see if my lady is home. Don't get up, Ramona. And forgive me for not making eye contact with you right now. But the Lord might send a bolt of lightning to strike me dead should these old shame-filled, leprous eyes gaze on the goodness of you right now."

He was out of the door quickly; the sound of the door closing sealed the quiet that hung over the living room. Ramona just sat on the couch. She could still smell his cologne as if it were suspended in the air in front of her. Now the scent reminded her of Tyrone's eyebrows. She jumped from the couch and ran to the phone to dial Tyrone's number.

His voice had that dizzy, just waking-up static to it. But the sound of his voice went right to Ramona's heart. It was a voice she was no longer willing to wait around for.

"Tyrone," she said, "good morning, Tyrone."

"Mona, baby doll—"

"Don't baby doll me, just listen to what I got to say, okay."

"Okay, I'm listening."

She took a deep breath, then let her words rush out with the breath. "I need you, okay, like I've never needed any man ever in my life, I need you. The girls are gone, ran away—"

"What, ran away—"

"Don't talk, listen." Her voice was starting to shake. "Yes, they're gone, all three of them, gone. So you tell that bitch you been laying up with, whoever she is, that your lady, Ramona, needs you, for now and until I say I don't need you no more. Tell her the little jive fling y'all was having is now over. So you gotta cut it off, hack it, sever it, baby, but you got to let it go for good. Because I need you, here, now. And if you can't be here with me, for me, right here and right now, you can't never be with me, ever again." Now she was crying. It was a soft cry that was trying not to moan.

"Mona, just hang up the phone," Tyrone said.

"What?" she wailed.

"Hang it up! Hang it up right now! I'm trying to get to you, baby, and I can't get to you fast enough if I'm talking on the phone."

25

CLARISE was back. Not back in the physical sense, with her dark, bushy-straight hair swept off her face, while a pure silk paisley skirt and blouse set, or cashmere walking suit, or gaberdine coat dress ensemble traipsed over her lithe proportions as she stepped out in the kind of style that had become natural for her over the years. She still wore the light blue hospital gown, the terry-cloth slippers with the rubber soles, the chain bracelet with the white plastic balls that spelled out "Clarise," her hair pulled in two puffs and wrapped tightly in rubber bands by some unknowing nurse's aide. Physically she still looked like that crazy lady, that rich caterer's widow who had tried to separate her hand from her wrist over a bad reaction to his death. To look at her, no one would know she was back. But her mind was back indeed. When the day was bright and floating into her room through the venetian blinds, she saw it for what it was: yellow, sunbathed air. At night, when the sky was black and moonless, and the lights were turned on in the courtyard below her bedroom window, she knew it was night, and that was the reason for the navy descending; she didn't have to fight the dark to push it out of the way so that she could see. No more variegated hazes confusing her, making her slice at her skin. She was back, completely, cinematically, and then more, much more than she could see through the air that was prone to change colors, that was now dripping gray all around her table as she sat in the multipurpose room and ate her breakfast. All of her senses were back: the salty taste of the bacon as she crunched it down between her teeth; the chirping sound of the ice chips hitting the bottom of her juice glass as she swirled the glass around in her hand; the cold, slick feel of the butter pat that plopped from between the waxy paper into her fingers as she tried to drop it into her grits. But it was the olfactory sense that was the strongest, that was greatly affecting her now, the smoke rising off the top of the brown 'n' serve roll and sifting up into her nose straight through to her brain, shaping itself in her brain until there it was, clear as the shine on her fingers from the butter pat, a sense of her girls and baking bread. It wasn't a comfortable sensation. It wasn't as if she could sit back and say, "Ah, my girls are in some grandmother's kitchen right now, and she's making them yeast rolls and telling them parables from the Bible." Instead it seemed as if the smoke curling so gently off the bread turned sharp, pointed, left her with a stabbing feeling that went all the way to her heart. She dabbed at the corners of her mouth. Then tilted her chin. Her hands shook; she held them together tightly in her lap, nodded and smiled at the woman who stayed in the room next to hers. She didn't want to appear nervous, might be cause for strapping her down, force-medicating her again if they decided she was exhibiting signs of agitation.

She was actually more excited than agitated because today was the day. The staff was buzzing all around her about the shortage of help because of the storm last night. That's why she was eating breakfast in the multipurpose room instead of in the chair by her window; most of the tray girls called in late or absent, so the kitchen just sent up the food in bowls and left it up to the floor nurses to dish it out. And the floor nurses were exhausted, couldn't leave until their replacements showed up. Even the night cleaning staff had been retained: Broom sweeps became receptionists; window shiners became telephone operators; trash collectors became messengers. But what really confirmed for Clarise that today was the day was the gem of information that she'd just heard as she bit into her toast and licked the crumbs from her lips: Four-eyed Jim, the thick glasses–wearing head of the linen collection crew, was down on the front desk, signing visitors in and out and checking off the staff as they came and went.

So Clarise was ready. She had Til's fox-foot–collared coat in her closet to cover her blue cotton gown. She'd just finished the purple shawl the night before for draping around her head. She'd complained about cold feet and legs and been given an extra pair of over-the-knee nylons. All she needed now were shoes, and they were on the way, once the day shift nurse finally made it in and left her shoes in the utility room to dry up from their coat of White-All shoe polish.

The silver-blue-haired, prone-to-throw-a-fit Emma was at the next table over and whispered to Clarise that the sky was going to fall. "Look at how gray," she said, pointing wildly at the window. "Gray is the heaviest color too; it sags so."

"Calm down, just calm down," Clarise said as she looked out of the window that took up a whole wall. "They're pink streams in the gray, see, look and you'll see them. The pink will act as a harness and hold the sky up to the heaven until it's strong enough to stand on its own."

"Really?" Emma asked, her voice sudsing up to cry.

"On my honor," Clarise said, and raised her fingers as if she were doing a Girl Scout pledge. "And with this Mickey Mouse hairdo"—she touched her puffs of hair wound tightly in the rubber bands—"my honor is all I have left."

Emma tilted her head to study Clarise's hair, and then Clarise heard the smudging walk of the day nurse. She looked quickly at the nurse's feet, saw her in her street shoes, put a blank look to her face as if she'd already had two doses of her medication, and then hated herself for what she did next.

"I was wrong," Clarise said as she pushed her chair back slowly and walked over to Emma as if she had lead in her slippers. She leaned down and whispered in Emma's ear, "That's not pink, it's lavender in the gray, and lavender will make the sky fall quicker than even yellow."

"It will?" Now Emma was crying. "What can we do? My God, we're going to be crushed. What can we do?"

"We can count to ten and scream our asses off," Clarise continued to whisper, and then backed up slowly as she listened to Emma count. Clarise was at the utility-room door by the time the screaming started, and the exhausted staff came from every direction and rushed past Clarise to restrain Emma.

Clarise could still hear the screaming in her head as she jammed her arms into her aunt's fox-foot–collared coat and stuffed her feet into the day nurse's shoes. She could still hear it as the exit door into the stairwell closed behind her and sounded like a yawn. She could even hear it as she smiled and said good morning to Four-eyed Jim. "God, am I glad my replacement got in here, so I can finally go home," she said to Jim as she leaned in and scribbled on the pad. "Caught without boots, so I have to wear my work shoes out in this snow," she said to draw his thick-lensed glasses from her face to her feet. She could hear the scream even as she walked right on out of the front door, across the courtyard under the window to the room that had been her home. And then, as she got to the corner of Market Street, which was absent cars or people or opened stores, grateful for the thick rubber soles on these nurse's shoes, and she could still hear the scream, she realized it was her own screaming going on in her own head. It was a silent scream that she didn't allow to leave her head. Help me, Jesus! she screamed. Help me to get home, get my bearings, call the aunts and uncles, and then please, Lord, you brought me this far, now please help me find my girls.

26

PERRY stood on Hettie's porch and called to his son as he saw him running up the block.

"Later, Pops. I got to get to Ramona," Tyrone yelled back.

"Only take a second, Ty." Now Perry was waving his keys. "You gonna need some transpo to take your lady out to hunt for those girls."

Tyrone's feet almost dented the pavement, he stopped so short. No way could his father be offering him his car. Not his brand-new deuce and a quarter that he never ever let Tyrone borrow because Perry maintained that if Tyrone were handed things on a silver-plated platter, he'd never work as hard as he was going to need to work in order to make it; not his father, who paid his son a notch over minimum wage to offset his room and board because it would make a man out of him; not his father, who wouldn't even give Tyrone an advance on his pay if he ran short because he said it would teach him how to live within his means.

Tyrone squinted. Yep, those were definitely keys dangling between Perry's fingers as he yelled, "Come on, boy, get over here, only take you a second."

Tyrone veered across the street and swept up the steps onto Hettie's porch. "Yo, Pops, what's up? You look like you're on the way to stepping out in your good shirt."

Perry looked away so his embarrassment wouldn't show. "You hear about those girls?"

"Mona just called. I'm trying to get over there now."

Perry threw the keys at Tyrone. "Take her out and help her look for them, you know, help her calm herself down."

Tyrone caught the keys in one hand, and then Perry reached into his pocket and pulled up a twenty. "Do something nice for her too. Buy her something to eat, maybe some flowers, something that smells sweet, you know what I mean?"

Tyrone's eyebrows were furrowed in deep confusion. "Scuse the cliché, Pops, but I'm gonna take the money and run before you change your mind. Even though I'm dying to ask why." He searched Perry's face when he asked it.

Perry looked up and down the steet, at the porch floor, at the keys dripping between Tyrone's fingers. He looked everywhere except at his son's face. "Why?" he said. He took a deep breath. "Because that's what a man does, Tyrone." Now he did look at his son. "A real man doesn't run his woman into the ground, lie and cheat, try to outhang every stupid ass who walks the Strip on Saturday nights. A real man is strong enough to go soft on his woman and knows that it doesn't take away from his manhood."

Now Tyrone was embarrassed. Now he couldn't meet his father's gaze. He took the twenty, and his father held on to his hand, shaking his hand, and Tyrone had the feeling that they were both learning how to be real men together.

B<small>LISS</small> was bored, waiting for Mister to return. Shern and Victoria were still huddled up against each other asleep on the couch, so there was no one to argue with, or complain to, no one even to console her should she start to cry again. There was no television, not even a transistor radio. So she went exploring. Crept around the corner from the main room where her sisters were sleeping, ended up at a white wood door with a glass handle. Started to open the door, then stopped. Decided to play ice skating on the smooth, cold floor. She propelled her body and spun herself around as if her double-stockinged feet really had blades attached. She curved out figure eights and double Lutzes all through this expansive and empty room. She hummed "Moon River" and pretended she skated with a partner, and now he was lifting her up and up and she was twirling like a fast-moving sundial on the palms of his hands. Then she was back on the floor, bowing gracefully to a standing ovation, grabbing for her partner's hand, presenting him to share in the accolades. She was holding the glass handle to the white wood door, pulling her partner out because he was shy; she pulled the handle instead, and the door creaked open.

Now she was Bliss again, not the gold medalist ice skater. She was her bold, curious self, looking inside the closet of a room on the other side of the door. She saw the baseball bat that was propped against the wall on an irregularly shaped patch of a red velvet rug. She picked up the bat and swung it around. It was a heavy bat, and she had to call on her strength to brandish it about. She scuffed her stockinged feet against the cold, slick floor, pretended to straighten out a cap on her head, rubbed her hands along the side of her corduroy pants, spit, straightened out the cap again, then spread her feet and swung the bat. "Strike one, strike two, you're out."

Now she was no longer playing baseball but was a sleuth in a murder mystery. "You're out!" she said to the butler who had done the crime. "I've cracked this case, and you're out."

"So are you, little one, I'm so sorry, but you're out too." The voice she made sounded so menacing that she caused the hair on her own scalp to recede with such velocity that it was like a push and pull against her head. She gripped at the gray air, trying to keep her balance, trying not to fall from the thudding weight pressing into the back of her head. But there were no anchors in the air that she clawed into now, no support. The air was empty and light and fell down with her, covered her even as she closed her eyes on its grayness and landed hard on the cold, slick floor.

She just lay there and listened to her heart beat. Then reached her hand behind her to feel her head, make sure it wasn't busted as hard as she'd fallen. She sat slowly, shook her head, put her hand down at her side, and chided herself for being so silly. But her fingers touched leather instead of the hard slick floor. She snatched her hand back, held down a yell, looked up to see Mister peering at her.

"You shouldn't be in here, little one," he said.

Bliss studied his face. Smiled, praying he would return the upturned lips.

He didn't. He grunted and leaned over to pick up the bat. "You should go in the main room with your sisters. Don't come back in here again, ever."

His tone was crisp, had lost that languishing quality that made his words flow into one another as if he were singing. Bliss was suddenly terrified of Mister, much beyond the skepticism that had shrouded their interactions up until this moment; she was now experiencing full-blown terror. She suddenly realized that this was the first time since they'd been pulled from their mother's reaching, flailing arms that one or the other of her sisters was not at her side, enabling her to be Bliss, bold, snappy, say-anything-she-wanted-to Bliss. She felt centerless without Victoria's gravity that held in place, Shern's friction that gave her her spark. She looked away from Mister, looked at her hands as they shook. Cried a scared little girl's cry as she mashed her stockinged feet into the cold, slick floor and ran into the other room, where her sisters were.

MISTER repropped the bat against the wall. Got down on his hands and knees and smoothed out the patch of red velvet rug. He didn't even know why he still kept this trinket of a young boy. Every time he had occasion to walk past this door, peep at the irregularly edged velvet sticking under the door, he told himself to dispose of the bat once and for all. Should have buried it all those years ago, when he came upon the boy, deep in the woods of the park, cold as steel and twice as hard, skin gone from pink to blue to what looked like gray. Even the foam around his mouth had dried to a crust that looked like steel wool. He turned his head back and forth, much the way he'd turned his head back and forth that evening eighteen years ago. He'd had a choice then. Could have left the body undisturbed; let the police find this dead white boy in the black side of the park; let every colored man in the city become a suspect; let the police come through there with handcuffs and vacuum cleaners, sucking up every able-bodied black man as if they were clumps of dust, might even start in on the women, maybe even the children. Or he could save the parents the funeral expense, bury the boy himself, say a prayer over the dirt, and ask the Lord to cleanse his no-good soul.

He picked up the bat, twirled it around in his hands. This was thick, solid wood, slow burning. Worth at least a couple of hours of glowing heat in his stove. Plus that little one might mention that she'd swung a heavy old bat at Mister's place. Might raise an eyebrow, a question here, a look-see there. Yeah. It was time. Eighteen years was long enough to honor the memory of a murdered white boy, especially one as hateful as Donald Booker.

He listened to Bliss crying in the other room, telling Shern that they should go; they should just leave right now and go back to Mae's. He was inclined to agree. Smitty wouldn't be able to get him the penicillin until the next day. Plus Mae's nephew was going into Smitty's just as he was leaving. He'd spotted the glove peeking from Mister's pocket, the one he hadn't even realized was in there. "Hey, that's Shern's glove," he'd said. "Gimme, I'mma tell. What you doing with her glove?" He'd snatched the glove right from Mister's pocket as if he were grabbing a chunk of gold.

Yeah, he agreed with that little one. As much as he believed in people's rights to be unconventional, drop out from the world so to speak as he himself had done, these were still children. They should go back to Mae's. He'd carry the middle one if need be. But they should go back to Mae's.

27

Mae's house was jumping. Typical of house-cramming gatherings kindled by some extreme event, happy or sad didn't matter: People laughed to lift the spirits if there'd been a death or other catastrophe, cried tears of joy if there'd been a wedding or birth. Somebody always came by with a four-layered yellow cake with coconut icing that they'd made from scratch, likewise a pan of fried chicken always showed, a bag of ice for the Kool-Aid, large jars of Nescafé and Maxwell House and Pream nondairy creamer. A deck of cards for the back room, a half gallon of Four Roses whiskey for the center of the kitchen table, and the talk got loud and loose, the forty-fives started spinning, and the converted called for prayer.

Such was the scene as the quality-dressed, coconut- and honey-scented quartet pushed through the crowded porch to get inside the house. Til led the line, her thick gray and black hair pulled back in a bun, a sterling silver ornamental comb nestled in one side; behind her Blue, undoing his cashmere Burberry scarf from around his neck and muttering, "My goodness, it's hot in here"; Ness was behind him, taking off her glasses, which had steamed up once she was inside the door; Show brought up the rear, his ten-gallon hat already off his head.

The ocean of people in the living room separated to allow the foursome through, the way it had been separating for the past hour whenever someone new came in to offer expressions of surprise and support over the missing girls. These four didn't maneuver back to the kitchen, though, the way Hettie had done, and Darlene from the hosiery shop, Beanie, Miss D, even card-playing Clara Jane from downtown. These four just made a line in the center of the living room, and then Til cleared her throat and asked, in her most authoritative voice, who among them had the name Mae.

A hush moved through the living room as people began to notice the oddity of the four, obviously not from around here, certainly not with the short one holding that ten-gallon hat in his hands. Someone pointed toward the kitchen, said Mae was in the back, playing cards, probably, to help keep her mind off of her crisis; who should they say is calling? Now muffled snickers replaced the hush. And Til sucked the air in through her teeth and headed toward the kitchen with her sister and brothers right at her heels.

"I'm looking for Mae," Til said as she walked all the way into the kitchen and stood right at the back of Mae's head.

Mae didn't turn around at first. She was too centered on the card game that was in fact keeping her from the moaning and hand wringing she'd be prone to right about now over her missing foster girls. "I said raise or fold, bitch"—she sneered across her kitchen table at her card-playing rival Clara Jane from downtown—" 'cause you getting ready to lose your motherfucking gold ring in here today."

Giggled comments about how that Mae can surely talk some shit circled the kitchen, and then Til's voice got in the middle of the circle and silenced it with her tone, which was sharp and serious and completely different from the jovial air hanging over the table.

"If you are Mae, please put down those got-damn cards and talk to me about my babies."

"Who might you be?" Mae asked as she started to turn around. "And who the hell are your babies?" She turned around slowly. She had to turn slowly because first she took in everybody's faces in her view. A cardplayer, she knew how to read faces, and their faces told her that there was a considerable threat standing over and behind her head right now. Now she was standing up. She was shorter than Til. Too much shorter, she had to concede.

Ness reached beyond Blue and grabbed Til's arm. Said, "Sister, whatever you thinking that's got the muscles behind your ears jumping like jackrabbits is not worth it; it's just not, let's just find out why Shern called and look our girls over and make sure they're okay."

"Lord have mercy," Mae said, clutching at her chest and thanking the God that she was sometimes prone to call in such situations for the substantial weasel room she'd just been blessed with, "are you the natural kin to those girls? Lord, forgive my lack of manners, please let me have your coats. Lord, yes, I am Mae, and those little pudding pies of yours been such a delight, such a pure delight. Now what can I offer you, all kinds of food here, something to drink? Some soda or a little taste?"

"I'll have one, thank you," Blue said as he slipped in the chair Mae had just gotten up from and took a shot glass and the Four Roses from a tray in the center of the table.

"You help yourself with your tall, good-looking self," Mae said, and let her hand rest on Blue's shoulder, and then lifted her hand quickly as if Blue's shoulder were a glowing coal. "Pardon me, please," she said to Til, "I didn't mean any disrespect if this is your man friend or intended—"

"My brother," Til said, putting all her weight on her feet so that her usually squared shoulders rounded out some. "His name is Blue, and behind me is my sister, Ness, and that's my other brother, Show."

"Mae, you in the game or out?" Clara Jane called from the table. " 'Cause I'm getting ready to deal your hand to this tall man with the pretty mouth who done took over your seat, he damned sure better to look at than you."

The crowd around the table laughed except for Til and Ness and Show. Then Clara went on. "Mae, thought you already knew about them anyhow. Didn't your cut buddy Vie tell you everything you needed to know about the kinfolk of those girls?"

"Vie?" Til said as her shoulders went square again.

"Vie?" Ness repeated behind her sister. "You a friend of Vie's?"

"Vie?" This from Blue as he drained the shot glass and stood at Mae's back.

"Vie?" Even the short, reserved brother, Show, added his questioning, threatening tone to the air in the kitchen that had gotten suddenly stark still.

"Vie?" Now Mae said it too. "What the hell you talking about, Clara Jane? I ain't seen nor talked to no fucking Vie!"

"You's a damned lie," Clara Jane said, incited by her several shots of the Four Roses and a decade and a half of harbored resentments over Mae's ability to get foster children over everybody else. "I can't even get a foster child placed with me but once or twice a year since you and that fat-assed Vie so chummie. Shit, between you and that no-good Bernie, it's a wonder any foster mother in this city gets work."

"Clara Jane, shut your big, lying mouth right now." Mae started moving through the kitchen toward Clara Jane. If she was going to have to fight in here today, she'd take her chances with Clara Jane over the square-shouldered Til.

"I ain't shutting shit." Clara Jane stood and grabbed the knife resting on the plate with the coconut cake. "And I hope once they find those girls, they take them right from your conniving ass. Ain't like they safe here. I live all the way downtown, and I heard about how some printer's son had to step to crazy-ass Larry about bothering those girls. And when I heard it, I said, 'Well, that conniving Mae ain't gonna say nothing. Shit, might mess up her good thing she got going with Vie.'"

The aunts and uncles gasped simultaneously at this information about needing to find the girls. Their lifestyle of contented isolation had kept this news from seeping under the door to their Queen Street row house. Now Til suppressed a horrified shriek at the mention of Larry in context with the girls. She knew not to get in between Clara Jane's words, though, even as Ness rubbed her arm to keep a fit from coming on. She knew Clara Jane was saying everything they'd need to hear to give their lawyer ammunition to go up against the judge's ruling. Hotheaded though she was, and as badly as she wanted an explanation about what all was being uttered, she let her weight go to her feet again, let her shoulders round out, and stood back between Ness and Show as Mae and Clara Jane called each other liars and cheaters and whores and were quickly running out of base phrases to sling at each other, which meant the "I'll kick your ass" threats would surely follow, and, as was inevitable at times like this, happy or sad didn't matter, there was laughter and tears, coconut cake, chicken, coffee and cream, Four Roses holding up the center of the kitchen table, and often, at times like this, there was a fight.

28

RAMONA sat back against the smooth leather interior of Perry's deuce and a quarter. Now she felt like a person. Her breaths were moving through her chest absent that block of granite that always surfaced when she tried to do something like this: be comfortable with a man in a way that was honest and precluded her having to look over her shoulder for somebody's wife or other love interest to jump out at her, maybe throw lye in her face, stab her with an ice pick, pitch a cherry bomb through her front window. The threats she'd endured in the name of what? Certainly not love, not even desire, more just living up to what she'd been told about herself for as long as she could remember. But this was love she was feeling now, as Tyrone clasped her hand and squeezed her fingers one by one, telling her not to worry; he just felt in his heart that the girls were okay.

They were almost to Chestnut Hill. Had just left the trolley tracks and shops of Germantown Avenue and were onto huge streets with no white or yellow lines that marked all the streets of this size in West Philly to hold the traffic in place. There was not much traffic here to hold in place. Just houses as large as the streets were wide, two-, three-storied, deep and long brick houses sitting back behind snow-draped trees; she couldn't even name these trees, they had such exotic shapes.

"No wonder those girls wanted to get back here." Ramona sighed. It was a tear-laced sigh. She'd cried such rivers today: for Mae, for those girls, for Donald Booker, for herself. She especially cried for herself.

Now Tyrone was going in between her fingers, taking his time, leaving no speck of her fingers untouched by his hand. "Well, of course, they wanted to get back here, Mona, not just because of their house; it's just that this is where their essence is. Don't matter how good or bad they were treated staying with you and your mother, they still would have wanted to get back here to, you know, to breathe."

Ramona squeezed his hand. Thought about how her essence had been left back in that park eighteen years ago and how she'd had to go back there, at least in her mind, so that she could breathe.

She rolled her window down. The air was still gray, and the temperature was dropping again. She rubbed her hands together and blew into them. She hoped the girls had doubled their socks. They were almost to where a tree had fallen and spread itself out halfway across the road. This was the block; Ramona could tell by the police cars, one marked, one unmarked, sitting in front of a grand stone Victorian.

"You think we need to get out of the car?" she asked. "That must be the house up there where the police cars are sitting. Maybe we could talk to the neighbors; maybe they'd tell us details they might leave out for the police."

"Sure, baby doll." Tyrone pointed out of the passenger-side window, motioning to a woman who'd just crossed their view. "We could start with her."

When Ramona looked at the tall, slender figure gliding up the street as if she were walking on velvet instead of ice-covered concrete and noticed the vintage fox-foot–collar coat she was wearing, she was getting ready to say to Tyrone that you can always tell people with money by the way they walk and the quality to their coats. She had her mouth all fixed to let go a barrage of observations about the rich. But then she noticed the purple wool blanketlike shawl hanging in a loose drape around the woman's head as if she were an Arabian princess. She couldn't even say anything after that.

It was the stitch. All through the shawl, that tight knit-purl cross-stitch, that stitch she'd never seen until she'd seen it woven through all of the hats and scarves and gloves that belonged to the girls. So all she could do was shriek, "Oh, my God! Stop the car right now, Tyrone. You gotta stop the car."

Tyrone almost ran up on the curb, unaccustomed as he was to driving Perry's fully loaded automatic transmission with power brakes.

"What? Ramona! What the hell is it?"

"That's her." Ramona pointed wildly toward the woman.

"Who?"

"Her, it's her. My God! She must have gotten out. They must have let her out."

"Who? Shern? Victoria? Bliss? Who? Who do you see?"

"Their mother, right there, that woman gliding up the street. That's their mother. My God, that's Clarise."

"That's Clarise?"

"I'm telling you, I'd know that stitch anywhere."

"You lost me, baby"

"Never mind, sit here. I'm getting out. I'm going to talk to her; I know that's her. I'll be right back. That's her. That's the girls' mother, Clarise."

Clarise drew into herself as Ramona approached. She balled her fists under her coat sleeve, deciding whether to run or try to fight her off. She couldn't run, damned tree was blocking her. It was the Pattersons' tree; the last ones to welcome them to the neighborhood, the first ones to point out all the business Finch was losing to the catering chains.

Clarise turned her back on the fallen tree and faced Ramona. She looked for her shoes. Darn, black rubber slip-on boots, so she couldn't tell if she was wearing the white oxford, rubber-soled shoes all the institute staff seemed to wear. Like the ones she was wearing now, borrowed from the day shift nurse who had left them in the utility room next to the opened bottle of White-All shoe polish and the three-tiered squeegee sponge. Good shoes too. Her feet had remained dry and fairly warm the whole walk here. She sniffed. No aura of wintergreen alcohol surrounded her. She unfurled her fists, then balled them again quickly. This woman was calling her name. Who was she, calling her name like this? She centered her weight. Took the stance taught her by the aunts. Fixed her eyes on Ramona like they were cannon loaded and ready to fire. "Who the hell are you?" she asked. "And how is it that you know my name and I don't know yours?"

"Um, miss, um, may I call you Clarise?"

Clarise dropped her fists. This was definitely no one from the institute.

"Um, I'm—my name is Ramona, and actually we're—" Ramona turned and pointed to Tyrone, who was halfway out of the car.

"Tell him to get back," Clarise commanded.

Ramona made a frantic motion with her hands, and Tyrone got back in the car.

"We're over here about your girls."

"Say their names," Clarise said.

"Shern, Victoria, and Bliss." Ramona said the names slowly, seeing each of the girls in this woman as she said the names. Shern had her mother's eyes for sure, probing, intense, watery, like half-wet circles of gray-black ink. The strong, straight nose was also Victoria's nose. And Bliss had certainly taken those fleshy lips, that pouty mouth.

Clarise felt a stabbing in her heart as Ramona said each girl's name. She sat down on the fallen pin oak and buried her face in her hands. "Just tell me. Tell me fast and tell me true. Just tell me right now. What happened? Please tell me what happened to my babies."

"Um, well, they were staying with me—that is, with my mother and me over in West Philly. Um, you know, my mother takes in foster kids—um, I mean children. And, well, we don't know all the details yet, but it looks like they ran away sometime late last night or early this morning."

Clarise was crying into her hands now. Her shoulders were going up and down, the fox-foot collar seeming to stroke her neck as she cried. "I knew something was wrong," she sobbed into her hands.

The pin oak made a cracking sound as Ramona sat down on the fallen tree next to Clarise. Ramona had her arm around Clarise's shoulder. It was a stiff arm, Ramona so unused to consoling people using physical contact.

"I've been smelling bread, all morning, a yeasty, buttery smell. The morning I woke and my husband wasn't next to me, hadn't been in the bed all night, first time ever I'd woke not knowing exactly where he'd spent the night, I woke to the smell of the sea, a sweet, oily smell that was coming to me in mists, and then in waves, and then I could barely catch my breath, as if my lungs were filling with water."

Now Clarise was starting to shiver under her aunt's faithful coat. She had walked from the institute to here. Most of it through snow-covered Fairmount Park, where she had the streets to herself, no cars, no people; the storm had even kept the stray animals and pesky park squirrels in. And she had done the eight miles in three hours and kept reasonably warm, even worked up a mild sweat. But now her heart had almost stopped at the news that her girls were missing, her blood froze a little, and the heat that had settled between her coat and her skin while she'd kept moving was quickly receding, and suddenly she was feeling the gray air for what it was, a dull, throbbing cold.

Clarise's shoulders felt so frail under Ramona's arms. So Ramona wrapped her arms fully around her. She rubbed her hand up and down her arm. "Um, uh, um, Clarise, why don't you come and get into the car with my boyfriend and me? We were riding around looking for your girls. We figured that they'd probably try to get home. Um, but the police look like they had the same idea. Um, maybe you know where else they would try to go. But first why don't you come and get in the car with us? Please, come on," she whispered, "let me help you into the car."

Clarise allowed Ramona to help her up. Because not only was she cold, but she was tired; more than tired, she was weak.

Tyrone had the back door opened when Ramona and Clarise got to the car, and Ramona climbed into the backseat with Clarise.

"Are you warm enough?" she asked her once they were both settled in.

"Much better, thank you," Clarise answered, and then let the loosely hanging shawl fall from her head and onto her shoulder. Ramona noticed how Clarise tossed her head as if she were royalty to encourage the shawl to fall. She took note. This is how refined people acted.

"Is this your young man?" Clarise asked as she leaned forward to get a better look at Tyrone.

"Um, yes, yes, he is," Ramona said.

"Can you tell him to drive slowly through this block? This is our block. Even though my girls wouldn't hide on this street. My Shern has a key. They would just use the key and go on in. Unless, of course, those dumb oxen police so visible in front of my door have scared them off."

They rode in silence through the block. Ramona respected the silence even though she was brimming over with questions for Clarise. When did she get out? Why hadn't they known she was getting out? Why was she just walking through the streets like that? How did it feel to go through life without any idea who her father was? She gasped as she thought this last question. Had never been aware of any yearnings to know her real father. Was just beginning to understand that that didn't mean the yearnings weren't there.

Clarise was sitting forward to get a better view of the snow-covered block, seeing her girls in strollers, then tricycles, then roller skates, then two-wheeler bikes with training wheels; splashing around in the inflatable toy pool on the front lawn that would make Clarise's jaws ache when she had to blow it up; posing for pictures on Easter Sunday and Mother's Day. The images were building one on the top of the other like a slide show in fast motion, she could even hear a clicking sound as her mind went from one scene to the next, and now she was screaming and startling the quiet in the car. "Oh, dear God. Dear, dear God," she hollered. "Please let them be safe. After my Finch, I just couldn't bear another loss. Not a loss like that, not my girls. Sweet Father in heaven, please, not my girls." She closed her eyes tightly. Then wrapped her arms around her chest.

"Why don't you sit back and try to relax?" Ramona said as she reached for Clarise's shoulder.

"Relax? How can I relax? I've run away from the institute, yes, that's right, run away," she said to the shock in Ramona's eyes. "My girls are God knows where, and you tell me to relax." She stared hard into Ramona's face. She lowered her voice. "My dear, if you think it is even remotely possible for me to try and relax right now, then the institute has a bed waiting for the wrong woman."

She saw Ramona's features recede to a hurtful downcast. Noticed then Ramona's red eyes, puffy nose. She sat back against the seat and closed her eyes and rubbed her forehead lightly with her long, slender fingers. She moved her fingers outward along her face and let them rest at her temples. "Well, at least you let me have a decent outburst without shooting me with that navy haze. I'm not crazy. Never was. It was the medication. Had me so bogged down all I could see was navy. The more I reacted to it, the more they gave me. Educated fools, those doctors. I stopped taking it on my own, you know. Look at me now. Or at least listen to me. Don't I sound as sane as the two of you?"

Tyrone caught Ramona's eyes through the rearview mirror. Did a questioning move with his eyebrow as if to ask Ramona if she was okay back there with this woman claiming not to be crazy. Clarise saw him too. She sat up again, tapped him on his shoulder, said, "My dear, I'd put my clarity of thought against yours any day of the week. I'll bet over the past week you've found yourself in situations and wondered why you were there, and knew you shouldn't be there, and continued to stay there. Personally I think *that's* crazy. Are you locked up somewhere forbidden time and space with the things you hold most dear?"

Tyrone thought about his week with Candy. How he'd started off unable to resist, humming all the way to her animal skin–covered walls. But after five, six, seven days in a row, the skins and the smoky mirrors made him dizzy, and even the way she so readily went wide open for him that had so excited him in the beginning he thought his natural head would burst, after a week straight, the predictability of their time together made him miss Ramona's hot and cold, hard and soft changeable nature.

"I didn't mean you any disrespect," Tyrone said. He fixed his eyes on the street unfolding in front of the car lest his guilty eyebrows show. "Any suggestion on where we should go?" he asked the hood of the car.

"To your house," Clarise said, and lightly touched Ramona's suede-trimmed trench coat. "That's where my girls left from. I believe that's where they'll return. I'll call my aunts and uncles when we get there. When I see what's what, I may even let them take me back. But they've got to understand about the medicine. I'll explain it to my aunt Til; she'll fight for me." She smiled weakly at the thought of Til fighting for her. And then she turned to face Ramona again. "Young lady," she said, "I need a favor. Can you please remove these tight-ass rubber bands from my hair. Why they did this, I certainly can't figure, they should have just left my hair be, let it go wild; the African bush seems a popular hair statement, don't you think?"

Ramona moved in closer and began unwinding the rubber bands. "I don't like that bush, no, I don't like it at all. And I want you to know that I've been keeping a good press in your daughters' hair, hot-curling their bangs every morning and giving them two thick plaits down the back. Except that Bliss has a softer grade, more like yours." She had the first rubber band out and smoothed through Clarise's thick, soft hair to get to the next one.

Clarise smiled and sighed. "She does, she really does. My baby Bliss." She nestled her head against Ramona's shoulder. Ramona's fingers through her hair reminded her of how Shern used to love to play in her hair, smooth through it to get to her scalp. Ramona had unwound the second rubber band now and was massaging Clarise's scalp. The car was warm, and the seat was soft and drawing her in. Ramona's fingers whooshing through her hair was affecting her; she actually was beginning to relax. What a powerfully intimate thing to do, she thought, the press of fingers against someone's scalp. She realized now why women told their hairdressers their deepest soul secrets, why mothers and daughters bonded so over the act of combing hair, why best friends always styled each other's hair. Why she suddenly felt so close to Ramona, even trusted her.

"Please tell me that you and your mother were good to my girls," she said in a voice that wanted to fall asleep. "Please tell me that they didn't run away because they were being mistreated. Please tell me, why do you think they left?"

Ramona took in a deep breath and picked up an end of the purple shawl. Her voice shook as she started to speak. "Because I couldn't act like you, you know, a real mother; because my mother couldn't either. Because we didn't even know how to be mother and daughter to each other. Because sometimes things happen to people that in an instant change who they are and they spend a lifetime trying to get back to who they used to be—" Ramona was crying again. She was pulling the sobs from her stomach, and her entire body convulsed, and she rocked back and forth and made choking sounds.

Clarise opened her blanket shawl, stretched it out for Ramona to lean into. "Or trying *not* to get back to who they were," Clarise said. "That institute I just left is teeming with people trying not to be who they really are." They nestled on each other's shoulders under the tight knit and purl cross-stitch that didn't let any cold in as Tyrone maneuvered through the ice along Lincoln Drive bound for West Philly and Mae's house.

Mae's block was crowded as Tyrone eased up Addison Street in Perry's deuce and a quarter, Clarise sleeping against Ramona's shoulder under the purple shawl. Anybody not already at Mae's over the girls missing had surely run out of their houses and into the street to watch Mae and Clara Jane curse at each other and get ready to fight. They never really exchanged slaps. Clara Jane held on to the coconut cake knife; Mae broke a wine bottle against her concrete porch for effect. Said she'd cut Clara Jane right in her lying mouth. But people like Beanie and Hettie separated them, said the newspeople were likely to show up to do a story about the girls, and why we always got to be acting like heathens when the newspeople show, Beanie said. So Clara Jane walked on down the street, Mae went back into her house, and the tide of people separated to let the car through.

Tyrone stopped in front of the door, told Ramona he'd let them out, then go park. He got out of the car and walked around to the back passenger side and was just about to open the door for Ramona and Clarise when he was met by Addison barreling down the street, legs and arms moving in big circles he was running so fast.

He was holding up the mitten that he'd snatched from Mister's pocket. "Look, look at what I have." He waved the mitten in Tyrone's face and then pulled it back. "You think this is worth a reward. I'mma show my aunts, ask her to hook it up for me."

Tyrone grabbed Addison by the collar. "Is that—?"

"Shern's, yepper," he said.

Tyrone glanced into the car, saw Ramona gently nudging Clarise awake. "Where?" he demanded. "Where did you find the glove?"

"Hey, man, get off of me or I ain't telling you jack."

Tyrone tightened his grip around Addison's collar. "Where'd you find the glove, you little shit? Tell me. Tell me right now."

He centered one hand under Addison's collar and balled his other, reared back, and was just about to bring his hand down on Addison's mouth.

"All right," Addison cried. "I found it on Mister. It was sticking from his coat pocket, and I snatched it out."

Ramona was tapping on the window, telling Tyrone to open the door, they were ready to get out of the car. Tyrone stuffed the glove in his pocket, didn't want Clarise to go hysterical when she saw it, Ramona, either, for that matter.

"Hey, man, I'mma tell my aunt Mae on your righteous ass." He bounded up the steps into Mae's.

Tyrone opened the door, and Ramona stepped out, and they both helped the elegant, poised Clarise. She just stood on the sidewalk once out of the car, covered her head loosely with her shawl, looked up at Mae's house, and then started her glide up the steps.

The cries of "Mommie!" "Mommie!" "Mommie!" floated through the gray air, turned it pink, warm. These cries were like a song filled with hope and promise that Mommie would hear, that she would stop midway into her climb onto Mae's porch, that she would turn, as if in slow motion her turn would be so deliberate; that she would raise her arms like a gospel choir belting out Hallelujah, not even noticing that her purple hand-knitted blanket-shawl had fallen to the ground; that she would make an arc of her arms, leaving her hands unclasped so her girls could spill into the arc, just seep into their mother's arms like circles of water frantically searching for larger parts of themselves: a lake, a stream, a river. These girls found an ocean in their mother's arms, as they all fell down on the blanket shawl covering the pavement in front of Mae's and cried and kissed and tasted one another's salt.

They were so absorbed in their mother, she in them, that they didn't even hear the aunts' and uncles' shouts reverberating all around them as they ran onto the porch, down the steps and added their own salt to the ocean Clarise and the girls made.

Ramona hadn't realized that she too was crying as she watched those girls in their high-quality plaid wool coats zoom up Addison Street, Victoria in Mister's arms as he panted and kept up with Shern and Bliss. Ramona couldn't see what everybody else saw as they were drawn from Mae's house by the commotion out front. She didn't know that she was jumping up and down and kicking and shouting unintelligible words like a baby who doesn't yet have words. She couldn't even feel Tyrone trying to pin her arms down, to still her, couldn't hear him whispering, "Mona, baby doll, what is it?"

Nor did she hear Clarise yelling from the ground, where she sat with her girls and now the aunts and uncles, "Young man, let her be. It's not you she needs right now, just let her be." Now Ramona's unintelligible shouts turned into a word, just one word over and over: "Mommie" was the word. It sifted up onto the porch, into the house, the kitchen, where Mae had just cut herself a slice of coconut cake and sat down to a new game of cards. Ramona's word fell on Mae's ear, went straight to her heart, hearing it over and over like that, as if her child were being pushed too high on a swing and taunted by a good-for-nothing. Mae got up from the table, moved with force and determination through the house, out onto the porch, saw the crowd circling her daughter, then parting as Mae walked down the steps, poker cards a fan in her hands. Now it was Mae who moved in slow motion, raising her arms like a gospel choir, letting the cards fall from her hands and drift into the pink and gray air.

"It's all right, lil darling. Mommie's with you. I'm right with you," Mae said as she covered Ramona with her own ocean. This Ramona did hear as she fell into the waves that lifted her up, up, up, into her mother's arms.